...urned to any branch of the
...y on or before the date shown

THE
BLACKEST
DEATH

———————

VOLUME I

THE
BLACKEST
DEATH

VOLUME I

Edited by
The Staff of
Black Death Books

Black Death Books
An imprint of
KHP Industries

THE BLACKEST DEATH
VOLUME I
Edited by the Staff of Black Death Books

Black Death Books
is an imprint of
KHP Industries
http://www.khpindustries.com

ISBN: 0-9679220-9-7

Cover art by KHP Studios

Printed in the United States of America

10 9 8 7 6 5 4 3 2 1

CONTENTS

Right Next Door to Hell
by
Mike Adamson

Chapter One

It was with nervous excitement that Janice Coulton watched her new neighbours moving in. It was nine-thirty on a wet Thursday evening. Strange time to be moving in, Janice thought. She squinted her eyes through the window as the new people walked up and down the driveway. Her new neighbours consisted of a man, a woman and a young boy. The boy had gone inside the house and not reappeared. The man and woman were unloading several bags and suitcases from the boot of their car and carrying them inside. The car was long and black, an estate of some kind. Janice wasn't very good on cars. She knew what it reminded her of though, a bloody hearse!
"Please don't let them be weirdo's," she said, her breath fogging the glass. The last lot had been an absolute disgrace. Scrubbers, was how Janice described them to anyone who asked. As she watched, her mind wandered back over the time she had spent living next door to the Griffin's.

Des Griffin, his wife Colleen and Alan, their little shit of a son. Under the reign of the Griffins, 132 Allerton Road, had been a mess. The small front garden couldn't even be classed as poorly kept. It wasn't kept at all. It was ridden with weeds and rubbish within a month. As for the back garden, well, the less said the better. It seemed to Janice that the Griffin's had spent almost the entirety of their one-year stay bickering and arguing. Des was a drunk. A loud-mouthed drunk. The worst kind. Colleen was also a heavy drinker and Janice was in no doubt that thirteen-year-old Alan knew what hangovers were all about.

It went without saying that she had warned her own daughter Katie to stay away from Alan Griffin. Katie was also thirteen, the same age as Alan, so contact at school was unavoidable. It turned out that Katie had the same ideas about the Griffins as her mother and did indeed steer well clear. The houses were relatively soundproof but no amount of insulation could prevent the noise of a Griffin row in full flow. The week was like a warm up for the weekend. Des coming in pissed at all hours usually started it. Janice believed that that man didn't know how to close a door. He could only slam them. One of the most curious things about the Griffins was that their rows would last about an hour and then the unmistakable sounds of sexual congress would come seeping through the walls.

Colleen Griffin didn't work and Alan seemed to go to school as and when he pleased, which wasn't often, according to Katie. Despite all that, Janice never had many face-to-face confrontations with them. She was definitely scared of Des and being a single mother, she wasn't about to go over there and start a war. They wouldn't have listened anyway. Then, last November, a For Sale sign had appeared in the dirty excuse for a garden. Janice had treated herself to a nice bottle of Chardonnay that night (and paid for it the next morning). She heard that, surprise, surprise, Des had lost his job. The Griffins were gone before Christmas. The estate agents sent a couple of men round to clean up the gardens. Janice happily lent them a hand. That was ten months ago. The house had sat empty for almost a year. Until now.

Janice wiped the condensation off her bedroom window and peered again at her new neighbours. The man was wearing a heavy looking leather jacket, the collar flipped up around his neck. He was tall and skinny looking. The woman, Janice presumed it was his wife, also wore a long black coat. Blonde hair spilled across her shoulders. Neither of them looked around the street, they didn't even glance in Janice's direction. They made one more trip and then went inside. Janice shrugged and closed her curtains. They were probably a little nervous themselves. After all, they had just moved in next door to a graveyard.

Chapter 2

On Friday morning Janice got up at eight o'clock as usual. As she crossed the landing she gave Katie a wake up shout, as usual. She went downstairs and made breakfast in her slippers and dressing gown, as usual. Katie strolled down about fifteen minutes later and they ate toast together and watched the morning news.

"Did you see the new neighbours last night?" Janice asked.

"Nope," Katie mumbled through a mouthful of toast. "Did you?"

"Yes. Well a little bit. Looks like a mum, a dad and a young son," Janice replied.

"It's not the Griffins come back, is it?" Katie said.

Janice laughed. "No."

"Good," Katie said, standing up. "Well, Mum, It's time I wasn't here." She kissed Janice on the cheek and picked up her school bag.

"Have a good day hon," Janice said.

"You too," Katie replied. Then she left the house and went off to school.

Janice finished her toast and then went upstairs to get dressed.

An hour later she was sitting at her desk, typing a letter to a patient. She was a medical secretary at Westbury Hospital, a job she had done for the last seventeen years. Her husband Carl had died of a heart attack when Katie was only two years old. For a while the bottom fell out of Janice's world. But she swiftly realised that she had a daughter to support and no amount of grieving would put food on the table. So she put her nose right up against the grindstone and her shoulder firmly to the wheel. Janice wouldn't have managed had it not been for her sister, Claire, and Carl's mum and dad. They all pitched in and took care of Katie whenever Janice couldn't manage. When Katie started school, things settled down and she began to live like a normal human being again.

In the coffee room at about eleven o'clock Janice sat with her friend and fellow secretary, Eve. Janice told her about the neighbours.

"So they're a family, huh?" Eve said.

"Looks that way. I don't know."

"Pity." Eve's mouth curled into a grin. "You could have done with a nice single dad."

"For god's sake, Eve."

They both started laughing.

The rest of the day passed by Janice like a plastic bag caught in a strong wind. She got home at five-thirty. As she pulled into her drive Janice looked at the house next door. The sleek black car was parked where it had been last night. No lights were on. Janice got out of her red Vauxhall and went into the house, but not of course before she had given her customary glance to the graveyard that lay only one house away from hers.

That was a spooky bugger of a place and no mistake. Janice had only been in it a couple of times and never at night. An old brainteaser flitted through her mind. If a tree falls over in a forest and there is no one to hear it, does it make a sound? Then she thought, If no one was around to see it, a dead body could very well rise from its grave and go wandering. Janice shivered and went inside.

Chapter 3

At half past eight Janice went next door to say hello to her new neighbours, despite Katie's pleas to at least let them settle in first. She carried with her a bottle of Californian red wine. Janice took a deep breath and brushed a bang of her long blonde hair away from her eye, tucking it behind her ear. She had spent ten minutes fixing herself up. She wore blue jeans and a black top and her heavy sheepskin jacket to kept out the cold. Janice was actually a little disappointed that it was a family that had moved in. A single father would have been nice. She knocked on the door; after a moment or two, the door opened.

A tall man stood before her. He had shoulder-length black hair. He was wearing a long black shirt and black jeans. He looked very fit. Janice found herself captivated by his blue eyes. He spoke first.

"Hello."

Janice caught herself and quickly made an introduction

"Hi, I'm Janice Coulton, I live next door. Just wanted to pop round and say hello."

"Well, hello, Mrs Coulton, I'm Mal Hutson, why don't you step in." He took a step back and Janice crossed the porch and stood in the hallway. She glanced around; the place needed a lot of decorating. An awful lot. Wallpaper was dangling from the walls and there were several patches of bare plaster. A scruffy brown carpet adorned the floor. The stairs were uncarpeted.

"We haven't even started yet," Hutson said.

"Hm," Janice mumbled. It was almost as if he'd read her mind.

"The decorating. My wife and I are terribly lazy when it comes to D.I.Y."

"Oh, erm, I brought you this, a little moving-in present." Janice held out the bottle of wine quickly. There was something about Hutson's gaze. Piercing. She felt as if he was looking into her.

"That's very kind of you, Mrs Coulton. Would you care for a glass?"

"I'd love one, and please call me Janice."

"OK, Janice it is. Let's go into the living room. Not much prettier in there, I'm afraid, but at least it's warm." They left the hallway and moved into the living room.

Hutson wasn't kidding. A big Persian rug sat in front of the fireplace. A real log fire was crackling away nicely. There were two black leather sofas and a television and video in the room. That was about it. A woman was curled up on one of the sofas. She rose as Janice entered.

"Honey, this our new neighbour, Janice."

Janice was hit with an inferiority complex as the woman got up. She was stunning. Long flame-red hair flowed over shoulders and spilled down her back. She was slim and curvaceous. She was wearing a pair of white shorts and a tight red tank top.

"Hello, Keeley Hutson." She held her hand out and Janice shook it.

"Um, hi, Janice Coulton." Janice had faltered slightly when she first saw Mal, but she was totally gob-smacked by Keeley. Janice was dying to ask if she was a model.

"Please excuse me, Janice, I just got back from the gym." Keeley's voice was husky yet soft; she was simply oozing with sex appeal. Janice resigned herself to listening to more sexual antics through the walls.

"Janice brought us a rather special bottle of red," Mal said.

"How nice. Well why don't you two open it up and I'll be back in a second," Keeley said. Her long tawny legs carried her swiftly from the room.

"Janice, have a seat, I'll be back with glasses," Mal said. With that he left and Janice sat down on the edge of the sofa. She removed her coat and placed it next to her.

Mal stepped into the kitchen where Keeley was waiting.

"Well?" He said.

"I think we may have struck gold here, Mal. She's got the look, alright."

"Shall we be gentle, though. We have to live next to her, remember."

"Always the gentleman. Let's just play it as we usually do," Keeley said.

Mal stepped around the circular wooden table and opened the big fridge in the corner of the kitchen. He placed Janice's bottle of wine inside and took out another one. He turned and Keeley handed him three glasses. He smiled and took them from her.

Then she pecked Mal on the cheek and hurried out of the kitchen and up the stairs.

"Here we are," Mal said. He held out a glass to Janice. "I thought I'd save your bottle for another time. I've had this in the fridge for a while and I've been dying to open it. Tonight seems like just the ticket."

"OK," Janice said, taking the glass. Mal opened the wine with long dexterous fingers. In moments Janice's glass was half full. He sat down next to Janice, clinked his glass to hers, and said, "So tell me, Janice, are you married?"

Chapter 4

Keeley entered the room just as Mal and Janice finished their first glass of red wine. She was now wearing white jeans and a white woolen roll-neck sweater. She looked resplendent.

"Janice was just telling me that she lives with her daughter. Her husband died," Mal said.   Janice had felt uncomfortable with Mal's opening question; now she'd have to go through it again with Keeley.

"Oh that's terrible. I'm very sorry, Janice," Keeley said. She picked up the wine bottle and poured a large glassful.

"Thank you," Janice said.

"I love a good red wine, dark and thick." Keeley raised the glass to her lips.

Over the course of the following hour Janice found out that Mal was actually short for Malvern, not Malcolm as she'd thought. He was a freelance writer and Keeley was a fitness instructor. Model, fitness instructor, same ballpark. They also had a seventeen-year-old son called Brandon. Janice told them about Katie. She repeated several stories about the Griffin's that got all the right responses from Mal and Keeley. Janice couldn't help wondering about them, though—Keeley in particular. She wasn't sure if she was being overtly sexual or if Janice was just reading two much into it. It was just that almost everything she said could be twisted into a sexy double-entendre. Even her body language was very profound. She constantly changed her sitting position. Tucking one leg beneath her buttocks seemed to be her favourite.

The conversation flowed pretty well, as did the wine. There came a lull in their chat, however, and Mal said, "So, Janice, please tell me about the graveyard next door. With me being a writer I find it terribly interesting that we live next to one. Are there any local myths about the place?"

"A few, yes," Janice replied. "Most of them, as you can imagine, are total bullshit." Janice almost blushed at her word choice but Mal and Keeley both laughed.

"There have been a couple of incidents that I know are true, grave desecration mostly—kids, you know. I heard that a girl was raped in there once. That was before I moved here, though. It's just a generally spooky place, harmless but spooky."

Mal grinned at her. "Sounds just the ticket. I'll have to investigate."

That seemed like a good enough place to leave it and Janice noted the time and stood. She thanked Mal and Keeley for having her over; they thanked her for the wine. Janice left and ran back to the warmth of her own house. The wind was getting up and the first spats of rain were starting to fall. She went inside her house, though not before she threw a quick glance at the graveyard.

Chapter 5

Janice had a nightmare that night: she dreamt that she was walking alone through the graveyard. She was barefoot and the grass was cold and wet. The air around her was still. She had no idea why she was wandering through the graveyard, what she was looking for or why. Eventually she stopped and looked at a gravestone. Janice's blood ran cold as she read the inscription. The name on it was hers and the date of her supposed death was the eleventh November 2003. That was in two days time! She staggered away from the headstone, and promptly tripping over another, she landed on her back. She was lying on freshly dug topsoil. Janice screamed as a bony, withered hand jabbed out of the soil and began clawing at her.

She woke with a start. A layer of cold sweat was frosted onto her spine.

She stumbled out of bed and glanced at the clock: eleven a.m. A rare lie in, she thought and went downstairs. Katie was sprawled on the couch with the TV on.

"Morning, hon," Janice said and bent over to give Katie a quick kiss. "Have you eaten?"

"Nah," Katie replied. Before Janice could ask what she wanted, Katie said, "Guess what happened last night?"

"What?"

"Somebody got killed in the graveyard."

"WHAT!" Janice spluttered. "Who was it? How…wait a minute, how do you know this?"

"Brandon from next door told me. I spoke to him this morning and he told me that someone found a gravestone covered in blood."

Janice sighed. "That's it, blood on a grave and you two instantly think murder, good god Katie." Janice laughed and headed for the kitchen.

"Oh yeah, how do you explain the hand then?" Katie called out.

Janice froze.

The hand. "What hand?" she asked in a very timid voice.

"Brandon said they found a guy's cut-off hand near the grave. Gross, huh?"

"Very gross. What have the police said?"

"Don't know. They asked Brandon's mum and dad a few questions, then they left."

"When did all this happen?"

"About half past eight."

"Why on earth didn't you wake me up?"

"I wanted you to have a lie in. You looked tired," Katie said.

Janice laughed again. "Well, thanks. Next time you can wake me, though."

"OK," Katie said and turned back to the TV. Amazing, Janice thought. She'd just had a conversation with her thirteen-year-old daughter about a murder not even one hundred yards from their home and Katie's main interest was a pop-band on the telly. Then she shivered as she remembered what she had said, *Next time you can wake me up.*

Next Time.

Chapter 6

Janice spotted Keeley out in the back garden that afternoon and went to talk to her. It turned out that the police had actually found a gravestone covered in blood and a hand. Keeley said the first thing she knew about it was when the police knocked on the door.

"Brandon was up for ages, watched them working over there and didn't say boo."

Janice laughed. "Katie did the exact same thing."

Janice peered over the fence. There was a square white tent in the middle of the graveyard.

The rest of Saturday drifted by. The police eventually called Janice and asked her if she had seen anything the night before. She had nothing to tell them.

Katie was in town somewhere with her friends and Janice was watching the TV herself when the doorbell rang. She opened it to find Mal standing on her doorstep.

"Hi, Janice, may I speak with you a moment," Mal said.

"Of course. Please, come on in," Janice replied.

They went through to the living room and sat down. Mal commented on how nice the place looked. They chatted idly for a few minutes, Janice mentioning that Katie and Brandon had met. Mal laughed and told Janice that he thought Brandon might have taken a liking to Katie.

"He's been talking about her all morning. I'm sure you'll meet him soon."

Mal looked as though he really had something to get off his chest, though, so Janice said, "So what's up?"

Mal stood and paced over to the mantelpiece. He fingered a photo of Janice and her husband, then he turned to face Janice.

"I was hoping you could help me."

"Oh, how?" Janice asked.

"I want to go into the graveyard tonight. This is too good an opportunity to miss. I have a story right on my doorstep."

A look of shock was slowly spreading across Janice's face.

Mal continued.

"Normally I'd take Keeley, but she's off out tonight. I'd need you to help me take some photos," he said.

"Mal, I don't know, what kind of photos?"

"Just some general shots of the graveyard. I like to put some snaps in with my work, if I can. We'll only be half an hour. We'll walk through the place together, get a feel for it. You hold the flash, I'll take the snaps, and we're done. C'mon it'll be fun!"

"Well, I don't know about fun, but alright. I'll help you. What time?"

"Come over to the house at ten."

Chapter 7

At ten o'clock that night Janice went next door. She had on her jeans, a sweater and her heavy sheepskin coat. The night air still managed to nip at her.

Mal opened the door, ready to go. He picked up his camera equipment and handed the flashcube and a small tripod to Janice; he carried the camera and a small Dictaphone. Together they walked along Allerton Road until they reached the big open gates of the graveyard. Mal stayed pretty quiet. Janice asked him where Keeley was. He replied that she was out with her gym friends. The way he said it, Janice imagined he didn't care much for Keeley's friends.

They pressed on into the graveyard. A soft amber glow from the streetlights penetrated only a few yards in so Mal pulled a torch from his coat. They walked along the grassy pathways, weaving between gravestones and monuments.

Janice's dream threatened to come back to her but she forced it away.

Mal played the torch across several headstones. Occasionally he would hold the Dictaphone to his mouth and say a few words.

"You alright, Janice?" Mal asked.

"Sure, just a bit cold," she lied. She hated this place and wanted to leave.

"Well, let's get started then. Quicker we're done, quicker we leave."

Mal told her the shots he wanted. "Keeley usually just shoots what she likes the look of; she'll spot something spooky or out of place," Mal said.

"OK," Janice said.

They penetrated deeper into the graveyard. Janice stopped occasionally to take a few shots. She was getting ready to take a snap looking out across the graveyard. She had the tripod set and although she couldn't see much through the viewfinder, the shot looked right. As she prepared to take the photo, Janice thought she caught movement from the corner of the viewfinder. She strained to see. Nothing.

It looked as though something had moved from behind one of the stones.

She took the shot. She didn't see anything as the graveyard was briefly illuminated.

Mal had asked her to save five shots. When she had only five left she went over to him. Mal was kneeling next to a small headstone. The grave was that of a child.

"Sad, isn't it," he said.

"Yeah. I'm down to five," Janice said. She didn't know why but her anxiety levels were steadily increasing.

"OK, I'll do the next bit if you want," Mal said.

"Why, what is it?" Janice asked.

"I want to see what's in that tent."

"Mal, you can't! It's a crime scene," Janice said.

"I know. That's why you don't have to go in. I don't want to get you in trouble."

They started walking towards the white tent. Mal kept looking over his shoulder. Maybe he's getting nervous, Janice thought.

This time Janice *heard* something move. It was a low stony sound like

(*the lid of a stone coffin sliding open*)

bricks scraping together.

"Mal! What was that?" Janice hissed.

"What?" Mal replied.

"Sssshhhh, I heard something. Oh god, I thought I saw something before too. Mal, what if someone is following us!"

"I can't hear anything. Come on, we're almost done." Mal scanned the torch over the ground near them. Nothing. Janice didn't catch him smile.

They got to the tent and Mal began to work one of the poles loose.

"OK, you wait here. I'll be two minutes. Here, take this." He handed Janice the torch.

Then taking the camera and flash, he wriggled under the sagging plastic and into the tent. Janice stood with her back to the tent. The torch beam shone directly ahead. A strong wind kicked up and blew her hair across her face.

She swung the beam left and right. Nothing.

Janice told herself to stop being a baby.

"Hurry up, Mal," she hissed at the tent. Mal didn't respond. The flash didn't go off inside the tent, either. Janice got on her knees, lifted the flap up and pushed her head inside the tent. She poked the torch inside and gasped.

The tent was empty. Mal was nowhere to be seen.

Janice jerked out of the tent as fast as she could. Her heart was pounding now. How could he leave her? Maybe it was just a joke. Janice decided that she was out of here and started away from the tent.

That was when a huge black form loomed out of nowhere and knocked her flying.

Chapter 8

Keeley saw the thing make its move. It hadn't been where she had thought, but close enough. She rose up from behind the headstone where she had been hiding.

She put her rifle to her eyes and peered into the laser sight. The sight was equipped with night vision and it presented Keeley with a sharp green view of Janice being attacked by what looked like a huge man in a long black coat. She saw Janice fall, saw the man cross to her and stand over her. Keeley took a deep breath and pulled the trigger. A silver, cyanide-tipped bullet exploded from the rifle and in less than a second it struck Janice's attacker in the back. He didn't go down.

Janice was screaming. The man raised his hands as if to strike Janice, then he toppled backwards. A gout of blood spewed from his neck.

Janice was struggling to her feet. Keeley stood up and sprinted towards her.

Keeley neatly sidestepped the headstones and was at Janice's side in seconds.

Seconds after that Mal appeared next to Keeley. He held a huge crossbow. They both covered the man on the ground.

"What the…who…oh my god!" Janice spluttered.

Mal looked at Keeley, then fired a volley of three silver bolts in the prostrate form on the grass.

Mal stepped back and Janice felt him tug her arm. The body at their feet ignited. It was consumed by fire in seconds. Blue smoke swirled up into the air and the night was tinged with the stench of burning flesh.

"I'm sorry we had to use you like this, Janice. I'm not really a writer. Keeley and I are vampire hunters."

Janice's mouth fell open.

"I know how it sounds, but I promise I'll explain everything for you," Mal said before Janice could speak. Keeley took her arm.

"It'll be fine, Janice, I promise. You were never in any danger, really. I had you covered the whole time."

Janice's mind was in a mad tangle. She could find no way to unravel what she had just witnessed. She had a million questions so she just opened her mouth and let the first one fly out.

"What if something had gone wrong? I could have been killed!"

Mal pointed to Janice's chest. "See that little red dot over your heart."

Janice saw it. It was like a laser pen was being shone on her.

"That's Brandon. He's our backup. That's why we bought the house. Its position is perfect," Mal said.

Janice looked over to the Hutson's house not fifty yards away. The red dot vanished.

"Plus we've been tracking this guy for three months," Keeley said and kicked at the pile of ash at her feet.

"VAMPIRES!" Janice yelled.

Keeley couldn't help it. She started laughing. Mal joined in moments later and for reasons she had no idea why, Janice began to laugh too.

The three of them stood there howling at the moon like lunatics for a good few minutes. Finally they calmed down. Janice quickly became afraid.

"You two are going to stick around for a while, aren't you?" she said.

"Oh yeah, that's the thing with vamp:, where there's one, there's usually another," Mal replied.

"We're not going anywhere yet, hon," Keeley said.

"I need a drink. No, I need 10, now," Janice said.

Mal started laughing again and together the three walked off toward their homes.

Mike Adamson

For as long as I can remember, there were only two choices of career that ever appealed to me. One was to be a writer. The other was to be a coroner. The length of time it would have taken me to become a coroner eventually put me off. Now I realise that to become a successful writer will take even longer. It is something that I am dedicated to doing, however, and writing has always been my passion. I am an avid reader of all things dark and dangerous. I am a complete horror junkie. I still don't know why I'm so attracted to the macabre and that is what intrigues me more than anything. I just love a good scare. To see this story published here is the biggest thrill of my writing career so far.

To date I have had three other stories published.

My first foray into horror was "Sleep Tight" and can be found on the website http://www.alternatespecies.com. My second story "Dog Day" was featured in the June episode of *Dangerous Creatures* E-zine. "End of the Line" will be published at http://www.themurderhole .com in December 2003.

When I'm not conjuring up new and exciting ways of killing my characters off, I am a keen football fan. I love going out on the town and am usually first in the queue at the cinema whenever a new horror film comes out.

Pretty normal lifestyle for a 26-year-old. Then I write something and people give me strange looks. That's my favourite part, scaring someone else. I hope my tale makes you look over your shoulder next time you walk home alone.

Visions
by
Douglas T. Araujo

Miguel jumped from the bus to the airport's gray asphalt. The strong smell of gasoline came immediately to him carried by the wind, which also brought the promise of rain that night. Miguel's brown hair fluttered, and he instinctively held more tightly to the briefcase full of documents he had in his right hand, suddenly afraid that a stronger blast of wind could take it out of his hand.

Almost twenty feet were between Miguel and the airplane, and while he followed the other passengers through this distance, he observed the plane he would fly in for the next three hours. Miguel used to travel frequently at work and to some degree was familiar with several commercial airplane models. He recognized this one immediately as a Fokker 100 and that it seemed to be a relatively new airplane.

Several people wearing the airport uniform were working near it. Some were carrying packages into the plane, while others were topping off the fuel tanks, which certainly explained the smell of gasoline he had noticed before.

The passenger line in front of him stopped for a moment while a smiling stewardess helped an old lady to climb the ladder's metal steps. Miguel used this time to close the last button of his shirt. He was starting to feel cold because of the wind, which was continuing to blow.

Slowly, the line resumed moving.

Miguel looked at his watch to confirm what time it was. The flight seemed to be on schedule.

Finally, he reached the ladder. Beside him, the stewardess who had helped the lady moments before looked at his ticket. Miguel thought she was very beautiful with her green eyes and dark hair tied in a bun. She couldn't be more than twenty-five years old, he thought.

"Welcome on board, sir."

"Thank you."

Something in his voice made her smile. At this time, however, her smile was a natural one, not that mechanical expression that stewardesses always had. Miguel was proud of himself. He was a handsome man, and he knew how to use his charm when he wanted to.

He started climbing the stairs, firmly holding the railing. He was only on the first step when a strange feeling came over him.

At first, it was only uneasiness, a sensation of light d iscomfort. But with each step, the feeling seemed to intensify, to grow. It seemed as if a cold fist was tightening in his stomach.

Miguel recognized the feeling immediately, even having felt it only once during his whole life. It was the same sensation he had twenty-two years ago. The same thing he sensed when he walked beside his father in that hospital row, the smell of disinfectant invading his nostrils and tears trickling down his cheeks.
The same thing he had felt when his father said to him that his mother was dying.

It was a deep grief, caused by the knowledge of losing something irreplaceable. Something nobody could give him again. A grief which seemed to grow at each step.

He still remembered that night perfectly, although he was only nine years old. And he remembered all of that because of a unique reason: he already knew his mother would die that night

At the current moment, however, there was no reason to feel that way.

Even so, the feeling remained and grew at each step, until the point where he reached the top of the ladder, and his eyes were filled with tears.

An uncontrollable desire to look behind him, to the ground, dominated him.

Miguel looked back from the top of the ladder to the landing strip and to the airport he was leaving behind him. The sun's last rays were shining on the horizon, and the lights were already on. The feeling of losing something was so strong at that moment that his chest ached.

He looked again to the plane, and suddenly the feeling disappeared as if by magic, as if it had never existed.

He sighed and entered the aircraft, disguising the tears and drying the corner of the eyes with his shirtsleeve. He verified his ticket and started looking for his seat, already feeling like an idiot.

His seat was 13B, and it didn't take long for him to find it. It was at the left side of the plane, near the corridor. There was nobody on the seat beside him, at least not yet. Miguel looked through the small window and noticed he was exactly over the left wing. Outside, the night had already fallen completely.

He opened the small compartment for the handheld luggage and put his briefcase inside. While he was doing this, a fat man passed by him in the corridor going somewhere to the back of the plane, and Miguel had to force himself against the seat in order to let him pass. He didn't even look at the man because he was focused on putting his briefcase inside the compartment and sitting down as fast as possible so he wouldn't obstruct the passage of the other passengers.

However, out of the corner of his eye, he saw something that attracted his attention.

The man's neck was bleeding. A red strain showed on his back.

Miguel, frightened, turned his head to see better and realized he had just fooled himself. The man was wearing a red scarf which finished in the middle of his back. He had thought of it as blood. He looked a moment longer until the man sat down.

Then he also sat, trying to calm down his heart that was thumping in his chest. While his heart came back to its normal rhythm, he started feeling a light headache, which seemed to radiate from behind his eyes. It was a very faint pain, which didn't even bother him. He closed his eyes and remained that way for some seconds. Only now he started perceiving how tired he was.

"Excuse me?"

Miguel opened his eyes. Beside him at the corridor stood an old man. His black shirt collar was the first thing Miguel noticed when he looked at him. The man was a priest.

He got up, leaving space for the man to pass and sit down on the seat beside him. While the old man sat, Miguel observed him. He was thin and feeble-looking with white hair, which contrasted with the black of his clothes. A silver crucifix hung from his neck. His face was thin with big brown eyes, the face of a very intelligent man. He appeared to be around sixty years old, maybe a little bit more. He had a small book in his right hand.

Miguel felt a little bit uncomfortable. Although he was a Catholic, it had been several years since he attended church. He wondered if the priest would want to chat about this subject. The last thing he wanted was a preaching during the whole three-hour flight.

But the man didn't do that. He only opened the book he had brought with him and started reading without a word. Miguel observed, curious, the book's cover and noticed it was Stephen King's *Carrie*. Miguel had heard about this author, although he had never read any of his books. He didn't like horror stories.

A metallic voice started coming through the loudspeakers, and at the same time a stewardess started the safety indoctrination. Miguel noticed she was the same stewardess from before who stood beside the ladder, and this made him smile.

He looked at his watch once more. The flight was well on schedule. They should be taking off in a few minutes.

He walked hurriedly through a corridor with high white walls. The smell of disinfectant made his nostrils burn and tears trickle down his face, dropping from his chin and wetting the front of his shirt. His father was beside him. They walked hand in hand, and he could feel the strength and the comfort of that rough hand on his own.

Miguel looked at his father. He was tall and was wearing the same red shirt he had worn the night his mother died. He walked with a steady step, hurriedly, as if he knew they had not much time left. His head was lowered, confirming his sorrow. An expression of defeat was stamped on his face. An expression of pain. Exactly the same expression he had on his face the night his mother died.

However, something was different.

While they walked, they passed through several people who stood in the corridor. Physicians, attendants, nurses. Everyone looked at them with frightened expressions, as if they didn't expect them. Some of them pressed themselves against the wall to let them pass, the green of their uniforms contrasting with the impeccable white of the hospital walls. He and his father never stopped. They didn't have time for this.

Finally, they were in front of a door at the corridor's end. Miguel looked at his father, and suddenly understood what was different. His father was older. He wasn't the same man that had taken him to see his moribund mother twenty-two years ago. His head was bald, and he had wrinkles under his eyes.

Miguel looked at himself, and noticed he also wasn't the same. He wasn't a nine year-old boy anymore. He was an adult. His father's hand didn't cover his own hand, as it had done that night.

His father looked at him, pain and grief totally apparent in his eyes. He opened the door, signaling with his head for Miguel to go in first.

Miguel walked through the door, and suddenly he wasn't in a hospital anymore. The disinfectant smell was gone, and the walls were not white. Instead, he was in a kind of chapel, with wooden seats and walls painted an austere gray. Soft religious music was playing. Some people were sitting in the seats, but he didn't recognize any of them. They were all wearing black and chatted among themselves in whispers.

At the end of the room, near what looked like an altar, there was a coffin.

Suddenly, Miguel understood where he was.

A wake.

He started walking toward the coffin as if pushed by an invisible force. The people in the seats didn't seem to notice him. None of them seemed to have even seen him.

When he passed by the last seat, the one nearest the coffin, he recognized the man that sat there.

His father.

He was sitting on the edge of the seat, almost kneeling, his back curved. Instead of the red shirt, he was now wearing a black suit. He had a handkerchief in his hand, and he was crying sorrowfully.

Miguel felt sorry and wanted to comfort him, but didn't stop walking. He doubted he could. He continued walking until he reached the coffin. There was a corpse inside it, surrounded by flowers, and he needed to know who it was.

He looked straight into the coffin and into the face of the deceased. The shock he felt was so overpowering he had to step back.

It was himself in the coffin.

His face was as white as wax. The hands crossed on the chest held a silver crucifix. He wore a black suit he recognized as the same he wore at his cousin's marriage, almost a month before.

It was he, Miguel.

He was dead.

Then he felt an irresistible desire to get out of there. He needed to go, to run away as far as possible. To go, to run…

Suddenly, everything changed, and he was again in the hospital room, looking at the same bed where twenty-two years before he had seen his mother for the last time. This time, however, the bed was empty.

A hand touched lightly on his shoulder. Miguel turned, frightened.

His mother was there, still in front of him, her hand holding his shoulder. She was wearing the same hospital green clothes she was wearing the last time he had seen her. Her face had the same injuries from the accident which had caused her death. Her brown hair was covered by blood-strained gauze, exactly like that night.

So she talked, and her voice was as hoarse as the sound of a scratched disc:

"Be careful, Miguel! Be careful!"

With each word, the hand in his shoulder tightened, making his whole body tremble.

"Be careful! Be careful!"

Miguel woke up frightened, holding tightly onto the arms of his chair. A few moments passed before he realized where he was. Some people were looking at him with frightened expressions. He noticed that a woman whispered something to a man on her left and pointed at him.

"Son?" The priest shook his shoulder again, and let him go. "Are you all right?"

Miguel passed his hand across his forehead. It was wet with sweat.

"Now I'm fine. I had a nightmare."

"I noticed it. That's why I was trying to wake you. It must have been quite a nightmare by the way you started struggling and talking."

"Did I say anything?" Miguel looked visibly uncomfortable.

"To tell the truth, it was nothing anybody could understand. Only disconnected words." The priest opened his book and concentrated on it again.

"Thanks for waking me." Miguel felt it was his obligation to say it.

The priest raised his eyes from the book once more and looked at him with an amused expression.

"Well, you're welcome."

And resumed reading.

Miguel looked at his watch. He had been flying for half an hour already, and his headache hadn't passed yet, even with his sleep.

Miguel leaned his head against the seat and closed his eyes. He had been like this for most of the last half-hour, but it didn't help his headache. The pain only got worse. What in the beginning was only a light discomfort behind his eyes had now become truly agonizing. The pain had increased enormously and spread across his temples and the region just over his eyebrows. He couldn't remember having felt a more intense headache in his whole life. It seemed his whole brain was throbbing.

Even with his eyes shut, he couldn't sleep. First, because the pain didn't allow him to relax, and second because he was afraid of having another nightmare and embarrassing himself again. It was not usual for him to have nightmares, but he didn't want to risk it.

After another minute, he decided it was time to call the stewardess and ask if she had any analgesic he could take. He should have done that at the beginning, but he was one of those people who avoided taking medicines if he possibly could. However, he couldn't endure this pain any more.

Slowly, he opened his eyes. First one, then the other, as if he was afraid that opening both at once would make him moan with pain. He noticed that when he opened his eyes, the priest looked at him with an expression which seemed a mixture of concern and curiosity. However, he didn't say anything, and Miguel was grateful for that.

Touching the panel over his head, he pushed the button to call the stewardess. A yellow light on the button went on immediately.

Miguel remained looking at the corridor, waiting for the stewardess to show up. For a moment, he wondered if she would be the same one who had offered him the smile at the stairs, but this didn't seem important to him now. All that mattered was to make the headache stop. Out of the corner of his eye, he noticed the priest was observing him with a curious expression. None of the other passengers were looking at him.

The stewardess was taking her time showing up. He was about to push the button again when she appeared in the corridor, coming from behind the drapes that separated the passenger section from the captain's cabin. She was not the same girl who had smiled to him before.

Then, with no warning, he felt a sharp pain in his eyes so strong it surpassed everything he had felt until that moment. The pain began behind his eyes and spread across his whole head. Miguel felt as if his brain would explode in that instant. Closing his eyes, he swallowed a cry of pain in his throat.

Curiously, the pain disappeared in the next instant. It happened as if that sharp pain was the last breath of a dying man. Miguel opened his eyes, suddenly relieved.

Then he saw her, and his blood became chilled water.

The stewardess was still coming down the corridor toward him. But it wasn't a stewardess anymore. It was a corpse, a dead woman. Its red uniform was reduced to strips. The right half of its face was black, burned, and where the eye should be there was only a dark hole. Its hair was burned too, disheveled and dirty with blood. One of its legs was visible through the torn uniform, and the bone was projecting through the flesh at an impossible angle.

Even so, none of the other passengers seemed to notice anything wrong. The thing stopped in the middle of the way and exchanged words with one of them. Eventually it continued down again and leaned close to Miguel.

"Do you need anything, mister?" The corpse smiled, contorting the burning flesh around its mouth in a repugnant grimace.

Miguel's voice disappeared. He was holding the arms of the seat so strongly it seemed he wanted to pull them out with his bare hands. His heart was racing, and his mouth was dry. He could smell the burned flesh, and this made him feel sick.

The corpse seemed to notice all this because suddenly its expression changed. It stopped smiling and asked in a more concerned tone:

"Are you feeling all right, mister?"

Then, as if somebody had simply pushed a button, everything became normal again. In a wink, the corpse wasn't there anymore, and a beautiful girl was in its place, looking worried. There wasn't blood and bones projecting from under torn clothes, or the smell of burned flesh any more. Miguel looked around, astonished. Nobody seemed to be looking at him, except the priest, who glanced at him with the same concerned expression as the stewardess.

Getting strength from God knows where, Miguel released his grip on the arms and said:

"Could you please give me an aspirin? This headache is killing me."

Relief showed on the girl's face as she heard his answer.

"Sure, sir. I will be back in a moment." And she went away, slowly, as she had come.

Miguel looked at his own hands, which were shaking badly. So he passed his hands across his face and onto his hair. He noticed this time the priest hadn't resumed reading but continued looking at him, as if he was waiting for Miguel to have a nervous attack at any instant

He leaned his head on the seat again. The pain was back. Weaker, but it was still there.

He needed to think, to decide what to do. He had to coordinate his thoughts. Now, everything was clear to him. It was happening again, the same way it had happened twenty-two years before.

A wave of desperation washed over him. He lowered the head between his hands without knowing what to do, what to think. Memories assaulted him. The headache seemed to worsen with each second.

"Are you feeling well, son?"

Miguel opened his eyes once more. The priest was looking at him with an anxious expression.

"Excuse me for my intrusion," he said, "but can I help you? You don't look very well."

Miguel remained looking at him for a second, in doubt about what to say.

Somehow, the big brown eyes of that man inspired confidence in him. In addition to that, it would be good to talk to somebody, to help him to arrange his thoughts. That damn headache kept him from thinking clearly.

And could anyone be better to listen to him and give him advice than a priest?

Making a decision, Miguel straightened again on the seat and passed his hand over his hair, as if this simple gesture could alleviate the pain he was feeling. With a low voice, so that nobody else would hear him, he asked:

"Father, do you believe in visions?"

The old man looked surprised at the question.

"Yes, I do. The Bible tells us of a lot of cases. See, for example, the vision Mary had when the angel Gabriel announced to her she was pregnant, or…"

"No, no, Father. Not this kind of vision. I am talking about…" he thought for a moment, without knowing how to say that better. "I am talking about seeing things that will happen."

"Do you mean clairvoyance?"

Miguel nodded. Talking seemed to make the pain worse.

The priest looked at him for a long time with a strange expression on his eyes, which Miguel wasn't able to recognize. Finally, he spoke:

"Why are you asking this?"

Miguel looked at his own hands, not sure again about what to say. He decided that he would tell everything.

"I am going to tell you a story, Father, one that happened several years ago, which I never told anybody. Not even my dad."

The priest straightened up in his seat, as if looking for a more comfortable position, but he didn't say anything.

"I was only nine years old at the time. I don't know what day of the week it was, but I remember it was a sunny day, and my mother closed the bedroom drapes, because I was sick, and the strong light bothered me, making my eyes ache. I don't know exactly what disease I had, but it had started when I woke up that morning. My head and my eyes had ached so much that I barely could leave the bed. At first my mother seemed worried, but after she took my temperature and saw I didn't have a fever, she calmed down a little. I remember her talking to my father before he went to his job. Probably, she thought I had a migraine or something similar. The fact is that I stayed home, lying in my bedroom's penumbra, trying to sleep without much success. My mother was in the kitchen, making lunch."

He paused, trying to put the ideas into sequence. His headache was getting worse with every minute that passed, and he was finding it difficult to concentrate. His eyes seemed want to jump from their sockets.

"I don't know how much time I remained there, lying in the penumbra. I think I must have slept a little. When I woke up, my mother was in the bedroom. She had her back turned to me and was putting something into the wardrobe. The bedroom was still dark. I talked to her and she turned to me. Then I saw her face."

Miguel looked to the priest again, trying to read the expression on the man's face. He remained impassive. It was impossible to say what he was thinking.

"It was the most terrible thing I had ever seen," he continued. "It was not my mother who was there. It was a monster. To be more accurate, a corpse. The upper part of its head was crushed, and its face was full of blood. Its eyes were wide. When it looked at me, I closed my eyes and started to yell."

"So what happened?" The priest spoke for the first time since Miguel had started his story. His voice sounded curious.

"It came to my bed and held me in its arms. It talked to me in a low tone, saying that everything was all right, all right. When I finally had the courage to open my eyes, it was my mother who was there holding me. Only my mother."

"You could have been dreaming. It was not real."

"That was exactly what she said when I told her what I had seen. And I believed her. That was my mistake."

Miguel looked at the priest, who didn't avert his eyes, and continued:

"On that afternoon, I was already feeling better. The headache was gone, and I was watching TV in my room. My mother came to where I was and said she was going to the market to buy some things, but she would come back soon. She went while I stayed watching cartoons. She didn't come back. One hour later, my father arrived at home, earlier than usual. He had an expression on his face I had never seen before, and I noticed immediately there was something wrong. He sat beside me on the couch, held me tightly and said my mother had had an accident and was in the hospital."

He paused and passed his hand across his forehead. The aspirin he had taken before didn't seem to be helping with the headache.

"At that time, I didn't know for sure what had happened. Only later, I understood that the car of a drunken driver had jumped onto the sidewalk and hit my mother while she was leaving the market. But that day, the only thing my father said to me was that she had had an accident. He took me to the hospital because he wanted me to see her. I think he wanted me to see her one last time, although he didn't say that to me, of course." Miguel wiped the tears from his eyes with his shirtsleeve.

"When we arrived at the hospital, she was unconscious and lying on the bed. There were several pieces of equipment around her and tubes going into her nostrils and mouth. But what attracted my attention even more was the gauze which covered her head."

Miguel paused and looked the priest straight in the eyes.

"When the car hit my mother, her head struck the sidewalk, and she had a cranial fracture. The location of the fracture, where her head was swaddled in gauze, was exactly the same as I had seen on the corpse's head that morning in my bedroom. Exactly the same. So I understood it had not been a dream..." He paused, breathing heavily. Then he continued. "Two hours later, she died. She never recovered consciousness. And I never told anybody I had had that vision, not even my father."

He leaned his head against the seat again. Definitely, the aspirin wasn't working. The pain seemed even worse than before.

The priest remained silent for some moments. Then said:

"Everything was a coincidence. You had a dream or maybe a delirium, and by coincidence your mother had a fatal accident that same day. Coincidence. Just that."

Miguel opened his eyes, ready to say it was not true, when a sharp, new pain spread from behind his eyes. For an instant all became blurred, as if someone had used the flash of a camera in front of his face. Then everything came back into focus again.

But it was not the priest he was looking at. In his place, a blackened corpse sat, looking at him through empty sockets. There was a big hole on its chest, as if some object had been projected through there, ripping flesh and bones.

Miguel looked the other way, trying to avoid that repugnant vision. However, what he saw on the other side made him even more terrified: Corpses occupied all the seats! Most of them were totally burned, with wrinkled flesh and blackened and empty eye sockets. Several had wounds, deep cuts, bones showing through. A few weren't totally burned, and in these he could see the blood of the wounds. The smell of burned flesh, blood and urine struck him.

Nearby, one of the corpses rose up from its seat, its intestines slipping out through a hole in his belly.

Miguel thought he was going to puke.

Then all of this was gone. The woman that had stood up continued her way toward the back of the plane, probably going to the restroom.

The priest was holding his arm and looking at him with a worried expression.

"Son, are you all right?"

Miguel took the priest's hands with strength.

"Father, you need to help me. I also believed it had been a dream, a coincidence. I had convinced myself of this through the years. But it is happening again. I can see them! They are all dead!"

"Calm down, son." The priest's voice was low and soft, the voice of a professional, accustomed to the task of comforting people. "This is not real…"

Miguel felt the tears appear in his eyes. The headache was terrible; it hadn't disappeared like the last time but continued even stronger than before.

Desperation started flooding him.

"This is real, father! I saw them! They are all dead! Even you are dead!"

"It's not real…"

"It is real! Everybody in this plane is going to die!"

Several people looked at him when he announced this. Only then did Miguel notice he had been shouting. The priest, however, remained calm.

"All right. I believe you. Let's see what we can do." And saying this, he pushed the button to call the stewardess.

Miguel felt a little bit relieved. Finally, someone was listening to him. He lowered his head and closed his eyes for a moment, trying to clear his mind. It was difficult to think with that headache. When he opened his eyes, the stewardess was coming through the corridor. He noticed, almost unconsciously, that she was the same girl who had smiled to him before.

When she approached them, the priest asked:

"Miss, my friend here is a little bit nervous about the progress of our trip, and he would like to know if the flight is going normally."

The stewardess looked slightly amused by the question. With a smile on her face, she answered:

"Yes, it is all right, sir. We will arrive at our destination at the appointed time."

"There isn't any problem, is there?"

"No, of course not."

"And if there were one, you would tell us. Right?"

"Sir, if any problem happened during the flight which could affect the safety of the passengers or the crew, this company must as a standard take all the precautions to land as fast as possible. In this case, surely the captain would announce that through the loudspeakers. This is our procedure."

"Thank you."

The girl went away slowly. Before she disappeared behind the drapes, she looked at Miguel over her shoulder and smiled.

The priest was looking at him, also smiling.

"See? There is nothing to worry about."

"But, Father, I saw them…they were all dead!"

"Son, you wouldn't believe what the human mind can do. Many times we think we see things that don't exist. I worked for a long time in a hospital, and I saw things like that several times. It is called self-suggestion, and it can happen during periods of great emotional stress. From the little I saw, you are undoubtedly passing through a period like this."

Miguel thought for a moment. He still found it difficult to believe what the old man was saying, but he really was fighting a period of great stress in his life. Maybe the trip had only stirred old memories…

"I suggest that you try to relax a little bit," the priest continued. "Nothing is going to happen. Nobody is going to die."

"I think you are right. I'm going to wash my face and try to sleep. And thank you for listening to me."

Miguel rose and went toward the restroom. While he walked, several people looked at him with frightened expressions, as if they thought he would attack them at any moment.

He entered the narrow restroom and closed the door. He turned the faucet, and started washing his face slowly. The piercing headache continued, and the back of his eyes seemed to throb.

Then he lifted his head and looked at himself in the mirror.

A yell locked in his throat.

He was also a corpse. His skin was blackened, wrinkled, and a big wound had been opened in his neck from one side to another. His eyes were empty holes. The smell of burned flesh and hair flooded the small restroom. He looked at his own hands, reduced to blackened lumps of coal.

Miguel opened the restroom door suddenly and jumped into the corridor, hitting the wall. With this sound, several corpses looked at him. Not controlling himself anymore, he started walking and stumbling towards the captain's cabin.

All he could think of was that he needed to do something, to warn someone.

Everybody was dead. Every one of them.

When he passed by his seat, he noticed that the corpse, which before had been a priest, tried to say something to him, but it didn't matter. He needed to go to the captain.

He walked three more steps, and another corpse emerged in front of him, coming from behind the drapes. Strangely, Miguel recognized her: it was the same stewardess who had smiled at him before.

"I need to talk to the captain," he said, hurriedly.

"You can't do that now," the corpse answered. "The captain has just turned on the lights to fasten belts. Everybody needs to go back to his seat."

Miguel looked at the signal, which now was on. When he looked again to the corpse, it was gone. The stewardess had returned. However, now she wasn't smiling.

"What is happening?" He asked.

"We are going to cross a turbulence zone. Everybody needs to go back to his seat and fasten his belt."

"I need to talk to the captain. I need to warn him."

"Unfortunately, this will not be possible now. You can talk to him after we cross the turbulence zone."

"Don't you understand?" Miguel started yelling desperately. "If I don't talk to him, we all are going to die!"

A sepulchral silence fell over the plane. Miguel could sense the eyes fixed on his back.

For a moment, the stewardess seemed to hesitate. He could see it in her eyes. But this moment of doubt disappeared when he heard a voice behind him:

"My friend is a little bit confused, Miss. But I am sure he is going to calm down now. There is nothing for us to worry about, is there?"

Miguel turned in a flash only to find the priest, who now glanced at him with eyes that seemed as cold as ice.

"I can guarantee you that everything is under control," the stewardess said. "There is no reason to worry."

The priest held Miguel by the arm with a strength that surprised him, and said in a low tone:

"Now, let's go back to our seats."

Miguel obeyed, not knowing what else to do. The headache didn't let him think clearly. He landed on the seat like a rock and fastened the belt mechanically. In an instant, the airplane started pitching as they passed through the turbulence.

"What were you trying to do?" The priest asked, nervous. "Put everyone in this plane in a panic?"

"I need to warn the captain. We are in danger!"

"No, we are not! It's only your imagination!"

"Don't you understand? This plane is going to crash! We all are going to die! I saw it!"

"All right." The priest suddenly changed his approach. "Let's say that you are right. Now, I'm not saying you *are* right, but let's suppose you are. In this case, what good will do to warn the captain? Do you think he can do something about it?"

"He can be more careful."

"Careful with what? Do you know why we are going to crash?"

"No," Miguel admitted.

"Even if you warn the captain, this would lead to nothing. Probably the captain would be more nervous, and that could make him become distracted."

Miguel was silent.

"In addition to that," he continued, "He surely won't believe you. Put yourself in his place. If a passenger talked to you and said he had a vision that the plane was going to crash and that everybody on board would die, would you believe him?"

Miguel remained silent. He knew the man was right. It didn't matter what he did, he couldn't avoid what would happen. Their fate was already determined, and there was nothing he could do.

Everyone on that plane was already dead.

He himself was already dead.

"You are right, Father," he said, his voice full of grief. "There's nothing I can do."

The man smiled, satisfied with himself.

Miguel laid his head down and started praying, silently.

The plane had been in turbulence for a half-hour and it showed no signs of diminishing. Instead, it seemed to be getting worse and worse. The airplane jumped up and down as if it was out of control. Sometimes it descended suddenly, only to go up again, making Miguel feel coldness in his stomach.

In addition to that, there was the headache which didn't pass. At least, it seemed to have stabilized.

The passengers were strangely quiet. When the plane first went into the turbulence, the chattering continued as always. He even heard some people complaining of the jumping. They had become quiet now, though, one by one. Now, the silence was complete.

Looking around, Miguel noticed a woman with her eyes shut, gripping the arms of the seat. A man behind her moved his lips silently, as if he was praying. The priest beside him slept. He was the only one who seemed calm.

In the plane's front, he saw two stewardesses talking, half hidden by the drape that separated them from the passenger area. He noticed by the way they whispered and by the expression on their faces that they were afraid too.

Something was wrong, and they knew that.

Everybody knew that. They all could feel the danger.

But knowledge wouldn't save them. They were all already dead. Including himself.

He closed his eyes, trying to sleep. But the strong turbulence and the headache didn't allow him this relief.

Miguel opened his eyes again when the captain's voice sounded through the loudspeakers. His tone was tense and hurried, as if he wanted to finish the task as soon as possible and go back to more important things which required his immediate attention. His voice sounded tinny on the loudspeaker, and there was some static in the background.

"Ladies and gentlemen, this is the captain speaking. Unfortunately, due to the storm we are fighting, we are going to make a route change. It will not be possible for us to get to our destination right now, and we are going to land soon at another airport where arrangements will be made to resume this trip. I thank you for your cooperation. Everything is under control."

Some murmurs could be heard through the airplane, but Miguel didn't pay them any attention. A phrase from the captain's statement had absorbed his total attention. "Everything is under control." Why did he say that? If the problem was the weather, why had he said everything was under control?

Suddenly, he knew.

The captain was lying.

It was not the weather which was making the plane deviate from its original route. It was something wrong *in the plane.* This explained everything: the whispers and fearful expression of the stewardesses, the captain's tense voice, the change in route and surprise landing. Even the turbulence. Maybe there was no turbulence, after all. Maybe it was only the airplane which couldn't be stabilized.

Miguel looked around. The other passengers seemed calmer now. The sound of voices started once more. People were chatting again, even with the turbulence.

But Miguel knew. He had seen what was going to happen to them.

They were all dead.

And there was nothing he could do. The priest was right. It wouldn't do any good to warn the captain. Whatever the problem was, the captain already knew about it. He was now sure of that.

He looked again to the priest beside him, who continued sleeping.

In that moment, Miguel envied him.

It would be better to die sleeping.

Some minutes later, the landing procedure started. The turbulence didn't stop, and the airplane jumped more than ever. Miguel's head throbbed, and his eyes burned.

Slowly, they started passing through the clouds. Through the small window, Miguel observed that a torrential rain was falling. The priest had finally awakened and looked at the rain with fear. Miguel wondered if he was finally starting to believe in his warnings.

Lighting cut the sky on the right side, illuminating the passengers' faces and causing some of them let out small, frightened shouts. With the lighting, Miguel's eyes seemed to light themselves.

Then the corpses were back. Every one of them, in all their repugnance. But something was different now. It was as if now everything looked more...*real*. It was as if there was no returning anymore.

Their fate was sealed.

The airplane continued going down, and the rain and the wind outside shook it from all sides. Miguel imagined the captain trying to control the plane, sweating and holding the controls with determination. He looked ahead, to the drapes, trying to see any of the stewardesses, but none of them was in sight.

The city lights became visible through the window. The corpse who was the priest turned to him, and his face contorted in which should be a smile.

Miguel closed his eyes. He didn't want to see that anymore. He *couldn't* see that anymore. While the plane approached the ground, going up and down like a roller coaster car, he prayed for a fast ending.

Then the plane touched down. It was a sudden stroke, more a fall than a landing. The impact made his body sink into the seat. Somehow, however, the captain was able to hold the plane on the ground, and Miguel could feel the great plane slowing down from application of the potent brakes. He held to the seat tightly, sure that something dreadful might happen at any moment.

The airplane decreased its forward velocity until it had stopped almost completely. Then the captain headed slowly toward the place for arriving flights.

His voice came through the speakers:

"Ladies and gentlemen, welcome." This time, his voice seemed happy, almost exultant, without even a shadow of the stress of the last message.

Some passengers applauded, and Miguel opened his eyes again.

There were no more corpses. Everything was back to normal again.

The plane glided slowly to the arrival deck and stopped. The "fasten belts" signs went off, and everybody rose, anxious to leave the flying machine.

The priest said to him jovially:

"Do you see? I told you nothing was going to happen…"

Miguel smiled back a weak smile. Thank God he was wrong. Thank God the priest was right, and everything had been only his own imagination fooling him.

He rose, opened the baggage compartment above his seat, and got his briefcase, which he had nearly forgotten about. Everything had returned to normal. Now, all that he needed was to make that damn headache go away.

In minutes, all the passengers were inside one of the two buses which would take them to the arrival room. Miguel stood, because the bus was full. He looked around but couldn't see the priest. Probably in the second bus behind his, he thought.

Powerful rain and wind continued outside. From time to time lightning cut the sky. His headache seemed finally to be going away. Miguel smiled, thinking of how he had been a fool.

Two stewardesses got onto the bus, chattering and giggling. The driver closed the door and started the engine. Miguel looked behind him and saw that the second bus was following them closely.

More lightning tore through the sky, this time very close, and the brightness made Miguel blink.

In that blink of an eye, everything changed.

The corpses were there again, blackened, mutilated. The smell of burned meat now mixed with the gasoline smell made his nostrils burn.

Miguel felt terror-stricken. But in the middle of all that, one thing attracted his attention.

The bus driver.

He was a corpse too.

Miguel understood immediately what that meant, and this knowledge seemed to burn inside his brain.

The problem was not in the plane, after all.

He opened his mouth to yell, to order the driver to stop the bus…but he didn't have time.

Another lightning bolt cut through the sky, blinding the driver for a second. At that same instant, a truck appeared, as if coming from nowhere. The bus hit it right in the middle, making the truck tumble and spilling gasoline onto the ground. The second bus tried to avoid it, but the wet strip made it skid. With the impact, the gasoline ignited. The explosion that followed broke several windows at the airport, injuring many people.

The fire was soon extinguished because the torrential rain helped to fight it. However, it was too late

There were no survivors among the people inside the buses. Only corpses were found among the debris.

Blackened and mutilated corpses.

Douglas T. Araujo

Douglas T. Araujo is a Brazilian writer who lives in Santos—a not so small city in Brazil's coast—with his wife, two children and a dog. Born during the Halloween night of 1970, he has been since his childhood an avid reader, with a strong preference for speculative fiction. It was during his childhood that he started writing his first stories, mainly in the Mystery and Science Fiction genres, but it was only in 1999, when he started writing horror, that he felt he had found his true vocation.

The Little Brother Puzzle
by
Jason Brannon

It all started when Preston dug up the corpse of his eight-year-old younger brother to see what damage time and worms had wrought. The body, not surprisingly, was much as Preston had imagined it, a heap of rotting limbs in a burlap sack, hardly the brother he remembered.

"You don't look so good, Mikey," he said, peeking into the sack as he hoisted his brother out of the cheap pine casket. "But I hope that we can fix that. The way I got it figured we're going to put you back together again and get some answers."

Something with multiple sets of legs ran across the back his hand as he let go of the bag, and he couldn't help wondering about how many organisms were currently sustaining themselves on his brother's rotting flesh. He pushed the thought out of his mind as he drove back to his house.

The others were waiting inside for Preston when he pulled up in the driveway. Every light in the house was off, yet in one of the rooms, there was a faint glow in the window. Candlelight.

Preston didn't go to any great lengths to conceal the fact that he had his dead brother's body in the trunk of his car. With the burlap sack, he really didn't have to. If anybody happened to look out the window at that moment, they would probably think that he was unloading a bagful of laundry. Nobody would ever consider the possibility that there was a mutilated eight-year old inside. Of course there would be quite a lot of explaining to do when Mikey was back to normal and the pieces of his eight-year old body were put back together again like a puzzle of flesh. But that was a problem Preston would worry about when it became a problem.

"I honestly didn't think you would actually go through with it," Johnny whispered, eyeing the sack with equal parts amazement and disgust. "Is that really him in there?"

"Yeah, that's him. Why are you whispering?" Preston asked. "I don't think any of the neighbors could hear you at this time of night."

"I'm just a little jumpy. After all, I'm not used to breaking the law," Johnny said. "Don't get me wrong, I'm willing to help you go through with this. I just hope you know what you're doing."

"I've been studying," Preston said with a wink and a smile. "We'll do fine."

Karen was sitting on the bed when Johnny and Preston struggled to get Mikey's dead weight through the door. Normally, she smiled when Preston entered the room. Not tonight. Tonight wasn't a night for smiling.

"Rankin's not here," she said after Preston kissed her softly.

"He won't be. Not while the festivities are going on, anyway. He should be here about thirty minutes from now. I wanted somebody to come in after everything was said and done just in case anything went wrong. He's our backup."

"What a comfort," Johnny said, crossing his thickly muscled arms.

"Don't worry. It's just a precaution."

"And Rankin is an expert on all of this stuff, right? He'll be able to make things right if this little conjuring of yours gets out of hand?"

Preston's eyes narrowed at the question. "Rankin doesn't know jack about the art. And, no, he won't be able to twitch his nose a few times and save us if anything happens. But don't worry. It won't come to that."

"Fine," Johnny conceded. "But it sounds to me like he's the clean-up boy."

"What will he have to clean up?" Karen asked.

"Us," Johnny said.

"Stop being such a wuss," Preston said sharply. "You act like I'm trying to call a demon or something. Mikey could be pretty obnoxious at times, but I hardly think that he's capable of mass destruction or serial killings."

"I'll just shut my mouth," Johnny replied with a sigh. "You do whatever you want. I'm the idiot here. You're the omniscient sorcerer."

Preston nodded like he heard Johnny, but it was clear that he wasn't listening.

"You got everything set up, Karen?" he said.

"The Ouija board's ready to go," she said with a hint of hesitation in her voice.

"What is it?" Preston asked.

"Are you sure you want to go through with this?"

Preston sighed as he maneuvered the bag containing Mikey's remains onto the bed. "You're jumping ship on me too? \We've already had this discussion. If you don't want to help, that's fine. I won't hold it against you. But don't hold it against me if I try to bring my brother back and find out who cut him into little pieces of fish-bait."

"I'm just afraid you might be getting in a little over your head," Karen said softly, kissing him lightly on the forehead. "I mean this isn't something you should take too lightly."

Preston was about to say something when Johnny put a hand on his shoulder.

"Look, man, we just want to make sure that you've considered every possibility here. We're trying to look out for you."

"I've been doing my homework," Preston maintained.

"This is the occult we're dealing with here," Johnny said. "Not some fairy tale out of a book. Things happen during these sorts of rituals. Things that you don't always plan on. I've watched enough movies to know that."

"I've been studying, Johnny. I've already explained that. Practicing too. I can control what's going to happen. And if you and Karen don't want any part of it, then leave. Nobody's holding a gun to your head or anything."

"I'm staying, man. Let's just get on with it."

"Fine," Preston said, taking what he hoped was one last look at his little brother as he was in death.

A small card table had been set up in one corner of the room, directly across from the bed. Three folding chairs were placed around it. Preston gestured for everyone to take a seat.

"I still don't understand why you need us," Karen said.

"This sort of ritual demands power, and I'm not strong enough to summon Mikey without a little help."

"I thought you had this under control. I thought we were mainly here for moral support," Johnny said, eyeing the Ouija board.

"Look, I promise this will all turn out well. We just have to attract Mikey's spirit into the room and then I can place it back into the body."

"But the body's all decayed and gross and in pieces," Karen said. There was a twitch of fear in her voice as she gave the dirty burlap sack a wide berth. "What good will it do to reanimate?"

"Once the spirit's been put back there are ways of making flesh whole again," Preston said, his eyes alive with a mad scientist's gleam. "But first a tiny prick."

Karen's eyes went wide at the sight of the knife, and Johnny stood up from his chair. Preston held up his hand, motioning for them to be patient, and put on his best smile like a carnival barker who is trying to draw in customers.

"Dude, you didn't say anything about any cutting," Johnny said.

"Just a few drops of blood," Preston protested. "Like I said before, we've got to attract Mikey's spirit. Blood is the best way."

"I wish Rankin would hurry up and get here," Karen said. "At least with three of us, we might be able to talk some sense into your thick skull. And if that didn't work, Rankin could just carry you out of here."

"Rankin agreed to help me. He would be on my side. I'm sure of it. Besides, he'll be here in a few minutes anyway. By then, we'll be finished."

Johnny and Karen winced as Preston uncinched the bag and poured out what was left of his little brother onto the bed. This was the first time Preston had seen Mikey since his death, but he didn't look away like the other two did. Instead, he forced himself to stare at the lifeless features, the severed limbs, the dried blood, the eyes that seemed to follow him wherever he was in the room, pleading for big brother to make him whole again.

Preston made a slash across one forearm, holding the knife firmly so the blade wouldn't cut too deep. A steady trickle of blood seeped out, and Preston held his arm out over what was left of Mikey's body. The thin red stream splashed across Mikey's decayed lips and ran down his parched throat.

"This is too weird for me," Karen exclaimed, slapping her hands over her eyes.

"Now you two," Preston ordered, motioning them over. Karen held tight to Johnny's hand as if to keep him away from the knife, but he pulled away, reluctant to desert his friend. The blood rained down on Mikey's face in a waterfall splatter. Sighing, Karen was the last to take the blade. Her eyes turned away from the atrocity as she made a small incision and let her blood drip.

"How can you be so sure that Mikey's the only one you'll attract?" Karen asked softly as she opened a gauze packet from a first aid kit that Preston had gotten from the bathroom cabinet. "The way I see it these spirits could be like sharks in bloody water. If you've got one around, you've got a hundred."

"My blood is familiar blood," Preston said as if that explained everything. "Mikey will know it's me. Just as a gag we did the whole blood brother thing a few months before he died. I'm sure he'll respond."

"Fine," Karen said doubtfully. "You're the expert."

"Thank you," Preston replied as he began to gather up the remains of his dead brother and systematically place each limb back into the burlap sack. The rotting flesh was greasy with blood.

That done, he sat down to the card table. Johnny and Karen took a chair on either side of him and carefully put their hands up to the planchette.

"We'll start with 'yes' or 'no' questions," Preston instructed, closing his eyes as he began moving the planchette in small, roving circles. "But first I've got to contact Oscar."

"Oscar?" Karen and Johnny said simultaneously.

"He's a spirit tracker. I found out about him on the Internet. He knows the other side like the back of his hand and can have Mikey here in a snap. Of course, it may cost us a little more."

"What do you mean?" Johnny asked hesitantly, looking at the sticky cut on his arm that had almost dried.

Keeping one hand on the planchette, Preston used the other to grab a silver goblet from beneath the table. "Let's just wait and see how this goes," he said. "Oscar may be in a generous mood today."

Johnny and Karen nodded nervously. Sitting the chalice on the table, Preston put his other hand back on the planchette and began.

"O.K., Oscar, it's me, Preston. I'm going to skip all the mumbo jumbo and get on with it. You already know what I'm planning to do. We've already discussed it. So will you find Mikey or not?"

Preston knew what Oscar's reply would be even before the spirit guide had finished spelling the word out on the Ouija board.

"Blood," Karen said in a whisper.

"Are you guys up for another cut?"

"You've got to be kidding me," Johnny shouted. "People are going to think we're masochists or something."

"Will you cut again or not?" Preston said firmly.

"I guess so," Johnny said as Preston handed him the knife.

The three of them emptied their blood into the cup and watched in amazement as it went from full to empty right before their eyes. Preston thought he heard someone burp and then realized that Johnny had done it as a joke.

"That better be good enough, Oscar," Preston said, ignoring Johnny. "We're not giving you any more. We want Mikey and we want him now."

Immediately, there was an undefinable warmth to the room. Under ordinary circumstances, the presence of spirits was an icy wind that chilled the skin and made the breath issue in wispy clouds. Mikey's spirit was a like an ember of coal, heating them against the coolness of the afterlife. Preston wasn't surprised. That was just the kind of kid Mikey had been.

"Mikey, it's me, Preston. Can you hear me?"

The planchette rested briefly on the word 'yes' and then continued making elliptical orbits around the board.

"Mikey," Preston said softly, tears brimming at the corners of his eyes. "You were taken away from Mom and Dad and me way too soon, and I want to change that. I'm going to fix things and give you another chance. You want that, don't you?"

Yes.

"I don't even like to think about the things that were done to you, but I want to nail the maniac who did this. That's why I need you to answer some questions. Is that O.K.?"

Yes.

Taking one of her hands off of the planchette, Karen wiped a tear away from Preston's cheek. He didn't try to move away.

"Who killed you, Mikey?" Preston whispered, his lower lip trembling at the thought of someone hacking Mikey up into little pieces. "Who cut you up like this?"

During the planning stages of the ritual, they had collectively decided that Karen should interpret the written responses since she was a receptionist. Her face went white as the name materialized from the letters like a word from a bowl of alphabet soup.

"Mikey says somebody named The Butcher killed him?" she said softly, the tiny hairs on her forearms standing at attention.

"Who is The Butcher?" Preston pushed, his face pale at the thought of what had been done to his brother. "Give me his name."

"That's what they call him. But it wouldn't be such a good idea to try and find him. He's not a man, you know. He's not anyone you would want to mess with. You almost met him one time before. That day I barged into your room and found you sitting inside that circle of candles. You called him that day. You told him where we were. He came back for me."

"Wait," Preston was quick to ask. "Are you saying that I'm to blame for what happened to you?"

"It's not your fault," the Ouija board answered. "There's no way you could have known."

Johnny and Karen watched as the tears slid down Preston's face. Despite the remorse he felt, Preston never took his hands away from the board to wipe the tears away. Maybe he wanted the grief, felt as though he deserved it.

"But why did he want to kill you, Mikey?" Johnny spoke up, giving Preston a moment to grieve for his mistakes.

Karen concentrated hard on the letters that were highlighted. "This is not a game," she said at last. "Mikey thought it was."

"Is there some reason that Mikey is referring to himself in the third person?" Johnny asked quietly, waiting for the significance of that question to fully sink in. The contents of the burlap sack began to rustle before anyone had a chance to reply. Although no one voiced their opinions aloud, each of them was reminded of the sound a snake makes when slithering through grass.

"Is this supposed to happen?" Karen asked uncertainly.

"Well, let's see," Preston answered sarcastically, his eyes red and puffy from crying. "Since I raise so many people from the dead on a daily basis, I guess I should have answer for that. But sadly, I don't really know."

"Mikey, is that you?" Johnny asked, ignoring the other two, his eyes focused exclusively on the bag of bones.

"It's Mikey all right," the spirit responded. And then the planchette stopped all at once.

"Did either of you do that?" Preston asked, a hint of concern in his voice.

"No way, man. That wasn't us."

Like a carousel just starting to spin, the planchette jumped to life, twirling around the board again in lazy, ever-quickening circles.

"We didn't do that either," Karen was quick to verify.

"Sorry, guys," the spirit spelled out. "Just a little joke. I thought I might lighten the mood by playing a trick, but I guess it didn't work."

"I guess not," Karen said dryly, looking uncertainly at Preston for some sort of reassurance. "I wish Rankin would hurry up and get here."

"Mikey, is that really you?" Preston said. "Tell me something to prove it."

"You mean like something else that nobody would know?"

"Yes," Preston confirmed. "Tell me something that only you might know."

"Your girlfriend and Johnny were kissing while waiting for you."

The surprised, guilty look on Karen's face was confirmation enough for Preston, but he wasn't about to take his hands away from the planchette just yet. Not when they were so close to reuniting Mikey's spirit with the rest of his mangled body.

"I'm sorry," Karen said softly. Johnny, knowing better than to say anything that he really didn't mean, remained silent and focused on the slow moving path of the planchette.

"We'll discuss this later," Preston said, noticing the apprehension on the faces of both former friends. "For now, keep your hands on the planchette and stay with the plan. After this sort of betrayal, you owe me that much at least."

Karen and Johnny nodded their heads and did as they were told. Preston took a deep breath and tried to concentrate.

"Mikey, tell me something about The Butcher."

"You don't want to meet him," Karen said as the letters slowly spelled out words. "He's the kind that will keep you company for all eternity."

Preston nearly took his hands away from the board. That wasn't a typical eight-year-old sort of answer.

"Is he keeping you company?" Preston asked hesitantly.

"Oh yeah. I'm never lonely with him around. Then again, I always hurt when he's around too."

The mention of pain was enough to push away any reservations Preston may have had about going through with what he had planned. If there was one thing he couldn't bear to consider it was someone torturing his kid brother.

"Would you like to get away from The Butcher?" Preston said softly, as if The Butcher might be able to hear him. This time Karen never got the chance to form the letters into words and speak them aloud.

"It's impossible," Mikey said from inside the bag. "He'll never let me get that far."

"Did you bring the salt?" Preston asked Johnny sharply, trying hard not to picture him and Karen together.

Johnny nodded solemnly. "Yeah, it's in the corner."

Hoping to finish this before The Butcher got wind of their plan, Preston hauled the burlap sack with Mikey's remains into the center of the room and drew a circle around it with a bottle of table salt that he pulled from an attaché case.

"Demons are supposed to hate this stuff," Preston explained, motioning them toward him with his hand. "So I'm making a circle of protection. Get inside."

"Are you still there, Mikey?" Karen asked softly, a little afraid of the reply she might receive.

"Yes, I'm here," the dead boy said from the burlap sack. The bones shifted and clattered together like a handful of dice. "And if you're going to do something you'd better do it quick. I can hear The Butcher coming now. I can hear his chains rattling and clanging together like a pocketful of money."

Preston quickly began reciting something in Latin, his voice rising and quickening with each passing second. Although there was no one in the room but the three of them and Mikey, there was an indefinable tension in the air like the kind that is ever-present in funeral parlors and psychiatric wards.

The air inside the circle immediately grew deep-freeze cold and the three of them joined hands for the small measure of comfort that it provided. The bag moved erratically at their feet as if it were full of snakes.

"I don't like this," Karen said, squeezing Preston's hand tightly enough to crush every bone.

"Me neither, man," Johnny said nervously. "I think we're getting in just a little too deep. Rankin better get here soon or I might bail."

"The circle will work. I bound it with the words and salt, and it will work. As long as we stay inside the perimeter, we will be safe. The Butcher won't be able to touch us."

"He's here," Mikey said ominously from the burlap sack. Karen and Johnny exchanged worried glance. No one looked at Preston.

Instinctively, they backed away from the bag as the heavy cloth opening was uncinched and a dark cloud of smoke roiled out. Karen's heel touched the edge of the circle of power and she felt something at her back. A barrier that she was incapable of crossing. She let go of Preston's hand and reached out to feel the invisible wall that separated them from the rest of the room.

"We can't get out," she said calmly. "We're trapped inside the circle."

"I can make it go away," Preston said, eyeing the black cloud that seeped out of the burlap sack like creeping death. "But not until I'm sure that we're out of danger."

"Will it take a lot of time?" Johnny said, his voice trembling in a way that Preston had never heard before.

"Yeah, it'll take some time," Preston replied. And then he realized that they didn't have a lot of time as he saw the black-nailed hand inch its way out of the burlap sack. It didn't take a genius to realize that Mikey wasn't coming back. Somehow Preston doubted that they had ever really been talking to Mikey in the first place. He had established contact all those months before with The Butcher, and now he was going to pay for his mistake. At this point, Karen's analogy of sharks in bloody waters didn't seem to be too far off the mark. They had summoned a spirit, only the wrong one had responded. As The Butcher pulled himself out of the bag, Preston realized that it was too late to do anything about it now but pray and die. The little brother puzzle, it seemed, was going to be left unfinished.

As the blood flowed and the screaming finally stopped, Preston barely heard the steady rumble of a car pulling into the driveway followed by the false reassurance of a door slamming shut. The last thing Preston ever saw was Rankin ambling through the door and stopping. The big guy's jaw dropped, and there was probably a scream tearing through the night like a sharp knife. Preston never heard it.

Jason Brannon

Jason Brannon is the author of over 120 published short stories, four short story collections, two novels, and two chapbooks. His writing has appeared in such diverse publications as *Dark Realms*, *The Best of Horrorfind II*, *Black Petals* and *Underworlds*. When not writing or attending to his duties as a book reviewer for *SpecFicWorld*, Jason can sometimes be found lurking in one of the dark corners of his webpage at http://www.angelfire.com/rant/puzzles/

And the Dead Shall Rise
by
Eric S. Brown

Chris ducked further into the brush surrounding the road as the police cruiser slowed. An officer leaned out of the passenger side window, shining a hand lamp across the tree line. Maggots slithered in and out of his pale, rotting cheeks. Chris held his breath and prayed that his luck would hold. The light moved over his face, burning his eyes, and moved on past him into the trees.

"Nothing here," the officer said in the hollow, cold voice of the dead. The cruiser picked up speed and disappeared over the nearby hill.

Chris started to breathe again, mopping at the sweat on his brow with the sleeve of his filthy and tattered flannel shirt. It had been close, too close. Only God knew what would've happened had the officers discovered him. Chris had heard stories that the last "Breathers" were being herded up, gathered into breeding centers so that they weren't forced completely into extinction as the society of the dead took their place as the rulers of the Earth.

Everything had changed so much over the past year; Chris still sometimes wondered if he was stuck inside one of his own nightmares. In the before times, he had been a powerful man, the owner of a chain of grocery stores which stretched from one coast of America to the other. He'd had money, women, respect, but none of that mattered now. Like anyone else left alive, he was merely food—an animal to be hunted and killed.

Chris jumped out of the brush onto the road and took off at a run in the opposite direction the cruiser had gone. His breath came in ragged gasps as he pushed his body beyond its limits. He remembered the days when the dead were slow pitiful things, lumbering around like mindless automatons. If only the world had awoken sooner to the danger they posed, they'd never have been allowed to evolve into what they were. Now, they spoke, drove cars, used weapons and did all the things "Breathers" used to.

Chris had not seen another living soul in weeks and he didn't know how much longer he could go on. He felt so very tired. The past few months, he'd managed to survive more through luck than skill.

Chris came to a jarring halt in the middle of the road as he saw a house up ahead. There were lights on inside it and smoke rolled out of its rock chimney towards the stars. Chris was not naive enough to believe that there could be real people inside its walls, but a gnawing curiosity made him approach it.

He ducked off the side of the road into the trees and crept towards the house's lawn. He could see someone or something moving above the sink through its kitchen window. Chris sank to his belly and crawled across the dark yard. He dug his .38 revolver from his jacket pocket, carrying it openly as he crawled.

He reached the side of the house and got to his feet, leaning against the wall, careful to stay out of view of the window. He could hear the sounds of leftovers being scraped off a plate into the sink. Chris snuck around the side of the house, searching for another window, wanting desperately to get a look inside.

The lights were off in the living room as he peeked through its window, only the dim glow of a TV screen lit the room. A man sat in a recliner, watching the screen intently. The man's flesh was gray and decayed. At his feet sat a young boy. The child paid no attention to the TV, staring directly out the window at Chris.

Chris jumped back as if he'd been physically struck, but when no alarm sounded from within the house, he found the nerve to peer inside once more. Then he noticed the boy's eyes. He looked into the child's empty sockets and watched as a worm worked it way free and fell to the wooden floor.

The tiny thing began to cry. The man yelled something Chris couldn't quite make out and got to his feet. He scooped the child up in his arms and yelled again. A woman entered the room from the kitchen, her long blonde hair matted to her scalp with blood and pus from an ancient wound on her forehead. She rested her hands on her hips and scowled at the man. Chris thought he heard her say something about bedtime.

Chris ducked below the window. The woman, despite being dead, had eyes that still saw. He remained motionless until the voices disappeared deeper into the house.

Chris felt sick, leaning over as he nearly vomited onto the grass. He'd never imagined the dead could really live like this. They were supposed to be monsters—hungry, evil things waiting to tear the flesh off your bones. Not a family tucking their child in for the night.

The bright lights of the cruiser topped the hill heading back toward Chris and the house. He stood in plain view of the road and there was no way he could cross the distance to the trees before the cruiser reached the house.

Inside his mind whatever remnants of sanity survived gave way. He charged out onto the road in front of the cruiser, shouting at the top of his lungs.

"Jesus!" The officer at the wheel screamed as he swerved the vehicle to the left, narrowly avoiding Chris. His partner snatched up the car radio. "This is car 71. We have a Breather down by the Peterson farm on Route 106, requesting back-up!"

Chris aimed and fired several times at the thing behind the wheel. The windshield shattered, spraying shards of glass into the car as the bullets tore into the officer's chest. The thing leapt out of the car as blackish goo leaked from the wounds staining the front of its uniform. "Drop your weapon!" it shouted, pointing its own handgun at Chris.

Chris turned to flee back towards the house as the front door swung open. The father-creature stood there with a 12 gauge leveled at Chris's stomach. He saw his own fear and hatred reflected in the thing's dull, glazed-over eyes. The night shook as the 12 gauge thundered. The blast knocked Chris off his feet, his intestines spilling onto the dirt as he fell.

The officer ran over to stand above him pointing his pistol into Chris's face. Chris smelt the officer's ripe state of decay as drops of black pus dripped from its wounds onto the bare skin of his face. The last thing Chris saw was the barrel exploding with light before the bullet ripped through his brain.

The mother-thing ran out of the house, shoving her husband aside as she made her way onto the lawn. "Oh God!" she wailed, seeing Chris's corpse sprawled before her. Blood dripped from Chris's forehead onto the asphalt as his body twitched, growing cold.

The officer turned to her, a smile on his withered lips, saying, "It's all right, ma'am. Everything's okay. The monster is dead now."

Eric S. Brown

Eric S. Brown is the author of *Dying Days*, now available from http://www.silverlakepublishing.com. He is also co-author of *Space Stations and Graveyards* which is presently available from Bn.com and Amazon.com. His e-book *Poisoned Graves* was also published by Double Dragon E-books this year and he is author of the chapbooks *Bad Mojo* (Undaunted Press) and *Flashes of Death* (pending publication from Naked Snake Press). He is 28 years old and live in NC with his loving wife Shanna Hall.

The Thief of Missouri
by
Mark Engle

"Tear the two bears from the flag of Missouri. Put thereon in place of them as more appropriate a thief blowing out the brains of an unarmed victim, and a brazen harlot, naked to the waist, and splashed to the brows in blood."
—John Edwards
The Sedalia News, 1892

Lieutenant Williamson loathed his new command. It wasn't the fact that he had no specific post. It wasn't even the fact that his weekly pay never reached his pocket except maybe, if he was lucky, once a month. It was people, lazy people, fat people and unruly people that truly made his life miserable. It was standard society that bereaved habits such as these and the main reason in which he sought out and joined the cavalry. A tightly ruled and strict regiment was the only solace, the only escape.

He stirred the campfire and cursed under his breath as embers slowly rose up, reaching the clear dark sky. This was to be his fourteenth trip across Missouri, and he was damned. It would become a self-made curse upon him quite frankly. Commanding officers praised him on the success upon his eighth trek across the state, breaking the previous record in the last decade. Now on his latest, his own testimony and goals toward perfection only increased the amount of travelers to seek his guide and means of providing safety. Thirty-one unruly souls depended on him this time around, unlike his first party of two families consisting of only eight.

It was only four years before that it all started. Large groups of travelers, families and opportunists heading west to seek a new life, new fortunes or a chance to start over. The expansion westward had been going on for decades but it was only short of half a decade that large parties disappeared without a trace. Experience did not make a difference, nor braveness or toughness. They all vanished. Children, pastors, farmers, parents and all other walks of life left this world without a trace, not a sign of their actions during their last breaths. And thanks to a sympathetic governor and public outcry, it was up to Williamson and others like himself to make sure that these people reached their new destinies unscathed or at least safe to the state border.

Williamson lit the remaining of his stogie and added wood to the fire, realizing that winter would soon be screaming its way in. Wrapping his uniform jacket a little tighter around his shoulders, he shuddered at the thought of another winter of traveling. Guiding the poor, the whining children, crying babies and the dreary trek across a frozen white landscape. It was the beginning of the second night after a brisk cold day of the trek and he was ready to leave all of them behind. If it weren't for his orders, he would leave them all to fend for themselves.

After only eight hours into the second day, his party had already informed him of missing items. Cash, small goods and other trinkets of value had mysteriously disappeared. Most of the party were families, the remaining: two clergymen, two elderly panhandlers who would be lucky to survive another year in the weather and three brothers traveling from home for the first time. Minus the three young men, the rest seemed hardly suspect material for a life of crime. Williamson contemplated the idea that the remaining trio may be responsible for stealing the missing items, but soon discarded the idea. They seemed more wild-eyed and frightened than anything else. Momma's boys on their way to some distant relative in the west where opportunity may strike more luck than home or immediate family offered. He had most of the day to watch the individuals talk, relate future dreams of a new life and found none of them to be suspect. Most were ignorant in their flights to a new life, but not the type to purposely victimize another despite his contempt for each one of them.

Looking across the clearing of their camp, Williamson came to a conclusion, the only real answer left. Not that he really cared what happened to these people's precious items. But the final thought might pose a possible threat to the party. Something he was ordered to prevent. Harm. He had read reports of it happening on prior treks, but never on his. Not on his watch. The idea of a thief or thieves stalking the party seemed contrived, almost silly to Williamson. An exasperated feeling came over him as now he had the responsibility of containing peace and safety among "his" civilians within their perimeters, but had to keep an eye out for one or more of the lowest common denominator.

Scum who would never conform to the rules intruding on his task at hand, bringing the possibility of scathing a perfect military record.

The remaining butt of Williamson's stogie hit the fire as he threw it in. Gazing out into the dark underbrush, he wondered if he would have to kill his unwelcome guests. It would be his first kill and something that he wondered about constantly since signing up. The strict rules of military life, the same pressed uniform, the tight regimental chain of command and the power to legally take the life of another all appealed to Williamson. So much different than his childhood, the idea of authority in his own hands added the delusional satisfaction of overpowering his long dead alcoholic father. At one time powerless under the strong hand that stung of pain and smelled of nightly foul odors he was now left to fantasies of reaching back into time, rising up and striking back. It wasn't reality and he knew it, but it did ease the pain and at times brought a quirky little smile to his face when his thoughts reached far enough from reality turning into revenge.

Another three hours had passed and most of the party finally stopped stirring and complaining of aches and pains from the day's hardships. Maybe an hour had passed since he embarrassed one of the daughters of the more prominent family in this particular outing. Obviously educated highly in the art of manners, the idea of a man escorting her to use a nearby bush to take care of certain unmentionables seem to horrify the very idea of her existence. She, even though elegantly dressed for the night, was only of fair beauty, but Williamson noticed that once she blushed, which even permeated through the dark shadows, a certain radiance gave light to a budding sexuality that was pleasing to look at. The sight of this discovery must have shown a change in his own expression, for soon after, using three fingers, she tried to hide a slight giggle that was forming between tightly shut lips. While returning to camp, her thoughts most likely went back to innocent dreams, meanwhile, Williamson daydreamed in the dark of sexual yearnings that the military could never provide. Yes, Williamson thought, it was going to be a long night.

Another stogie and what was left over from dinner resting peacefully in his stomach, the night grew brighter from the moon closing in and time seemed to stand still. No breeze and only the sound of crackling fire to keep Williamson awake. It wasn't until he had cursed the stars for the hundredth time that it happened; enough noise off in the distance to raise the hair on the back of his neck. Just what he had been waiting for! Get your ass off your bed roll and out of site was all that came to mind, but the shock of the moment froze his legs in a half crouched position, just enough to stare over the flames into the trees. Give it time, stand still and wait for it. Another crack, branches breaking underfoot only a few paces from where he originally stared. Struggling with the smoke and heat in his eyes, he widened them to take in the dark when the third sound of brittle limbs burst underfoot, shooting out only a few feet from the tree line that encompassed the camp's clearing. This time he jumped enough to startle himself and reached for his pistol, stopping just before opening the holster. Unfortunately, as stable as his hands were, his boot shot forward into the fire. Branches in the distance exploded simultaneously while burning coals shot up into the air over his head. The chase was on.

Williamson hit the underbrush with enough force to awaken all his senses. Only two thoughts entered his mind at the moment. One, he surprised himself by already having his gun out, pointed forward, cocked and ready to kill without even thinking about it, and second, that he would feel damn foolish if he was chasing some wild animal. Another thirty yards in a straight line, branches whipping at his face and clothes, it definitely wasn't an animal. The sounds of his own footsteps echoed those in front of him along with distinct groans in between the heavy breathing of his would-be assailant. Thank goodness he was gaining on the stranger, because another five minutes of this tomfoolery and he would lose him. Williamson kicked in that extra inertia before realizing that the only breath he was hearing was his own. Stopping in his tracks, he hunched over to catch up with his lungs. Tilting his head up to look straight ahead, he could feel the burn of exertion in his throat rising up from his chest. As his lungs finally stopped drowning out his hearing, he realized that nothing but the forest was in front of him. Whoever he was chasing was somehow behind him, somewhere. The gun in his hand, he turned and soon his body followed, now standing up straight. Full alert took over every muscle. In the moonlight, he could barely make out where he tore through the underbrush, and no sign of the camp or the fire. Not sure how long he had been running, he slowly marched back from which he had come. He needed to get back to those he was in charge of, but his own stubbornness kept him from quickening his step. He wanted this bastard and he wanted him bad.

Ten minutes of walking and still no sign of the fire's glow. He was sure he wasn't lost, but then again, every tree started to look more unfamiliar than the last. Eleven years of impeccable service and now he was lost. He pictured the people back at camp waiting for him in the morning. He could see the confusion in their eyes as they argued whether to move on or continue looking for him after a week had gone by. Would they starve to death or freeze? Ultimately, he was responsible for their safety and he threw it all away in the glory of the chase. No matter how he rationalized it in his mind, those in command would not be forgiving, but neither would he if the shoe was on the other foot. Perfection was all he strived for and expected of himself, as misguided as his chase may have been, he was unsuccessful and that was his downfall. Sitting down on a large rock, he looked around in hope of some sign to gain his footing. Not a sound nor glow of campfire, his breathing creating the only movement in sight as it evaporated into the cold of the night. Swallowing what little moisture was left, his breathing came to a standstill, and that's when he heard it. His breath held back in his lungs but the noise continued. Someone was exhaling next to him.

Slowly rising, he turned around to focus on the boulder he had been resting on. Nobody in sight, but the breathing continued and it wasn't coming from him. The burning came back into his lungs as he fought it back, but relented and he slowly let air escape from his mouth. Looking at the boulder he saw nothing out of the ordinary. White granite filled with gray speckles and jagged edges, it stood about four feet wide and five feet in length. Only three feet off the ground, it made the perfect bench to rest a lost Williamson. With the gun in his hand, never replaced in its holster from the chase, he slowly walked around the stone. Whatever or whoever was breathing was just behind the rock where he had been sitting. Looking around, he crept up on the culprit while slowly cocking his gun, ready to fire at any sudden movement. As he walked down a slight slope through autumn leaves that the wind had brushed up against the side, there half buried in the dead foliage was a man, sound asleep.

Upon a closer look, Williamson noticed the man wasn't actually sleeping, but knocked unconscious. A large gash above the man's left eyebrow and blood from an obvious broken nose gave quick evidence to the contrary. This stranger was in no kind of decent condition even before his unfortunate accident. Most of his outfit was made of tattered leather full of creases and cracks giving away its time in weather and age. Next to the rock was the man's hat made of the same coarse skin and above that on the stone itself was more blood, most likely where the man hit face-first. So, he was on the right track and thank goodness, not lost. Contemplating the events, Williamson figured this was the same man that had sent him on his wild goose chase. Well, that was the end and he had gotten his man. Using his foot, he turned the man completely on his back, bent down and shoved the end of his gun up against the broken nose with enough force to create a new flow of blood. The stranger's scream was short lived once he noticed the barrel in his face.

The heat of dawn was creeping upwards over the distant mountains. Williamson's breath was slowly fading from sight as the air went from dark to a misty gray of morning. Johnson, or at least that was what he claimed his name was, still displayed a large vaporous trail from his nose caused by a combination of unsettling nerves due to a gun at his back and trying to breathe through the clogging mixture of blood and mucous which of course doesn't help when one is walking on a twisted ankle. Johnson kept looking nervously over his shoulder for any way to escape, as well as worrying about the soldier behind him being trigger-happy. He figured it wouldn't hurt to ask, "Where are you taking me?"

Laughing at the nasal-sounding question, Williamson told him that they were headed back to camp.

"Well, I figured that, Captain, but where to after that?"

"Tie you up and take you along until we run across a military post on the way. No time to lose and I'm already a half day behind, not too mention losing a night's sleep chasing you across the countryside."

Relief swarmed over Johnson's face and Williamson noticed it, "That is if I don't have to shoot you on the way." Worry returned and Williamson grinned at his newfound power over his captive.

The sun pierced the back of their necks as they headed towards camp. A welcome relief of warmth and familiarity crept over him this morning as Williamson could not wait to show off his new trophy. He only hoped that someone had enough brains to make coffee in his absence. Finally over the hill, he could make out small bellows of smoke from the fire he built last night. A swift kick in the rear to Johnson and about 60 more yards, some rope to tie him and a hearty breakfast was all that he could think of. His feet felt heavy and sleep would also be a plus, but he knew that the trek had to keep moving in order to make their deadline. Making out the clearing just ahead, he pushed Johnson through the last set of trees only to have the thief jump right back at him. It wasn't an attack on Johnson's part but more of a fright that knocked both of them to the ground. Grasping his gun, he picked himself up and pushed the two of them through the tree line. Johnson muttered "Jesus" in such a way that Williamson felt as if he just swallowed the blasphemy whole and choked on it. His legs buckled at the sight, he dropped his gun and it was a good thing that Johnson was too shocked to pick it up.

The camp was torn to pieces, literally with pots and pans strewn everywhere, some torn in half, the jagged metal edges soaked in blood. The wagons looked like loose piles of kindling. Tattered rags that were once clothes now hung from trees, some covered in the morning dew while other pieces sparkled in the new sun, soaked with fresh blood. Williamson walked closer to what he believed was part of a nightgown worn by the young lady he escorted the night before. It was hanging from a limb. It weighed heavily on the branch as he reached for it and gave a pull. Something didn't feel right and Williamson dropped the cloth as quickly as he had pulled it from the tree. It did not flutter to the ground but fell like a dead weight hitting the dirt, pattern side down. He immediately backed up a step and raised his arm over his mouth. The underside of the nightgown, sticky with blood, had a large chunk of flesh fused with what remained of the threading. Quickly kicking it away, Williamson started to choke on his empty stomach and forced himself to bite down on his sleeve as he turned around.

The smell of cooking meat. "Jesus, they were killed while eating breakfast," was all that Williamson could muster as he walked over to the dying coals. Unfortunately, this wasn't the case as he discovered upon closer examination. On the far side of the fire, almost the same color as the burnt and black wood, was an arm, smoking fingers curling upwards, small burning embers of what was left of the elbow still feeding the flames. The hand was still grasping a melted crucifix now embedded in the palm. The chain attached to the cross laying far enough away from the fire was covered in dry blood from where it must have been torn from one of the clergymen's neck. What was left of the poor man sat only a few feet from the arm; a pile of intestines with the man's head buried up to the bottom of his nose. His eyes were open, glaring upwards while the morning sun created a steam of gaseous mist rising upward. Most of the remaining body parts were near or on what was left of the bedding. Obviously, to Williamson, they had been killed in their sleep. Picking up a piece of wagon wheel, he turned over the heavy wool of the closest bedding only to find a portion of rib cage, broken like twigs; all that remained was about three inches of each rib, ripped flesh and what may have been at one time part of a spinal cord. Backing slowly from which he came, he bent down and picked up his gun, turned and pointed it at Johnson.

"OK, Captain, I'm just going to back up slowly and get the hell out of here."

The words sounded quiet.

Williamson contemplated for a moment and told him to sit down. Confused and frightened, Johnson seemed to just sort of plop straight to the ground without realizing he was doing so. Anger stormed over Williamson's face and he rushed over, kicking. Johnson slumped over from the blows to his arm and ribs. Confused, he reached forward to try to get away as Williamson screamed, "Who the hell did this?" Johnson saw another blow coming his way and quickly replied, "I don't know. Stop, I don't know!" Johnson now curled into a ball as Williamson stopped kicking. He was too tired to keep it up and somehow knew that further blows weren't going to get him any real answers. He looked over the camp he was responsible for and let out a moan that turned into a scream. All that returned was the echo of his cries.

Johnson didn't like his current situation one bit. The last six months had been hell as it was, but he didn't know what to make of all of this! For five hours he sat in total shock. Not just at the aftermath before him, but at his captor as well. Williamson was constantly screaming at himself, the trees, the bodies and even the shovel and pick he used to bury the remains. The only time he didn't scream was when he muttered some sort of bizarre ritual that could only be described as a perverse last rights. After the fifth hour he decided to chance standing up and mill around. The minute he moved anywhere, Williamson's gun was on him as well as the warning, "I'm not done with you yet. Sit Down!" Then back to his fits of outrage or biblical mutterings. Nope, sizing up his predicament at the moment didn't add up to all that much. Clearly, if Williamson was almost over the edge last night, he definitely seemed off his rocker now. Sizing up the ordeal that lay before him, he decided that the Captain was indeed insane, but not capable of the atrocity before him. He was, however, deranged enough to pull that trigger.

It was only last May that he arrived in Missouri from New York. Receiving a letter, from his cousin, promising massive fortunes to be made, he packed up what little he owned, used the last of his small savings and headed into the country to make a new beginning. Only disappointment followed when he discovered that his cousin and a few friends made a living robbing and killing travelers heading west. Even less glamorous than stage coach robbery, this wasn't Johnson's idea of a golden opportunity. Not wanting to be part of such a scheme, but out of necessity, he went on a few of these so-called adventures only to plead for the sparing of lives before and after. Enough had been enough; last night he had planned on warning the soldier and turn himself in. Unfortunately, before he could get into their camp and do his good deed, all he could see was a blast of flame and what looked to be a man with the devil in his eyes coming right at him! Panic stricken, all he could do was run. The last thing he remembered was what felt like a hand reaching up from hell and grabbing a hold of his ankle. Turned out the next morning, superstitions of darkness aside, it wasn't the devil chasing him, but a lunatic doing his job, and it wasn't anything with a pitchfork and horns that grabbed him from the fiery depths of hell, but a large branch that sent him pummeling forward, face first, into a large boulder. One thing was for sure, though. If this madman didn't kill these poor folk, it definitely wasn't his cousin's group either. Yes, they shot their victims and yes, they buried them way off in the woods and yes, they cleaned up everything, kept the goods, sold the rest, but tearing people apart into pieces no bigger than a fist? Nobody was capable of this and if that was the case, what the hell was?

"Captain...excuse me. sir, but what do we do now?" Johnson said, in the utmost quiet and nervous tone he could muster. A few moments of silence followed except the slight whistle sound that escaped from his throbbing nose. "Surely we should go get help or tell someone about this?" Johnson thought it would be a good idea to be around other people at the moment even if it meant jail rather than hang around with present company.

Williamson stood silently looking upward, sweat and blood dripping from his brow, back towards his prisoner, his gun now back in his hand. What do we do, he thought to himself. He wasn't sure if he had heard someone whisper those words or if he had been talking to himself. Didn't matter really, the answer was always there.

"We wait and kill the bastards that did this. I'm not going back empty-handed. No way. We'll stay here for now and if they don't show up tonight, we'll hunt them down and take them in."

Johnson stood there for a moment with both arms out in amazement. Careful, he thought to himself, you don't want to set this guy off. But hanging around here seemed like a bad idea. Johnson had to think of something reasonable. "Umm, Captain, wouldn't it be easier to get some help? I mean, look around Cap...there were at least two dozen people..."

"Thirty-one," Williamson corrected.

"OK, over thirty people here last night, and what was left barely fit the small grave you made! We're not dealing with a man here. I dunno what we are dealing with, but I don't think your gun will help you much tonight or tomorrow. What we need to do is get as far away from here as possible, tell this tale to your superiors, lock me up where it is safe, and try to forget what happened!"

Williamson looked around at the situation and for a moment, Johnson thought he had reached him. Putting his gun back in its holster he answered, "There's some tins of food over there." Williamson pointed toward what was left of one of the wagons. "I'll build a fire." Johnson knew only two things for sure at that moment, the sinking feeling in his stomach left little appetite to eat and if he had a chance, no matter how small, he wanted to kick the living shit out of this man.

Johnson stared at Williamson with heavy lids as nightfall set in. The tinned beef wasn't sitting well and neither were his nerves. Williamson just sat and stared into the trees, gun in hand, half cocked and tilted halfway into the air while the weight of his wrist balanced on his leg. If only the bastard would fall asleep, Johnson thought to himself. Both lacked any decent rest for at least 36 hours and he knew if there was any chance of escape it would be if Williamson collapsed from exhaustion. Wrapping himself up tighter in the blanket given to him, he scooted towards the fire and figured some idle chatter might just be enough to calm the man down. "So, how long you've been a cowboy there, Cap? You do rank Captain, yes?"

Williamson's head stood fast, but his eyes slowly diverted over and replied, "Yes, Captain is correct, not Cap, but Captain to you. If you must know, I've been in the service going on 11 years now, last four years with this lousy assignment."

There seemed to be a depression to his answer, and for a moment, Johnson realized that there was a hint of humanity in the madness somewhere. It came as a relief, if only momentarily.

"Captain it is, sorry if the nickname bothered you. I have a tendency to shorten things up a bit when things go bad."

"How long have you been a thief?" Any amount of accepting Johnson's apology was missing from Williamson's reply.

"I'm not really a thief, actually. I was originally a guy who could barely read and write, looking for a decent job. My cousin talked me into coming out here. As for thieving, you'd have to talk to him. I was on my way to give myself up and warn you when you decided to chase me through the damn woods."

"Your cousin may have done this?"

"No way any man could've done this Cap—er—I mean Captain," Johnson said, partially lying to Williamson and himself. He honestly didn't think his cousin was capable of this, but couldn't imagine a pack of wolves doing it either. It was the only logical answer that was possible, even if it was wrong. "He's never killed anyone that I know of." Lying again. "Maybe wolves. I don't know."

The banter and theorizing went on for a good half hour and Johnson was glad to see Williamson responding and calming down. It did him some good as well. Conversation brought some normalcy back into the events of the day. Some sanity coming from Williamson also helped. After the long episode of Williamson ranting like a crazed madman, he honestly didn't think he had a chance of getting out of these woods alive. He still had no clue what was to become of him, but did start to feel a little better as he noticed Williamson's gun resting completely on his knee as his eyelids fell shut.

Slowly rising, he knew this was his chance. Walking backward toward the tree line, he kept his eyes on Williamson until the bush surrounded him and only the campfire poked through. Thirty yards out, he finally turned around and quickened his step and then came to an abrupt stop. A sense of guilt overcame him as well as realization that he was now only surrounded by complete darkness. A strong urge came over him to head back. Somehow his odds seemed to diminish being alone, in the dark and without any sort of weapon. He argued almost aloud to himself with this new dilemma, trying to make up his mind only to have it made up for him when the shrieking pierced his ears.

Running back towards the camp, he could hear Williamson screaming like he had never heard before. It sounded unnatural, especially coming from a man, who, only hours before, was vowing revenge and displaying an unbent anger that could not only be heard but felt vibrating through your nerves just by watching his eyes. A single gunshot fired and before it could echo, Johnson stopped, only for a moment his arms outstretched behind him past his own body weight as if to help immobilize his step. When his arms caught up with the rest of him, without even thinking about it, he started running again, this time screaming Williamson's name at the top of his lungs, his voice only slightly muffled by his broken nose.

Just upon entering the clearing he heard a loud tearing noise and a high-pitched whimper, then silence. Through the last bush, the very same he escaped through, he came to a skidding halt, this time his arms overshooting his body as he tried to stop and keep his balance. What was left of Williamson lay before him. His head was completely gone and so was the hand that had been holding the gun. From the neck down, Williamson had been torn completely in half, both pieces separated by six inches of ground and steam rising from the center. His intestines slowly oozed outwards by gravity as if attempting to become a single functioning whole again. His uniform was torn up the middle of course, but both sides of his shirt were pulled back to expose his chest with a caved-in look. If Johnson had inspected further, he would have discovered that Williamson's rib cage had been completely removed, leaving only an open cavity for his skin to fall away as his muscles gave out. Looking downwards at the body, Johnson noticed one foot still wore a boot, while the other was bare or at least what was left of it. Everything after the heel was gone, toes and all. From the jagged bite mark, a pool of black blood congealed with the dirt forming a sick pasty mud.

Johnson barely had enough time to take this in before he shuddered and looked up. At the opposite end of the clearing came a deep low hissing sound from the trees. Branches cracking and moving around the circle of the camp. His eyes followed the noise as it moved around behind the piles of what were once the wagons. He could make out the violent rustling of branches as it grew closer to his side of the camp where he stood. A small fir, only about eight feet high, snapped at the base and fell directly into the clearing. The dull hissing came again, only closer. "Fuck this," was all that Johnson could muster before turning to run.

"Fuck this. Fuck this, holy shit and Fuck this!" Johnson shot straight through the same bush he came through for the third and hopefully final time and back into the darkness. Whatever it was, it was directly behind him and Johnson guessed that it wasn't done eating yet. If "eating" was what it was doing? He didn't know and didn't want to know! This seemed to a be a direct repeat of the previous night, only this time, even though his body was exhausted, his step moved quicker, his stride wider than ever before. It wasn't Williamson chasing him this time. Not human or animal, Johnson knew this for sure. Whatever creature was behind him, it came from some other place or nightmare for which Johnson couldn't even begin to fathom. The hissing now turned into a dull menacing roar and if it wasn't for the cool wind Johnson could have sworn he felt it right on the back of his neck. The roar was seamless, as if the creature's breathing didn't even interrupt the noise emanating from its mouth. He could even hear the creature's footsteps that almost sounded like a light whistle through the underbrush, not thudding or stepping but almost as if it were barely scratching the surface of the dead leaves and twigs on the ground.

Johnson wasn't sure where he was nor the creature, but he did recognize the large slab of granite coming up. This time, he avoided the dead branches on the ground and swung his whole body around the boulder and changed his direction completely. Through the moonlight he could see the outline of the mountainside straight ahead and hoped that the creature wasn't able to hear or smell his change in direction. His breathing grew heavier and louder and he was no longer sure if he had lost the monster behind him or if the pounding between his ears kept him from hearing it. Either way, the pain in his nose swelled, his lungs burned, his legs screamed, his head throbbed, his mouth swelled and felt like it was full of cotton, but he wasn't going to stop running. He did however; he had to dodge several more boulders along the way. Large rocks of granite seemed as if they were sprouting up everywhere. Hopefully this meant he was getting closer to the mountain range.

His pace slowed considerably as the ground sloped upwards. Now surrounded by granite, Johnson used his hands on each stone to help push him forward. There were fewer trees now and he took the opportunity to look behind him, but saw nothing but the dark. The only shapes that stood out were dark outlines of a few trees and several boulders that sparkled with a gray white tone barely visible from the light reflection of the moon. He stopped and turned. His breathing became so heavy he sat down against another rock and looked down the mountainside. Whatever that thing was that was chasing him wasn't in his sight, but he knew it was out there somewhere and that was enough. Catching a little of his breath, he balanced himself into a hunched-over standing position and began to climb, only slower. Looking upwards, he noticed a large overhang that was impossible to climb. He would have to go around. Changing his direction, he carefully made it around the overhang and happily changed course again towards it. Johnson was relieved to see what looked like a twelve-foot ledge that he could look over the whole valley with, and better yet, the mouth to a cave that he could hide in and rest.

Johnson, now on both knees, put both hands at the very ends of the ledge and peered over. He was actually very surprised at how far he had climbed up the mountain. There didn't seem to be anything coming up towards him so he let out a large sigh and then realized how cold he was. The sweat from his run and climb now felt as if it were freezing on his skin as his clothes stuck to his body. His breathing finally relaxed; he wished he had that campfire up here with him. Well, wait just a damn minute, he thought to himself as he reached into a pocket that was halfway down the side of his pant leg. He took a quick inventory of a small pouch of tobacco, rolling papers and, thank goodness, a small box of wooden matches. Looking around for wood was another story. With only two sticks on the whole ledge, a fire was out, but at least he could build a small torch and seek refuge within the cave.

The warmth of flame felt good on his face as he entered. The cave looked a lot bigger on the inside than it originally had from the outside. The first thing that hit Johnson was the stench. This was bad, real bad. Smell or no smell, though, he was determined to make his personal safety a priority and that meant a good place to hide. The bad smell aside, something else was odd about the whole thing. Moving his torch closer to the wall, the whole side was made from pure granite. Little speckles of silver danced and sparkled off the stone. Johnson had never seen a cave like this before. Actually, he had never been in a cave in his entire life, but didn't expect it to look anything like this.

As he ventured farther in, the cave became damp, the air stale and the stench grew stronger. The walls of the cave still sparkled and seemed smooth in appearance. A slight shudder came over him as he held the torch over his head and looked up at the ceiling. Relief, no bats. Thank God for small favors. That was all he needed on top of everything else. Bringing the torch back down in front of him, he squinted and peered in front of him to see what looked like the back end of the cave. Ten feet farther and he stopped in amazement. He had reached the wall, but the ceiling above had all but disappeared. Looking upward, he saw pure blackness as if the whole mountain above him was hollow. A wave of stench penetrated his broken nose with a blast that recoiled his whole face in disgust. He lowered the torch, turned to the right, and then he saw it. The floor was covered in bones. Skulls, rib cages full and in pieces, arms, feet and even sections of joints, some from the knee, others from parts of the elbow, completely littered the ground at least six inches deep.

Backing up a good foot or two, Johnson raised the torch and peeked around a corner where the bones were piled even higher. There, perched in a corner, it was sleeping. At least eight feet tall the creature must have stood. Only now it was hunched up to its knees, head resting sideways. The skin was almost as white as the cave walls, only without the sparkle. Johnson stood very still and stared at the creature. Obviously female, its breasts were large and just as white as the rest of the body, only with a more translucent look to them. You could see small purple veins by the thousands just underneath the skin. The veins seem to disappear inside the body where the breasts ended and the rest of the chest began. Its stomach was thin like a starving child's and the waist seemed to almost cave into the long legs. Three joints or kneecaps per leg for a total of six, and Johnson couldn't even imagine what that looked like standing up. The feet were large and led to three very sharp light brown claws. A forth prong-like claw protruded from the heels. As strange as this was, it was nothing like the head and arms. The creature's face was almost pointed, but not enough to make it a snout, almost cone-like with two small nostrils just above the point. Below the end of the cone-like face was the thing's mouth. The skin ended where the teeth began, no lips, and just four sharp teeth from the top of its mouth interwoven with another four from the bottom. It had eyelids, but they were completely translucent in texture, exposing two small eyes that were a beautiful golden brown, no whites to the eyes, but solid in color. The head was bald, in fact the thing had no body hair at all, and the creature's ears were jagged with several points on the top of both of them. No earlobes, but instead the ears came down rounding to a smooth long neck that led to its shoulders.

Johnson moved the torch the length of the creature's shoulders and found that it had extremely thin arms at the end of two very broad shoulders covered with what looked like thorns. Both arms and shoulders met with paper-thin skin that hung several feet below and attached to the creature's rib cage. The damn thing had wings, yet they didn't look finished or at least not complete enough for full flight. Here again, Johnson could see the same type of veins as the breasts, only these particular veins looked thicker than the skin and more visible. At the end of each wing was the creepiest thing Johnson had ever seen in his life. The hands looked almost human. If it weren't for an extra large thumb and long sharp brown nails, he would have sworn the creature had stolen someone's hands and sewn them on!

The cave was a bad idea. Johnson now knew what had killed everyone in the camp, including Williamson. He knew what had been chasing him across the countryside. He knew it was time to get the hell out of there. He knew nobody was going to believe him. He didn't care. What he needed to do was high tail his ass out of the cave and never look back.

Johnson turned and looked face-first into terror. Another creature stood there in front of him. This one at least ten feet tall and awake. It let out the same growl he had heard behind him in the woods. The only other difference from the sleeping creature was that this one had no breasts, but more of a hard shelled plate that lead to a point just above the crotch. Obviously, this was the male of the species and it was pissed off. The creature reached out its long arm-like wing and grabbed the top of Johnson's head. He felt the sharp nails enter his skull. The creature's thumb was long enough to run the length of Johnson's face and curl up under his chin. The thumbnail punctured through the jaw into his open mouth and he dropped the torch. The cave went black and all Johnson heard before he died was the creature waking up behind him. Her growl wasn't angry like the male. The noise he heard sounded satisfied, like the one a person makes before sitting down to a nice big meal.

Mark Edward Engle

Owner, Writer, Managing Editor and Head of Publicity of *Cultcuts Magazine*, Mark Engle also publishes short stories and articles for other magazines, including *Ultra Violent* and *Hacker's Source* as well as short stories in upcoming anthology books available this year. He is currently working on his first novel, *Townfolk*, and is producer and screenplay writer for the upcoming film *Decay*, starring James Lew and Mark Dacascos. He recently finished writing, producing and directing his first short film, *In the Loaming* for the upcoming anthology film, *Evil Anthology*. Mr. Engle has been promoting film professionally for over fifteen years.

Encounter on Old Temple Road
by
Christopher Fulbright

Just as Samuel spotted a light through the trees in the darkness of the back road wilderness, the *thing* suddenly appeared in front of his car.

He'd been clipping along I-35 south from Ft. Worth to Austin at a good 75 mph. He'd passed Waco sometime back, and there weren't many prospects within driving distance when the orange light that looked like a gas pump came on, glowing at him from the confines of the dashboard. Samuel looked for a place to pull over.

Miles of road unrolled before him like black satin ribbon. Night pressed in. He couldn't see anything in the near vicinity—no lights, nothing. The needle went precariously closer to dipping below "E."

The reflective green road sign glowed in the headlights, soared nearer, then slipped by.

Next Exit: Old Temple Road.

The exit came and he took it at 50 mph.

The pavement ended as he went down the exit ramp onto a ragged dirt road. Washboards rattled the frame of his Mustang. He eased onto the brake. The car shuddered so badly that it spent half its time in the air, wanting to go sideways instead of forward.

Samuel turned down the radio so he could better hear the sounds of his car shaking to pieces.

He slowed to a crawl and came to a four-way stop. The road on which he traveled was washed out ahead; the frontage road had become a drainage ditch, leaving only two choices. Right, into darkness and trees, or left, under the interstate and into more darkness. There were no signs of civilization either way.

Samuel went right.

He rolled down his window. The sound of tires crunching over gravel popped in the night. His headlights swept the wilderness to his left as he made the turn. A field was neck-deep with late summer grass to the right. Directly ahead there didn't seem to be anything at all. And then…wait—there was a light far back in the trees.

Ahh, thank you God, Samuel thought.

His eyes searched the primeval woods for a driveway.

The thing appeared out of nowhere.

Shocked, blood-drenched eyes shone in the beams. Half-human features. Scaly black skin. One clawed hand spread webbed fingers at the car, trying to stop it with a motion.

It appeared in a flash of horror, and then hit the front bumper of the Mustang. An inhuman shriek filled the night. It echoed through the woods like a cross between a falcon's caw and the pained growl of a dying feline.

Samuel screamed and turned the wheel.

The left front tire of the car bounced up and over the thing before he could skid to a halt. Dust billowed through the headlight beams. Samuel's heart thumped in his chest like war drums. His eyes flicked to the side mirror, almost not wanting to see what was there.

He lifted his eyes slowly, on level with the mirror so he could see the road behind him.

The curled-up form of what looked like a man—a man with black scales and spines along the center of his back—lay wounded. The back of its head looked wet in the scarlet glow of his taillights. He couldn't see the full form of the thing in the mirror. The light from the brakes washed the whole night behind him the luminous color of blood.

"Damn it!"

He put the car in park and stepped out, leaving his door open. One foot landed on the gravel and crunched loud in the night. He kept one hand on the car, tracing it with his fingertips as he went to take a look at the thing.

He drew nearer but couldn't see much now that just the running lights were on. A mass of scaly flesh shone like the meaty curve of a snake, and the back of the thing did seem to have spines, like some kind of amphibious creature. Its head was misshapen…too long and too wide in back. It seemed to have…no, he thought, but yes…it had *horns*…

The car suddenly died; the engine burned its last vapor of fuel and fell silent. The lights stayed on but went a shade dimmer.

Samuel paused. He listened.

He stood only a few feet from the thing. His fingertips had dragged themselves a trail to the trunk of the car. He could grab the crowbar, and wanted to, but that meant going back to the front driver's side to open the latch, and that suddenly seemed like a long way to travel.

He studied the creature's head, tried to discern more of its features. There wasn't a moon out, so shadows swallowed the details. The back of the head was wet with something…an oily substance like—

He reached his hand down to touch the thing's shoulder. He intended to roll it over and get a better look. As soon as his fingertips made contact, the thing screeched.

Alive!

Samuel cried out and jumped back, but not in time.

In a final death throe the creature bared long vamphyrric fangs that ripped Samuel's hand, drawing blood and leaving a deep wound.

Samuel fell back onto the ground.

The thing flipped over toward him like a fish out of water. He saw its tail rise in the shadows. One arm was mangled and trapped beneath it. Its eyes were wide, filmy, and full of blood. The teeth were yellow and sharp. Its growl was a mewling symphony of anguish and rage. Its mouth opened wider than it had any right to, and the creature gagged on its own swollen tongue.

The head, dripping with black ichor that leaked from a crack in its skull, fell limp and lay still.

Samuel clutched his ravaged hand. *Damn thing bit me.* He squinted to inspect the wound in the glow of headlights. He could feel the pulse of warm blood as it flowed between his fingers. It was deep; fat pushed through the torn flesh. He needed help—stitches and maybe even a tetanus shot. God only knew what that thing might have been carrying in its vile saliva.

Samuel turned off his headlights, clicked on the hazards and, with the amber glow of his emergency signals blinking behind him, started off through the forest toward the dim light he'd spotted from the road.

He crossed a drainage ditch full of knee-deep weeds and moved through the wall of trees. He figured there must be a driveway here somewhere.

Samuel realized his breath had become shallow in his lungs. A painful lump had formed in his throat. It crossed his mind that he might be getting sick from the bite.

He paused just beyond the edge of the woods and scanned the forest, still clutching his hand, still seeing that vague light in the distance. He looked back at the car and could barely see the black heap of corpse that lay behind it. A snapflash memory of the creature in his headlights was enough to elicit a shudder. While there wasn't much he could do back there, there wasn't much he could do back on the interstate either. He had the sinking feeling that there was nothing out here.

Nothing but the glow.

And that thing.

He perked his ears, suddenly more cautious about proceeding blithely into the woods. He thought he heard a snapping twig. A disturbed rustle of brush, not more than a whisper.

What if there are more of them out there? he thought.

If there were more of them out there, his only option was to get to the house, and quickly. Should another one of those things come along and he didn't die of fright, he'd surely be killed.

Samuel pushed ahead into the trees.

Mighty oaks towered above him, thirty and forty feet on each side. No moon and only a few visible stars made the going difficult. Brush snagged his feet and his own steps became the loudest sounds under the blanket of night. His breaths still came in short gasps. He had to remind himself to breathe deeply. Branches, unseen in the blackness, reached out like bony claws to snag his shirt or scratch an arm or cheek. He paused only a moment now and then to listen. Echoes of nocturnal life drifted through the foliage, whispered in a fragrant wind.

There was a shudder in the brush nearby.

A twig snapped.

Samuel froze, ears like radar tuning into some deeper fathom of the night.

A hiss from behind him.

As he turned around, an angry feline growl came from another direction.

He bolted. Brush snagged his shoes as he ran toward the house, eyes focusing only on the dim glow from an upstairs window. Only now as he came closer to the structure could he see that another source of illumination existed beyond the house. Deep violet light emanated from a grove of trees behind the house itself, but—

His haste made him reckless and he crashed face first into the brush. Samuel fell. He reached to catch himself with his bad hand and cried out. He bit his tongue. Squeezed his eyes shut with the sudden pain of the re-inflicted wound.

The sounds of pursuit closed in on him. His cries had awakened whatever wickedness dwelt in the forested depths. Sounds in weird throats growled and grunted nearby as Samuel forged onward to the house. An unseen hand seemed to grip the girth of his chest and literally push him through the overgrown yard. The dilapidated condition of the home didn't give him much pause. He thundered up the decaying wood steps. He steadied himself against a rotting pole of the overhang and hammered on the door.

Samuel looked back into the woods. No sign of his pursuers…at least none that he could see in the pitch black that filled the woods like inky clouds. But he could hear them, hear their hints of feline discontent, the subtle growls, deep lionic purrs.

Samuel beat on the door with his good hand. No sound came from within the house, so he rattled the doorknob.

Just as he did so the door came open.

He stood suddenly face-to-face with a man his same height, with ruddy features, a wide bearded jaw, a bushy mustache concealing his firm-set mouth, deep haunted eyes, and long hair streaked with gray.

"Come in," the gruff man said with urgency, grabbing Samuel by the arm. He stumbled into a narrow foyer, supporting himself against the wall as the man shot urgent looks of fright over his shoulder into the night. He slammed the door and slid a bolt home, following that up with a chain.

"Thank God," Samuel breathed. "Something…those creatures—chasing me." He was out of breath. Spent and afraid. His heart continued to hammer away as the old man faced him. The old man seemed angry.

"Are you mad?" The man barked at him.

Samuel caught his balance in the hall only so he could take a step back from the imposing man, who seemed suddenly much taller than he had originally appeared. The foyer was quite small; and from a cursory glance so was the rest of the house. Small, and poorly decorated. There didn't seem to be much furniture, and a little light overflowed from a candle-powered lantern near the door. Samuel backed away from the man and ended up in a small kitchen. He felt the chill of porcelain beneath his palm, felt the open air of another room behind him.

The old man came at him. "What are you doing here?"

"Car—ran out of gas—" Samuel swallowed. He'd just been chased—*attacked*. More scared than he'd been in a helluva long time. Car out of gas, crashed into some freakin' creature that *bit* him. Anger rose up in him, clouding the pervasive fear that had been driving him on since the incident on the road and the chase through the woods. "They were after me! Those things!" Samuel spat the words. Accusatory in tone. Suddenly he felt like he might be on the wrong track here, that this guy could be anybody in any kind of state of mind for all he knew, but there wasn't much to work with now; the creatures outside, or this guy here.

The old man's brow came together in rage and fear. He seemed undecided on which to go with right now.

"Look!" Samuel lifted his bleeding hand, now crusted with dirt and leaves. Blood caked between his fingers and was splashed down his arm. Fat still pushed through the deep wound, and he could see a bit of bone through the laceration, sticky wet with new blood. "This was the only place I could come...the only place there is for miles around! I need help!"

The old man stepped forward, reluctantly accepting this bit of reason. His mouth beneath the thick coat of mustache twitched, wanting to say something harsh, and yet his eyes glinted beneath untrimmed brows, rheumy with a strange mixture of sleeplessness, concern, anger, and fear.

The old man took a few more steps toward Samuel, who backed completely into the small kitchen. Violet light poured in through two long windows above the sink, providing the only illumination since he'd left the candle near the front door in the other room. Samuel recalled the scant illumination that had been emanating from beyond the house—a luminescent fog, violet and pungent.

The old man's eyes flicked to the scene through the windows. Samuel looked but doubted what he saw; a nightmare collage of movement and madness.

In what passed for the back yard of the house, many of the black-tailed, scaly creatures danced like furious demons as if to the beat of unheard voodoo drums. They hopped in the violet glow—the fog which seemed to be a kind of effluence from some otherworldly portal. The creatures moved like exotic dancers of death, thick, double-jointed legs ending in talons. Long tails, spined and spiked with shiny black scales unfurled and slashed like whips of the sadomasochist. The horned, misshapen skulls reared back in malevolent delight, jaws opening wide and flickering with forked tongues, eyes flashing electric blue.

Samuel stared in gape-mouthed awe, for what they were was not all there was to behold.

The fog did not just emanate from some ethereal hole in the darkness that led to the Abyss. There was an object around which they danced. Something that could barely be seen but seemed to pulsate like an enormous balloon of amorphous flesh, gray and mottled. Tentacles sprouted from it in unlikely configurations, curling out from the lavender fog to join the demonic dance of madness. Growths that he couldn't quite make out—like vegetation almost—could be seen atop the central mass of throbbing horror.

The circle of abysmal madness continued to swirl, dancing demons and vile pulsating heart.

Samuel was horrified and yet couldn't turn away. Couldn't pull his eyes from the vision of—

"You had a better chance out there! On the road!" The old man whispered urgently.

"I didn't. I couldn't go anywhere. There wasn't a choice."

"You don't have one here, either," he hissed. His teeth were black and broken. His breath smelled like fetid trash. "Go back to your car. Wait for help—you're in more danger here!"

"What?" Samuel pulled away from the old man's vice-like grip. His age in no way determined his strength. "What about *that?* Them? I'll never make it."

The old man glanced at the otherworldly visage. His beady eyes flashed with anger but softened in realization of the truth.

"What is that?" Samuel asked him. "What's happening out there?"

The old man looked at him squarely. His pitted cheeks relaxed, the bristles of his beard and mustache twitched as his snarl gave way to flat acceptance, even remorse.

The air in the kitchen between them was taut, musty, and full of strange anticipation. Samuel breathed deep, holding his hand between them in the purple shadows, blood black and dripping from his wound. The old man seemed to smile—a painful effort from the looks of it— but not for long. He reached out and grasped Samuel's wrist, peering down at it with concern. They washed the wound under the sink, in some brown looking water that burned.

They went back into the living room to take a closer look when there was a footstep in the hallway that led up through the stairwell.

A second slow step. Then a third.

Someone—or something—was coming down from upstairs.

Samuel looked up at the old man, but he hadn't budged. He was staring intently at the wound.

The skin at the back of Samuel's neck crawled—the hair prickled and raised all along the back of his skull.

Someone was coming down to meet them.

"We're going to have to cut it off," The old man said.

Samuel jerked his head around at the old man.

"Like hell!"

The look in the elder's eyes said he was dead serious.

The walker on the stairs emerged into the shadowy back hall near the kitchen.

It was a lithe figure in a robe, wearing a hooded cowl that shaded its face. The figure moved like a phantom into the front room. All that was visible as it emerged into the flickering circle of candlelight was a ruby hint of wet lips deep in the hood. Its hands were concealed in the sleeves of the robe, folded together in front.

"Father," the figure said; a woman's voice issued from the darkness of the cowl. Soothing and calm. "Not now. Let us talk with him."

She turned toward Samuel.

"What is your name?"

"Hannah," the old man said in stern remonstration. "This is not appropriate."

"Father," the woman's voice—Hannah's voice—was soothing, almost balmy. "We don't have visitors, let me know him…"

"Samuel," he said, "My name is Samuel."

"My name is Hannah," the dark figure said. "And this is my father, Eli."

The old man grumbled under his breath. "This is neither the time nor the place for this…"

"When is it ever the time or place, Father?" Hannah asked. "When is there ever a visitor here because of what you've done?"

The old man, Eli, slammed his fist down on the arm of the couch and stood. His beady eyes flashed with indignation as he stormed off and went upstairs, grumbling about "ceremony," and "damn the rest." He paused at the base of the stairs and turned toward Samuel, a warning on his lips.

Samuel met Eli's maddened gaze.

He seemed on the verge of speaking but then changed his mind and disappeared up the stairs.

Hannah sat across from Samuel. The flicker of candlelight caught now and then a slant of her chin above the neck of the robe, the glimmer of supple lips, the glint of a dark eye.

Samuel wanted very much to confide in her, but the robe set him ill at ease. He felt pretty certain he'd left the sane world behind when he drove off the interstate and come right through hell's foyer the moment he'd stepped through these doors. And here before him, in black robes, now sat some kind of evil sorceress or something. Some devil-worshipping priestess of the night.

His choices were slim. His hand was bleeding. Throbbing.

He looked at the wound.

Samuel did a sudden double take.

"What the hell?" The skin at the edges of his wound had begun to get hard and darken. Shingle-like scabs had begun to form. He had an awful feeling he knew what those were too—black scales, like the reptilian skin of his victim. Fear pooled deeper in his gut. "What's happening here? What is all of this...am I—?" And suddenly the entirely possible thought came to him that, "I must be dreaming. This is too freakin' crazy to be real...you're not real."

"Oh," Hannah said, in her sweet, sultry tones. "But I am real. See?"

Her hands emerged from the sleeves of her robe. They were the dainty hands of a perfect woman, slender fingers and fragile bones— except that her skin was ebon and scaly, smooth and shining like satin, with black fingernails that curled like talons.

As she pulled the hood from her face, Samuel began to push himself away from her, eyes scanning the room in the immediate vicinity for a weapon, or anything, to use to escape. Nothing immediately came to mind, and he didn't have any kind of plan.

And yet, despite his fear, he couldn't look away from her face.

Hannah was a phantasmagoric statue of twisted beauty. Her eyes were electric blue, hair in long dark curls that cascaded from inside of the robe. Her face was very much that of a beautiful woman save for gray tinted skin and the nubbed protrusions of horns. Her ruby red lips pulled away in a lethal smile to reveal a double row of razor-sharp fangs. Her neck was thin and beautiful, almost kissable, until it came down and blended with the black, scaly skin of her hands, and, presumably, the rest of her body.

She presented herself before him.

"I am as real as you are...as real as my father is."

"Eli?" Samuel swallowed. He had to buy time with words. "He's your father?"

"Yes, he's a...how shall I say? Not quite a warlock, and yet, a formidable conjurer in his own right. Especially in this age, as my mother tells me. Anyway, it's rare that a man knows what he's doing in the realm of the dark arts. Sadly—as it has always been—the price of sorcery is greater than he bargained for."

Samuel leaned slowly forward, eyes scanning the room. The candle might be used for a weapon, but anything he tried in the way of burning her would probably be futile.

"I am the product of his unholy lust," and she hissed the word 'lust' like a serpent. "All his years of solitary study combined with the whispering suggestion of demonic influence drove him to satiate his sexual desire...my mother and I, we are succubi. He called her out of sinful lust. She devoured him, and gave birth to me."

Hannah leaned forward and gripped Samuel's chin with two nail-pointed scaled fingers and one taloned thumb. Her eyes were swirling whirlpools that drew him in, electric blue flashes of power flickering out from her eyes, reaching deep into his mind from the depths of her sinuous manipulations...

"She is coming now, and bringing her demon fathers through the open portal—the portal that my father opened for her to come through. There is nothing he can do to close it now, you see; he is hers, completely, just as you will be mine."

She smiled, revealing again the rows of razor fangs, the forked tongue that licked her shimmering lips, the magical gleam in her eyes...

"Hannah! Get back!"

In a flash Hannah's head whipped around. She emitted a monstrous roar in sudden Jekyll and Hyde contrast to her seductions.

The old man stood at the bottom of the stairs. He had changed into long red robes covered with the gold embroidery of magical symbols and hieroglyphs, a hood pulled up over his head, face painted with white streaks above the scraggly beard. He held in his hands a long axe.

Hannah turned swiftly to face him. Her black robes whirled.

Samuel's eyes flashed between the half-human succubus and her father, but focused in on the double-bladed woodcutter's axe. Its metal gleamed dull orange in the light of the candle from the living room, backlit by the violet glow of the demonic festival beyond the house.

We're going to have to cut it off, the old man had said.

Samuel looked at his hand where he'd been bit.

The wound was now completely black with crust, the skin around the bite quickly developing a scaly texture.

"No!" Hannah hissed at her father. "I want him for my own!"

"I won't allow it!" Eli said. "He doesn't belong here."

Hannah's answer was a cry of rage that filled the house like a lioness's roar. She leaped at her father. Her body impacted his in full force and knocked him back into the shadowy hallway. The old man yelled some words that Samuel couldn't understand. The succubus's head lashed down like a striking serpent, fangs ripping into his neck. She went down again, teeth bared, deep within the old man's cowl. Her face emerged a second time in a bright spray of crimson. She roared and seethed and attacked again in an increasing frenzy of bloodlust. Soon, the walls ran thick with scarlet. Dark rivulets dripped down the walls of the hallway, splashing out from her vicious attack.

Samuel seized the opportunity. The situation was madness, and he feared he had begun to go mad himself. He had no choice but to act. It was certain death either way, but better to die trying.

The double-bladed axe had fallen from Eli's hand onto the threshold of the hallway from the kitchen. It gleamed next to the two fighting forms on the edge of the living room. Samuel lunged, grabbed, and hefted the weapon into the air.

The succubus was still busy ravaging her father, back heaving with the strength of its hunger. Claws raised wet with bodily fluids as she went down and then rose again from the body, intestines and guts streaming from a cavity torn into the old man's torso.

She caught the image in the corner of an eye, turned to see that Samuel towered behind her in the hallway; the weapon held high above his head, a maniacal gleam in his own eye.

He brought it down with a heavy stroke.

It sank deep into her spine.

Hannah roared. She thrashed into the hallway and tried to roll away.

Samuel struggled to keep hold of the double-bladed axe that almost jerked from his hands. He tried to pull it from where it had been lodged. He fell with the force of the yank, but scrambled to his feet, dashing toward the front door.

She thrashed across the floor toward him, like a wounded fish out of water, a quivering mess of dripping blood and broken spine, her tail thrashing out from a tangle of bloody robes. She leaped to her feet with a sudden rush of supernatural strength and met him at the door, swiping the air with a taloned claw, roaring in his face with fetid breath and eyes burning with anger.

Samuel dodged the attack and stepped back to raise the axe high. He dropped the weight of the weapon with the added strength of surging adrenaline.

The downward stroke was swift. His arms shuddered with the sudden impact of the strike. The blade planted deep in her skull. Her forehead opened in a gushing black fissure. The body of the beautiful blood-drenched succubus fell to the ground, dead.

A rumble sounded deep within the earth.

The entire house began to tremble. Windows shook in their panes. The floorboards beneath his feet shuddered as in the early tremors of a massive earthquake. The rumble grew louder, rising in volume like the sound of high tide, when the surf just keeps coming. A rushing sound of wind, a tidal wave of madness from the darkness of another world.

Looking down at her, struggling to remain on both feet, he remembered what she had said about her demonic mother from another world:

She is coming now.

Samuel shoved the broken body out of his way to open the front door of the house and, wielding the double-bladed axe in one hand like a blood-crazed barbarian, made his way over the heaving earth back through the forest, down along the overgrown path he'd followed here from the road. He ran with both feet pumping like the pistons of a steam engine. When he spotted the shining scales of black in the darkness, he swung a mighty blow and kept going. Twice he struck the reptilian creatures in the pitch darkness of the forest. He didn't stop to see if they lived or died. His only purpose was to reach the car, the road…where sanity had ended for him tonight, on Old Temple Road.

He forged ahead through the forest. The earth beneath his feet became unstable. It shuddered as if mountains were ready to burst forth from the terrain. Trees cracked and swayed, roots snapping beneath the earth, ripping apart in explosions of dirt and deadfall. The sound of wind behind him again rose like a rushing wave.

Samuel ran. He kept on running for what seemed like many long minutes. He reached the edge of the woods and glanced back to see the distant silhouette of the house completely engulfed in the violet glow. The forest seemed to waver then, like a desert mirage in the dead of night, the paper-thin film of reality fluttering in the thrashing heat-blast of hellish winds.

There was an explosion then, unlike anything he'd ever seen before, as if the house had gone supernova—a brilliant burst of blue and violet that filled his eyes and seared his vision. The flash grew in size, and then disappeared in an abrupt vacuum.

A black hole swallowed that section of forest. The air grew wintry cold. Trees were uprooted and sucked in, crashing against one another as they were pulled into the void. A blast of wind knocked Samuel off his feet. He scrambled across the ground, gripping handholds, anything he could use to make it the rest of the way beyond the edge of the woods and across the ditch.

Samuel crawled out into the road. He searched both directions for the shape of his Mustang in the distance. He struggled to his feet and ran toward it with all his remaining strength. The creature he'd first struck was still curled in its hideous rigor of death.

He struggled with the door handle. His hand was stiffening. His heart leaped as he realized his entire left hand had become a black scaly claw at the end of his arm.

With a cry of fright, his heart and lungs near capacity with fear, he leaped into the front seat of his car and slammed the door, throwing the gore-smeared axe into the passenger seat and closing his eyes. Tears issued out from between his tightly closed lids, and he had to take deep breaths. He reminded himself to breathe.

He knew what he had to do. Before the rest of him became the same way...like *them.*

He ripped a strip of cloth from his shirt. He placed his infected left arm upon the dash, and took the axe in his right hand.

He hacked down quickly—without thinking about it. To think about it would have been a mistake.

Blood spurted against the inside of the windshield.

He hacked again, not quite cutting through the bone. Again. And a fourth time. He was crying and didn't know it. Blood was dripping down his face by the time he had cut through his own wrist and removed the blackened claw that had once been his hand.

He managed to tie off the stump with the tourniquet.

He vaguely remembered a final flash from the woods where the house had been glowing in the distance. A strong wind buffeted the car as darkness overtook him.

When the state police found him the next morning, they opened the door of his car with guns in their hands and horrified looks on their faces. The black reptilian creature still lay dead at the back of the Mustang. Blood covered him and the inside of the car. Black ichor was splashed across his face and shirt. The severed claw that had been Samuel's left hand lay in a soggy pool in the passenger's seat, where the gore-soaked axe was leaning.

Samuel looked up at them. They stared back. Gray shocks of hair had pushed out in stripes on each side of his head. His eyes seemed wild and lost.

He smiled, a wide maniacal grin. He started to giggle. And then he started laughing.

It was a long time before he stopped.

Christopher Fulbright

Christopher Fulbright is a freelance journalist, ghostwriter, technical writer, and the author of more than 50 stories published in *Haunts, Dark Tome, Whispers from the Shattered Forum, Outer Darkness, Thirteen Stories,* the recent anthologies *Blasphemy, Deathgrip: Legacy of Terror,* and more. His sci-fi novella *Sometimes Women are so Cold* was published in the UK in a numbered limited edition in 2002, and his horror novel *Of Wolf and Man* was recently published in trade paperback in the USA. He currently lives in Grand Prairie, Texas with his wife and two children. Visit his website at http://www.mindovermedium.com/chfulbright

A Taste of Power
by
Bill Glose

Wary shopkeepers closed their doors and shuttered their windows to prepare for the coming storm, but not Hamlin. It wasn't that he mistrusted the predictions—far from it. He, too, recognized the gusting winds as a precursor to the coming onslaught. But the weathermen had only predicted a tropical storm, and *that* he could withstand. Had they called for a hurricane, then he would have buttoned up. Certainly, the gathering storm carried risks, but cash flow outweighed those dangers. Lightning flashed in the sky as if to rebuke his thoughts, and as he shuddered, he once again reminded himself that he *had* to stay open.

Business had been light lately. Unseasonably cold weather had kept vacationers away from the city and the indigenous crowd was hoarding their money to splurge once spring finally arrived. Although Hamlin's Shop of Oddities was not a seasonal business, his profits rose with the temperature. When warmer weather brought tourists to town, few were able to pass his shop without at least wandering through to peek at his wares.

And so it was that Hamlin was alone when the two scraggly youths entered his front door. Garbed in all black, they strode in confidently, not bothering to glance around at the items on display. A stout boy of about 19 years walked up to the counter with a lean kid about two years his junior trailing behind. They both wore sunglasses, and Hamlin briefly thought, *Yes, of course they would.* Their type always wore shades regardless of the lighting. Water poured from their matted hair and streaked from their leather jackets, but neither seemed to care. Hamlin eyed the puddles they created on his shop floor but didn't mention them. Perhaps he would have said something on another day with other customers present.

"Helluva day, ain't it?" the leader said to Hamlin in a tone implying he didn't really want a response. Hamlin stayed quiet and studied the teardrop tattoo high up on his cheekbone. He remembered hearing that type of marking was a gang sign. It meant he had killed for his colors.

"Whatcha doing open, Pops? Everyone else is closing up for the day." Hamlin figured this question was rhetorical too, so he stood deathly still, awaiting the inevitable. The tall boy continued, "When we saw all the other stores shut up tight, we figured it must be fate. I mean, we're the only ones out there and you're the only one open." The smaller one chuckled, sidling up to his companion and unzipping his jacket as he moved, revealing a wiry frame sheathed in a ribbed white tank top. A striking tattoo of a panther tearing at some hapless and indiscernible prey might have caught Hamlin's eye more if not for the silver gun butt jutting out from his waistband.

"You believe in destiny, Pops?"

"Sure." Hamlin tried to keep his voice even. He thought a sudden move might spook the two boys so he remained calm.

"Well, then, why do you think we were brought here? You must have some good stuff to sell us, right? And I'm sure you're going to have a very reasonable price for us too. I mean, if fate brought us here, we should get some hefty discount, dontcha think?" The smaller one giggled some more. He'd removed his shades and his eyes flitted back and forth from his cohort to Hamlin and back again. Though Hamlin could barely discern the tall one's eyes through the dark lenses, he knew they remained fixed and icy. His companion didn't possess the same steely fortitude, though, and Hamlin was glad the tall boy was present. He would have had more trouble controlling the situation had the young skittish lad come in by himself.

The tall one continued in his deep and powerful voice, "So, what kind of discount do you think we should get? Half off?" Hamlin didn't move, not that there was anywhere to go. They stood between him and the front entrance, intending to block off his escape. "No response, huh? Must mean you think that's too low. So how about 100 percent?" He smiled for the first time, showing perfect teeth that seemed out of place with his blocky face. Hamlin could picture those teeth smiling out at him from a billboard ad with the words, *Got Milk?* written across the bottom.

Hamlin glanced furtively to the unshuttered windows. Fat drops of rain pelted the panes but there were no passersby. "Get it over with," he said.

The younger one pulled out his gun and revealed a smile that would never be on a milk poster. Two front teeth were missing and the others pressed in on the vacant space, creating a snaggle-toothed grin. He looked over at his partner and asked, "Now, Bull?" When the tall one nodded his head, the young boy darted behind the counter with his gun raised. He snarled as he pistol-whipped Hamlin, slashing the barrel hard across the bridge of his nose. Hamlin crumpled to the floor and the young boy kicked him a few times. When Hamlin didn't fight back, he stepped over him to open the register.

"Crap," he yelped in a staccato pitch. "There's only fifty bucks in here. Where's the dough, old man?" His boot put an exclamation mark on his question as he struck the balled-up shopkeeper once more.

"With the storm, nobody's really been in here today. Just a few people looking for batteries and whatnot. This is all I've got." Hamlin thought the kid believed him, but that didn't prevent a hail of kicks from showering down upon him.

"Ease up, Mouse," the tall one said, then turned his attention to Hamlin again. "We got a problem here, Pops. See, we walked through that door for something memorable, something more significant than fifty bucks. Now, if you ain't got nothing for us, then maybe *you* are the something significant. You might be Mouse's first teardrop." He paused a moment to let his words sink in. "Unless you got another idea. A memorable one." He flashed the movie-star smile again to let Hamlin know that whatever happened next was up to him.

Mouse paced in a tight circle without turning his back, dancing a waltz with some unseen partner. When the tall one finished talking, Mouse stopped and peered at Hamlin. His tongue darted through the ugly gap in his teeth as he licked his lips and stared at the shopkeeper.

Hamlin knew this kid would do whatever the tall boy asked. He hung his head down and spoke almost in a whisper. "I have a storage room."

"There you go, Pops. See, I knew it was fate."

They hauled him up roughly and followed him to the back of the store. Hamlin wheezed as he limped toward the back wall, jerking now and then as Mouse poked him in the ribs. When he reached the end, he paused for a moment to look back at the boys. The younger one smiled his grotesque sneer again and Hamlin told him, "You'll have to give me a hand moving this."

The sneer disappeared as his lips pinched together. He thought maybe the old man was somehow giving him a hard time. But Hamlin put his hands on the bookcase and waited, so he shrugged and joined in. Together, they shoved the bookcase, and though it was heavy, it moved fairly easily on the scuff-marked floor. As soon as the shelves were out of the way, Mouse jumped toward the secret basement entrance and twisted the door's handle. He grunted and slapped at the door with his hand, but it didn't budge, so he turned back toward Hamlin wearing his tight *he's-screwing-with-me-somehow* expression.

His partner intervened, grabbing one of his shoulders. "Mouse," he said. "Why don't you step back and let Pops have a go at it." He looked at the shopkeeper and nodded at the door. "Pops?"

Hamlin nodded back, then dug through his jacket pockets. The key he produced was hefty and weathered, a thick shaft with one notched end and another that terminated in a bulbous knot resembling a fist. He slipped it into the sturdy lock, then pushed the door. It creaked open, revealing a dark, descending stairwell. Mouse pushed Hamlin aside but didn't step down any of the stairs. A dull light glowed from whatever room lay at the bottom, but the staircase twisted and Mouse couldn't see the source. When the door had been revealed, he'd been eager to burst through and claim their prize. But now he hesitated. He swallowed once, peered down the stairs, then grabbed Hamlin's arm and shoved him ahead. He held onto Hamlin's collar as he followed closely behind, peering over his shoulder to see the room, but keeping Hamlin between him and whatever lay ahead. When he finally saw the room, he released Hamlin's collar and almost forgot about the man altogether.

The ornate interior starkly contrasted with the run-down storefront, as if the door had been a portal to another realm, a darker and richer world. The crown molding consisted of colorful serpents jutting out from the wall with torches clenched in their mouths. Torchlight flickered and cast dancing shadows across the room, making it difficult to distinguish what lay at the room's other end. The long room's vaulted ceiling created a tunneling sensation, and Mouse had the unnerving feeling that this passage bored deep into the earth. Ivory statues of men with bull's heads lined the two side walls and a plush red carpet led from the entrance to a shiny steel seat thirty or so feet ahead of him.

But, the one thing that captured his attention, that absolutely compelled him to stare like a rubbernecker ogling an accident scene, was a six-foot totem pole standing before the throne. Two slender foot-long wooden columns supported the totem's thick torso as a person's legs might, but any human comparison ended there. Above the peg legs, the totem was crudely fashioned from jagged slats that resembled deer antlers with unevenly spaced knobby protuberances. The slats comprised the bulk of the figure, joined together in a cylindrical weave, and bulging at the midsection as a snake might after swallowing a large animal. Unlike the clean and polished Minotaurs, the slats were discolored and coated with speckled grimy ooze. The visible portions seemed to be made of bone, giving the totem the appearance of a skeleton torn from an otherworldly corpse. The stench of long forgotten and now mildewed meat accompanied the pole to complete the image of unnatural death.

Sitting atop this object was a lit glass case. The teens approached, mesmerized by the strange green aura emanating from the case, until they were standing a foot from the container. Inside they saw a hand carved from an ivory tusk with a golden ring on one finger, a green emerald bigger than a half-dollar set into the band.

The tall one was the first to look away, remembering they were not alone. "Get your ass up here, Pops." Hamlin heard a slight crack in the thug's voice but said nothing of it. Instead, he got up from the floor and shuffled toward them.

"What the hell is this?"

Hamlin didn't wait to reach the boys before responding, "That ivory hand was created for Count Pedulla in the Tenth Century. The gold trim is merely paint, but the hand is a relic. A collector's item."

"Expensive?"

"Yes. It's probably worth between five and ten grand. More if you can find the right collector."

Mouse let out a loud yelp, "Yeeeaahhhaaaa!"

The tall one had regained enough composure to ask the important question, "What about the ring, Pops? Is that stone real?"

"Real as they come. But if you were smart, you'd just take the hand and leave the ring well enough alone."

Mouse, perhaps buoyed from their big score, didn't wait for his superior to respond. "Man, you better can the advice! When we want your opinion, we'll beat it out of you."

The tall one kept his gaze fixed on Hamlin, but he shot an elbow out to the side catching Mouse off-guard. The blow hit him in the gut and he let out a breathy, "Umph." Mouse moved back a couple of steps, glaring at his partner, but he did nothing to retaliate.

The tall one ignored Mouse's whimpers and leaned in toward Hamlin. His voice softened into a neighborly tone as if the two of them were standing at their fence, pleasantly chatting over local gossip. "Now, why do you say we should leave it alone, Pops? Out of the kindness of your heart?" He was toying with Hamlin again, this time expecting an answer.

"Simple," Hamlin replied, "the ring's cursed."

Mouse tried forcing out a chuckle, but came up short, partly because his stomach still ached from the shot he'd taken and partly because he knew Hamlin wasn't joking. Of course, he didn't believe any of Hamlin's crap, but he could tell that Hamlin did. He could see it in his eyes.

The tall one dropped the convivial manner and finally removed his sunglasses, standing before Hamlin for a full minute. He set his jaw and drilled his eyes into Hamlin with the type of challenging stare bullies often use to start brawls, daring a weaker foe to do something—anything—to give them an excuse to strike. The silence grew heavy, the weight of it creating its own presence in the room. Hamlin said nothing, but didn't flinch either. He stood his ground and waited for the tall one to make his next move.

The next move was not what Hamlin expected. The tall one let out a howling belly laugh, as if just now getting the punch line to a hilarious joke told earlier. Mouse followed suit, but without the same gusto. His head cowered in the valley between his shoulders as he giggled nervously, eyes darting from side to side. The tall one clasped his partner's shoulder, the earlier incident all but forgotten. "You almost had me there, Pops," he said. "You see what he's doing, Mouse? *Cursed*, he says, so we won't want it…so we'll just leave it here and let him be. He must think we're retarded or something."

Mouse's head bobbed in agreement like one of those silly spring-mounted car accessories. "Cursed…retarded." Mouse mimicked in between giggles. Hamlin could see where he got the nickname.

"Now, Pops, I got one more question for you, and then you can file this whole incident away as a bedtime story for the grandkids. And my question ain't got nothing to do with curses or ghosts." He held out both arms to his side and shook them in the air in a mocking gesture when he said *ghosts*, followed by a warbling whistling sound. "I wanna know something a little more practical, Pops. I wanna know if you got any alarms rigged up on that case.

"See, I don't think you're a dummy, Pops. But, I do think you're a little scared, and scared people can do dumb things even though they know better. Now, letting us trip an alarm—that would be *very* dumb." He paused, letting this sink in before continuing. "The choice is yours. Smart and alive—" He paused and his smile melted away, "—or dumb and dead."

"No," said Hamlin, shaking his head. "There's no security device."

"You absolutely sure?"

"The ring is guarded by something much more powerful than police. I can give you no more warning than that."

Bull's fist shot out lightning quick, catching Hamlin on his left temple. He laughed again, but this time it was more menacing than jovial. "Fair enough, Pops. I'm warned." He then stepped away toward the gleaming case with Mouse in tow. "Open it up," he told Mouse.

"You sure? What if he was lying? I mean, about the alarm. I don't trust him."

"Then we can cap him and still be outta here before anyone can respond."

Mouse did his strange, nervous dance again, eyeing the case as he had done to Hamlin earlier. His tongue darted out and licked both corners of his mouth, shot back inside, and then repeated the process all over again. He rolled his fingers together before reaching up with shaky hands to grip the exterior metal handle. The hair on Mouse's arms stood up and a tingling sensation ran up and down his spine. He tapped at the handle once first, not quite sure what to expect—a loud siren, an electric jolt, something. But nothing happened. Relieved, he grasped the handle and pulled the front door open with a gentle tug.

Once the case was open, he looked inside and discovered the source of the strange green glow. Recessed lighting just inside the case's edge shot beams upward to reflect off the gemstone, creating the illusion that the gem glowed naturally. More confident now, Mouse reached in and grabbed the ivory hand. "Cursed, yeah right," he mumbled.

The ivory hand was slightly smaller than Mouse's and not nearly as heavy as he'd expected. He tossed it up in the air a few times like it was a new toy.

"Careful, Braindead," scolded the tall one, smacking Mouse on the back of his head after the second toss. "If this thing's anywhere near as valuable as he claims, you don't wanna go cracking it up on the floor."

He turned away from Mouse and strolled back towards the shopkeeper. Hamlin lay still, propped up on one elbow. Blood from the gash in his head flowed across his face, blurring his vision and caking his beard. The tall one lowered himself a few feet away to rest on his haunches. "How's your memory, Pops?"

Hamlin stared back with a puzzled expression etched on his face. After a moment, the expression dissolved and he replied. "Very bad," he said.

The tall one cupped Hamlin's face in a vise-like grip, shaking his head a few times. He released Hamlin's jaw and said, "There ya go, knew you were smart."

He got up, jerking his head in a *follow-me* gesture to Mouse, and then they left.

Bull grabbed the top bar of the chain link fence and vaulted over in one fluid motion. He held out his hand and Mouse pushed their booty through a small hole in the fence. A stray wire snagged Mouse's wrist as he pulled his hand back through the small opening, leaving a dot of blood as a reminder. He winced, but didn't dare do more than that lest he show any weakness, possibly earning him another shot in the gut from Bull. He simply shook his hand, then grabbed the fence, slipping once from a misstep then scrabbling over on his second try.

Once he landed on the far side, Bull returned the load for him to tote. Mouse accepted the large plastic shopping bag that they'd confiscated, shifting its weight under his arm to rest on his hip. Stenciled on the bag was the store logo, a large black raven with horns encircled by red wavy words reading, *Hamlin's House of Oddities and Curious Creations.*

Bull turned and Mouse followed. The rain was still coming down hard, fueling the oily brown river that gushed through the alley. Bull strode onward, undaunted by the flowing muck, but the grimy stream sucked at Mouse's heels and threatened to knock him down. The gap between the two widened as Mouse slowed his pace, considerably afraid of falling—not for the damage it might cause him, but because he didn't want to appear foolish.

Bull stopped in front of a ramshackle building whose windows and doorways were boarded up. Spray paint coated the walls from ground level to a height of six feet. At that point, the artwork petered out but a few comments splattered the second floor face and some enterprising youths had even painted a four-foot pig wearing a police uniform just outside one of the third floor windows. The THIS BUILDING CONDEMNED notice decorating the front entrance had been modified too, select letters blacked out or altered to spell out THIS BIG CONDOM. Various phallic symbols decorated the sign, completing the montage.

Bull yanked at the door and said, "Into your hole, Mouse."

Mouse ducked inside, saying nothing. He hated his nickname but endured it quietly. Only the leader of the Black Widows could change a member's name. That was part of their tradition, their code. Mouse had been called plenty of names before—pipsqueak, runt, speck, girly-man. But, these were his chosen brothers. They weren't supposed to pick on him the way everyone else had. He thought that joining the Black Widows would have been the end of those hassles.

He put up with the name, silently hoping to change it someday. He'd heard stories that Bull hadn't always been called Bull, though it was hard for Mouse to imagine calling him anything but that. With his thick neck resting atop a barrel chest, the name suited him perfectly. Of course, Bull liked to brag that one of his girlfriends gave him that nickname for another reason.

Mouse hadn't dared to ask what he'd been called before but the others mentioned it when Bull wasn't around. Zephyr said Bull was called Stump when he first joined the gang ten years ago. "Short and squat—just like a stump," he'd said. Then he'd doubled over laughing, spitting soda out his nose, so Mouse figured maybe he was just joking. It was possible, though. After all, Bull had been a Black Widow since his tenth birthday and Mouse cheered considerably thinking of him as Stump. It gave him hope that he, too, might one day grow out of his nickname. In fact, he already had a new name picked out.

Mouse rubbed his hand wistfully over the ink panther roaring on his shoulder, its teeth and claws dripping with the gore from its hapless victim. The needle had hurt like hell when it bit into his shoulder, injecting ink into his soft flesh, but the pain was well worth it. *Awesome, bitchin, bad-to-the-bone.* That's how others reacted when they first saw the panther, and they said it with respect. One day, Mouse hoped, his name would change from Mouse to Panther.

Mouse crawled through the opening and the inky darkness swallowed him. Bull stepped inside next, flicking his palm across his lighter as he entered. The flame invaded the thick gloom, but dispelled little. The building was huge, but without any depth perception the walls seemed to close in on Mouse. He hung back hoping to gain some vision from the dull halo surrounding Bull.

"Move it, Mouse," he said, giving him a jab in the side.

Mouse did as he was told, stepping gingerly and feeling the floor with his extended foot. The building offered protection from the raging storm outside, but at the same time provided more imminent dangers. Familiar with the perils, Mouse proceeded with extreme caution. His toes pressed against the rotten and spongy floorboards, which responded with creaks and groans. Bitter bile crept up from his stomach and he swallowed to keep it down while searching for the gaping hole he knew to be there. But the putrid taste kept rising in protest anyway. When his foot finally pressed down into empty space he relaxed his clenched jaw and quietly sucked in some air. He was glad Bull couldn't see the set of his face and didn't want to make any unbecoming noises.

He backed up against the left wall and edged around the chasm, clutching the slick bag to his chest. Splinters from the wall scraped the back of his neck but he refused to pull his head away from the wall. In fifteen seconds he was across and continuing toward the back of the building. Bull followed, hopping across the slim ledge in two quick steps.

Once in the back room, Bull exchanged the lighter for the shopping bag and Mouse busied himself lighting candles. His hands shook a little as he lit the candles and he took his time, hoping for the shakes to subside. Afterwards, he grabbed some rags from the corner to wipe his face, then offered them to Bull.

Bull wasn't interested in toweling off, though. He'd pulled the ivory hand from the bag and was turning it over in his grasp, looking at it curiously. After studying the hand for a few minutes he did something entirely out of character. He asked his partner's opinion. "Whatcha think about what that old man said? You think the ring's cursed?"

Mouse wasn't sure how to respond. The old man had freaked him out and he wanted to say so. It wasn't just the way he told them with such conviction that the ring was cursed; everything about his manner had changed once they got into that strange room. No one stood up to Bull the way he did down there. Bull gave him the icy stare and he just stood there indifferently.

Now that he thought about it, nothing in that basement was right. While Bull was interrogating the shopkeeper, Mouse had tried toppling one of the Bull-man statues but found he couldn't budge it, even when he lowered his shoulder and shoved hard. True, he was no Arnold Schwarzenegger, but he should have been able to move the statue a little bit. It must have weighed over a ton. Sturdy statues like that are found in museums or on display in front of government buildings, not tucked away in some shopkeeper's storeroom.

But the thing that creeped Mouse the most was that strange creation holding the case. The statues simply seemed out of place but that totem was downright unnatural. When he grabbed the hand from the case, he was so worried about an alarm that he hadn't paid enough attention to it. He remembered how his hair stood up on end like there was some sort of static energy emanating from within. The room's whole setup was like an altar of sacrifice.

Mouse wanted to say all this, and more, to Bull. But this could just be one of the many character tests of which he was so fond. Failing those tests often meant punishment, or at least being humiliated in front of the gang. He remembered how Bull had laughed out loud when the old man told them the ring was cursed and knew how he was supposed to respond. "Cursed my ass!" he said. "That crazy old dude musta been on drugs or something."

Bull smiled and Mouse knew he'd said the right thing, the *cool* thing. Bull leaned against a rusty metal desk, still turning the ivory relic over in his hands. Mouse noticed that he held onto it at the base, at the wrist, never touching the ring. "My thoughts exactly, Mouse. I thought maybe you bought into his line though. You seemed scared back there."

"Not a chance, man. Black Widows ain't scared of nothing." Mouse thumped his chest a couple of times while he said this, trying to sound tough but failing.

"Uh huh," said Bull. "Well, if you ain't scared of nothing, why don't you try the ring on, then?" He said this nonchalantly, no hint of challenge in his voice, and then passed the hand to Mouse, still avoiding the ring.

Bile raced up Mouse's throat again. He didn't want anything to do with the hand or the ring. He wanted to tell Bull that, but he also didn't want to fail the test. Or was this a test? For a moment back in the storeroom, when the old man first said the ring was cursed, Bull had lost his composure. He'd been relaxed up until that point and then he gave Pops the ice eyes. Bull only gave someone the ice eyes when they were causing problems, and an old man rambling about ghosts and goblins wasn't any trouble.

However, Mouse didn't think the old man was simply telling ghost stories. And Mouse thought the old man actually believed what he'd told them. Either way, it was pretty strange. Maybe Bull knew this too, or maybe Bull was actually scared of the ring.

Mouse took the hand. There was something disproportionate about it but he wasn't quite sure what it was. He turned it over and held it next to his own hand and then he saw it. Each of the fingers on the ivory hand had an extra knuckle. The fingers weren't bent, so it was hard to notice at first. "Something ain't right about this hand," he said to Bull.

Bull's tone became menacing. "Are you gonna be a wuss your whole life, or you gonna be a Black Widow?" Mouse's chin dropped at the rebuke and he caught sight of his tattoo again. *You're a panther and there's no such thing as curses,* he told himself, then grabbed the ring.

Just as when he'd grabbed the case's handle, he expected a shock of some kind, but there was nothing. He slid the ring on his fourth finger like a wedding band and noticed Bull staring at him. "Well," he asked, "you feel anything strange?"

Mouse responded with bravado that wasn't faked this time. "Like I said, man. Old man musta been smokin' dope."

Bull eyed him a little more and Mouse could tell he was checking him out for some sort of reaction, like a medieval food taster. Bull *had* believed the old man. He'd been too scared to put the ring on himself and used Mouse to test it out. *Well, who's the wuss now?* he thought, noticing the quizzical look on Bull's face.

"You know," Mouse said, "if that hand is worth 10 big, then this ring must be worth at least 50. I mean, look at the size of it. When are we gonna tell the others about this score?"

Bull's curious expression hardened before he replied, "No reason for them to know." Mouse didn't understand. "OK, you can take it off now," he continued.

Now that Bull was sure there was no curse on the ring, he seemed eager to get his hands on it. *But what would happen then?* Mouse wondered. If he wasn't willing to share the loot with the rest of the gang, was there any chance he'd actually want to split it with Mouse? Mouse knew the answer and his stomach started churning all over again.

Bull stepped forward menacingly. "C'mon Mouse, take...it...off... now!"

Bull was giving him the icy stare and Mouse knew he had to do something. A thunderclap boomed nearby, causing Mouse to jump. He reached for his Beretta but Bull grabbed his wrist before he could grip the handle. He twisted hard and Mouse fell to the floor. He pulled Mouse up by his scruff and yanked the automatic from his waistband. "You ain't gonna be needing this," he said. "Ain't gonna be needing that ring either."

Tears welled up in Mouse's eyes but refused to spill over. He tucked his lower lip in his mouth, biting down with his front teeth to stifle a cry. "But...but...I'm a Black Widow, Bull. We're brothers."

"You ain't nothing to me, Mouse. You're a rodent, a speck. Now give it to me or I'll shoot you and pry it off your dead finger." He knew Bull wasn't kidding. *Bluff* was not a word in Bull's vocabulary. Mouse looked around for something to grab. He saw a brick on the desk and formed an idea. Maybe he could drop the ring to distract Bull, then grab the brick. A brick against a gun was hardly fair, but he couldn't think of anything else.

Mouse tugged at the ring but it wouldn't come off. The gold loop gripped at his finger, refusing to let go. "I'm getting impatient," Bull prodded.

"It...It won't come off, Bull."

Bull chopped him in the temple as he had with Hamlin earlier, but used the barrel this time. Mouse collapsed and cartoon stars danced in his field of vision. He tried to lift his arm to protect his head from the next blow he knew would be coming, but couldn't find the energy to lift his arm. His whole body felt like jelly. The brick might as well be a mile away for all the good it would do him now. His head lolled and he saw the panther again. "I wish I really was a panther instead of a mouse," he mumbled to himself, starting to cry. "Then I could deal with Bull. I could rip his throat out."

Mouse waited for the next thud on top of his head, the one that would end everything. Huddled on the floor in anticipation, blackness overcame him.

When Mouse awoke, he wasn't sure how much time had passed. Except for a thrumming in his own head, silence greeted him. The candles had burned out and the room was pitch black. That was no indication of time, though. With the building boarded up, this room was just as dark at noon as midnight. However, the lack of rain and thunder told him that he'd slept through the storm and that he'd probably been out of it for a significant amount of time.

He tried to sit up but fell back when the stars came again, appearing as light blotches in the dark. His head thundered and there was a sharp pain in his side. He lay still for a few moments, breathing deeply, trying to regain control of his body. Using his elbow to prop himself up, he slowly scooted into a sitting position. He sought the source of the pounding in his head but was unprepared for the sticky tangle of hair and crusted blood his fingers discovered. He swooned and felt something swirling in his head again. If there had been anything in his stomach, he might have thrown up.

He sat motionless and tried piecing together all that had happened. He was sure Bull would have killed him. *Why hadn't he?* He gazed around his pitch-black surroundings. Maybe Bull had killed him. Maybe he was dead and this was Hell. He hadn't been to church in years, but even when he had gone, he never imagined Heaven and Hell to be anything like the preachers described. The dark void engulfing him now was more terrible than anything they had conjured up in sermons.

That thought roused him into action. He bent down on his hands and knees and started crawling. He had to find something, anything, to get a reference. After crawling a few feet, his efforts were rewarded when his shoulder bumped into the desk. Finally, there was an object to add substance to the prevailing darkness. He released a long sigh. Mouse knew his fears were stupid but was unable to control his emotions. He needed to calm down and think things through. Just because he wasn't dead now didn't mean Bull wouldn't come back to finish the job later. He had to get out of the building.

Mouse crawled around the desk and headed toward the doorway—at least where he thought it was. He should be able to just crawl along the wall all the way to the front door, but he wasn't sure how he was going to cross the hole. Before he could even exit the room, Mouse halted when his hand touched something wet and pulpy. He froze with his hand pressed against this unknown item while his mind searched for an explanation. There hadn't been anything else in the room when he'd lit the candles. Just the desk, a patio chair with only three legs, and some old magazines. The mushy texture told him this was not an inanimate object though. He told himself it could be a dead rat or something like that, but he knew it was too large for typical vermin.

Mouse really didn't want to know what it was. He withdrew his hand and shuffled back a bit, then aimed his course in another direction. This time his hand slipped on something slick. His first thought was that it was milk, because it felt too gummy to be rainwater. Then he knew what it was—blood.

Mouse reached up to his head to feel how bad the wound had been. It still felt tender, but not too wide or deep. He couldn't imagine all this blood coming from him. But what other explanation was there?

He didn't want to think about it any more. He had to get out of there. He crawled through the sloppy floor and found the wall, then followed that to the doorway out into the hall. Once outside the room, he slowed to search for the dangerous trap ahead. He had no idea how he was going to make it across this time. It was tough enough to cross at full strength, but now, he would certainly fall in.

He'd held back his tears before, but they streamed freely now. "Dammit!" he sniffled. "I wish I could just catch one lousy break! No hole to crawl over or a little light. Something, anything!" A searing sensation ripped through his side and Mouse screamed in pain.

"Who's in there?" a voice yelled from outside, followed by some loud thumps on the door. Moments later it came crashing down and Mouse squinted at the bright light that streamed in. It was daytime after all. Heavy footsteps ran towards him but he couldn't tell whom they belonged to.

Mouse couldn't think any more. This was just too much. His head was still pounding and now his side was on fire too. The man leaned over him and asked him questions. *Who was he? What was he doing here? What day was it?*

Mouse heard the questions and wanted to answer, but nothing came out of his mouth. It was just too hard to talk. His eyes adjusted slowly and he could make out the outline of a hat on the stranger's head, and centered on that, a badge. The man talked into a microphone clipped to his vest, then turned back to Mouse. "You're going to be OK, son," he said. "Just hang in there."

Mouse heard this but he didn't believe him. If everything *were* going to be all right, the room wouldn't be spinning so much.

The police officer knelt by Mouse and stayed with him until EMTs entered to treat him. Mouse's vision swam and he saw blurry white contrails fill the EMT's wakes as they moved efficiently around him, pushing, probing, and questioning, searching for injuries. His mouth still wouldn't function so he just stared up at them dumbfounded, catching snippets of conversation. *Where's it hurt...too much blood...only superficial ...going into shock.*

They lowered a gurney next to him, then plopped him on top of it with the cop's assistance. He felt something prick his arm and a cold sensation oozed up his arm. He hoped it would travel all the way to his mouth, which felt unbelievably dry.

More men wandered around his portable bed but they made way for the medics who rushed Mouse along the floor and out the door. Mouse tried to focus, but everyone's bodies seemed to vibrate with double and sometimes triple images. It was all too confusing for Mouse, so he shut his eyes.

As he was being wheeled out, the last thing he heard was a voice asking, "Hey, when did they fix the floor?"

The next time Mouse awoke he was in a hospital bed surrounded by light pastel walls with white cabinets. Décor was minimal with functional items spread throughout the room, though none of them were in use right now. Idle machinery sat atop a rolling cart pushed against an unoccupied bed and other high-tech gadgets littered the counters on the far wall. Gummy liquid from an IV bag provided the room's only motion, dripping down a tube that fed into his arm.

He watched the liquid flow through the tube, merging with his own bodily fluids. *Where did all that liquid go?* he wondered, and *How much he could hold?* Watching the steady drip, his mind raced back to the condemned building. *Had he actually crawled through blood, or did he just dream that?* It all seemed so hazy to him now.

His lips were chapped and his throat sandpaper scratchy, but at least the drumming in his head had stopped. There was just a dull thrumming where Bull had smashed his skull. When he'd first woken in the dark building, he'd touched his hand to the side of his head and worried that maybe some of his brains had leaked out. The gritty, globby texture of caked blood in his hair was one thing he wouldn't soon forget. Though repulsed from the memory, he once more felt the need to touch his wound, to feel the split in his head. He reached up tentatively to check out the damage only to find out he couldn't since both wrists were handcuffed to the bedrails. He was a prisoner.

Seeing his manacled wrists was a shock, but an understandable one. He could accept it, even. But the other thing he saw when staring down at the cuffs biting into his wrist made absolutely no sense. The ring with the large emerald stone still rested on his finger.

His chest hitched as the breath caught in his throat. *Hadn't Bull taken that?* Before he could ponder that thought too much, a nurse walked in—barged in actually. Pink tails fluttered in her wake as she rushed across the room carrying a plastic tray in one hand, reaching his bedside before the door swung shut. She was a mountainous woman who moved with surprising grace, swinging a metal arm up and around from the bed frame and setting the tray on top before Mouse knew what she was doing. Shortly cropped bright red hair contrasted with her cottage cheese complexion and blushless flabby cheeks surrounded a tiny mouth that worked overtime to compensate for its lack of size. "Well, looks like our guest is awake now," she said as if chatting with an imaginary friend.

"And how are we feeling today?" She was bereft of jewelry except for the watch on her wrist, which she consulted now without waiting for an answer. Plump fingers from her other hand probed under the cuffs before settling on Mouse's wrist. "Much better," she said, referring to his pulse. "You should be up on your feet in no time, honey."

The industrial strength supports on the bed creaked in protest as she sat on one edge. Mouse saw the corner of a nametag high up on her pink uniform shirt, but her gown covered too much for him to read it. "Here you go, honey, just take a sip of this." She leaned in with the bigger of two cups from the tray, pushing the bent end of a flexible straw into his mouth.

Pursing his cracked lips was painful, but when he suckled at the straw Mouse was rewarded with a cool sensation that ran down his throat and radiated through his body. It might only be tap water, but Mouse couldn't ever recall tasting anything more refreshing.

The nurse pulled back the cup, admonishing him lightly. "Don't gulp now. There you go. That's it. Now, open wide." Mouse obliged and she placed a green gel capsule from the smaller cup on his tongue and let him drain the remainder. "Mmm mmm, you sure were thirsty. Nothing like a glass of cold water to get you off on the good foot. So, what's your name, honey?"

"Mou…" he croaked.

Mouse licked his lips and was ready to try again but she stopped him. "Oh, don't you worry. I'll just keep calling you *honey* until you get your voice back. Though you might not be here long enough for us to chat." She patted his cheek once and then got up from the bed, which groaned its appreciation. "You're going to be just fine," she added, picking up the tray and disappearing in the same pink flutter that marked her arrival.

Mouse wondered what she meant by her comment that he wouldn't be here long. Did she mean he was going to be released? He looked around the room and for the first time noticed something peculiar just outside his window. There were bars there. Though they weren't the industrial-sized iron rungs you might find on storefronts, the thin mesh was just as impenetrable. He glanced down at the bracelets chaining him to the rails and understood that she meant something else all together.

Detention was fine with Mouse, though. Where would he go if they released him? He didn't have a home and he couldn't risk going back to the Widow's lair. For some reason Bull had spared him and it seemed unwise to give him another chance at it.

With the nurse gone, he looked at his hand again. Why hadn't Bull taken the ring? Some of the fog left his weary head so he concentrated hard, trying to piece it all back together. Just before Bull whacked him on the head, Mouse had tried to remove it himself, but the ring wouldn't budge. Was it stuck on his finger? That might explain things. Maybe Bull left to get something to loosen it from his finger when the cop had wandered by.

Mouse recoiled as another thought slapped its way into his mind. Maybe Bull went to get something to *cut* it off. The idea of Bull getting a blade to cut off his finger seemed more plausible to Mouse than him going out for a bucket of Parkay. Although efficient air conditioning chilled the room, sweat trickled down his face and his pulse quickened as he gazed at the ring. It had an animal presence about it. The gemstone peered back at him with an aqua eye while the loop dug into his finger. It was a beast that he wanted as far away from him as possible. But all he could do was stare at it through the perspiration stinging his eyes.

A short while later, two tall men dressed in suits entered his room with considerably less fanfare than the nurse. Both were calm and casual as they approached. *Plain clothes cops*, Mouse thought. *Pigs in a blanket.*

The first one, a very dark black man with broad shoulders and GQ features, sat on the bed. He looked at Mouse with intense obsidian eyes and wasted no time getting to the point. "We just heard you were up. Do you remember how you got here?" His voice was deep and powerful, the kind that commanded respect.

The second cop was just as tall as the first but that's where the similarity ended. Saucer-shaped spectacles rested on his ski-slope nose and an awful toupee topped his diminutive head, one that Mouse thought could actually be a rat hair weave. His thin frame seemed as brittle as uncooked spaghetti, and he stood in an expectant pose, notebook flipped open and pen at the ready, eyebrows arched as he awaited Mouse's response.

"Yeah...kinda," Mouse said. His voice was still gravelly but was adjusting some. He figured that a little more liquid would rinse away the sandpaper taste all together. Water?" he asked.

The thin cop slid his notebook into a pocket and stepped outside, returning moments later with a much larger cup than the one Mouse drank from before, but without the silly safety lid used to teach toddlers how to drink. He passed it to his partner, then resumed his ready-and-waiting pose.

The GQ cop offered Mouse no rebuke as he slurped greedily at the straw. After allowing him to empty half the cup in a minute, he picked up where he left off, gently prodding Mouse. "You were saying..."

Mouse knew this was wrong. Even if Bull had turned on him, the cops were the enemy. That was one fact of life he knew for certain. If he could work up enough saliva, the Widow thing to do would be to spit in his face. "I wasn't saying anything at all." Mouse glared at him, but averted his eyes from the policeman's unwavering gaze after only a brief moment.

The cop remained calm and relaxed, unfazed by Mouse's pitiful attempt at defiance. "That's all right. We've got time." His stoic appearance told Mouse he would wait around as long as necessary too.

Mouse bent his head and addressed his comments down into his chest, much softer than before. "Who the hell are you guys anyway?"

"I'm Detective First Class Dubois," replied GQ, opening his wallet for Mouse to inspect. "Go on with your story, son. You'll feel better if you get this off your chest." He paused, then repeated his initial question. "Do you remember how you got here?"

Mouse lifted his chin and bounced his gaze between the two inquisitors before finally settling on a less-threatening object, one of the cream colored cabinets. His puffed-up chest deflated as he sighed. Finally, he answered the question. "Well, I was alone in that abandoned house, trying to crawl out when I felt something on the floor." The recollection forced Mouse to pause briefly with an involuntary shudder. "I wasn't sure what it was. When I yelled, I heard someone call from outside the front door. Next thing I know, a cop busted the door in and rushed up to my side."

"What happened next?"

"I'm a little hazy on the time after that. I was lying there for a while. The cop stayed with me and some others joined him—I don't know how many. They wheeled me out of there and then I woke up here." Mouse was feeling much better now, but his throat still felt scorched. "Can I get some more water?"

Now that Detective Dubois had the kid talking, he didn't want him to stop. He pushed the half-full cup to the far edge of the bed tray and continued. "In a moment. Go back a little further. What happened before? What were you doing in that building? And was anyone else in there with you?"

When Mouse first saw his wrists cuffed to the bed, he figured he was being detained for what they had done to the shopkeeper. But that was just grand theft. They didn't send detectives to investigate robbery, especially when the suspect was already in custody. Something else was going on here.

"Why am I cuffed to the bed?" Mouse asked.

"Partly because we don't understand your involvement with events that occurred in that building."

"What do you mean? I don't know about any *events* that happened in that building. I crawled in there to get away from the storm, and when I woke up that cop busted in and brought me here."

Dubois' eyebrows arched. "Is that so? We won't know that for certain until you tell us the full story. However, you're also being detained for your own safety."

Mouse clanged the cuffs against the bedrails. They bit into his wrists, but he ignored the pain to emphasize his point. "My own safety? What does chaining me to a bed have to do with my own safety?"

"You had extensive injuries when we found you and we had no idea how you got them. For all we know you could be suicidal."

"No way, man. Someone else did that to me."

Detective Dubois smiled and spread his hands in an expansive gesture. "Who? You just told us you were in there by yourself."

Mouse quieted. He wasn't sure what he wanted to tell the cops and what would be better to keep to himself. "Am I under arrest?" he asked.

GQ paused, then replied, "No."

Mouse yanked the handcuffs harder than the previous time and yelled at the policeman, "Then I wish you would take these damn cuffs off me."

Detective Dubois was debating whether or not to comply—he wanted his questions answered first—but then the kid screamed in pain. Though he didn't know what was wrong with him, he knew he'd be in serious trouble if the kid being chained to the bed complicated matters. Dubois hurried to the kid's side, knocking the cup on the floor as he grabbed for his keys. He quickly removed them from a pocket and unlocked the cuffs.

A terrible pain scorched Mouse's side much like the searing sensation he'd felt on the floor of the darkened building. As the detective removed the cuffs, Mouse reached for his abdomen in search of a wound, but found no holes. The skin was unusually soft and as his fingers pushed and probed, he winced from his own touch.

The pink nurse rushed into the room. "Where's it hurt, honey? What happened?" She glared at Dubois who backed away, shrugging his shoulders. She pushed past him to the bedside monitor that graphed erratic peaks and valleys. Her pudgy hands raced expertly over his body, searching for any sign of trouble. She saw Mouse's hands clutched to his side and felt underneath for damage. Something was amiss, but there was no bleeding and nothing protruding. It must be an internal injury. Mouse saw the puzzled look on her face and knew something wasn't right.

An Asian man in a white lab coat entered next, trailed closely by a wispy nurse who looked too young to even be out of high school. The doctor also scanned the monitor first before asking, "What's going on here, Nurse Redding?"

"Pain in his abdomen," she replied. The doctor probed in the same manner as the nurse, but when he touched Mouse's ribcage he pulled his hands back as if receiving a shock. Mouse was really scared now. *What the hell was going on?* he wondered.

The doctor slowly put his hands back and felt more carefully, pushing and prodding gently at Mouse's gut. His brow furrowed with the same confused curl as the nurse, and just like her, he maintained a professional manner. Regardless, Mouse didn't feel bolstered. His pulse raced when the doctor called out, "Get him to x-ray quick."

Nurse Redding rushed out and returned with a gurney in her usual efficient manner. With Dubois' assistance, they hoisted Mouse up onto the cart and rolled him out of the room. Detective Dubois escorted them down the hall, hovering over the doctor's shoulder. "What is it, Doc?" he asked.

"I'd like to wait until the x-rays come back before commenting."

Dubois gripped the doctor's arm. "I'm just asking for your opinion. Nothing official. I'm just curious." The doctor didn't seem the type to take flak, but he also realized the quickest way to get rid of Dubois was to simply answer his question.

"I'm really not sure. It doesn't make sense, but it seems like he's missing some of his ribs."

Dubois released the doctor's arm and swiveled his gaze in Mouse's direction. They spoke of Mouse's condition as if he was in another room even though they were never more than a step from the gurney. "Are you saying his ribs got smashed in? I thought the only injury was to his head."

"You weren't listening to me," said the frantic doctor. He spoke haltingly, as if trying to make sense of it himself. "I'm not talking about fractured ribs, I mean gone altogether."

"Gone? Is that possible?"

Two police officers tugged a struggling prisoner to one side, making room for the speeding gurney. The doctor stopped talking momentarily as they exited the security wing and moved into the radiology wing. The rolling bed was used to smash open doors along their path as if time wasted by pushing them with hands was too precious. "An abnormality to be sure, but I assure you, I've seen stranger birth defects. However, something this critical would normally be a life-threatening event. I can't imagine how he was able to live this long."

If the heart monitor would have been attached to Mouse, the racing beat could have substituted for a drum solo. The ache in his head was long forgotten. He knew there was no birth defect. Other than his tiny stature, he was an ordinary boy. He was complete, whole. Nothing was there that shouldn't be and nothing was missing—until now. He thought back to the blood on the building's floor. My God! Had Bull cut him open and removed some ribs as a trophy? Something to show the gang? Evidence for another teardrop?

That thought bounced through his head as the gurney slammed through a final set of doors. It didn't make sense. No one had mentioned any holes in him. The detective had just mentioned that the only injury was to his head and the doctor seemed surprised by the discovery. If Bull had operated on him, there was no way a hole in his side would have gone unnoticed. He would have been gutted. So, what was the answer then?

Mouse was wheeled under a large gray machine resembling a Xerox that hung from the ceiling. Everyone left except one technician who donned a heavy lead apron to shield her from the damaging rays. Mouse was offered no protection, but he feared something other than the electromagnetic radiation. He concentrated to put a face to the unknown threat, the source of his pain.

The Xerox flashed and made a copy of Mouse's bones. Goosebumps shot up Mouse's arms but not from the x-ray. The pain in his side was suddenly gone, replaced with a strange surge of power coming from his hand. Of course, he realized. The ring!

Mouse reconstructed what little he could recollect clearly as the others streamed back into the room. He remembered the sharp pain, a sudden stab in his side coming from nowhere, unlike anything he had ever felt before. As far as he could remember, nothing had set it off. He had been lying on the bed, needling the cops, when he asked them to take the cuffs off. Though he hadn't really asked them, he simply said he wished they would take them off.

The goosebumps raced up Mouse's body again as a fuzzy image took form in his head. He saw himself being wheeled out of the house. How in the world did they roll him through that hazard-filled building? Mouse knew it was dangerous enough for one person to navigate, but they had pushed a gurney through there. The fog in his mind burned away and he saw two cops standing in the doorway. *When did they fix the floor?* one of them had asked.

Like everything else, that made no sense either. Mouse remembered edging around that gaping hole on his way to the back room. There was no way anyone could have repaired it in that short a time. He also remembered crawling around searching for the hole. That was the first time the pain had struck him, causing him to cry out.

But, no, that wasn't quite right either. He had said something just before that, just before calling out in agony. When he realized that he couldn't make it around the hole with his head split open, he had broken down. He was on the verge of tears and he had said something. He *wished* that there wasn't a hole to crawl over. He also wished for some light, and right afterwards the cop had busted the door down, bringing in the daylight.

The ring thrummed on his finger as the pieces fell into place. He remembered the static charge he'd felt earlier while reaching for the case. He thought it had come from an alarm system, but now he realized the source was something else entirely. *Was it possible?* No, there was no way. But, what other explanation was there?

Lying on his back, he watched fluorescent lights pass by overhead. Nurse Redding had run ahead to get his bed ready but the remainder of the entourage surrounding him provided plenty of targets on whom to test his theory. If he was right, he might feel some pain, but he knew that would pass. The earlier pain was gone already. Whispering under his breath he said, "I wish Detective Dubois would shoot his partner."

Mouse screamed as the now-familiar pain tore through him, causing everyone in the hall to jump, including an unfortunate guard from county lockup. Since the county jail didn't have its own infirmary, seriously injured prisoners had to be transferred to the hospital's security wing for treatment. The paunchy guard lost the argument with his superior about getting any backup assistance. "We need every available man for the bus ride," his boss had said, leaving the skittish deputy alone to escort his injured prisoner—Jeb Thornton.

Thornton—AKA, The Madman—was facing a life sentence for his latest endeavor. A three-time loser, his chances of seeing the outside again were slim, good behavior or not. Once they moved him to his new maximum-security home, the chances of escape would be slimmer yet. So an hour before the transfer, he picked a fight with another captive, making sure he lost. Though the hapless stooge he battled had little chance of even landing a blow, when the guards opened the cage, his confused cellmate was left holding a handmade shiv while a bleeding Thornton screamed bloody murder.

Thornton's injuries were not nearly as threatening as he portrayed, of course, and Mouse's distraction provided him with a perfect opportunity. When Mouse screamed, the nervous officer transporting Thornton released his hold to reach for his gun. Although the officer hadn't pulled his gun from the holster, he had unsnapped the restraining strap. Thornton easily overpowered the clueless guard, slamming his manacled fists into his side and grabbing at the revolver. As he tugged the gun from the holster, the deputy's finger tightened on the trigger, shooting himself in his leg.

Detective Dubois immediately went for his gun though his partner stood frozen in place with his eyes growing wide as half-dollars. As the prisoner turned his gun toward them, Dubois pulled back on his own trigger. Nurse Redding, hearing the first shot, came bursting into the hall to find out what was going on, hitting Dubois' arm and jolting it enough so that his gun no longer pointed at the prisoner.

The bullet tore through his partner's shoulder and slammed him into the wall. A geyser of blood erupted from the fastidious notetaker, spraying the walls around him. He stood plastered against the wall with his mouth in an *O* of surprise to match the wide eyes behind his saucer-shaped lenses.

Another shot from the downed officer's gun hit the wall above Nurse Redding's head, who then added her shrieks to the growing clamor. With catlike reflexes, Dubois recovered enough to retrain his aim on his opponent's heart. He squeezed the trigger three more times, putting a tight grouping of slugs into the man's chest.

Mouse was all but forgotten in the ensuing pandemonium. The brief skirmish left one man dead and two wounded in its wake—two wounded officers at that. Mouse was of little consequence. He sat up as groups of white and pink gowns rushed through the hall, bandaging wounds and transporting victims to treatment rooms. One man in green scrubs pushed against Thornton's chest in a futile attempt to revive him, his orange jumpsuit quickly changing to red as the life leaked out of him.

Unlike the revulsion Mouse felt from the blood on the abandoned building's floor, this red pool gave him strength. He felt a dizzying sense of power. This was *his* doing. He glanced around at the bedlam and knew he had to get out of there. The pain in his side was receding already so he should be safe to travel. First though, he had to get out of the silly hospital gown.

He reentered his room, ignoring the commotion surrounding him. Slipping off the gown, he grabbed his street clothes which hung neatly in the closet on plastic hangers. Just as he finished shrugging into his jacket, someone entered the room. "Oh, dearie. Are you all right? I almost forgot all about you. You really shouldn't be up and about. You need your rest, honey."

Mouse glared at Nurse Redding. What could this tub of lard be thinking? He *wasn't* her honey. His glare turned to a sneer as he approached the woman. "I'm fine," he spat. "But I'm not too sure about you."

She ignored his comment and pulled the sheets back from Mouse's bed, tilting her head in a *come-here* gesture. If the bloody affair in the hall hadn't ruffled her feathers, a nasty rebuke from a rebellious teen wasn't likely to set her aback. "Now, now, honey, I know it was shocking what happened out there, but everything's going to be all right. You're perfectly safe in here."

"Yes, I am," Mouse replied. "You on the other hand…well, that's an entirely different matter." For the first time, Mouse saw her composure fail when he loosed an evil laugh. Raw energy coursed through him. He now understood the power that came with strength, the power that had been held over him with Bull's iron fist. Along with this realization came a perverse need to discover his boundaries. He prepared to determine exactly that as he planned a final test on the poor woman. Gritting his teeth to prepare for the coming pain, he made his wish. "I wish the bed would eat Nurse Redding."

The pain gripped him, but he was coming to terms with it. It wasn't nearly as bad now that he knew when to expect it. Nurse Redding however, had no idea what was happening. His manic tone and absurd babbling caused her to shuffle backwards into the puddle created by Detective Dubois. Her right foot shot out from under her, and in an attempt to maintain balance, her arms darted out to the sides, causing slabs of flesh underneath to shake uncontrollably. She fell hard against the joint of the still-open bed tray, which snapped shut on one of her waving arms.

Nurse Redding screamed in agony and struggled to get up, calling to Mouse for assistance. While trying to stand, her foot slipped once more and she fell to the floor, this time accompanied by a loud crack. The metal framework retained its grasp on her arm, devouring the abundant folds with mechanical disdain and snapping the ulna underneath. Mouse howled with laughter for just a brief moment. His howls intensified his own pain though, so he winced and resorted to petting the bed. "Good boy," he said. "Hope you enjoyed your meal."

Although her own ripped flesh coated with blood hung from the hinge, Nurse Redding stopped screaming. Terror won the battle over pain on her tear-coated flabby face. Her eyes got huge and she cried out as though testifying at a church revival, "Lord Jesus, help me, help me!"

Mouse was captivated by this impossible feat. He had wished it, and it had happened. His side still ached but that was inconsequential. The raw power of the ring was all that mattered.

Mouse laughed again and left the room, leaving a shivering Nurse Redding in the mechanical mouth. She aired the sign of the cross over her chest as he left and said to his back, "You've got the Devil in you, boy." Mouse ignored her just as the busy occupants of the congested hallway ignored him as he left the building.

The sun greeted him warmly as he stepped outside, the storm long gone. Branches, leaves and trash littered the curbs, bunching together in newly formed ponds beside overfilled drains. The world, so different than the mayhem of the hallway, seemed calm and peaceful. Mouse intended to change that.

The pain in his side had receded to a dull throbbing as he strolled down Broadway. It was somewhat reminiscent of the time he'd lost two teeth in a brawl. There was discomfort associated with it, but the feeling was more strange than painful—there was a void. His tongue darted to the gap in his mouth and he wondered what could possibly be missing inside his belly.

Regardless, the pain and the odd accompanying feeling were tolerable. He could handle anything as long as he could recreate the look of pure terror etched on Nurse Redding's face. He'd seen the look before, but he had always been a witness to it, not the cause. The omnipotent sense was intoxicating; he was drunk on it.

He walked two blocks from the hospital, lost in his fanciful daydream without realizing it. Looking up, he saw the sign for Jackson's Jewelers and smiled. The sign on Jackson's doorway stated, *If diamonds are a girl's best friend, then Jackson's is where your friends call home.*

Mouse chuckled at the corny words. It was time he made some new friends.

DeJean DuBois hovered over his partner. The mound of reddened gauze taped to his shoulder had choked off the bleeding, but his partner was still in great pain. The nine-millimeter bullet had shattered Nick's collarbone before bouncing up and out of his body. Most of the bleeding had come from the quarter-sized exit wound in his back near his shoulder blade. Though there had been a lot of blood, the damage could have been much worse. If the slug had deflected downwards instead, it could have ripped through vital organs instead of tearing through non-vital flesh and muscle.

DeJean still couldn't believe the amazing sequence of events that had produced this injury. He was a skilled marksman and frowned on those who waved their guns about frivolously. But DeJean was sure he had been anything but frivolous. The prisoner was about to fire, of that he was certain. It was just dumb luck that Nurse Redding had opened the door at just that precise moment. By the same token, it was pure chance that the prisoner got his hands on a weapon in the first place. He could understand the other officer going for his gun—after all, he had jumped when the kid had screamed as well and he had already heard the kid perform that act already.

DeJean's eyebrows arched. What was going on with that kid anyway? Figuring his partner would be fine, he left the room and entered the hallway, scanning up and down its length. He walked back to the kid's room and was stunned by what he saw there.

Several nurses stood around a berserk Nurse Redding, trying to dress her bleeding arm and force her to take some medication. She yelled at Dubois as he entered the room. "He's the Spawn of Satan! The demon seed!" One of her arms was bent at an awkward angle, and Dubois figured it must be broken. She ignored the arm and her coworkers, staring at Dubois through fevered eyes. "He is possessed…the demon seed…he's the Devil, I tell you."

Dubois didn't have to ask whom she was talking about. Her voice triggered invisible fingers that crept up Dubois' spine, tickling his vertebrae. He knew all about possession. His father was a Houngan, a Haitian Voodoo Priest, well versed in casting spells and creating potions. He hadn't disclosed his religion to the close-minded police community but still obeyed its laws and wore a medallion bearing Dumballah—a benevolent Loa in serpentine form. He felt at his neck for the medallion and received comfort from its outline.

DeJean knew some things could not be explained no matter how long they were examined, unless you accepted that supernatural forces caused the events to happen. Most cops had a sixth sense about things like this, but explained it away as coincidence or delusion. DeJean knew better, though. He knew that spirits and demons often caused unexplained events to happen, and though this particular one might not be Voodoo at work, DeJean knew it had to be some form of black magic.

The invisible fingers still clutched his spine when his radio crackled, pulling him out of his stupor. *All units vicinity of Broadway and 8th, 10-35. Please respond.* 10-35 was the national 10-code for a major crime alert, and the location cited was just down the road from the hospital. It had to be related to the kid.

"Don't you worry," he told Nurse Redding. "I'm going to get that kid now and then I'll straighten this whole thing out."

The drained nurse pulled away from the others. Throbbing veins flared out from her temples as she gripped his elbow with her good arm. "Let him be Detective. That boy's got the Devil in him."

"I understand. I will be careful." His strong baritone reassured her, and realizing that someone finally hadn't told her she imagined the whole thing, she succumbed to the other nurse's wishes, taking her pills and lying back on the bed.

Detective Dubois passed the elevator and ran down the stairwell, taking the steps three at a time, galloping past stunned visitors. His car was parked behind the hospital's service entrance but was buried deep in back. By the time he got there and started it up, he could already be at the scene. So, he ignored the parking lot and continued his frantic journey on foot out of the hospital's front entrance.

Proper procedure required him to stay put until another officer could take his statement. Even though the hallway shooting was by a police officer in the line of duty, there were still mountains of paperwork to be filed. All the T's had to be crossed and the I's dotted. That would just have to wait, though.

Sweat bristled his forehead as his pace slowed to a trot. His gun was drawn as he ran up Broadway approaching 18th Street, the handgun's grip much less comforting than usual. As he neared the intersection he saw a familiar character exiting a jewelry store. The boy strode out confidently clutching a large velvet sack.

Dubois had the drop on him and this time no one was going to jolt his firing hand. He squared up his stance and eyed the boy's chest over the firing post. "Freeze!" he yelled.

Mouse snapped his head around at the unexpected shout. Years spent blending into the background urged him to drop the bag and follow instructions, but after his jerky reaction, he turned to face the officer. The old habits meant nothing to him now and his natural reaction to flee passed as this realization took hold. He returned the policeman's gaze without flinching, the corners of his mouth creeping upward in a slight grin.

"Drop the bag and put your hands up in the air." DeJean would follow proper procedure until he was certain the boy was possessed. There wasn't anyone in the line of fire and as far as he could tell the kid wasn't carrying any weapons. He ran through the next steps in his head to keep the situation under control. *Have the perpetrator lie down, hands on his head, then cuff him using the same handcuffs he'd had on his wrists earlier.*

Mouse ignored the cop and released a throaty belly laugh.

"I'm not kidding." DeJean had over 100 pounds on the lanky teenager and considered rushing him. He should be able to flatten him with a good hard tackle. But he hesitated, remembering his father's warnings of black magic and Nurse Redding's protestation—*that boy has the Devil in him.* He also recalled the condition of the body they had found in the abandoned building. It had been torn up worse than the chainsawed body they had found last year—gored, as if by some jungle creature.

The kid mumbled something and DeJean felt the steel in his hand bite his flesh. His cried out and dropped his gun that now glowed as hot as a branding iron. The barrel melted, turning into lava-like slag while the cartridges cooked off with loud pops. He yelped when the blistering weapon burned his hand, but his cries were soon drowned out by tormented screams from the anguished kid, and DeJean quickly forgot his own pain.

DeJean had involuntarily backed up a few paces. He was certain the kid was possessed, perhaps mounted by a black magic Loa. He could tell from the crazed look on the kid's face that he had no clue what was going on. The kid gripped his side and tried to control his grimace, failing miserably. DeJean swallowed the lump in his throat and asked, "Do you know why your side hurts so much?"

The kid looked at him, jaw slightly agape.

"The Doc said you had a birth defect, but I think it's something else entirely." DeJean maintained his position. He didn't want to approach the kid and scare him. He didn't want to back away, either. He kept his chin up and gazed forward, striving for an air of control even though his knees were weak.

"What are you talking about?" Mouse asked in a slightly trembling voice.

"Pull your shirt up and take a look for yourself."

Mouse did as Dubois suggested, exposing a concave area on his ribcage. Though DeJean hadn't seen anything amiss before, the change was visibly noticeable now, even at a distance. The skin on his abdomen flapped uselessly with bulbous lumps dotting the area where ribs should protrude. Instead of solid bone outlines though, the bulges had a viscous flowing appearance. An open-mawed expression replaced Mouse's self-assured sneer when he saw his body. Malleable substance met his touch when he pressed areas on his torso that should have been covered with protective bone.

Dubois yelled, "Whatever it is you're doing, I beg you to stop. Look what it's doing to you. Come with me and we can try to get you some help. You've got a black magic curse on you."

Mouse studied the cop, took a step toward him, and then stopped. There was nothing this detective could do for him. The hospital couldn't help either. As he tugged hopelessly at the ring, the old man's words echoed through his head, *cursed*. There was only one place where this damage could be repaired.

Dubois took a step toward Mouse. "Please, son. Let me help you."

"Stay away if you know what's good for you. I won't warn you again."

Detective Dubois knew not to push his luck. He stood aside and Mouse walked away.

"Come again," Hamlin said, handing change to his patron. "And don't forget to mention us to your friends."

"You bet," the customer replied with a smile, turning away from the counter and exiting the store. Mouse entered at the same time and the departing customer held the door open for him before heading on his way. Hamlin looked at Mouse, recognized the boy's frenzied expression, and smiled. Mouse's face bore the look of someone who saw death approaching but was helpless to move from its path. It was a look Hamlin had seen many times before.

Mouse stood in the doorway, wanting to approach the counter but unsure of himself. He stared at the shopkeeper and saw that his nose bore no scar from the pistol-whipping. Mouse was shaking and felt like his knees were about to give out. The sense of power had long since left him. "What...what's happening to me?" Mouse asked.

"I'm sure you've got some idea of that yourself, young man. Otherwise, you wouldn't have come back here, would you?"

"Please. Is there something you can do?"

"Lift your shirt," he instructed. Only the top few ribs on either side of Mouse's abdomen still produced an outline on his body. Hamlin dotted the air while counting the missing bones and nodded in deference to Mouse. "Impressive. That's the most I've ever seen. Most get anxious after their first couple of wishes. They realize that, just as they stole the ring, something is being stolen from them. Sure, it's okay for them to rob others of their possessions, but the thought of someone stealing from them sends their minds reeling in a panic."

"Why would someone want to steal my ribs?" asked Mouse, not really wanting his question answered.

"We'll get to that soon enough." Hamlin walked past the boy to the door, flipping over the 'open' sign and locking the door. "Guess that's all the business for the day. Follow me. All your questions will be answered shortly." His manner was calm, as if discussing the weather. This offhanded manner disturbed Mouse more than anything else could have. Mouse still had the ring and certainly Hamlin knew of its powers, yet he was unconcerned.

Mouse finally worked up the courage to ask him, "Please. Can you take the ring off for me?"

"Certainly. But, it's going to cost you. As you can see, my store is fairly meager to those who don't know better. But, I've got rich tastes. You were ready to steal from me, so now you must pay me before I will free you."

Mouse had forgotten about the bag of precious gems. He now opened the bag, eagerly displaying the contents. "Here, take these. You can have them all."

"Ah, very nice. You've done well." He accepted the sack and moved to the rear of the store. As before, he uncovered the basement door and unlocked it. Mouse followed him through the heavy door once more, hopeful that the gems would be payment enough. The room seemed more ominous than before, thrumming with energy as if it was a living organism and he was its meal.

Hamlin walked across the room and dropped the sack beside the throne. He moved over to the case, then invited Mouse to approach with a nod of his head. "Before I answer your questions, you must do something for me."

"Anything."

"Bring me the ring."

Mouse approached with caution. "The ring...it's stuck...it won't come off."

"Don't worry. I will take care of everything."

Thoughts of Bull cutting the ring from his finger were still fresh in his mind, so Mouse offered his hand tentatively, ready to withdraw it if he saw the gleam of a knife. Instead, Hamlin pointed to two of the slats jutting out from the totem. "Grab hold of these." Mouse complied and Hamlin closed his eyes, chanting in a foreign tongue.

"Good boy," he said, patting Mouse on the cheek. Mouse tried to pull his hands from the totem, but they were stuck just as the ring had been stuck on his hand. Tears streamed from his eyes, mixing with the salty sweat that coated his face.

Hamlin strode back to the throne and sat down. "Now, I imagine you want to know why this has all happened. You're not the first to wonder why. For years, decades, centuries, whimpering thieves such as yourself have asked the same question: *Why me?* It's simple. I didn't *choose* you. You made the decision yourself. I even tried to warn you. But you wouldn't listen. Your type never does. That's what makes you such good targets."

He leaned forward, elbows on knees, and lowered his voice to a hushed tone. "Do you know what happens when a simple thief disappears? Nothing. No one asks any questions. The public is content. And I can go about my business without being disturbed."

Hamlin laughed heartily and stood up, kicking the velvet sack aside as he approached the shivering boy. "All your wishes have been granted, but as you can see, it has cost you. Not by these meaningless gems. The payment has been marked—one rib for each wish." Mouse smelled a fetid odor on Hamlin's breath as he leaned against his back and whispered in his ear. "Look closely at the sculpture before you. Can you guess what it's made of?"

Mouse studied the totem. He thought of the hollow area in his abdomen and the gritty slats comprising its surface suddenly made sense to him. "No," he moaned, "please, no."

"That's right...the ribs of all those who have come before you. You've set a new record, young lad. No one has ever gone quite as far as you. Unfortunately, I think none will suffer as much, either. Those ribs, they also represent the life force you must pay to cover your debt. And your payment is due now."

Ear-splitting screams pierced the room as Hamlin chanted another foreign phrase. Green light enveloped the boy, whirling about him and sucking at his limp body. Emerald tendrils stretched from the tornado lashing at Mouse with cracking pops, tearing through fabric where they made contact and leaving behind sizzling scars. After just a few moments, his clothes were stripped away and his flesh was a bubbling liquid mass.

A bright stream of white light formed a bridge between his eyes and Hamlin's. Black dots streamed across this span rushing away from Mouse. The dots flowed in legions at first, but gradually trickled to an infrequent few. After the last of the spots finished its journey, the green whirlwind increased its pitch. The eye of the tornado centered on the ring, which greedily sucked it inside, Mouse along with it.

The sequence of events lasted only a few minutes, and by the time it was over all that remained of Mouse was a gritty pile of ribs, one for each wish. Hamlin breathed in, feeling refreshed. A burnt odor permeated the room, but otherwise all was fine. He placed the ring back inside its case and wondered how long he would have to wait until the next thief paid him a visit. Not long, he mused. It never was.

A Little Nest Egg
by
Kenneth C. Goldman

The old farmhouse lay hidden behind a fortress of neglected shrubbery, and had it not been for the freckled brown and white cat, Willy McCorkle would have sped right past it. The animal had darted out into the road from nowhere and Willy never even saw it. He heard only the sharp crunch of bones and the thick squoosh of innards as the animal thumped beneath the front tire of the Ford pick-up and burst open. The cat rolled a few yards like a small furry sack, then lay soaking in its own thick gravy, leaking its guts into the cracked asphalt fifty yards behind him.

Willy noticed the weather-beaten old house peeking through the thatch of bushes that separated it from the road and wondered if perhaps inside some withered prune of a woman would be expecting her tabby to be lapping up a dish of milk in her kitchen right about now. The thought curled his lips into a toothy smile. This was almost too easy.

Just weeks earlier Willy would have had little use for a jerkwater town like Loomis Falls, excepting those times he had pulled his truck off the Interstate to guzzle down a few cold ones or to take a dump behind a tree. But six months of dipping into the cash receipts at Al Kelly's Service Depot in Piedmont had convinced him that he was not cut out for time-clock employment. Al had been one of those grizzled old duffers who were easy to fool, but still Willy had to waste his days on oil changes and wheel alignments. This seemed unnecessarily time consuming when there were so many other old folks living just off the southern exit ramps of Interstate 95 who could more quickly improve his circumstances the moment he shoved his .22 into their mouth. Old women especially scared easily, and they were usually more than happy to empty their jewelry boxes for a young man holding a gun. That flattened cat baking on the asphalt might just as well have been an engraved invitation to come pay one of them a visit.

The buzz among the Piedmont cowboys was that these old farmhouses were deceptive because many of these hovels hid gold mines behind their doors. Every second story man this side of Georgia knew that inside the decaying shacks lived the sort of frumps who placed Uncle Sam's Federal Reserve System in the same category with the greaseball who might slit your throat for a cold beer. To them, the bank vault had not been built that was as trustworthy as the tattered mattress upon which they slept.

In helping Willy McCorkle to locate the human fossils who shared this logic, so far Lady Luck had been with him, and he had acquired some decent pocket change. Inside one of these old farmhouses he knew some real pay dirt awaited, and Lady Luck would be throwing in her own blow job. Somewhere in an old house like this one those riches were his for the taking.

"Like eatin' corn outa the can," Willy whispered to the empty cab, and pulled the dusty pick-up into reverse. He parked alongside the soft shoulder to inspect the dead animal for any source of identification. It was a chubby calico, and although a mangy creature, it did not seem very old. He knew that in places like Loomis Falls where you might wind up porking your own sister it was unlikely any resident would think to place an ID on a dumb cat. The tubby fur-ball he had smeared into the road might not even have been a house cat judging from the look of its coat.

But then again two tons of truck had just passed over it. Cats and old women just seemed to go together, and Willy figured it might be worth a shot to see who was home and to humbly offer the lady of the house some restitution for the pet he had unfortunately killed.

If I might come in for just a moment, ma'am, why I'd be much obliged if you'd allow me to pay you for your beloved pet lyin' out there on the road. Thank you kindly, and I am so sorry for what I done, ma'am, I truly am. So if you'd be kind enough to just open the door…

The name on the rusty mailbox read Hammond. Except for his pick-up, Willy saw no other vehicles parked near-by, although there might be one inside the shed behind the house. Whether there was a Mr. Hammond around Willy could not tell. It was Sunday and farmers usually did no work on the Lord's Day.

But Willy McCorkle did. He followed the crooked path through the weeds to the house and stepped onto the rickety front porch. A floorboard was missing near the screen door, and the half-rotted door behind it had been left ajar. Judging from what Willy could see through the dirty windows and the torn screen, the grey furniture inside looked like early American garage sale. No one very young lived here, that much was damned sure.

He rang the bell. Nothing. He rang again. Still no answer. This was going to be easier than he thought. He pulled the screen door open.

Old people's homes always had that same musty smell. No matter where they lived, you walked into a house that had elderly residents and you were assaulted by that rancid liver-and-onions stench of rotting flesh. It was embedded in the walls and saturated itself into every fiber of fabric. But the smell made Willy smile. It meant that he had come to the right place.

Daylight had a hard time finding its way through the grimy windows and filthy drapes, and most of the parlor was shrouded in dusty shadows. This too was good. Willy quickly headed for the staircase.

...and just as quickly he stopped himself cold.

"Jesus—!"

An old woman sat half hidden silhouetted in the shadows, motionless upon a wooden rocker in the far corner of the room. Wrapped in a colorless shawl, she must have been staring directly at Willy all along. Her shriveled hands rested in her lap upon a thick patch quilt blanket, and the dark rodent eyes that followed him were set deep inside a head that did not move. The woman's creased gray-crowned face expressed nothing except its age. Only her eyes differentiated her from someone who was dead, but not very much. Standing before her was a complete stranger who had come uninvited into her home, yet the old woman simply sat in her rocker and stared at him as if she were watching a housefly that had somehow got inside her parlor.

Willy had to gulp air just to catch his breath. "Sorry, ma'am," he said trying to swallow his gasps as he approached her rocking chair. "I didn't mean to startle you, but I guess you sure have returned the favor. See, I think that I just run over what might be your cat out there on the road, and so I figured—"

Nothing. No reaction at all. If not for her eyes Willy would have sworn a corpse sat in the old rocker. He reached into his jeans jacket and whipped out his revolver, pointing the small pistol directly at her forehead. The woman did not even flinch.

"Look, lady, let's fuck the formalities. I don't want to hurt you, okay? Just show me where you keep the money and I'll be out of here in no time flat, and no one gets hurt. You understand what I'm sayin'?"

The woman stared at him yet did not seem to know he was there.

"Hun'reds and hun'reds. Prob'ly over a hun'red thousand of 'em ev'ry goddamned day," she said through pale lips that hardly moved as she spoke. Her voice croaked at Willy from somewhere deep inside her throat.

"What?"

For the first time the woman stirred. Although she had been watching him the entire time, her head finally came into alignment with her eyes. "…a hun'red thousand of 'em ev'ry day since my Jake passed on, that's how many I'm losin'. Even while ol' Nettie Hammond is just settin' here doin' nothin', doin' nothin' but just settin' here countin' 'em as they go, she's losin' hun'reds of 'em. Maybe thousands of 'em."

Willy smiled and slowly let the .22 drop to his side. He wouldn't need it. Ol' Nettie was clearly a few eggs short of a dozen.

"Okay, lady, I hear what you're sayin'. You're losin' hun'reds and hun'reds of 'em, yes sir, that's just what's happenin'. So while you're busy countin' up all those figures of whatever the fuck it is you're losin', I'm just goin' to step upstairs for a moment and rob your crinkled old ass blind, if that's okay with you. You just stay down here sittin' in that ol' rocker doin' your figurin' loud enough for me to hear you, and I won't have to come back down to blow your goddamned lunatic brains out through your ears. That's a good ol' girl, Nettie, yes indeed…"

"Just hun'reds and hun'reds of 'em, and me just settin' here countin' 'em…" the old woman continued as Willy headed up the stairs. She was still babbling when he reached the top, and this suited him just fine. The crazy bitch would have probably done the same if he had dropped a grenade into her lap.

Although there were two bedrooms, only one of them contained a bed. The other was littered with junk piled clear to the ceiling, and Willy figured there was not much point in rummaging for more than a few seconds through the cheap lamps, broken pieces of furniture, and the countless boxes of dusty magazines.

Ol' Nettie must have been quite fond of medical journals. There were hundreds of them in piles wrapped in tight cord and packed to brimming inside dozens of dirty cardboard cartons. Willy picked up a handful of loose copies from a stack of *The Journal of the American Medical Association* and blew the dust from them, rifling through articles on health and diseases, human anatomy and surgical procedures, features on the brain and the whole shebang.

"Hun'reds, just hun'reds of 'em…" he could still hear the woman repeating downstairs.

"Crazy old buzzard," he mumbled.

The woman had kept a regular medical library in the small bedroom, but Willy did not find much of interest in any publication that did not come with a centerfold. Maybe this was exciting stuff for a prune-faced hag who probably had not seen daylight since the Nixon Administration, but otherwise the old magazines were completely worthless.

He tossed the dusty journals to the floor and headed for the main bedroom. There was this unwritten law that every person this side of Georgia over the age of eighty understood, a law with dubious logic that stated one's nest egg became automatically untouchable if someone were sleeping near it. Willy McCorkle intended to dispute that logic.

He swung open the bedroom door and stopped dead where he stood.

"Whoa!"

The room reeked with a foul odor that was worse than any other part of the house and Willy had to force himself to enter. He opened a window, hoping the stench would not cause him to woof his breakfast. It stank as if some animal had crawled into the room to die, but first decided to spend some time inside a toaster oven. The room probably had not been aired out in months, and the open window did not help very much. It was the kind of smell that clung to your clothes and forced itself through your nostrils to imprint its fetid memory into every fiber of your consciousness, a stink so powerful that Willy had to shove his head out the window to fill his lungs with fresh air.

Waiting for his breathing to return to normal, he yanked out the drawer of the rickety nightstand alongside the woman's bed. When he flipped it over, two pairs of eyeglasses, a dozen pencils, and a set of yellowed dentures spilled to the floor. No gold mine here.

The old bat had to be hoarding something, he thought. They always did.

A sudden breeze blew open the pages of another medical journal that was on the nightstand. Willy would have completely disregarded the magazine, but the woman had apparently marked off a section, underlining a paragraph with a thick red marker. The article was titled "Memory Functions of the Brain" and it was written in 1985 by some gray-matter genius named Tolbert whose first and middle names had been reduced to initials.

Human brain cells are finite in number. They gradually deteriorate with advanced age, and as many as one hundred thousand of them a day—cells that can never be replaced—simply disappear, taking with them fragments of memory and intelligence.

Inside Willy's head a red flare suddenly exploded. Hun'reds and hun'reds, a hun'red thousand of 'em a day, he thought, turning the old woman's ravings over again in his memory. His mouth went dry as the synapses within his brain connected to formulate a thought too grotesque to share with his conscious mind.

That smell! That god-awful foul smell was coming from beneath the old woman's bed! Oh, yes indeed, the woman was hoarding something under there, all right…!

He tore the sheets and blankets from the mattress, stopping to cover his mouth and nose against the putrescence that assaulted his nostrils in thick waves and kick-boxed with his stomach. Clawing at the stained mattress in several aborted attempts at separating it from the screeching assortment of box springs below, he managed to dislodge the whole assembly of rusted springs and musty coverings, and looked into the black space below the area where the old woman had rested her head.

"Sweet Mother of Christ…!"

Willy gagged up a taste of his own vomit.

They were in there, all right, clumped together in lumpy piles like stinking clusters of dried sponges, a crazy old woman's hedge against the day when her mind had finally subtracted all those dying cells from her brain and left her with neither the memories nor sanity to soothe her. Some of the gray chunks contained long tail-like stems as if Willy had uncovered a cache of disfigured reptile remains. Others lay in fragmented bloodstained nuggets, like misshapen globs of dark clay that had been molded by an insane child.

There were dozens of them.

Maybe even a hundred.

Hun'reds of 'em.

A lunatic's nest egg of human brains!

Willy suddenly realized how quiet the house had become. The loopy old bitch had stopped counting! Some cloudy signal passed through his own brain and told him maybe he ought to turn around. When he did, the old woman was standing directly behind him, hovering over him.

"There's just hun'reds of 'em dyin' inside my head even while I'm just standin' here," the old woman croaked. "And Lord knows, a body's got to save 'em as best a body can!"

For a fleeting moment Willy forced a crooked smile at the woman standing over him. Then he saw what she held in her hands.

With both hands grasping the object tightly, old Nettie Hammond held a baseball bat high over her head.

"What the—?"

A thought raced through his mind that the crazy old broad could not possibly have the strength to do very much damage, not even with the heavy bat. For Christ's sake, he could knock this old crow over with a goddamned feather, so how could the senile bitch ever manage to—?

It was the last thought Willy McCorkle had before the woman brought the thick bat down like a mallet and shattered his skull.

The young man's truck presented no problem for the old woman. She still remembered how to drive one of those four-on-the-floor jobs, and she wasn't so far gone that she had forgotten the way to Marshall's Swamp. Even a toothless relic like her could still remember how to do that much. Besides, she'd done it so many times before with the others.

But those blasted brain cells were drying up so fast, and sometimes it was hard to remember how to work that damned threshing machine the way Jake had showed her. Luckily, enough of the little buggers had remained inside her head for her to recollect what she had to do. The thresher was supposed to be only for grain, really, and Jake had warned her she couldn't put anything too bulky into that thing, else the machine might choke. So she had to cut up everything she stuck into the thresher's long chute, cut it up real careful into little chunks so that the machine could chew it up real nice for the cats.

The cats...all those poor little cats in the shed...

She didn't really mind chopping this new one up so much. He wasn't a nice fella like some of the others, talking to her like she was some kind of fool. Still, she had to be careful with the young man's head, 'cause those brain cells were so damned important. She had read about the part of the skull that was easiest to crush and she pretty much knew how to bring her bat down directly at that spot near the base at the neck. Maybe she hadn't done too much damage. Brain cells were getting mighty hard to come by, and she was still losing so many of them. A hundred thousand a day, that article had said.

Soon it would be time to set another one of the cats out on the road. She felt sad that she had to do that; they seemed to trust her so. But folks usually stopped because of the cats. Most folks were so kind about animals and old people, it could almost make you cry.

She felt truly sorry about that too, but sometimes a body's got to do as best a body can. After all, she was just saving up all that gray matter for a rainy day. People would understand that. They always did. People always forgave a lonely old woman, even if she was missing a few brain cells.

Even if she was missing hundreds and hundreds of them…

Ken Goldman

Ken Goldman, a former high school English and Film Studies teacher, resides in homes in Bucks County Pennsylvania and the Jersey shore, as suits his mood, and has published stories in over 300 publications. In 1992 he placed second in the Rod Serling Memorial Foundation Writing Contest, in 1994 received the Small Press Genre Association's nomination for Best New Writer, in 1995 The Genre Writer's Association nomination for Best New Writer, and received honorable mention in Ellen Datlow and Terry Windling's *The Year's Best Fantasy and Horror 7th* and *9th Annual Collections.* In 1997 he won Preditors & Editors Best Poem On The Internet Contest, and in 1999 won second place "silver" in the Salivan Short Story Contest (Horror Division). His work appears in the anthologies *New Traditions in Terror, The MOTA: Truth 2002 Anthology, Freaks, Geeks, & Sideshow Floozies, The Witching Hour First* and *Second Editions,* and the UK's *Darkness Rising 5: Black Shroud of Fear.* Coming soon and featuring more of his work are the anthologies *The Fear Within, Vicious Shivers, Underworlds,* and Justus Roux's *Erotic Tales Anthology.* More than 20 other publications containing his tales are due in 2003-2004. Ken is a current member of the Horror Writers Association.

To Save a Dynasty
by
Angeline Hawkes-Craig

His name was Rasputin. And he might have faded away into historical obscurity had he not had the unfortunate notoriety of being the Empress Alexandra Feodorovna Romanov's ailing son's apparent unintentional savior. Savior. Holy man. Monster. Devil. Rasputin was called by many names. Some said he was a Holy Devil. Some said he was just a devil.

The Romanov's inhabited a glittering world full of sparkling crystal chandeliers and all the gilded trappings that come with being Emperor or Tsar, as in this case. The palaces were lavish, the food was perfection; and life went by blissfully unaware of the harsh and extreme poverty that had befallen the Russian people. Alexandra had four gorgeous daughters who were all lovely to look upon. Her heart's desire and her duty were to produce an heir, a male child, a son. This she finally accomplished with little Alexei who was born in 1904; but her happiness would prove short-lived when it became painfully clear that she had passed onto her long-awaited son the cursed disease of Hemophilia. She had had uncles die of it, and a brother die of it. She was full aware of the fatal disease and the terrible suffering it bestowed on its hapless victim. It was the beginning of a long and terrible nightmare. No doctors could cure him. No doctors could ease his immense suffering. Suffer, the poor boy did. Bouts of internal bleeding would cause his tiny body to swell, pushing the small boy to beg for death—his screams piercing the stillness of the palace. "Mama!" He must have cried in the midst of his agony. "Help me!" He must have anguished as she stood by wringing her hands, tears coursing down her lovely cheeks, heart breaking for the child she so long waited for, and now so wished to keep alive despite his tortured existence.

What was a mother to do? Alexandra was a princess, then an Empress, but above all, she was a mother. What mother would cease in her efforts to ease her child's suffering?

Enter Rasputin. A Starets—not a monk—but a drifter of a holy man, unrecognized or ordained by the church, but tolerated in his strange particular brand of holiness. Dirty, rank, he wore the untidy and coarse clothes of a wandering Russian monk. Bathing was a foreign thing to him. He was everything vile and lewd, and yet he attracted the highborn women with his rough and coarse ways. He sought out and found the primal desires suppressed in a woman's heart. He was no stranger to the addiction of the flesh. It was said he said what he should not say, and touched what he should not touch. Rasputin did not care. It was all performed under the guise of his ministry, his powers, and his divine abilities to help those wretched afflicted souls struggling on this earth.

He was called the Holy Devil.

And that's where the story began to unfold. Unravel. Just like the Romanov dynasty.

"I think you should reconsider the position you are affording this peasant, that is all I am suggesting," the Empress' friend said softly, over tea.

Alexandra bristled and sat up stiffly in her whale-boned corset and in her gilded chair. She said nothing.

"It's not that I believe the rumors. They are most foul and the indecent murmurings of the crass and the lowbred that drive these tall tales onward. But—think of the damage to the Tsar and your own reputation. Certainly you don't want to allow a simple mouzhik (Siberian peasant) to cause so much trouble for you?" The friend sat her gold and blue cup down with a delicate clink on the saucer before her.

Alexandra stared hard at her friend in the ostrich plumed hat, in the soft, fluttery lavender dress that hovered and rustled above the chair cushion in its fineness. At last she spoke, "The Tsar and I thank you for your heart-felt concern, I assure you; but, Father Grigory has a place in our hearts and our home that we have no plans to deny him now or in the future. We care not for false talk or vicious gossip." Alexandra heaved a great sigh, her tightly corseted white lace laden bosom heaving upward then down again in the process. She sipped her steaming tea and glanced down at the biscuit on her plate.

"I just thought that I should warn you," the friend said with a weak smile, absently tapping her slender fingertips on the rim of her teacup, tracing it's delicate gold rim around and around as she waited for the Empress to respond.

"Your thoughtfulness is noted," Alexandra said with a genuine smile. The topic was changed. The issue was dead.

Later that evening, while the children scuffled off to bed, Nicholas and Alexandra sat discussing this thing and that together before the blazing fire that warmed the chilly night air that circulated through the vast chamber, however lavish it might be.

"The rumors continue to grow, Sunny," Nicholas said gently to his wife, tempering the introduction of the topic with her pet name.

"Yes. I know. I had this conversation earlier today during tea with Ekaterina. It seems some people will believe any heap of rubbish that is passed by their ears." Alexandra reached for her knitting basket and sighed.

"I thought perhaps we should ask the Father to stay away—only for a short duration, of course." Nicholas hastily added the latter half of his statement, sensing his wife's sudden displeasure at the statement.

Alexandra's eyebrows flew up. "You KNOW that Alexei depends on Grishka when he is ill. There is no other who can give our wee one the relief that he can." Alexandra's voice raised an octave or two while her fingers and needles seemed to pick up a furious pace clinking and clicking ferociously against each other as the knitting progressed steadily along.

Nicholas shook his head. "Surely, you and the girls can sustain Alexei now. Grigory has assured me that all of you are complete now; you no longer need his ministrations. He has fulfilled his role. It is now up to you and the daughters to relieve Alexei's suffering."

Alexandra frowned. She did not like discussing this topic. It was because of the matter of Alexei's survival that she and her daughters had consented to Grigory Rasputin's methods—foul though they were. It was also the only thing that could save her son, and so she had consented. His sisters who adored him and also saw the necessity of their decisions consented only on these grounds as well. Given any other option, this would not have been the road they would have chosen to travel. There were no other options.

"I'm sorry, Sunny. I should not have brought this up." Nicholas saw the deep concern etched onto his prematurely aging wife's face. Concern, terror and heartbreak shouted from each and every one of those deep lines. He could see the pain and horror on his daughter's somber faces and in their serious manners. Rasputin's method had changed them. Had taken away the familiar personalities Nicholas had always known, and substituted in their place new personalities of a different sort. Cold. Quiet. Joyless. They had all sacrificed, perhaps their very souls, for the life of Alexei.

"No. No. You are my husband. You alone are untouched directly by this abomination, but you must live with our decisions. You should be free to question and discuss whatever lies heavy on your heart. I cannot deny you this. But know that neither your daughters nor I relish our roles. We simply know that there was, there is, no other choice for our little Alexei, and the fate of Russia lies in his survival." Alexandra, laying aside her knitting, reached across the massive carved wood desk and grasped Nicholas' strong hand in her own porcelain white one.

Nicholas smiled, his mustache twitching. He looked down at his wife's hand and raised it to his lips, kissing her fingers. "Your skin. It is so cold," he said quietly.

"An unfortunate side effect of Rasputin's method." Alexandra smiled slightly and withdrew her hand somewhat self-consciously. She resumed her knitting. She liked to knit scarves. She could not abide sloth, and knitting, though some called it common, was a productive skill to busy one's hands.

The Tsar sighed; resigned to the fate his wife and girls had resigned themselves to as well. He only knew briefly what Rasputin had done to transform them and bestow these certain abilities on them. He didn't know all of the gory details. Alexandra did not want him to know and so he did not press the issue.

Sometime in the following week, Alexandra's close friend, Anna, burst into Alexandra's mauve-colored bedroom like a frenzied whirlwind. She waved a tattered paper in her hand and rambled loudly about something incoherently. Alexandra had to calm her down to make sense of it all.

"Anna! Calm yourself! What is all of this?" Alexandra grasped her friend by each arm firmly, shaking her back to her senses.

Anna blinked and then slowly began again, "I found this. This filth tacked up on the gate. The palace gate!" She began to wildly wave the tattered, dirty paper around in the air again.

Alexandra snatched the paper from Anna's hand that was still flailing about in the air, now paperless.

The paper bore a cartoon. A lewd cartoon of a blood-drinking Rasputin and Alexandra drawn as a naked follower of Rasputin the monster. Alexandra stiffened.

"They KNOW!" Anna said shrilly. "Somehow, someone knows! They've told the masses! You and your daughters will be found out!"

Anna broke down into a round of unintelligible sobs and shuddered ranting.

Alexandra studied the cartoon and then chucked it on the fire. "They know nothing."

"But, the paper!" Anna wailed again, pointing weakly at the fire-engulfed sheet that was now curling and black, flaking away in the orange licking flames.

"The paper means nothing. Rude comments. Lewd jokes. That is all. A wild imagination bent on destructive ends. No one knows anything," Alexandra said with such force that Anna almost believed her. Almost believed that Alexandra believed herself.

"I think Rasputin has given his gift to too many now, Empress. I don't think his powers are a secret any longer," Anna moaned piteously as Alexandra stroked her head.

"Perhaps. But there is no evidence to support my part in his circle of friends." Alexandra smiled at Anna.

"You are the very center of the circle!" Anna wailed and broke down into body-shaking sobs once again.

Alexandra embraced her dear friend and let her cry it out. Sometimes great relief could be found in tears.

"Anna," Alexandra said softly when Anna had calmed down. "There will always be rumors and wild accusations against the Tsar and myself. You must be strong and do as I do. Pretend these evils do not exist." Alexandra stroked Anna's head like one would a crying child's.

"But, we know these rumors are true! How much longer can it be until someone discovers these truths?" Anna looked into Alexandra's face with much sorrow.

"Do you judge me, Anna, for my choice?" Alexandra asked, unblinking, staring her friend directly into the eyes.

"No. No. You are a mother. You do what you do to save your son," Anna said without any hesitation.

"Then we will let God decide our fates." Alexandra smiled.

Anna shivered. The Holy Devil—she knew what God did with devils. She nodded anyway.

News reached Alexandra of the attempted assassination of Rasputin. He had been severely stabbed several times by a lunatic prostitute who screamed incoherently while plunging the blade into his gut. Rasputin, miraculously it was claimed, had survived. Alexandra knew a stabbing couldn't kill him. The incident only fueled the gossip of his unearthly, unholy, power. He did not die.

Nicholas did not like the stirring up of the masses. There was already all together too much unrest in the country as it was. He did not like the murmurs that reached his ears. He had to protect his family at all costs. They no longer needed Rasputin. It might be time for him to go elsewhere. The separation would do them good.

"Alexandra. It is decided. I'm not discussing the matter further. After he recovers he can go on a pilgrimage or something of equal importance. The important thing is he will be far away from you, away from here. Away from the crowds of those who want to link you and he in these foul and devilish deeds. Let things die down some. Let the gossipmongers find a new topic." Nicholas paced the room as Alexandra sat mortified before him.

"You did not consult me at all!" she raged, a flashing glint of something not human, more animal-like, in her eyes.

"Because when it comes to the Father, you will hear no reason! The stories are coming too close to home. Too close to the truth. Too close to you and the girls. What I do, I do to protect my family." Nicholas pointed at her.

"But, who will bring us the necessary participants?" Alexandra asked, concerned. It was always so much easier when Rasputin brought the other party to them.

"You don't need Grigory for that. Anna and Nagorny have been doing an excellent job of finding less desirables from the streets and then of disposing of the bodies afterwards. You will have what you need," Nicholas said firmly. He knew of this part—of some sort of ritual involving some form of murder. He knew that it sounded unholy, terrifying, and diabolical. That was all he knew.

Alexandra knew that what he said was true, but it was her last effort to keep Rasputin close to her. She could not bear the thought of his soothing powers not being available to calm Alexei should he have a hemophiliac episode, a terrifying hemorrhage. She and the girls could sustain his life, but none of them had attained the level of hypnosis that Rasputin was capable of. One look into his dark eyes and one felt lost, carried away in a serene and blissful wave of lightness, of nothingness, of perfect calm. It was these powers that Rasputin utilized to calm Alexei during the worst of his bleeding bouts. Rasputin had told Alexandra it would take many more years for her to attain this level of power in her new life.

"Alexei can get his sustenance from you and the girls—alone—as he has done before. You do not need Rasputin to continue as we have been. Alexei will be fine. He has you and his sisters to nourish and protect him." Nicholas knelt down on his knees before Alexandra and the chair she sat in regally. He took her face in his hands and kissed both of her cheeks, her forehead, and her lips. "Trust me," he said softly. "Trust me as you do him."

Alexandra leaned her weary head upon his shoulder and wept. Her blood red tears rolled down Nicholas' shoulder and splattered in large drips on the white marble floor beneath them. Nicholas noticed the bloody tears, somewhat startled and shocked.

Alexandra laughed self-consciously. "This is why I seldom cry."

Nicholas was unaware of all of the transformations that Alexandra's body had gone through; each time he noticed something new he tried his very best to seem unsurprised by whatever it was he had witnessed, but he didn't think he had done a very good job of trying to seem untouched by it all. Nicholas wiped at the bloody tears with his handkerchief.

"I did not know," he said, still sounding startled by the blood that flowed from his wife's eyes.

"It is better that you do not know everything, husband." Alexandra smiled again and watched as the Tsar of all Russia crawled around on the marble floor, soaking up her coagulating bloody puddles of tears with his spotlessly white, starched handkerchief.

Anna did not take the news as calmly as Alexandra. She, typically, burst into a fit of tears. Alexandra rocked her friend in her arms just as she had done each of her children many times over the years. "Anna. Anna. It will be fine. We will carry on as usual. You will see," Alexandra cooed. "Rasputin will always be with us in spirit."

Anna wailed piteously louder still at that comment. "You say it like he is dead!" she cried, anguished.

Alexandra sighed. "That's not what I meant. Part of him lives in me, in the girls; he is always with us. Remember that."

Anna smiled at this thought. "Yes. Yes. That is true." She seemed to calm down and her body relaxed in Alexandra's motherly embrace.

"Now. Tonight is one of those nights. You will knock when all is set like always?" Alexandra pulled her friend back at arm's length and studied Anna's somewhat worried face.

"Yes. Yes. Of course. You will have the girls with you this time?" Anna asked, concerned.

"Yes. And Nagorny will wait to take it away—afterwards," Alexandra added the last word after a slight, hesitant, pause. No one liked discussing the particulars of this process.

Anna nodded and seemed to collect herself. She knew that Alexei's survival depended on the supply given to Alexandra and the girls, and that supply depended on herself and Nagorny. She lured the hapless vagrant to the palace, plied he or she with enough expensive liquor to cause unconsciousness, and then summoned Alexandra. Nagorny cleaned up the remains and disposed of what was left. So, essentially, Anna knew Alexei, the little Tsarevitch's survival, depended on her and Nagorny just as much as it did on his mother and sisters. Her heart lightened at the thought. She had to do what she did to save Alexei. She smiled. She was vital to the survival of the motherland, mother Russia.

Anna got up and straightened her dress, put on her hat, and kissed the Empress. Neither spoke. There were no more words necessary.

The knock came at half past ten that night. Plied with the usual liquor, drunk and unconscious, the man lay on the table in the locked room. Naked, the Empress and her four daughters approached the man. Alexandra paused for a moment, watching him take rattling breaths so slowly. Almost as if he were dead already. Silently she approached and saw in the corners of her eyes her hungry children stealthily creeping up to the man's side as well. There was something slow about it all. Every action seemed somehow prolonged and drawn out, as if she was watching herself from above her body. Watching the beasts she and her daughters had become. Together they grasped the man, neck, arms, legs, it didn't matter, as long as there was a pulsating vein accessible to their razor sharp teeth. Together they sank their fangs into the warm flesh of the unsuspecting man on the table. Flesh tore, blood spurted. They were covered in a warm, salty fountain of life's essence. Over them, through their tangled hair, over their china white skin, the blood trickled and flowed until together they drained the man dry. He was dead before he knew what had hit him. He had never even blinked an eyelid. Silently, they each slipped into the individual bath tubs awaiting them, prepared by loyal Anna during their ghastly supper. The blood rinsed off in pink-tinged waters as each one of them quietly stirred the baths to cleanse themselves of the remnants of their feasting. No one spoke. No one wanted to. What was done must be done. They thirsted for blood the same way alcoholics thirsted for just one more drink. Just one more drink.

Alexandra smiled at her girls as they dressed behind the dressing screens supplied by Anna. Anna, always so conscientious of their needs. Olga looked near tears.

Alexandra stepped towards Olga and lifted her smooth, youthful chin upwards, looking lovingly into her eldest child's eyes. "Remember why it is we do what we do."

Olga nodded silently and then hung her head sorrowfully.

"So many have died," she said softly, barely above a whisper.

"So that Alexei—and Russia—may live," Alexandra said gently, but firmly. Olga nodded in agreement. This was the plain, horrible truth.

The pierced, ripped, gashed, and bloodied body of the drunken man laid limply, gore-smeared and ghostly white on the table. Nagorny nodded at each of the girls as he passed them in the hall on their way to their rooms. It was his turn now in this dance of life and death to prolong Alexei's life. He would do anything for the little Tsarevitch, no matter how vile and gruesome.

He wrapped the body in some battered canvas and bound it with ropes. Under the cover of darkness he carted the body to the river and forced the body under the ice, hoping against the odds that it would remain there, rotting, until the thaw. He had lost count of how many bodies and in how many different ways he had disposed of them all. He did it for Russia. The Empress and the Tsarinas had the vilest aspect of the bargain for Alexei's life. He would not complain about his petty part in the matter.

1916 was not a good year for Rasputin—the monster—the Holy Devil. Alexandra learned of the details somewhat sketchily, finally piecing them all together. Rasputin had been poisoned, but that did not kill him. He had been shot several times, but it was finally a stab in the heart with a bayonet that finished him off—the bayonet had pierced through his body with the wood of the rifle following it. They didn't know that it was the wood of the gun that had killed him, not the bayonet. Staked through, twitching, flopping, left to flounder and perish like a speared fish. Bound, wrapped in a curtain and shoved under the ice of the Neva River. He popped up the next day, rather battered, and still dead. The Tsar saw to it that Rasputin had a proper burial, but later when the whole truth came out about the monster Rasputin really was, well, the masses dug him up and burned his evil body and cut off his wicked head so that he might never return.

Alexei's savior was no more. Or so Alexandra believed. Really, it was her blood and the blood that flowed copiously from his sister's china white skin into the gaping mouth of their wretched little brother that saved him, or prolonged the inevitable. For Alexandra would not permit Nicholas to be tainted by their sacrifice, nor would she allow Alexei to fully cross over to their cold existence. Their blood sustained him. Drove away his pain. Replaced his own vital fluids and kept him alive. Alive. Alexandra hoped she could keep him alive so that someday he would inherit the throne. That was why all four girls were necessary in the scheme, so that Alexei always would have a source of survival. It was necessary. His secret must always be kept.

But, the secret leaked out. Rasputin had created too many like her and her daughters. Too many people knew what Rasputin was and how he had converted his followers. The truth was ever so slowly exposed. Why did the Empress stay in her bedroom so much of the time? Why were the Tsarinas never seen, always secluded only with each other? There were far too many questions and the answers were too well known now. Rasputin had left behind too many disciples. Angry mobs hunted the unfortunate women, and some men, down like dogs and staked them through the heart, took their heads, and burned their bodies. Shouting throngs of people found out who had "the gift"—and rich or poor, dragged them from their homes, stripped them naked in the freezing Russian air, held them down, and staked their hearts. Over and over the crusade found their monsters. Nicholas had denied all of the accusations against his wife and children, but when they came for his family it was hard to deny the truth any longer. But how do you do away with a royal family? They can't simply vanish like the unknown unfortunates the crowd dispatched in their mob-style hunting expeditions.

The Revolution provided a good cover for hiding the hideous truth of what the Romanov family had become. A good cover so that the world wouldn't think Russia backwards and superstitious. Who would believe such things? But, they knew the truth. The Romanov family were monsters feeding on the blood of fellow Russians to feed their dying heir, to keep alive the future Tsar who was cursed at birth with his ailment.

The Empress and her daughters took upon themselves the curse out of love, out of devotion. They had been led astray by a devil, a monster that provided false hopes for a dying boy and a dying dynasty.

It all had to be covered up. Done away with. Swept away. Rasputin's followers all faded into nothingness in the din of the revolutionary cries—in the chaos of a country ripped asunder. It was hard to destroy the Romanov family and the heir, but they too went away in the end. Shot, staked and burned up in the middle of nowhere. All of them—lest they miss one of Rasputin's monsters. And, almost a century later, science could identify the bodies, but never uncover the horrifying truth of what really led to their demise. What mother would cease in her efforts to put an end to her child's suffering? A sacrifice that in the end killed the child and the country that she had sold her soul to protect. All because she was in league with a Holy Devil.

Used for reference: Kirth, Peter. *Tsar: The Lost World of Nicholas and Alexandra*. Little, Brown & co. 1995.

Angeline Hawkes-Craig

Angeline Hawkes-Craig's stories appear in several 2003/04 anthologies: *Femmes de La Brume* [Double Dragon Publishing], *The Decay Within* [3f Publications], *The Blackest Death* [KHP Industries], *Cyber-Pulp Halloween Anthology*, *Fantastical Visions* [Fantasist Enterprises], *Scriptures of the Damned* [DDP], *The Unknown: Otherworlds Sci-Fi Anthology* [Branch & Vine Publishers], *E-Macabre: Tales of Horror and Dark Fantasy* [SpecFicWorld], and *Monstrous!* [Cyber-Pulp], *F/SF Vol. II* [Cyber-Pulp]. In May 2003, Scars Publications released her latest book, entitled, *Momento Mori: A Collection of Short Fiction*. Double Dragon Publishing will release the book in e-book format in 2004. Her story "The Board" won Horror-Web's Best of 2002 Contest Fiction. Angeline Hawkes-Craig's fantasy novel, *The Swan Road*, [Scars] was released in 2002. She is a member of the Horror Writer's Association and of The Writer's League of Texas. Angeline Hawkes-Craig received a B.A. in Composite English Language Arts from East Texas State University in 1991. Visit her works at her website www.angelinehawkes-craig.com

It Came in the Night
by
Nicholas Knight

The screech of rubber on pavement, followed by the harsh slam of a door, brought Emmanuelle Vascez's gaze up from the book he was reading to the open living room window. The noise had brought a scowl to his face, but it quickly gave way to a smile when he recognized the vehicle in his driveway. It was Jake Raleigh's ice-cream truck, which meant that his long-time friend was paying him an unexpected visit. Emmanuelle had just settled down in his favorite chair with a brand new paperback and a hot cup of coffee, but shooting pool with Jake would be an even more enjoyable way for him to spend the evening.

Emmanuelle's smile vanished when Jake burst through the front door and raced in like a crazed gazelle with a lion at its heels. Jake's t-shirt was caked in red and yellow gore, and his eyes looked twice as big as their sockets.

"Manny—you've got to help me, man," Jake said in a trembling voice just short of hysteria.

"What the hell happened to you?" he asked. There was putrescent gook smeared across Jake's nose and cheeks, and the right side of his lips twitched violently.

As he asked the question, Manny tried to come up with an answer of his own, but nothing came to mind. The guy looked like he'd walked straight off the set of a horror/slasher movie, only the stench was so bad that there was no way it could have been staged. Manny felt weak at the knees, but he was too much of a man to let it show. "Help you with what?" he continued when Jake said nothing. "This had better be important—not like the time you thought you'd killed an intruder, when really you'd just stabbed the jack-o-lantern on your kitchen counter in the dark. I haven't taken a break all week, and I'm dead tired."

"You have to help me, Manny," Jake said again, as if Manny's words hadn't even registered. "There's something in my ice-cream truck…something savage."

Manny peered out his window and blinked several times. The truck looked like it was shaking, but since that obviously wasn't possible, Manny decided that his eyes were just playing tricks on him from being so worn out.

"It's not like any animal I've ever seen before," Jake rattled on. "I think I hurt it—but the damn thing won't die. I slashed it with my utility knife, pummeled it with my tire iron, and blasted it with my shotgun. I'm telling ya, Manny, it won't die. It WON'T die…IT WON'T DIE…"

He repeated the words over and over in a crescendo until he was shouting at the top of his lungs.

Manny gently forced him into a chair, walked through the dining room to the kitchen, and returned with a bottle of brandy and a glass. He gave Jake a shot to calm his nerves, but it wasn't until Jake had downed his fifth that he finally quieted down.

When Jake spoke again, Manny noticed an uncharacteristic urgency in his friend's voice. "Please, Manny," he begged, "You've got to help me."

"I'll try, Jake, I will. But you have to tell me what happened first."

Jake's shoulders relaxed, and his voice actually sounded calmer. "I was on my way home from my after-dinner round when it happened," he said. Jake did great business on warm nights just before dark; the ice-cream truck's familiar chimes a natural magnet to children playing outside. "It was a good night, the freezer's practically empty. But the bells wouldn't turn off. It wasn't that dark out yet, so there was still the possibility of attracting potential customers. I was wiped out and I just wanted to go home. I fiddled with the controls for a while, but the stupid thing was stuck or something. I reached down to pull out the fuse—took my eyes off the road for half-a-second—when *BAM*, I hit something."

Manny's first instinct was to yell at his friend for being such an idiot, for being so careless. But then, he knew it was just an accident, and that Jake was already upset enough as it was. Yelling at him would only make matters worse. Still, it took every nerve and all of his will to simply remain silent.

"Of course, my first thought was that I'd just run over a kid—my worst nightmare come true, you know? With all the kids that are always running out to the truck, I—"

"Yes, yes, I know," Manny said. "*What did you hit?*" Jake always liked to take the long way around the block, but this was not the time for storytelling. It seemed obvious that Jake didn't have some lunatic *child* locked up in his truck. At least, Manny hoped he didn't.

"I don't know! I really don't know. I can barely begin to describe it."

"Well, try." Chances were it was just a porcupine, or maybe a cougar. Jake had lived near Grouse Mountain all his life, but he'd never ventured outside of suburbia. His little brother had been mauled to death by a bear at the age of seven, and Jake had steered clear of any wooded area ever since.

"Of course, I pulled over and got out to see what I'd hit—I'm not the type of scum to hit 'n run, y'know. Anyway, when I saw the thing, I nearly dropped a load in my pants. It was truly that horrendous a sight. Sure, it was only about four or five feet tall—I think anyway, it was lying on its side at the time—but its eyes were this bright yellow, like two miniature suns that would burn my eyes out if I looked at 'em too long. And it was black as night, with slick, oily fur, and huge claws."

Sounded like a small black bear to Manny. The sight of the wild animal that had killed his brother must have caused something in Jake's brain to snap, causing him to see monsters.

"I didn't know what to do," Jake said. "I still don't know what to do. All that blood…and he's gone, all gone, not a single bone left."

"Who's gone? You're skipping stuff Jake, start from the beginning."

Well, I hit it. That was the beginning, the rest all happened so fast. Like I was a spectator in my own body."

Jake had been loath to approach the animal. He'd thought about calling the police, or maybe the SPCA, but mainly he'd thought about getting as far away from the thing as possible. As he stood there staring at it, a teenaged boy approached from the sidewalk. The teenager's sloppy attire and glazed eyes led Jake to the snap conclusion that he was high on drugs.

"Hey, Ice-cream Dude," the stoner said. "You really crunched that doggie good." He walked right past Jake, straight towards the animal.

"It's not a dog," Jake said, "It's a…" He wanted to say *monster*, but it seemed too absurd to say out loud. Not that it mattered what Jake thought it was anyway; he was sure the kid would ignore him even if he said it was rabid.

The stoner walked up to the animal and nudged it with his foot, babbling the whole while. "This doggie is *messed* up, Ice-cream Dude. It's like bumpy and shit. Hey, doggie, doggie. Are you dead, doggie?" He nudged it some more, then gave up and turned toward Jake. "Hey, how about some free ice-cream if I help you get this major road-kill off the road?"

Just then, Jake heard a low, rasping growl. It wasn't loud, but it sounded primal, and it gave him goosebumps on top of the ones he already had.

The stoner's glazed eyes widened ever so slightly...and then the creature grabbed his leg. The teenager screamed, and it felt to Jake like razor blades had been shoved viciously into his ears. He'd never known such a high-pitched sound could come from any human's mouth, male or female.

The teenager looked to weigh a good 180 pounds, but he was yanked backwards like a feather-filled rag-doll. *"It's biting me!"* he screamed. *"Oh shit, it hurts. Help me, Ice-cream Dude, help meeeee—"*

Jake wanted to run over and help him. That's what he *knew* he should do in any case, but his mind refused to send the signal to his legs—which were like useless slabs of heavy rubber anyway.

The monster growled and bit, growled and bit. The stoner screamed and used his good leg to propel himself away from the beast. He fell forward onto his face almost immediately, and Jake realized with a sick feeling that the bottom half of the teenager's left leg was gone. Where his shin should have been hung the tattered remnants of his baggy jeans, turned purply-red with blood. Where skin was visible, Jake could see ice-cream scoop-shaped bite marks.

Jake looked at the stoner's face, and the pain and fear he saw there was incredible. He finally overcame his own fear and lunged forward. He grabbed the teenager's arms, and hauled him away from the monster. The creature snarled and leapt onto the stoner's good leg. The sudden force knocked the teenager out of Jake's grasp. Jake nearly ran then, but didn't. He grabbed the teenager's right arm and pulled. The creature dug its rear claws into the asphalt, wrapped its front claws around the teenager's leg, and snarled at Jake.

Jake yanked hard enough to throw out his bum shoulder, but he might as well have been pulling on his truck for all the good it would have done him; he couldn't budge the stoner. He kept pulling anyway, and the creature suddenly lashed out at him. Thankfully, it missed his hand...but the stoner wasn't so lucky. Jake fell backward, holding the teenager's severed arm.

The stoner screamed again—an unending, gurgling sound that seemed to bounce off the stucco houses and assault Jake's ears from all directions. Jake noticed that the teenager had a tongue-ring, and ludicrously wondered if getting it pierced had hurt.

Jake dropped the arm and stumbled backward, staring in disbelief at the scene before him. Blood spurted out from all over the stoner's body, forming an expanding pool of thick liquid that seeped towards Jake. The teenager's eyes rolled up into his head, and Jake knew there was no hope left.

But the creature wasn't finished with its prey. It growled non-stop and gnashed its teeth on bones. Its head became lost inside the teenager's stomach, and Jake could've sworn he heard its tongue lapping up every last drop of blood and God knows what else. He looked around, hoping to see faces at windows, holding phones that'd been used to call the police. But he saw no one. Nothing moved save for one flapping curtain in an open window. Where was everyone? Hiding under their pillows, trying to convince themselves that they hadn't just witnessed a living nightmare in their front yards?

He knew he couldn't wait for the police or anyone else. At the speed the monster was going, it would be finished with the stoner and coming after Jake within seconds. He ran back to his truck and grabbed the closest thing to a weapon he had—a tire iron. Then he nerved himself to walk back over to the nightmare creature from hell.

What little was left of the teenager's body shook grotesquely, like a bone in a hungry dog's mouth. The creature tilted back its head and gulped down the crushed remains of the stoner's skull. Jake raised the tire iron over his head. The motion caused the monster to look up. For a moment, its savage yellow eyes stared into Jake's, then its nose snuffled the air, and it dropped its head to the ground. It wolfed down an eyeball and the arm that Jake had dropped, then it lapped up the pooled blood like it was gravy.

Surprised that the monster paid him no heed, Jake brought the tire iron down hard upon its head. There was a dull thud as the creature's head sandwiched between the weapon and the road. Jake pummeled it over and over relentlessly until his arms grew tired. He knew he'd done some damage, because bits and pieces of the monster's brain matter covered his clothes, but the moment he let up, it lunged at him.

Jake whacked its snout, and the beast tore the iron out of his hands with giant, slobbering teeth. Jake ran to the truck, hopped in the back, and tried to close the door behind him. The creature leapt in beside him before he could reach for the door. Acting purely on adrenaline, Jake grabbed a utility knife, extended the blade and slashed the beast's neck.

The creature howled and wailed and clutched at its neck as yellow goo spewed out.

Jake jumped out of the truck, slammed the door closed, and locked it. He ran around to the front, and drove home with a lead foot. He parked in his driveway, dashed out and grabbed a shotgun from the garage. His hands shook as he reached for the latch that opened the truck's rear door. He was terrified, but he needed to be sure the monster was dead.

Jake yanked the door open, and brought the gun to bear just as the creature pounced.

"And I shot the damned thing square in the chest," Jake said.

"Come on, Jake," Manny said. "You expect me to believe that you sliced this *monster's* neck open, and it still had the strength to attack you?"

"I'm just telling you what happened."

Jake looked so sincere at that point that a shiver ran down Manny's spine. *God help us if he's telling the truth*, Manny thought.

Jake pointed at some crusty yellow stuff on his t-shirt. "Look at how hard this is," he said. "The thing's blood must congeal super fast. Not to mention that it must have an amazing pain threshold, because it came at me again! I mean, the blow to the chest threw it back hard against the wall of the truck, but it just got right back up and jumped at me as I reloaded. I aimed at its head, but it slashed at the gun as I pulled the trigger. The bullet caught it somewhere and knocked it back again, but I'd lost my grip on the gun. When I reached down for it, the monster stirred, so I made a quick judgment call—I slammed the door shut again.

"Then I came here."

Manny scowled at him. If there was even a shred of truth to what Jake was saying, Manny was not pleased that his friend had chosen to bring him aboard his ferry ride to hell. "Why the heck didn't you go to the police?"

"What if the thing got away somehow, and all I was left with was my unbelievable story? I've no doubt I'd wind up in the loony bin, or thrown in the slammer on suspicion of murdering that stoned teenager. No thank you. We have to get rid of this thing, and then…and then that's it—we go on with our lives and tell no one. Okay?"

"No, it's not okay. None of this is *okay*. What exactly do you expect me to do? I mean, you've already tried practically everything…"

"Please, Manny—your head's clearer than mine. What can we do?"

Manny walked back to the kitchen and pulled out a pack of cigarettes from the far reaches of the cupboard under the sink. He took out a stale cigarette, along with the lighter that he kept in the half-empty pack.

As he returned to the living room, Jake shot him a funny look. "I thought you—"

"Quit? Yeah, well…it helps me think." Manny stuck the cigarette between his lips, flicked the lighter on, then paused with the flame still an inch away from the cigarette. "See, I didn't even have to light it, and I already have an idea."

"Well, what is it? Shit, Manny, at this point the suspense could literally kill me."

Manny waved the lighter. "Fire, my friend, fire. We'll roast that sucker and see how it tastes."

"You're sick. If you believed me, you wouldn't be making jokes. But I like your idea."

"I'm not sick, but smoking this would have made me." Manny extinguished the lighter and tossed the cigarette onto the dining room table. "I think the safest bet would be to drive up towards Whistler," he said. "We'll pull over at one of those viewpoints, douse your truck with gas, light her up, and give her a shove over the edge."

"Do we have to torch the truck?"

"You have insurance, right? Look, why take any chances of the thing escaping?" Manny truly wanted to help his friend, but he knew he'd sleep better if he never actually laid eyes on Jake's monster.

"Fine, let's just get this over with."

Manny slipped the lighter into his pocket and grinned as an odd feeling of anticipation took hold of him.

They left the house through the garage, picking up a gas canister on the way. The grass had been growing like weeds that summer, so Manny had had to refill the can for the lawnmower on a regular basis. Fortunately, he'd made a trip to the gas station earlier that day.

The warm September night was quiet and still. As he approached the truck, which was weakly bathed in yellowish light from a nearby streetlamp, Manny couldn't help but question the veracity of Jake's story. He racked his mind for possible alternative reasons for Jake getting him into his truck…Manny's fortieth birthday was months off, so a surprise party was out of the question, and it wasn't April Fool's day, Halloween, or Friday the thirteenth. And Jake wasn't much of a practical joker. Still, Manny was on edge—expecting someone in a boogieman costume to jump out of the shadows at any moment.

"Can you hear that?" Jake asked.

"What?"

Jake tugged Manny alongside the truck, and placed a finger to his lips.

At first, Manny didn't hear anything. Then, something low worked its way into his ears—a soft whistle-wheeze, like the sound of someone or some*thing* sleeping…only…it sounded a little off…disjointed, like the sleeper's windpipes were ragged. Manny shuddered, and stepped away from the truck.

"God help us if fire won't kill it," Jake muttered.

Took the words right out of my mouth, Manny thought as he nodded silently and climbed into the passenger-side seat.

Jake joined him in the truck's cab, started the engine, and backed out of the driveway. He tore down the street like a bat out of hell, far too fast for a residential neighborhood, but Manny never even considered telling him to slow down.

About ten minutes later, Manny came out of an unwitting daze to realize that he was unsure of where they were. The landmarks were familiar, of course—he knew every strip mall, apartment building, and gas station within a twenty-mile radius of his house—yet he couldn't quite put his finger on their exact location. It was as if his mind refused to believe that Jake's monster could exist in the same plane of reality as his favorite taco joint and regular barbershop.

As he tried to lift the veil of fog from his mind, he discovered a peculiar noise coming from the freezer section of the truck—a scrape-thump, scrape-thump sound, as of metal raking across metal, followed by something heavy making impact.

The entire truck began to shake. Manny glanced over at Jake. His face was as white as his knuckles, which were holding a death-grip on the steering wheel. He had a determined look in his eyes and beads of sweat glistened across his forehead. Without speaking, Manny knew that Jake intended to make it to one of the viewpoint pull-offs before the monster tore through the wall separating them. Or die trying.

By this point, they were already ascending the mountain, and there was no shoulder along the highway—nowhere to safely pull over.

Suddenly, Jake yelled out in pain. He arced his back away from the seat, and Manny saw fresh blood stream from a gash in Jake's already stained t-shirt. In a blur of speed, something came through a hole in the seat and tore another chunk out of Jake's back.

Jake stopped concentrating on the road as he fumbled with his seatbelt, trying frantically to get away from his unnatural attacker.

The truck veered off the highway and flattened a "rock-fall hazard" sign as it scraped up against the mountainside. Trying to avoid the hole in the seat and Jake's squirming body, Manny reached for the steering wheel. His seatbelt restricted him, but he was able to give the wheel a shove to the left. A sharp curve in the road, combined with the sudden jerk to the left, caused the truck to swerve across the oncoming traffic lane. Manny tried to reach for the wheel again before the truck smashed through the protective railing and launched off the cliff. *I'm going to die now*, Manny thought matter-of-factly, as the truck flew through the air, tires spinning.

The truck didn't stay airborne long—a matter of seconds really—before it hit the embankment at an angle. Jake's tire hit first, exploding on impact, and the truck flipped over cornerwise. Manny thanked God for the seatbelt that tightened painfully on his chest, the life-saving device that held him in place as the truck rolled—*bounced?*—down the side of the mountain like a giant pinball against the rocks and trees.

Manny squeezed his eyes shut and tried to ignore the sounds of crunching metal and shattering glass, and the accompanying jabs of pain as shards of glass pelted his body. The truck stopped rolling, then slid a few more feet on the driver's side before coming to a jolting stop on a narrow gravel road. A few more feet and the truck would have gone off another cliff into the Pacific Ocean.

Manny tried to open his eyes, but a wave of dizziness and nausea forced him to close them again. As he hung there, uncomfortably strapped in place, the strong smell of gasoline wafted up to his nose. He wondered if it was the gas that they'd brought, or if the truck had sprung a leak. *Probably both.* If the battery was still intact, the possibility of a spark igniting the fumes seemed imminent. He was still alive, but fate seemed to be offering him two choices: get disemboweled by a mutant animal or get blown to smithereens. He didn't care for either choice all that much.

Manny willed his eyes open, released his seatbelt, and disentangled himself from the straps, while his mind tried to process what was wrong. The whole cab was a twisted mess, so it took his rattled gray cells a few seconds to realize that Jake was no longer beside him—*below* him, rather. The steering wheel had disappeared as well.

He didn't bother trying to push his door open, since the lack of glass in the window provided a quicker exit. He stepped on the dash and climbed out of the wreckage. He dropped down beside the truck, stumbled a few feet, then tripped over a hubcap that had wedged itself into the ground. As Manny picked himself up, a shriek of rage ripped through the night, so savage, so filled with blood lust, that it brought him back down to his knees. He covered his ears to block out the monster's howl—which seemed too loud to be coming from inside the truck—only to realize that the outburst was over. He pulled his hands away and a new sound greeted his ringing ears. He could hear the beast pounding and clawing against metal. Somewhere in the twisted wreckage, the monster was trapped. But for how long?

Manny's instinct was to run, to get as far away as possible. But he knew he couldn't leave that thing alive. Forget the noble notion of not unleashing the monster on the rest of the world—he knew in his gut that it had his *scent*. It would hunt him down relentlessly, then tear him asunder.

Manny pulled out his lighter. All he had to do was toss it through the window into the gas-soaked cab, and...no, the lighter would go out in the air. He quickly searched the area for something to use as a makeshift torch. A paperback book caught his eye. It was a romance novel. Did this fly out of Jake's truck? Shit, *Jake!* Manny realized he'd clean forgotten about his friend. He had to be sure Jake wasn't anywhere near the truck before he torched it.

The book's pages were dry. Manny held the lighter to a corner, and was pleased to see it readily catch fire. He never would have pictured himself a book-burner.

Smoldering book in hand, he circled around to the "top" of the truck. The sounds of the monster battering against its temporary prison made Manny's legs wobble. Jake was not in the vicinity. Manny peered in through the cracked windshield to make sure that he hadn't been hallucinating earlier. Apparently not—the cab was empty. Was it just his imagination, or was the hole in the driver's seat bigger than before? Big enough to pull a man through. Big enough for the monster to *get out* through...

Manny looked closer. Something metallic was jammed into the hole. A corner of one of the freezers? The object shook violently, and Manny had a feeling that whatever it was wouldn't be there much longer. Then there'd be nothing between him and the beast.

Doesn't matter now, that critter's toast. Doing his best impression of an NBA player going for the winning point in a basketball game from hell, Manny jumped up and slam-dunked the flaming book through the passenger-side window.

He backed away hastily, but refused to take his eyes off the truck. He needed to see it blow, needed to know that Jake's nightmare creature hadn't escaped.

The gasoline ignited, and bluish orange flames shot up through the glassless window. A great explosion followed, and a wall of hot air pushed Manny backward off his feet. He covered his head with his arms as several more explosions followed, and shrapnel of varying shapes and sizes rained over him.

When the worst of it was over, Manny stood up with the intention of checking the burning rubble for remains. He'd barely taken a step when something clubbed him hard in the head from behind. He crumpled to the ground unconscious.

Manny opened his eyes to the sight of towering hemlock trees dancing over him. He quickly realized that it wasn't the trees that were moving…it was he. Something had a hold of his feet, and was dragging him across the forest floor. As he tried to lift his head to see who'd abducted him, a large rock in the path smashed into the base of his skull, and the world went black again.

The next time Manny opened his eyes, he was still on his back, but the trees had been replaced by a dark ceiling. Once his eyes adjusted to the gloom, he deduced that he was in a cave—a shallow cave, in which he would surely hit his head if he stood up. Not that he *could* stand up—his arms and legs were pinned to the ground, spread-eagled, a heavy boulder at each wrist and ankle. The bones beneath the boulders were most likely broken, evidenced by the sharp jabs of pain that shot up and down whichever appendage he tried to move.

Who had done this to him? And *why*?

Manny was able to lift his head enough to peer a few feet past his legs. He was not alone. Moonlight seeped in through a crevice somewhere above, concentrating like a bizarre spotlight on the monstrous animal form that lay before him. Its muscular back moved slightly up and down. As Manny stared in mounting horror, a familiar disjointed whistle-wheeze sound reached his ears. He lowered his head and closed his eyes. Jake was right. It wasn't like any animal he'd ever seen before.

Could that beast actually withstand fire? No, wait—it hit me from behind. Right? Manny's head still spun from the recent wallops. It was hard to think straight. And the pain in his wrists and ankles didn't help matters. *But I heard it* inside *the truck, trying to escape.*

Heard something—someone—trying to escape.

The hole in the seat…Jake…

Why am I still alive? Is the monster full from eating the stoner? Taking a little nap between meals? Still, why spread me out like this? Why not just kill me?

Something had caught Manny's eye when he'd looked down his body earlier, something that he hadn't given much thought to. As he gingerly raised his head again, he took a closer look at his clothes. His pants and boxers had been torn away at the groin. *Could have snagged on a branch while I was being dragged.* Maybe. Razor-sharp branches?

The sleeping creature shifted its haunches ever so slightly and Manny took in a view that caused his stomach to roil. The light in the cavern was dim, and his fear could have been playing tricks on his mind, but he was sure he knew what he was looking at.

Manny strained at the boulders in a frenzied, excruciatingly painful attempt to free himself. It was no use. He probably wouldn't have been able to move the rocks if he'd been standing over them, much less from pinned below them with broken bones.

The more he thought about the way his body had been positioned, and the way his privates had been exposed, the more he was convinced that the creature had a desire to fill something other than its stomach.

The thought repulsed him to no end.

Manny lay back and shut his eyes in defeat. *Oh please God,* he prayed, *not that. Please...I'd rather be eaten alive that...* that.

Nicholas Knight

Nicholas Knight's stories can be found in *Black Petals, Camp Horror, Futures Mysterious Anthology Magazine, H.P. Lovecraft's Magazine of Horror, Midnighters Club, Mystery in Mind, Open Space, Side Show, The Witching Hour,* and *Underworlds,* among other publications. Readers can contact him at knight@darktales.zzn.com.

Mirrorwalker

by
Karen Koehler and Grave Mistake

9-11: In remembrance.

I suppose what bothers me most about Shatiel is that he has no soul.

The woman was weeping. No, not woman—girl, for she surely could not have been more than seventeen. And she did not weep outwardly, but inside, her face all wounded stone like a brownstone in this old city hardened by years and weather, the dampness kept beneath its skin like an eternal sorrow. And yet, Shatiel did not see, did not look. He stood at the curtainless window and peered out over Jerome Avenue, maybe seeing the rush-hour traffic crawl by in insectoid little patterns under the telephone wires, maybe seeing nothing at all.

I looked at the girl sitting on the old flattened futon, the card table and my half-finished game of solitaire off to the side of her. Eve's lost daughter, I thought. Her grief burned me; it turned her aura the color of pyre smoke. I offered her tea I knew she had no stomach to drink.

"Tell us everything that happened," I said, because Shatiel, that well of wordless souls, could not.

The girl-woman in her grief and her crown of rain-pale hair drew her coat close around her shoulders. The coat was an old befurred thing like a slain animal, something probably sprung from the bowels of the Salvation Army. She turned her head as if she could not bear to see the memory. "It was the Park. I put Theo down. He wanted to play with the Slinky, make it walk the bench. I was doing my term paper, you know, right there, next to him. I never meant, but…" And off trailed her voice.

I hunkered down beside her. The street lamp outside had come on, the peachy unwell light turning her pale face to bronze and hollowing out her cheeks, making her mascara-scarred eyes Egyptian in their darkness. I took her hand because Shatiel, I knew, would not; it felt cold, mummified. "And he disappeared?"

She nodded.

"How long ago was this?"

I could hear the huskiness of the city in her voice. "Three days…"

"And the police…?"

She was a silent testament to the ineptness of the human race to protect its own. So damn useless, I wanted to say. "Never fear," I said instead.

She looked to me, this child of Eve. I thought perhaps Shatiel had moved at the window, but without looking I couldn't be sure.

"They told you about us?" I said.

Again she nodded. "They said…"

I put my finger to my lips. Shhh. "All bad. Very skeptical, but of course."

"Not all bad. They said…you find lost things."

She looked at me. I knew that look: I saw it in every soup kitchen, every midnight mission in the city; I remember that look painted on every grungy face in every juvie hall and foster home I'd ever done time in. The look that blackens the eyes with fear, that can burn away the flesh over your heart to reveal the emptiness beneath. It made grown men crawl. It made innocent kids steal and kill. It was called Desperation, and I hated that look.

"You do find things?"

"Well…*I* don't," I told her truthfully, and the look deepened. "I mean, Shatiel does, not me," I quickly amended.

She looked to him. "Shatiel," she uttered like some half-remembered prayer.

Shatiel had not moved, after all, but his shoulders tightened at the sound of his name.

"I was raised Catholic," the girl said with faint hollowness. "I remember the name…"

She sounded so sincere, so Desperate. "The angel of voices and art, the father of the muses," I said. I'd been Catholic once, a long time ago, too. "But he fell and lost his voice."

I did not look at Shatiel; I looked at the girl instead. But she looked only sad, as if she mourned her missing son as dead, which he might very well be. Not that it mattered. Dead or alive, nothing went missing indefinitely, for everything existed somewhere, at some time. The property of matter. That was what Shatiel always said, not that that clever axiom made Shatiel necessarily human, mind you.

I straightened up, bringing the girl to her feet. "But we—Shatiel, I mean—requires time. You understand."

Another listless nod. Her eyes looked so cold, so dark, like reflective obsidian, like the mirrored surface of the Atlantic Bay at midnight.

"How much?" she whispered. I was aware of her chewed, jagged nails denting my forearm even through my thick-hided old leather bomber jacket, another ragged Salvation Army refugee dragged around for far too many years.

I looked to Shatiel standing as still as a manikin in the storefront windows on Fifth Avenue I remember as a child, pressing my palms to the frosted winter glass, pretending those figures were real. It was always the dream. Maybe Shatiel was the dream—choosing me to be his Keeper in this lifetime, bringing me into the dream with him. Sometimes I found the lines dimmed, overlapped. Anyway, that was what the counselors were always fond of saying when I explained my visions, or the auras I saw or the thoughts I caught in my head which were not my own. The lines sometimes dim for some of us, Stevie. Our thoughts sometimes overlap, causing...

Such shit. I held to the girl, looked into the mirrors of her eyes. "Will you give us an hour?"

The words seemed to stagger her. "An hour?"

Shatiel did not protest, so I went on. "There's a little coffee house a couple of blocks west of here. It's called Shannon's Garden, on Christopher Street. Do you know it?"

She swallowed. "I can find it."

"Good. I want you to go there. Order espresso and croissants, but not the cheese Danish. Ask about the fountain's history. Stay there one hour. One hour exactly. Do you understand?"

She nodded.

"Good."

"And Theo—?"

"You're son will be waiting here for you when you return."

Like a cat who has been fed and scorched too many times, she blinked up at me. Uncertain.

"Trust me," I said and closed my palm over her bony shoulder. "Trust us."

Without another word, Eve's lost daughter turned on her broken heels and left us to the Work.

The Work, as Shatiel always called it. And I thought the name was funny, as if what we did was Public Service, like cleaning park benches or oiling church pews at St. Patrick's, the way the probation kids were supposed to do. Except that our Work was a fulfilling thing most of the time and not a degrading punishment for one offense or another.

I pushed aside the solitaire game and lit a stunted, bone-white candle on the card table. I felt its small, fragile warmth grow on my face. It was not enough light to fill the room, but it was enough to meet our needs. Enough to do the Work by.

Shatiel was there, beside my crouching form. I hadn't even seen him move from the window. He was just suddenly there, as if the candlelight only illuminated what had been waiting there all along. Tall and dusty and enshrouded in his broken raincoat like the old folded wings of a king bat. Shatiel reminded me, as always, of a gothic hero in a British magazine—just with the cobwebs brushed out of his eyes. His long paper white hair lay in loose tangles over his shoulders, like his face turned the color of aged parchment by the greasy light of my candle. His amber eyes looked the same. His face was like the death mask of a thousand-years-dead Pharaoh prince. Nobody human could look as Shatiel looked, and it was this fact, I think, above all, which made me indispensable to him. It wasn't really possible for Shatiel to face even the bravest, most desperate, client without putting them off.

He would have terrified that little girl.

Sometimes he terrified me.

He touched my shoulder and I didn't quite start. I looked up at him, one hand cupped around my little uncertain flame. "Did you get an image from her?" I asked.

Shatiel nodded.

I smiled apologetically. "I was afraid I hadn't kept her long enough."

The natural commas which punctuated the corners of Shatiel's mouth deepened slightly.

My flame guttered. "Something wrong?"

He looked away. His aura was deep and white, like smoky ice. He was worried and he was breaking my heart.

"I know," I said. "This isn't like Miz Arkady's dog or that brooch last week. This is so much…bigger."

His fingers tightened over my shoulder.

"You're afraid you can't do it," I guessed. Sometimes I wished Shatiel wasn't really mute and could say exactly what troubled him without signing or implication.

But now Shatiel frowned to show I was mistaken. He made the sign for "home."

"Oh." What else could I say, really? Shatiel was wondering if this challenge would be enough to complete his sentence. If the others were willing to welcome him back at last...

But I didn't want to think about that and shut it off immediately. I didn't know what I would do if Shatiel left me. I *knew*, of course: I would be alone again, my services no longer needed. I knew I was being completely selfish, but Shatiel had been better to me than any foster parent or social worker. I almost wished the Work would fail this time.

But then I pushed *that* thought away and stood up, feeling Shatiel draw away from me a little, as if repelled by my selfish thoughts. I felt guilty for my secret little sin, for thinking I could own him in some way. What did I know? I was a seventeen-year-old runaway from Lodi who might have wound up pimp meat or just plain dead were it not for my "talents." It was the purpose of the Keepers to keep, not own. I knew the rules. I ran a hand through my cropped, spiky hair, tightened the edges of my jacket as if I had something to hide. And turned. "Ready?"

Shatiel nodded.

I went to fetch the equipment. We kept most of it in the big tarnished steamer trunk under the window of the loft: the paints and palette and an old wool cloth. That was it. Shatiel, unlike the other SoHo artisans, had no use for brushes and short spades, preferring to shape the oils and gouaches with his naked fingers—it was the intimacy that all great creators share with their creations, I guess. I brought the equipment over to where Shatiel hovered before the full length Victorian mirror set up in a dark corner of the loft. The mirror was milk glass and deeply etched with morning glories and doves, but blank and mysterious and waiting, too. Shatiel cast no reflection in the glass.

Shatiel was inanimately patient as I squeezed out the various sour-smelling oils onto the palette. Dove grey and the green of a fertile medieval forest, azure like shadow cast upon the wing of a swan and the changeable orange of a guttering flame. When I had filled the palette with a carousel of primary and tertiary colors, I handed it back to him.

Balancing the palette on one hand, Shatiel dipped two fingers into two different oils, drawing the two webs of color into one. Commingled, their mark on the waiting glass was like a wound, a wound quickly joined by another.

And another.

Shatiel's fingers paused. He closed his eyes.

And then the true magic. The Work. His long spindly fingers drew the oils of the palette into a webwork of colors like shattered crystals set in an invisible pattern, a broken mosaic. He laid his stained fingertips to the glass, transferring his inner vision to that tableau.

I waited, watched. It never ceased to amaze me, as many times as I'd seen it done. It was not art-making; it was the stripping away of a curtain of emptiness to reveal the art beneath.

Shatiel was done in moments.

He opened his eyes. And sighed silently.

The picture in its angled Picasso darks was a slice of autumn green; Sheep's Meadow, if I wasn't mistaken. Above, rising like a copper-colored missile, was the Empire State Building. But what caught and held my eye lay near the bottom border—the girl in her sad befurred dead thing of a coat, a textbook in her lap and her face scowling over it. A copper leaf lay caught on the girl's cardigan over her heart like a badge. Her boy knelt on the gravel bicycle path in the far southeastern corner. There he was, small and too fragile for this world, like his mother. He had a wonderful aura, the color of the clear heavens after a storm. Small children and animals always have auras like that.

I came up beside Shatiel and took the palette from him. He stood beside his work, his eyes appraising bits of amber glass.

Now to open the Door.

Shatiel held up his hands, palms outward and fingers spread. Passing his hands down the length of the painted mirror, he rotated his wrists and raised his hands in a gesture of summoning.

A low, waxing hum throbbed alive inside my head and blood like an ache. I braced myself for the intensity of it. The octave grew so that I could feel the ache in the back of my teeth and in the roots of my hair and in the tips of my fingers. The floor of the loft carried the rhythm like a quake. The empty Coke bottle on the card table did a musical little jig and fell over. I locked my teeth to keep them from chattering. And just when it seemed the very warps and wefts of the atmosphere around us were about to unravel, Shatiel pushed outward and touched the surface of the glass and stopped the quake.

The last metallic quiver left me. I made myself stop scratching the tips of my fingers on my jacket and watched the Door open.

That was what Shatiel called it. The Door. But a door was the last thing it made me think of. More like a pond of water arrogantly defying gravity. The touch of Shatiel's hand caused ripples to spiral outward over the picture, distorting its deep, sure lines and shadows. Then it passed through so that for a moment he stood with his hand buried up to the wrist in the glass, testing the waters, so to speak. He withdrew it, stood aside, and nodded once to me.

I stepped up next to him and peered in. As always, the world on the other side of the Door looked distorted, the colors runny and weak, and the darks and lights reversed, like a negative that had suffered water damage. On top of that, everything was in motion. The dogwoods swayed to and fro; the traffic, seized up on Madison Avenue only moments ago, began its snaily pace onward; a pigeon picked at the wrapper of a candy bar beside a busy fountain. At a distance, The Pond looked as murky as a skin of oil as it lapped with languorous interest at its muddy banks, its great white water birds as dark as a coven of crow. I've found it difficult to stay in the Otherworld (as I call it) for very long; its dissimilarities grate on the nerves and the mind's eye. The wrongness of it is as painful as one of those optical illusions where the parallel lines are of the same length but are angled so they don't look it.

I blinked, trying to adjust my point of view, trying to take in and negate the *alienness* of the landscape. It wasn't easy. Finally, I felt Shatiel's hand close around my wrist, indicating we were about to make the crossing. I clenched my hand, feeling...fear. Shatiel, by the unwritten laws, could come and go from the Otherworld as he pleased, but a Keeper could be lost in the narrow, uncertain place between, the place I thought of with dark respect as Oblivion, should she lose her grip on her Finder. She would find herself in a place not quite heaven and not quite hell, destined (I believe, anyway) to fall forever. I shivered a little. Returning was likewise as treacherous; impossible—or nearly so—for someone or something that had not first crossed with a Finder. But of course it could be done, or we wouldn't now be doing it. Yes, it could be done. For a price.

But I didn't want to think about that now.

Shatiel went through first, his creation accepting its creator with watery reverence until all that remained on this side was the hand I clung to. I hesitated a moment before following, feeling like a kid on a sturdy dock crossing over into a gently swaying rowboat. But then I took a hard breath, held it, and stepped through the Door.

The surface stung my face. My teeth rang. And then—nothing. It was all gone, the reality I knew. Darkness. I couldn't see. Where was the ground? I couldn't find the ground—!

I stopped myself. I was panicking. Stupid, Stevie, I thought. And willed myself forward.

The blindness fell off my face like a black sheet.

Shatiel had not let me go. His hand had guided me through the Door into the Otherworld with a single, steady tug.

This I've found: the Otherworld is strange to see, stranger to be in. Like sliding beneath exotic silver waters, all sound is deadened; the weight of noise nestling against the ear is like a murmur.

Shatiel released my hand. He began to move across the alien landscape in slow, broken steps, the motion clicking along in frames like a decrepit film reel. I followed after, my motions no better—as sharp and faulty as a windup doll that had lost its tension. The wind did not affect us, removed as we were from the moment. The pigeon with its bit of sticky wrapper didn't notice us at all.

We passed the girl on the bench, and I paused a moment to watch her turn the page of her textbook. I looked down at the black pages with their inked writing bleached white by this world. The writing was indecipherable—as always, backwards. The badgelike leaf twisted off the girl's sweater in magical slow motion.

I moved unnoticed past her and caught up to Shatiel where he stood by a second park bench. In our present state we could be touched, sensed, but only fleetingly. Shatiel had touched me once while I stood in the real world, and he had felt like a wind in the door, no more than that.

That was probably all that the girl's little boy felt where he knelt on the gravel path with his Slinky. He was making it walk in its weird mechanical way, top over top, and Shatiel watched as if the little metal spring fascinated him. Shatiel's shadow was white, like a fallen sheet; it covered the little boy like the long wing of a white bird.

I waited at a distance, thinking of Shatiel's adage that everything and everyone must exist somewhere, at some time. Nothing had always been lost, and because of that, anything could be found. And that made me think of this pixie-like child lost, possibly dead, in our world, but alive and found here.

The Slinky disappeared into a overgrown mimosa at the side of the path. I narrowed my eyes, and...yes, he did as I guessed he would and pushed back a plumed leaf and reached into its shady depths.

The boy scowled.

The toy was gone.

The boy went in after it.

But Shatiel didn't watch the boy now. He watched the stretch of darkness beyond the bicycle path. I strained to see what he saw, and after a moment I noticed the movement of something at the foot of a thickly whorled dogwood. It moved with casual agility, the body of a man with the mind of a predator. I watched this creature—general looking, even forgettable—as he moved in an unwavering path toward the boy. I wondered who he was. I wondered why he even existed. I suppose it didn't matter. I would never know.

Ten feet before he reached the boy.

My fingers curled inside the pockets of my jacket.

Eight feet.

Silently, he moved. Like a stalking tiger. Like a man-eater.

Six feet.

I thought maybe Shatiel had moved, couldn't be sure.

Five feet.

I couldn't look away, couldn't.

Three.

Shatiel had raised one hand. I was sure of it.

Two feet.

I heard the Door rasp open.

One.

The creature, quick-minded as the predator he was, saw the Door open blackly beneath him. He tried to step around it.

It just spread wider, like a hungry grin.

The man began the long fall. I knew the fall would never end. He would never catch up to the others who had gone into Oblivion before him. He was alone, and falling, and in the dark, forever and ever.

The wind sighed.

The man vanished.

The Door rasped closed.

I needed the Queen of Spades; without it, the game was over. I went through the reservoir deck once more, but there was none to be had. Game over.

Shatiel shook his head in sympathy.

"You can do better, I suppose?"

Shatiel took the deck from me and began to shuffle the cards. When he showed me the bottom card it was the one I expected, needed.

"So you found it." I took the cards from him.

But the card on the top of the deck was the Queen of Spades too. And the one under that one, and the one under that one...

"Parlor tricks," I said with a smile.

Shatiel gave me the smallest smile back.

"Blackstone beware," I whispered, and it was then that the first knock fell upon the door of the loft. My humor disappeared like a coin in a magician's hand. The cards bent beneath the pressure of my fingers. I set them down and rose.

I passed Shatiel's sheeted mirror and unlocked and opened the door.

The girl stood there, silent.

"I almost didn't come," she said in time. "What you said…" She shook her head.

I reached for her hand. "I'm glad you did. Shatiel just hates it when people give up on him." I wrinkled my nose, trying to be girlfriendly with her. "Shows so little faith."

She came with the encouragement of a little tug, came uncertainly, with the sting of faith not yet fulfilled. She looked around searchingly.

"It was an easy case, as cases go," I explained as I closed the door. "Not like Miz Monroe's brooch last week. You wouldn't believe where we found it. It took days." I rolled my eyes for emphasis, but she seemed neither amused nor convinced. Only lost. I looked to Shatiel, who nodded.

It was time.

"Come on." I led her to the mirror, and there we stood together like a pair of preening sisters, as sisters seemed to do in all the old Victorian fiction. I pulled away the sheet, fully prepared for the girl's shock; I experienced it every time a client looked upon Shatiel's work. I felt it myself and I had been doing this forever. Or nearly so.

The boy stood opposite us, his hands flat against the invisible barrier of the Door, peering in at us like a kid window-shopping. Beyond, the park had taken on dusky, irregular (for it) tones as Oblivion leaked into the Otherworld. In about another half an hour the painting would grow dark as Oblivion reclaimed the land like the tyrant it was. Then the glass would turn black and that would be that.

Theo's face was salt-scarred with his tears.

I looked away at last.

"Oh. My. God." Barely a whisper. The girl drifted toward the mirror. She whispered her supplication again and again. Finally, she fell to a stinted sobbing. Her chipped, painted fingernails made a metallic rasp against the Door as she slipped to her knees.

Shatiel had pulled away into himself, distancing himself from her and from me. She would receive no comfort from him, so I went to her and put my hand on her shoulder as I had before when she had first come to us. She laid her forehead tiredly to the Door. "What is he?" she asked, and I almost didn't hear her, so soft was her voice. "He's done this."

"No," I told her. "Not him."

The girl moved her hands so that they fitted her son's perfectly. The barrier alone lay between them. Theo cried for his mother and his voice was as soundless as Shatiel's.

"How do I get him out?" she demanded to know. She was now past the point of fear—all that remained were her best instincts, a mother's desire to protect her young. And it was then that I knew she would do just fine, regardless of the sacrifice Shatiel asked of her. I looked to him, unafraid now. He beckoned me forward, and I went to him.

Shatiel reached into the pocket of his coat and withdrew a gold dagger.

I paused halfway to him.

I've seen all kinds of cases. A year ago, when Mr. and Mrs. Vanderdaam came to us with their bizarre request—could we find the lost element that was destroying their marriage of fifteen years?—we had found them happy to sacrifice a little of the success they knew at their partnership-run travel agency to find what they were missing. And last week, when we'd confronted Miz Arkady with the price of donating a small percentage of her vast fortune to an animal-rescue service for the successful return of her precious Pekinese, we had found her uncooperative and the poor dog was lost to Oblivion. It taught me an interesting lesson: I could never judge a client until that final moment when they were confronted with the sacrifice, when all they presented to the world fell away with a single request and I was left staring at the beauty or the monster beneath. It had become one of the greatest—and hardest—lessons of my life.

I looked at the knife gleaming dully in Shatiel's hand. But this price…

I looked at Shatiel. Unchanging. Waiting.

I took the dagger. It seemed to throb in my hand. "Are you sure?" I asked. A stupid question.

He nodded.

I took a deep breath. Dutifully, being the Keeper that I was, I returned to where the girl was kneeling before the Door and murmuring the words of comfort I knew her son could not hear.

"It's getting so dark in there," she said, her voice a knife in her throat.

"It does that," I said. "We won't be able to get him out soon."

She looked to me, frayed yellow hair lying as harsh as straw against her white face, mascara raccooning her eyes, her dead fur trailing after her on the floor like an ancient and loyal pet.

"There's a price," I whispered, "a sacrifice that must be made for the Otherw—the place over there—before it'll release him."

She watched me unblinkingly. "What price?"

I opened my mouth but nothing came. Damn you, I wanted to say to Shatiel. Damn you and damn the Otherworld and damn this whole damnable system…

The dagger burned like heated brass in my hand.

"What price?" she prompted.

I turned the instrument over in my hands. "Shatiel says he wants…" I looked at my sneakered feet. So many times I'd made the proposal, so many times. But never this price. Never this. "He wants…wants your life for the life of your boy."

"My life."

I was stunned. No fear. A sharp-edged surprise, but no hate. I glanced up. She seemed to grow pale against the darkening landscape of the Otherworld. It was getting so late.

My expression was enough to make her turn and look. Theo seemed to sob half-asleep, his darkening face pressed to the barrier.

So little time left…

"How?" the girl demanded, flashing her eyes back on me. They were stained, beautiful, savage. I so envied Theo. And for all I felt for Shatiel, I found I could hate him too.

I offered her the gold dagger like a gift.

She hesitated only a moment, then took it from me. "He'll be free?" she asked, watching the eclipsing face of her son.

"I promise. He'll be free."

"He'll be alone."

"No," I told her, putting my back to Shatiel. "He'll be raised by someone who loves him very much. I promise."

So little light left. Only a few minutes more and Theo would begin the long fall that would never end. But the girl seemed to understand her son's fate innately, for she placed the nose of the dagger to her belly, cupping the elaborate, bejeweled hilt with her two hands.

She looked into the eyes of her son. It was such a private moment that I looked away.

I heard the soft fall of her body but refused to turn around. She had made no sound. It was awful and romantic and it gave me a chill; pain for the child's birth, pain for his rebirth. Death for his life. How I hated Shatiel.

I lifted my eyes to him. I saw him through a veil of tears. "Are you happy?"

He made no gesture. Any would have belittled the moment. Instead, he brushed past me like a dark lord down the dusty halls of a keep which was his lair and his prison. His eyes were set forward with purpose. He paused before the mirror, very straight and tall over the small fetal form of the girl, and, breaking through the silvery barrier to the Otherworld, he took the boy by both wrists and midwifed him through.

I stepped forward to catch the boy, to take his shuddering, sodden form with me to the futon. I held his face away from the sight of his mother's lifeless body and whispered all the words of comfort I knew to him, any I could remember from my own childhood. I guess I wept in tandem with Theo, I don't know.

Shatiel went to one knee before the girl and turned her huddled body over on the floor. He smoothed her hair by passing his hands over her face and body like a benediction. It was such a tired motion, and done with such reverence I could almost forgive Shatiel. Then he curled his fingers around the hilt of the dagger and pulled the instrument from the girl's body.

Shatiel's dagger left no mark on her.

The girl opened her eyes. "Theo," she said hoarsely, like someone rising from deep sleep.

Shatiel gently lifted her tired body into his arms, almost making me forget he had no soul to speak of, and carried her to where I sat with Theo on my lap. To the place of reunions.

Karen Koehler

Karen Koehler's versatility in many different genres has helped her create a number of compelling science fiction, fantasy, horror and action/adventure novels. Her past works include the critically acclaimed industrial gothic novel *Slayer, Slayer: Black Miracles, Slayer: Stigmata, Scarabus,* and *The Maiden #1: Out of the Ashes,* all from Black Death Books. She works as an editor and publishing consultant. Her website is located at http://www.covenhouse.com and you may contact her at the_vampire_akisha@yahoo.com.

Grave Mistake

Grave Mistake has been involved in the Industrial Gothic Underground movement for several years. He is an independent film director and scriptwriter. He spends most of his waking nights involved in music production, writing, and script development. His present projects include bringing the novel *Slayer* to the big screen as well as several other personal projects. "I enjoy bringing shadows to life and exploring the darkest regions of the mind. The dark holds the deceptions of life. The things people find disturbing and morbid, dark and frozen are what make up my visions. In the end the Truth of the grave is stone cold." Contact Grave Mistake c/o Black Death Multimedia.

The Eternal Reich
by
Christopher Lee

God's chosen people.

Burrmann watched them line up at the lip of the hole; they shuffled there through the snow, looking like nothing so much as a band of scarecrows, lost now without a field to silently attend. There were no tears, eyes long dried, and hunger was on them like a predator.

"Stand!" Burrmann commanded.

They turned to face him and they made no attempt to run, said not a word, just stood in the freezing Polish woods, the gray of their skin indistinguishable from the gray of their uniforms. The only thing that stood out under the pale, wan moon was the tattoo on their arms…their numbers, the remainder of what they used to be.

Burrmann raised his rifle and carefully squeezed off a round. A child gripped its stomach, weak blood pulsing from between clenched fingers. The others never even turned to look. They were as the dead, cold and locked in a rictus that only resembled life.

The bundle of pain and fear fell into the pit, blood shooting into the night, spilling like scarlet rain. The others never even moved, just bowed their heads. Some of them prayed silently in their mysterious, guttural tongue.

The rifle sang its venomous song once more, and an old woman fell to her knees, screaming, clutching at her belly, and feeling the nourishing blood fall into the snow, in pain beyond pain. Burrmann strode forward and thrust his boot into her face with a vicious motion, feeling the smooth shock of pulverized bone rising up his leg from her smashed face. He kicked her into the pit and returned to his position.

One by one they fell.

Klaus Gollden. He owned a small toy store in Prague where, once a year, he would make dolls for the children from old rags, sometimes lying in bed freezing because he used his blanket to make a dress for some little girl's "baby".

Kurt Bremen. He loved the children too...he was a monster, a rapist, a killer of the suckling babe. There was, however, no suave police inspector to capture him, no romantic dash through the cold Berlin night, trailed by a ravening mob like in the Gothic fiction that he loved so. He would just die here, with all the others, just a number.

Magda Ploiste. She had suckled four starving children at her breast, crying and wishing for a scrap of food in the Warsaw ghetto. She had survived for a time by giving herself to the men of the ghetto, but it was never enough, and her children grew stiff and cold and died in her arms, one by one.

Nickolaus Boerne. A homosexual. He lived in Berlin proper, loved too much in the wrong time. His lover had been a physician who had given him to the authorities in exchange for enough money to buy a new watch.

Too many names, each life a candle flame snuffed in the night, coldly, no rage no animosity. Simply crushed and lost. Burrmann bore them no real feeling. They were meat.

The last Jew fell into the ragged hole and Burrmann walked to the lip, staring down into the pile of bodies, blood and vomit and snow mixed in a trinity of sorrow. He felt nothing, nothing at all.

The only sound in the woods now was the crunch of his boots in the fresh snow, and his labored breathing as he gathered his pack and prepared for the march back to the camp. Then...

A stirring.

He stopped, listening to the silent woods. Far away in the night he could swear he heard a sound, first very soft and then rising like summertime air, the sound of thousands of insensate voices moaning in unison, in pain. It was a sound that he knew VERY well indeed. There weren't many expressions of pain that Burmann didn't know VERY intimately.

There was a sliding, a sibilant tone almost like a hundred people making violent love, flesh on flesh. Burrmann raised his rifle again, scanning the woods, looking for what he couldn't say—perhaps the telltale glint of moonlight from the muzzle of some partisan's rifle, perhaps something...else. He felt a cool hand of fear slide up his back.

Suddenly he saw movement at the pit, and chuckled at his fear. It was just the Jews holding on to the last of their parasitic lives. Let them struggle. The snow would take the fight from them. He would return in the morning and relieve his bowels on them.

He finished with his pack and hefted it on to his broad shoulders, pulling the fur of his cap down over his ears.

Fucking kike detail...

Then, that sound again...but much stronger. Much stronger, a sound like a hundred sleepers awakening, stretching catlike, or a pit of vipers roiling in the darkness now and then punctuated the moans of pain.

The night was no longer just a cold place, or darkness to hide the disposal from prying locals. It was the heart of cold.

Burrmann straightened himself, his face flushing in shame...afraid of a dying Jew! Boldly he walked to the edge of the pit, chambering a shell to finish off the struggling creature. He stared down the sight of the rifle and froze. They were moving. Not just one of them, but ALL of them, in a sort of mad danse macabre. They were dead, their skin blue, horrendous gunshot wounds oozing and spurting blood into the sodden earth, but they were moving, and speaking as one, a sullen groan of loss and weariness and hunger.

A bony hand shot from the pit, grasping his leg, tearing away the thick cloth of his uniform, and the nails pierced Burrmann's skin like razors, ripping through him. Burrmann screamed into the night and tried to pull away, and then he was falling forward into the pit. Within moments they were on him, pulling back his uniform, exposing his skin and his soft, well-fed belly. An old woman plunged her face into it, growling with infinite, dead hunger as she pierced his flesh and his red warmth filled her mouth. They were many, and they were hungry.

They pulled him apart like fresh bread, gnarled, dead hands tearing holes in his softness, teeth tearing into his arms. He wallowed in a pool of the dead, and they tore him apart, his blood a consecration, his flesh a sweet taste of life to keep back the cold of death. He screamed for a very long time.

Finally it was done, and one by one they pulled themselves from the pit stiffly, but with a newfound purpose.

Feeding.

They had been hungry for a very long time, and now in this empty wooded place they glistened redly under Luna's gaze and some of them carried pieces of meat, tearing, gnawing, but the hunger did not abate. God had been so kind to his Chosen. Even after death, their suffering did not stop.

The camp was near. And they were so hungry.

The ragged band shuffled into the night, a hundred strong, toward the heat and light. Inside, the guards sat at card tables, eating and smoking while their charges shivered and starved nearby and the furnaces roared ceaselessly.

With the ash of the dead, now dead forever, smeared on their tortured faces, the Chosen Ones tore through the fence through sheer force of numbers and fell on them all, guards and prisoners. The dead bore the no real feeling. They were meat.

Into the long hours, God's chosen ones fed, but the hunger never EVER went away.

And so began the second Exodus.

Mary

by

Rebecca Lloyd

She came walking out of the hills one night, up to the torch-lit gates of
the town, with a foul hot wind at her back that scattered the drifts of
autumn leaves. Wrapped in a ragged cloak gone colorless from the road,
once-pretty face now thin and drawn and sunken, with fevered eyes
rimmed with tears. They took her for a beggar afoot, or possibly a
wandering widow gone mad from desolation. She pleaded for entry, this
thin fragile creature with the wavering voice who claimed she was cold
despite the strange heat that rose off of her and swirled the road-dust. It
was the dead hours, just past the false dawn, and the guards were tired
and half in their cups (or more than half), so despite her strangeness
they threw the massive bolt and she walked past them with hesitant
steps.

The town's Inn was full, but there was a place by the fire granted her
by the barmaid who mopped the filth from the floor around the revelers
and guests who snored away on benches and tables. The woman choked
down the crusted gruel from the bottom of the pot over the fire and
smiled gratefully for it, for she had gone a long time without a hot meal.
The barmaid, her labors done, tarried a few minutes to talk to the
strange guest, whose delirious whispers bespoke the loneliness of long
wandering, and of terrible loss. The barmaid noted a strange smell about
her, but dismissed it as road-dirt and offered to draw her a bath in the
old washtub before she turned in for the day. This the woman accepted
gratefully, but she insisted on washing in privacy, and so water was
boiled and the tub set out in the stables for her. The barmaid went
sleepily to bed, and when the woman was finished she redonned her
worn dress and cloak and returned to watch the embers in the hearth
dim and flicker as the dawn light strengthened.

In the full light of day a great wailing went up in the town, for flies
had gathered in droves about the Inn, and upon peering cautiously

through the shutters the people were met with a shocking sight. The sleepers in the common room had never awakened, and now their bodies were bloating and blackening as the heat of the day rose. Pox stood out on their distended skins, and the smell of sickness drifted through the slats and poisoned the air for yards around.

Guards soaked facecloths with rosemary oil and tied them over their noses and mouths before braving entry into that place. They found all the guests dead of some swift and terrible illness, their faces still relaxed into the lines of deep sleep. In an upper bedroom reserved for the staff, though, they found the woman alive, weeping and rocking and holding the ravaged corpse of the kind barmaid in her thin and wasted arms. Not a single pustule of the pox that had killed all others in that place could be found on her by rough examination, which she submitted to with strange-smelling tears running down her narrow face.

They called her a witch and threw her in the town gaol, alongside two leering, burly burglars who seemed ready to amuse themselves with her until the guardsmen told them of the atrocity at the Inn. Then they sat as far from her as possible, while she crouched in a corner pleading with the gaol's keepers to destroy the key and wall her in with bricks. The burglars died within the hour, raving and screaming as the pustules rose and broke on their flesh swift as bubbles in boiling water. They lurched across the cell and tried to strangle her at the end, falling short and collapsing at her feet while she sobbed and begged their forgiveness. Again she asked the guards to wall her in, but they were swaying on their feet with fever and many had gone home to their beds. One brave man gathered stones and mortar and struggled to begin the task himself, but he had barely started laying the foundation when he choked and his limbs seized and he fell to the floor with black fluid pouring from his mouth and nostrils.

The woman, desperate for the town's survival, took the key from his belt, freed herself and limped as fast as she could for the wilderness, but already flies were thick as dust all through the town, and vultures circled over many houses. The illness swept from family to family, killing all whom it touched, no matter whether they had laid eyes on the woman herself or not. She cried for them, and for herself, and found torches and oil and set the town afire after the last of the townsfolk had let out his death rattle.

A few of the village Elders released message-hawks before the fever took their minds, and so word of the atrocity reached the surrounding towns, who locked their gates and sent out militiamen to find and destroy the strange woman before she could spread her sickness further.

They found her in a muddy copse, still weeping, and closed on her with swords, but the stout blades snapped against her pale and fragile-looking skin. Red-eyed and desperate, she screamed at them to leave her be for the sake of their own safety. They took that as a threat despite the pleading in her tone, and took hold of her roughly and bore her away to the gallows hill of the County seat, an hour's hard ride through the woods.

But when they brought her forth for execution, Death once again would not take her. The hanging-rope snapped, and the axe-blade shattered when it struck her neck, and the thrown stones of the crowd merely bounced off of her and fell in the dust. They strapped her to a post and piled hay-bales around her thin legs while the crowd of the curious swelled through the deepening afternoon. At last they put a torch to the pyre, but though the fire rose high enough to mask her body and drive the crowd back with its heat, and though they fed the flames with more bales until darkness had fallen, her weeping and pleading never once rose to heights of agony, nor were silenced by oblivion. Finally, ropes and post and clothes all burned away, she stumbled ash-coated from the conflagration, hunched and cross-armed to cover her shame.

The priests attending this strange execution made the signs of their God against her shuddering approach, and hurried to their coaches and the safety of town. One of the farm-maids, though, declared that it was a miracle, and ran for her best clean shift to replace the burned-off dress. She was given a sad smile of gratitude, but like the priests and all who visited Gallows Hill that day, she did not live past dawn.

The rulers of the land, outraged by this horror, sent their armies to hew the woman to pieces and bury what was left in salted graves. The troops surrounded her as she padded across the plain at the base of Gallows Hill, seeking the wildwoods again. Archers blackened the sky with their arrows, but not a one struck its mark. Horse-soldiers bore down on her with lances, but their steeds panicked at her scent and threw their riders in the mire. A thousand sword- and spearmen charged that one thin figure with a battle-cry like the roar of storm-surf, but though she never fought back once and was captured a dozen times, no weapon could break her skin, nor fist raise bruises. And in the end she walked from the battlefield the only one still living, mourning the deaths she left in her wake.

Stories of the horror spread to the surrounding lands, and with them all the rumors that arise around such things. Some said she was a demoness come to spread death among them. Others said that she had been cursed by the gods, or even was a Goddess herself, a minor one gone mad from some conflict among the Divine that mortals were not privy to. Some said that she was the Creator's vengeance come for them. Others claimed she was a sorceress whose own power had cursed and infected her, an immortal plague-carrier forced to wander the earth eternally.

She herself could not remember.

She recalled the endless wastes she wandered, and knew now afresh what happened when she touched or spoke with other people. But that was all. Sometimes, as she curled in fitful sleep on a hummock or beneath some thorny bush, she found torment in images of comfort, belonging and joy. Sometimes there were soft gowns that caressed her clean skin. Sometimes a healthy baby suckled at her breast. Sometimes she tumbled laughing through castles of cloud. What was true of these? Did any of them ever actually happen? She only knew that she woke in agony from such dreams, and was haunted by them for many days afterward.

She knew that she was death to those around her, and that she could not die. And so she wandered the wild places, far off beaten paths or signs of men, and shied from towns and caravans when she came across them. Sometimes a highwayman or wanderer would find her, but they died before they could carry the plague's ugly gifts to the flesh of others.

She did her best to keep these things from happening, for she was tenderhearted and had no love of the death and horror that came endlessly in her wake. Neither plants nor beasts were harmed by the sickness, and so she lived among them, and timidly enjoyed what little company birds and lizards and deer could grant her. She ate berries from wild bushes and fish from streams, and thrived impossibly on such meager fare as she contemplated the whys and wherefores of some possible relief, however temporary, from her agonizing fate.

In the meantime the cities grew, and the forests shrank, and the stories of her and of the dead towns and fallen armies she had left in her wake faded into legend. Wonders arose in the cities, and rumors of strange inventions she had never seen before sometimes tugged at her curiosity. And always there was loneliness, and the sweet ephemeral dreams that made her weep.

And after a long time, the memory of those long-ago horrors faded even from her mind, and she forgot why she was hiding from the eyes of men. She forgot, and the loneliness gnawed at her, until finally she set her feet to a road and followed it to the gated town at its end.

And came to the gate in the quiet hours of night, and stood in torchlight, begging the drunk and sleepy guardsmen for entry, and perhaps a bowl of gruel...

Rebecca Lloyd

A native of the San Francisco Bay Area, Rebecca Lloyd was first published in *Marion Zimmer Bradley's Fantasy Magazine* in 1994. She is part of the local poetry scene, has several nonfiction articles under her belt and is working on her first novel. She lives in Oakland with her fiancé, two cats, and two rats. She can be reached by e-mail at writerhelp@yahoo.com.

Angel
by
Aurelio Rico Lopez III

He gripped the steering wheel with his sweaty palms, kneading the leather with his hands. Squeeze, release, squeeze, release...unable to keep still. He watched the children on the swing, on the jungle gym, and on the slide. More of them were playing hopscotch and tag. Some girls were playing jump rope, and a group of boys were crouched on the ground like giant spiders, engaged in a game of marbles. Laughter and squeals of delight carried through the afternoon air and into the black van parked by the curb.

Glen Howards adjusted the rearview mirror and studied his reflection. He decided he wasn't such a bad-looking guy after all. His hair was thinning at the top, but he had other assets—compassionate dark brown eyes and a pudgy face that gave him a church choirboy look—the kind of look that got people elected... and reelected.

Maybe he should consider running for office.

Glen chuckled at that last thought.

He returned his attention to the playground, surveying the area for *the one.*

Most of the children were in groups of threes, fours, and fives, so they wouldn't do. Others were under the watchful eyes of a parent or guardian. Too dangerous. Too many complications. Too many chances for a slip-up.

You need help, Glen!

That was what Aileen had told him when she caught him alone in the bathroom with that children's magazine. He had tried desperately to explain, but the bitch would hear none of it. He was sick, she said, and he needed help.

Aileen had left him that day.

Moments passed. Maybe he had to go somewhere else—like the shopping mall.

He was about to start the van when he glanced at the side mirror. A little girl had come out of the west side entrance, about twenty meters from where he was parked. She was sucking on her thumb, and she looked left and right before she turned in the direction of the van.

Jackpot!

Glen let out a rush of air and blotted his hands on his Levi's. He got out of the van and slammed the door shut, walked around the front end, and stepped onto the curb. He gently kicked the front wheel with the toe of his boot, as if checking the tire's air pressure. In the corner of his eye, he saw the child approaching. She was no more than five meters away now.

He turned to face her and smiled. "Hello there, little lady."

She stopped, looked up at him, looked behind her, and turned to him again. "You talking to me, Mister?"

He got down on one knee like a man proposing marriage. "Well, who else would I be talking to?" He tilted his head a little to the side and raised his eyebrows.

She giggled, and her ears and cheeks turned bright red. She was lovelier than he had imagined, certainly lovelier than the last one, but a little younger; she couldn't have been over seven years old.

Her golden brown hair grew to her shoulders, and a few bangs draped across her face. Her matching hazel eyes were attractively large, and her lips were light red, almost pinkish. She wore pink shorts and a loose, white shirt with a large picture of Sesame Street's Elmo printed on the front.

And then he noticed the doll. She clutched it in her right hand. He didn't see it at first because it was no larger than a softball. It was faded orange and looked very much the way kids' storybooks illustrated the gingerbread man. Its head was twice the size of its body. White threadwork made up two round, pupil-less eyes, and the nose and mouth were fashioned out of black thread to form an inverted letter T. The doll neither smiled nor frowned; it just looked at Glen with that poker face expression.

"Mister, are you okay?" the girl asked.

He managed to tear his gaze from the doll and look at the girl. "Uh, sure. Listen, where's your mommy? I sure would like to talk to her."

Worry lines creased the little girl's forehead, and Glen was afraid she would burst into sobs.

"Mommy said she'd be back in a few minutes," she sniffed, her lips trembling. "She told me to wait by the sandbox. I tried to, but I got tired."

He looked past the girl. So far, no one had noticed them. A couple sat on a wooden bench by the west side entrance, but they didn't even give Glen and his companion so much as a glance. As far as they knew, he was Daddy picking up his daughter.

Glen knew he'd already been on the curb too long. He had to act fast.

"I think I know where your mom is," he said.

The girl's face brightened. "You do? Really, Mister?"

"Oh, sure! But…well, I don't know if I should tell you."

"Tell me what?" The worry returned to her face.

"About your surprise."

"My surprise?"

"Uh, huh," Glen said, nodding. "Your mom asked me to keep a present for you. I left it at my place. That's probably where your mom went."

She jumped up and down like a kangaroo on amphetamines. Glen was worried that she was going to attract too much unwanted attention.

"I'll bet it's a bunny rabbit," she said. "I really wanted a pony, but Mommy said they poo all over the place. I don't like poo. It stinks." She pinched her nose with a thumb and forefinger to emphasize her point.

Glen stood up and opened the passenger door of the van. "Well, why don't we go over to my place so you can see your surprise? If we hurry, we might be able to catch your mom."

She seemed unsure whether to get in the van or not.

"What's wrong?" Glen asked.

She held the odd-looking doll against her breast. "Angel said I should wait by the sandbox."

Angel.

That was probably the name of her mother, Glen thought.

"Don't you want to see your gift?"

She nodded mutely.

"Well then, get in," he urged, hoping he didn't sound so impatient. "Your mom's probably waiting for us by now."

He watched her slowly get into the van. She wasn't even properly seated when he slammed the door. He took one quick look around to check if anyone had seen them.

The playground continued to bustle with the sounds of children at play. No one had noticed that a little girl in an Elmo t-shirt was missing.

He hurried to the driver's side of the van and opened the door. He thought he heard the girl talking to someone, but when he looked, she was quiet, sitting comfortably with the tiny doll resting on her lap.

Glen got in and slammed the door. The van's windows were tinted so that no one could see who was driving. Or riding.

He turned the key on the ignition, and the engine came to life. Glen turned to his new passenger and grinned. "Here we go."

She smiled back with those pretty lips.

Glen shifted to first gear and slowly pulled away from the sidewalk. He drove, accelerating little by little.

He suppressed the urge to grin.

She was his now.

He turned right at the next corner, avoiding crowded streets and traffic. Only a few more blocks to go. The sun had begun to set, painting the sky with hemorrhagic streaks of red, orange, and blue.

"Gee, Mister, we sure are driving really far." She was kneeling on the seat, looking back the way they had driven. "Are you sure you know where Mommy is?"

"Of course I do," he said. "She just wanted a safe place to keep your present."

"I guess you're right," she conceded, slumping on the seat and facing forward.

"A lot of other girls would want a bunny too, you know," he added.

"I knew it!" She giggled and hugged her doll. She placed her left hand on his lap. "What color is it? Can you tell me? Pleeeaase?"

Glen felt her small hand squeeze his thigh, and something inside him stirred. "White, I think."

"Oh." She sounded disappointed. Her hand left his thigh, and Glen almost whined in protest. "I told Mommy I wanted a gray bunny. Bugs Bunny is gray. Mommy probably forgot."

Glen couldn't have cared less if Bugs were pink or any other color for that matter. His need was gnawing at him urgently, demanding to be satisfied. He leaned forward and shifted uneasily in his seat.

"Bugs Bunny is gray." She pouted.

Glen thought quickly. "The other one is gray."

She raised her eyebrows, and her jaw dropped. "The *other* one?"

"The other one," Glen echoed. "Did I forget to say your mom got you two bunnies?"

"Two bunnies?" she asked, raising her voice in disbelief.

Glen drove between two rows of condemned warehouses at the outskirts of the city. The concrete facades had turned a dark gray color; paint was chipping off; and in certain buildings, windows were boarded shut.

He pulled over in front of a half-raised steel gate and killed the van's engine.

The girl craned her neck and peered out her window. "I can't see my mommy anywhere."

"That's because she's inside. That's where the bunnies are. Let's not keep her waiting."

He opened his door and stepped outside. As he shut the door, he felt the gnawing sensation again, more urgent now.

He heard the other door open and close. When he rounded the van, the girl was waiting for him, clutching her doll around one arm.

"Come on, come on!" she cried, gesturing with her other arm. "I wanna see the bunnies!"

Glen allowed her to grab him by the hand and lead him through the steel gate. He looked like a master being towed by an untrained pet dog. A young, female dog. Glen smiled.

The warehouse was empty. It smelled faintly of stale air and urine. What was left of daylight seeped through broken glass panes that resembled the maws of ravenous prehistoric beasts.

"Mister, where's Mommy? You said she would be here with the bunnies. You said!"

"She must be in there," Glen said, pointing to a shut door on the left side of the room. "I'm sure of it." A pale light from an inner room shone under the door.

The little girl hurried to the door, and Glen followed close behind. "Mommy?" she called out as she turned the doorknob.

Glen shoved the girl inside the moment the door was partially open. With a yelp, she stumbled face forward onto a worn mattress, dropping her doll onto the floor. The doll bounced off the ground with a soft thump and rolled to the right end of the room.

The room was much smaller that the one they had just come from. It had previously been used as a storeroom for brooms and other miscellaneous items. Now, it was empty, save for the old mattress and a bulb hanging overhead.

He shut the door and locked it as the girl slowly began to get up. He tried furiously to take off his belt, but his fingers fumbled continuously. Cursing, he finally managed to unfasten it. He saw the girl turn around. Her eyes widened. With the whimper of a frightened animal, she scrambled on her hands and knees and wedged herself in one corner of the room.

"If you scream, I'll fucking kill you," he warned, unzipping his jeans and pulling them down. He was bluffing of course; he wanted her alive. He would kill her later when he was through with her.

"An-juh-juh-gel," she pleaded in a voice that barely sounded hers. "An-juh-juh-gel...p-p-puh-lease..." She pushed harder against the corner as if she believed she could magically mold herself into the wall.

Glen took a step forward...then another. The child was weeping now and shielding herself with her arms.

Suddenly, there came a scuttling sound from behind. When he spun around, he was confronted by something that made his bladder go.

The doll had gotten up and was glaring at him. At first, Glen thought it was a trick of light—an illusion cast by the overhead bulb.

Then he saw its mouth. The stitches had come apart, revealing dozens of shiny, serrated teeth.

A flood of thoughts washed over Glen's mind.

Angel said I should wait by the sandbox.

Angel was not her mother's name. It was the doll's. And when he had heard the girl talking to someone in the van...Jesus! Had she been talking to it?

It bared its teeth and hissed.

Glen took a step back. His foot got caught in his jeans. His hands windmilled before he fell over on the mattress.

The doll pounced on him in an instant. Glen caught the thing inches before it landed on his face. It squirmed in his hands, snapping its mouth at him. It was terribly strong. And unbelievably heavy for something its size.

Glen's elbows buckled as they slowly gave in. The creature seemed to grow heavier and heavier. The doll drew closer and closer to his neck.

"Get it off me!" he yelled. His eyes searched frantically for the girl. She slowly raised herself from the corner and casually walked up to Glen. She was smiling, and there was something about that smile that scared him.

"Help me!" he cried.

"Don't worry, Mister," she said. "Angel will take care of you."

"You fucking bitch! Help me!"

She crouched down and stared at him, the smile never leaving her face. "What's the matter, Mister? I thought you liked it rough."

Her voice had changed. He could still hear her voice, but in the background it was as though there were a dozen of voices speaking at once. Children. Not just little girls. Boys too. Like voices coming from the end of a long metal pipe.

The doll hissed, and Glen felt its hot breath on his skin.

"Please! I'm sorry. Make it stop!" he begged.

A dozen children laughed at him. The little girl squealed in delight.

He screamed for help as the doll tore at his carotid artery. "Help me for Christ's sake!"

The last thing Glen remembered hearing was Aileen's voice. That self-righteous bitch inside his head.

You're sick, Glen. You need help.

Aurelio Rico Lopez III

Aurelio Rico Lopez III is a scribble junkie whose other addictions include cheesecake and coffee. His works have appeared in *Lunatic Chameleon, Electric Velocipede,* the e-book *Julia, daughter of...,* and the scifaiku anthology *Random Planets.* His writings have also been featured in various e-zines, including *Horrorfind, Savage Night, The Murder Hole, Decompositions, The House of Pain,* and *October Moon.* More of his work will see print in future issues of *Dark Animus, Lunatic Chameleon, Scared Naked Magazine, Scifaikuest, Night to Dawn, Beyond Centauri,* and *Shadowland.* Aurelio is from Iloilo City, Philippines. E-mail him at thirdylopez2001@yahoo.com.

A Prick of Skin
by
Paul Melniczek

Martin held the small wood block in his sweating palm, the needles protruding from the object like a miniature bed of nails.

He shifted beady eyes past his telemarketer cubicle, scanning to see if any fellow workers were nearby. The office hummed with the normal background of solicited telephone conversations. Persistent employees pecked away at the nerves of people, the vast majority wanting to be left alone, while some would break down under the breathless rhetoric vomited into their ears, and approve the credit card protection plan that was being offered.

Martin saw that the aisle was clear, and he slowly pressed the needles into his palm, his tongue slitting between thin lips, probing outward like a prowling snake. Tiny droplets of blood welled forth from dotted puncture wounds, pocked ripe holes of penetrated flesh, the mild pain giving him a quick flash of euphoric contentment, his pulse quickening in perverted response. His gray eyes darted back and forth, in appearance more fish-like than human, but contained within an environment of air, not water.

Harder he pressed, sending the needles deeper.

The urge was powerful, edging him to continue, but Martin held back, knowing the danger of creating any noticeable wounds. Grabbing a tissue, he gently wiped the block clean of any staining crimson and patted his palm gently.

It was becoming increasingly difficult for him to back away from the tantalizing brink, to fully consume himself in the erotic pleasure that called to him. With every waking day, the compulsion threatened to drown Martin, take him down the road to self-immolation, and cast aside his shrinking fingernail grip on sanity. He concealed the instrument which gave him partial satisfaction, a teasing respite that kept back the hounds of sadism. The thirty-year-old man was a captive to invisible shackles which grew stronger by the day.

Martin looked at the small, white company clock sitting on his clutter-free desk. Ten more minutes left in his afternoon break, and then he needed to resume the scheduled calls. Seldom did he leave the office, not wishing to enter the lounge area, and risk mingling with other workers. The stares he received were mildly curious, but the possibilities loomed underneath for deeper scrutiny if he permitted doubts to surface about his true nature.

Only his impeccable appearance and youthful, darkly handsome looks saved him from blacker suspicions, and he knew that people considered him shy. Quiet, but always polite. Martin craned his neck past the work area, staring up at Cindy's desk. For the last two days, Martin had been disturbed by the actions of the girl.

She constantly smiled at him, and he caught her looking back at his cubicle. He tried to ignore the implications, but Cindy was showing some obvious interest in his direction. And that was creating problems in Martin's swirling head. He couldn't sleep, but tossed in fitful unrest, filled with dreams of Cindy.

What he wanted to do to her.

Visions of blood, pain, ecstasy, all mingled together. Until now, Martin only inflicted pain on himself, but the desire to expand his dark fetish was testing the man's self-control. Eroding the barriers of restraint.

Cindy turned around, her long black hair cradling her thin, white neck. A playful grin covered the girl's perky face, and Martin felt his mouth go dry, a subtle tingle caressing his back. Without wanting to, he found himself smiling in response, that simple gesture leading him one step closer to darkness.

When she looked away, it took Martin every ounce of effort he had not to impale his skin on the block of needles.

Martin walked down the gloomy flight of steps, his shiny opaque dress shoes clicking at the heels, echoing dully in the shrouded staircase. He tried to veer his thoughts away from Cindy, pushing away her pleasing image with an assortment of mind-pictures designed to distract the unwanted suggestions. His stomach growled like a disturbed tomcat, although nourishment could not be blamed for the restless agitation. It was a hunger of dark emotions, an appetite of lurid obsession. He passed down a section of stairs, and was startled when the hall door opened.

Standing there was Cindy.

"Sorry, did I scare you?" Martin's mouth dropped.

Her face was clear, beaming with a flawless complexion. The ruby lips were full, alluring, painted in a hue of beckoning red. Martin stood in silence for a moment. Surprise, excitement, and revulsion all spinning in his mind, a vortex of clashing sensations.

"I know that you like to take the stairs. Is it all right if I join you?"

"Uh, sure." He was amazed at how easily the words came out from his parched throat.

They walked together, Martin feeling nervous and uncomfortable.

"I was wondering if you would like to do something Friday night?"

He was stunned by her question, unable to form a response.

"Are you busy?" Cindy hesitated, mistaking his reluctance. "Do you have a girlfriend, maybe?" she answered quietly, tilting her head down.

"No, no," Martin stammered. "I mean, no, I don't have any plans. Or a girlfriend," he answered.

Cindy's eyes widened, and a cute blush passed over her face. "Good."

The pair continued down the steps, and Martin couldn't believe what he was hearing; from Cindy or himself. The stairs ended, and he opened the door to let the girl through, his eyes savoring the slope of her body as she passed seductively before him.

"Thank you."

He followed her into the parking garage, gritting his teeth to quench the rising stem of desire flooding his mind. To hold her, touch her.

Hurt her.

Cindy turned around, rummaging in her small, brown purse. She handed him a piece of paper.

"I was hoping you would say yes. Here's my phone number and address. Maybe we can go out for a pizza; there's a little sub shop down the block from my apartment."

"How about eight o'clock, I'll meet you there?" Martin was feeling bolder, caving in to the whispered ramblings in his mind.

"Fine. I'm off tomorrow. I'll see you then."

She turned on her heels and walked over to a small blue sedan. Martin couldn't take his eyes off her. He watched her get into the car, and he finally broke his stare, heading towards his own vehicle. Cindy drove away, leaving Martin shuffling about with eyes boring into the concrete, creating invisible mental holes.

After several minutes of roaming around the garage, he realized that his car was parked on the next level.

Martin paced the floors of his modest apartment that night. Anxiety crushed in on his chest, and at times he found himself breathing heavily, almost forgetting to inhale. Three times he poked needles into his thigh, the last time going in nearly an inch. He felt keyed up, the hairs on his arms tingled. His whole body felt vibrant, alive.

Cindy liked him, asked him out on a date.

He walked over to the phone, stared at the receiver, willing it to ring. Call me, he thought. Tell me you can't make it tomorrow. Martin picked up the phone, and dialed the first three digits of her number. He slammed the receiver down, torn by indecision. He wanted her, but was afraid of what he would do to her.

The feelings were gaining strength, like a funneling whirlpool, dragging him down and down, closer to the inevitable core, and at the bottom lurked pain, ecstasy, and death. Martin imagined holding her smooth body in his arms. He envisioned sharp objects, wicked and luscious knives, pricking her unwilling form.

"No!" he shouted to himself. "I can't do this!"

Martin knew that he desperately needed help, and should have looked for some years ago.

He thought the longing would be controllable, and diminish over time. It became more powerful. To the point now that he was certain of seeing Cindy tomorrow. There would be no canceled date. He lay in bed that night, eyes glued to the distant ceiling, Cindy's naked body hovering before his ephemeral vision, appealing and inviting, the image ingrained into the black corridors of his mind's eye.

The hours dragged by on Friday, and Martin failed to complete any phone sales. He couldn't stay focused on the screen in front of him, the lines of numbers melting, turning to crimson, the face of a raven-haired girl overlapping the pixels. The impulse to feel pain was unbearable.

Martin stepped into the men's room in the waning afternoon hours, staring at an ashen-faced reflection, haunted watery eyes slicing through his conscience and gouging at the sinister desires coming to the surface.

He slapped cool liquid on his skin, trying to dampen more than just flesh.

"She's innocent of anything, I can't let her get close to me."

Martin gripped the sides of the basin, enjoying the light crack of his fingers and knuckles. The sensation only reminded him of much darker feelings, ones that could become more than just fantasy soon.

Tonight. With Cindy. How would her skin feel? What morbid expression would cross her unsuspecting face? Would the coming night's events bring his imprisonment to an end at last? A release from deeply buried, stifled emotions? Martin felt the wheels of his fate rolling along, steaming to a conclusion. Cindy would be the catalyst. She held within her lithe hands the keys to set him free.

There would surely be consequences that waited for him down that path, but Martin was willing to take the risk.

Martin raised a glass mug of frothy beer to his mouth, the alcohol bitter and flat to his numb sense of taste. Cindy sat across from him, chattering away. After two servings of wine, she had loosened up considerably and was rambling on about clients at the firm. Martin engaged her readily, to his own wonder, and ordered another draught from the waiter. He looked at her slender frame, his hands imagining the edge of a razor brushing against the quivering flesh.

A broad smile creased his face, and she returned with a sheepish look.

"I don't drink too often," she said. "Hardly ever, actually."

"Me neither. But it's going down pretty good tonight."

Cindy giggled, letting her guard down further. "Would you like to stop over at my place for a little? There's a bunch of movies on every weekend, and I have pay channels."

Martin bit his tongue, attempting to appease the hunger he felt. "Sounds like fun."

Cindy's apartment was slightly larger than his, tidy and warm, with books filling two shelves, and throw rugs covering the hardwood flooring. A short hall led into the kitchen, and a comfortable sofa sat in front of a mid-size screen. Hanging from the ceiling was a metal cage containing a pair of lovebirds.

"Do you want a drink? I have a new bottle of red wine in the kitchen."

"That's fine," Martin answered.

He stared at the harmless birds, struck by pangs of guilt. They were so innocent, fragile, just like Cindy. Martin felt sick at what he wanted to do to the girl, but at the same time, felt greatly compelled by those same virtues that emanated from her.

Drawing him closer.

"Here you go." She handed him a tall glass of wine, holding one herself. She picked up the remote, flicking through several channels.

"A mystery is on soon. I like watching them. How about you?"

"Great," he lied. Cindy sat down on the far end of the sofa, staring at the screen.

A commercial for soap products came on, followed by a shaving advertisement.

Martin's eyes gazed at the blade cutting away the hairs on the model's legs, and he imagined the cuts going deeper into her flesh, bringing oozing drops of blood to the surface, cascading down the tender skin.

Down Cindy's skin...

He chanced a glance over to her, and she smiled back. Martin swallowed some of his wine, hoping to find strength for his foul purpose in its clouded depths. They said little for the next few minutes, and the movie started. Martin gazed at the actors, his thoughts drifting past their fleeting figures, and circling back to the girl sitting at arm's length. The people on the screen were phantoms to his hazy mind, meaningless as he waged a silent, internal battle. He finished the rest of his wine, the alcohol a companion now, lending Martin the resolve needed to take action.

"Another one?" Cindy looked at him, sipping her own drink.

"Yeah, that would be great. Might as well bring the whole bottle, looks like you're ready for some more too."

Cindy took his glass, her hand lingering briefly over his palm, sending a tingle of exhilaration through him. She left the room, heading for the kitchen. Martin reached into his pocket, pulling out a small switchblade.

He was feeling confident, burning inside. She looked so luscious he was beyond restraint. His head swooned in anticipation of cutting her, seeing the look in her eyes, defenseless, terrified, pained. The flow of precious blood would be a cloak of rapture, fulfilling his evil fetish.

Martin stood up, nearly tripping in the dimly lighted room as he walked to the hall. She would be returning any minute, and then he would act.

He waited, hearing her move about in the kitchen, the sound of drawers being opened.

"I spilled some of the wine, be back in a minute," Cindy called to him, and Martin nodded, looking more ghoul than man in the shadows, teeth showing in a primeval smile. He closed his eyes, sinking into the corners of his mind, blocking out a voice that emerged to chastise him. Scorning him for what he was about to do. What he would become. It was murder—despicable, the voice said.

Martin squeezed his eyes shut, trying to purge away the accusations. Evil, monstrous, inhuman. Don't do it. You can still stop... Martin leaned against the wall, holding the knife so tight that his knuckles were turning white. She didn't deserve this. No one deserves it. What was he doing? The knife dropped from his hand, and he looked up at the hall.

The last thing he remembered was a crushing blow against his head, and everything went dark.

Martin regained consciousness, slowly, painfully.

His temple felt like it was split open, throbbing like a tribal drum, his veins coursing with flaming spikes of agony. He moaned, unable to focus his eyes.

"You're coming around, I see." A familiar voice, he thought.

Cindy.

"That wasn't nice, you know. What were you trying to do with that knife? Help me slice cheese for the wine?"

The laughter was low, humorous.

"I guess I just don't know you that well yet. Can you see me? Sorry about that whack on the head."

Martin noticed a glare of light, from the side. He felt something soft under him, a bed. He was looking up at the ceiling, most likely Cindy's bedroom.

"You know, call me gullible, but I really believe you didn't want to hurt me. Am I right?"

"Yeah." Martin rasped out the words, dry and toneless from his barren lips.

"I thought so. I do like you, Martin. Actually, I would like to get this little episode behind us, and forgive you."

"Yes, I'm sorry." He didn't know what else to say.

"You're forgiven. Forgive and forget, like they say. Do you forgive me too, for hurting you?"

"Yes." His voice was stronger, and for the first time in a while, it contained another quality.

Honesty.

There was light at the end of his shrouded tunnel, and he saw how close to the precipice the obsession had dragged him. Martin thought that now it might be possible to overcome the darkness.

"I'm so glad, really. Are you trying to get up?"

Martin lifted his head, sending new waves of pain through hid bruised nerve endings. He was unable to get out of bed.

"That's all right, don't bother. You're just fine where you are. Relax."

His vision was clearing. Cindy stood next to the bed, and in the background he heard a scratching noise.

"It makes me feel a lot better, knowing that you forgive me. It would be tough to live with it otherwise."

Martin craned his neck upward as the noise became louder. It sounded like the whole room was alive.

"I'm going to leave the bedroom, but I'll be right outside, watching. I didn't want to tell you earlier, but I have the strangest fetish, you see."

Cindy walked towards the closet, opening it a crack, as the noise grew in intensity.

"It has to do with rats. I can't explain it, but just seeing them crawling all over men drives me wild."

Martin tried to leave, but realized that his arms and legs were held down by tight straps. He started to scream. She quickly went out, slamming the door behind her.

"You can't see it, but I have a peep hole, and I can watch from here."

The closet door was pushed open, and hordes of rodents scrambled madly into the bedroom.

"And one more thing, Martin. Did I tell you, there's something else about the rats…"

Martin watched the first of the bodies climb onto the bed. Cruel ravenous eyes glared at him hungrily, one already creeping onto his leg, biting into the exposed flesh of his thigh. He shuddered.

"Not like this," he whimpered, the desire for pain and blood a thing of the past.

Cindy giggled outside the door.

"They're starving."

Favors
by
Megan Powell

"Can you do me a favor?"

I rolled my eyes. Fortunately my brother couldn't make a show of being offended by something he couldn't see. "What sort of favor?"

"Well, my car's been stolen..."

"Then call the police."

"You find lost things," Ekundayo said, as if I should perhaps be flattered that he'd called me.

"Not usually stolen vehicles. Unless you know who stole it...?"

"No."

"Well, there you go," I said happily. "You've got better odds if you call the police."

"Why should they give a shit about a nine year old Accord?"

I almost said "Because they're paid to give a shit," but refrained. I awarded myself some good brother points, and spent them immediately: "Maybe this is a sign. Maybe you're not meant to have the car."

Since he started grad school, Ekundayo's made a show of interest in the otherworldly. Oddly enough, he seemed not to have considered the possibility of divine intervention in his own life. "Look," he snapped. "I'm not asking you to drop everything. I'm just asking if you can keep an eye out for it."

"Fine, okay. I'll keep an eye out for it."

I assumed that would be the end of it. A city filled with millions of people is also filled with a lot of cars. I figured that anyone who stole an Accord had probably taken it to his friendly neighborhood chop shop. So I was rather surprised a couple of days later when I saw the car parked two blocks from my office.

My girlfriend was out of town visiting a sick aunt. In her absence I'd been working later, gathering photographic evidence of adultery, so it was after ten when I saw the car. It was tucked down a little alley, the sort directors love to use for chase scenes with the car scraping the walls and shooting sparks. If it wasn't for the shadows, I might have walked past it. Ekundayo's rear driver side door had acquired a sizeable dent— he swore someone hit the car in a parking lot—and I recognized that first.

In the interests of playing the good brother (or perhaps one-upmanship, should the opportunity present itself), I'd written down the VIN and license numbers and had been carrying them around. The license plate matched. I approached the car carefully, in the spirit of common sense rather than specific fear of lurking car thieves. No one was sitting in the car and externally at least it seemed to be in good shape. The windows were intact and the front door was unlocked. I took advantage of the opportunity to check the VIN number.

If the thief hadn't taken the car to a chop shop, then it had probably been used in the commission of a crime. That meant I was sitting in Evidence, but I didn't feel particularly uneasy. Since the criminals in question hadn't even bothered switching license plates, I assumed they had dumped the car before getting too attached to it.

I exited the Evidence and pulled out my cell phone, but I didn't dial. It occurred to me that I hadn't looked in the trunk, and I had a really bad feeling about doing so. It was ridiculous, of course. I'd seen too many movies. I went ahead and popped the trunk. By checking, I was either being mature (thoroughly examining the vehicle) or childish (looking for the boogeyman). I reached the trunk before I could decide which applied, and at that point the debate was moot.

There was a dead man in the trunk.

I just stared at him for a few seconds. Seeing dead bodies is not a daily occurrence. For that matter, I don't normally find living people sitting in the trunks of cars. So I just stood there until my brain deigned to process the information coming from my eyes.

This particular dead man had a small, round hole in the middle of his forehead. I didn't recognize him, and if I'd just passed him on the street I probably wouldn't have remembered much about him. Dark skin, tattoo, jeans, okay shoes, worn shirt—maybe an old favorite. It was very strange to think of the dead man having a favorite shirt, but I preferred looking at the shirt rather than the glassy eyes.

I knew he was dead, but I always hate the part in movies when someone turns their back on the apparently dead bad guy and is then shocked when he turns out not to be dead. How much effort does it take to check a pulse? Looking at the dead man in the trunk, I had a little more sympathy for the dumb characters in movies. I really didn't want to touch him. But I reached in, decided that the wrist was moderately less disgusting than the neck, and held my fingers against the cold skin long enough to confirm that there was no pulse.

I turned away from the trunk and, using my untainted left hand, pulled out my cell phone again. I stared at it for a few seconds. This wasn't just a case of a stolen vehicle; there was a dead man in the trunk. Clearly I should call the police. But it also dawned on me that it was quite a coincidence that the car had been dumped so close to my office. What if the choice of cars had been intentional?

I decided that being a good brother took priority over being a good citizen; the police could wait. But before I hit the speed dial I heard a noise behind me and turned.

The dead man in the trunk was now standing next to the car. He didn't seem any less dead, aside from the increased mobility. I was significantly less mobile, and gaped as he swung at me.

I came to flat on my back, wondering why I was lying in an alley. Clearly I couldn't have been knocked out by a dead man.

The brain's powers of recovery are, unfortunately, quite remarkable, so within a few seconds I'd scrambled to my feet. The trunk was empty and the dead man was nowhere in sight. I didn't find that particularly encouraging. If a dead man could get up and walk around, I saw no reason why he couldn't also turn invisible, teleport, fly or use any number of other superpowers.

I made haste to my office and locked myself in, trying to take comfort from being on my own turf. Calling the police was no longer an option. I tried to entertain myself with the thought of how such a report would read, but utterly failed to distract myself from a very strong desire to take a shower. Being hit by a dead man's fist seemed impossibly gross. I'm generally a slob, but I border on obsessive-compulsive when it comes to a select number of things, and it seemed that contact with dead human flesh could be added to the list somewhere between silverfish and lumpy milk.

I picked up the phone—I could always incinerate it later—and called Ekundayo. "It's me," I said to the answering machine. "Pick up the damn phone—"

"Hey," he said. "What's wrong?"

And here I thought I'd managed a non-hysterical tone. "What the hell is going on?"

"You called me—"

"I just got punched out by a dead guy. What's going on?"

"Are you all right?"

"*No,* I'm not all right!"

"Iyapo, calm down."

I took a deep breath. "I'm as calm as possible, under the circumstances."

"Okay. Are you hurt?"

"No."

"Where are you?"

"I'm in my office. Two blocks from your car, which until recently contained a dead man."

"Okay, yeah, I got that part. Are you on your cell?"

"Dropped it outside." Maybe the dead man was running up charges.

"Okay, I'll call you back at your main number. Give me five minutes."

"What the hell is going on?"

"I don't know for sure," he said in a tone of voice that indicated he had a pretty good idea. "But I think I probably don't want to be in my apartment right now, and if you don't currently have any visitors your office seems like an okay place to be."

And then the bastard hung up, leaving me to imagine all the improbable spaces dead men could hide. I did make use of the lava soap in the bathroom, but even after rubbing my skin raw I couldn't forget the feel of cold dead flesh.

I jumped when the phone rang. Picking up the receiver, I realized that the dead man cooties had just transferred back to me.

"It's me," Ekundayo said. "I'm on my way over."

"Okay. What's your best guess for what's happening?"

A deep breath. He was either in a taxi or on public transportation, neither of which lent themselves to private conversations. Of course, Ekundayo's always taken a certain amount of pleasure in being publicly unconventional. "I'm sort of unpopular with some people right now."

"Yeah, like me. More information, please."

"What did he look like?"

"Aside from dead?" I bit my tongue. It was possible he'd known the guy. "Mid-twenties, medium build…"

"Tattoos?"

"Something on the arm. I didn't look that closely. He was wearing jeans and a purple shirt—"

"Yeah. Damn. Okay, I think I know who he is. Was."

"A friend?" I prepared to dispense sympathy.

"Acquaintance. I was doing some research…"

Oh, shit, I thought. Ekundayo's idea of research usually involves poking things with sticks to see if they bite. It's a good thing his interests run to the occult rather than nuclear physics.

"You'll probably find it difficult to believe," he continued in preachy-mode, "but there's some weird shit out there."

"More things in heaven and earth. Yeah, I know."

He seemed a little put out. "Okay. Well, there's this guy who's got an interesting take on Voudun."

Terrific. But not surprising. "So I can officially start saying 'zombie,' then?"

"Yeeess…"

I sensed a thesis in that syllable. "Am I correct in assuming that the dead man is walking around because of something this guy did?"

"Yes. But it's not authentic Voudun at all," Ekundayo said. I had a feeling that the inauthenticity, rather than the animated corpse, offended his sensibilities.

"Okay. So we've got an inauthentic zombie walking around—"

"Don't mock me, all right? I'm trying to explain this."

I took a deep breath. "Let's ignore the weird shit for a second. Somebody shot the guy."

"Well, they don't subscribe to the drug theory."

I waited as patiently as possible.

"One of the theories about authentic zombies is that they're living people in a drugged state," Ekundayo said after it became clear I wasn't going to take the bait. "Tetrodotoxin's been suggested as giving the appearance of death—"

"He had no pulse."

"But if you buy into the drug theory—"

"Which neither you, I nor the hougan in question do, apparently."

"More of a bokor, really," Ekundayo said. "His stuff's pretty black. Though I'm reluctant even to use that term, since he diverges so far from mainstream Voudun."

"Can you do me a favor and drop the authenticity tangent?" I asked. "Just be glad I'm the sort of enlightened person who doesn't start laughing when you say things like 'mainstream Voudun.'"

"All right," he sighed. "Anyway, I heard about this bokor, and I wanted to interview him but he wasn't interested. One of his associates was."

"The guy in the trunk."

"The guy in the trunk."

"Who's currently wandering around aimlessly."

"Not aimlessly. He's probably headed for my apartment. I'm here," he added, and broke the connection. A moment later he unlocked the door, reminding me that I'd meant to confiscate his keys weeks ago.

"So the bokor kills his associate and sics him on you," I said. "Why bother with the car? And why leave him two blocks from my office and not outside your building?"

Ekundayo shrugged and dumped a bag and an armload of books and notepads on my desk. I plunked myself back down in my comfy chair before he could think about it, and left him with a choice of client chairs. "I'm not completely careless. I watch out for weird shit, especially the black stuff. I'd have tried to neutralize the zombie. Did you touch him?"

"Yes."

Ekundayo nodded wisely. "That was probably what triggered it. You shouldn't touch things—"

"I was looking for a pulse," I grated. "And until I opened the trunk I thought we were just talking about a stolen vehicle."

He had the grace to look sheepish. "I didn't think it was related. It's a little prosaic when you think about it. Stealing cars, I mean. Not to mention shooting people." He bent down over the books. "This isn't exactly a well-documented phenomena—"

I swatted the back of his head, and got an "Ow!" that was equal parts outrage and whine. "What was that for?"

"You mean aside from the zombie? How about sticking *gris-gris* in my computer?"

"Oh." The sheepish look again. "But it did work…"

"It certainly stank up my office," I said. "What were you thinking, getting involved with inauthentic psychotic bokors?" Not that I'm one to cast stones on the matter of undesirable business associates, but for tonight at least I felt like I held the moral high ground.

"He didn't seem psychotic."

I swatted him again, and this time he was smart enough to push his chair out of easy reach. "I interview lots of people," he pouted.

"The *gris-gris* was a lab project, not an interview. What other shit are you into?"

A shrug. "Enough that I think I know how the zombie was animated, and how to stop it. Theoretically."

Lovely. "Worst comes to worst, we can always go for the traditional torch-bearing mob."

Ekundayo frowned. The frown deepened when I pulled the gun out of my drawer. "That won't work."

"I'm not planning on trying to kill it again, just slow it down." The zombie seemed dependent on bones and tendons and muscles for its mobility, and I was pretty confident about my aim.

"I thought you hate guns."

"I do. But I hate the idea of my idiot brother getting killed by a psycho bokor's zombie even more."

"I can do this," he told me, flipping through a notebook filled with his tight scrawl. I'd have had an easier time reading Sanskrit.

I glanced at the phone. I could probably call in a couple of favors. It wasn't the sort of thing I wanted to do, and there wasn't any guarantee that it would work...but if the alternative was trusting in Ekundayo's abilities...

"I said I can do this," he repeated, and I wondered if he was teaching himself telepathy as well.

"All right," I said without much conviction. "How about a name?"

"Name?"

"The psycho bokor?"

"Jean-Claude Balan-Gaubert is his legal name, so far as I know. Says he's Haitian."

"I thought you were studying the American South." I booted up the computer, and wished he'd thought to call me when all he wanted was a background check.

"I got distracted by a shiny thing."

"A shiny thing?"

"Yeah. He seemed interesting, and not completely unrelated to what I was working on."

Of course not. An inauthentic modern-day bokor was exactly like Marie Laveau.

"Why is Ogun wearing a fedora?" Ekundayo frowned at the partially obscured statue he'd given me as an office-warming present.

"Because it was a gift from my girlfriend and deserves to be prominently displayed." I wished Lota was in town. I could be having sex at this very moment, rather than sitting around with my idiot brother waiting for a zombie to show up. "What's our time frame?"

He shrugged. "If I'm right, Balan-Gaubert's not directly controlling the zombie. It's more like he programmed it. So it'll probably just keep going till it finds me, sort of like the Terminator. Putrification may become an issue eventually; I'm not sure."

I did not take heart, especially since it would be just like Ekundayo to turn this into a lab project rather than a monster hunt. "Do you remember the body count in that movie?"

"Huh? Oh, yeah. No. It knows who I am. He'd have given it something to identify me, like a bloodhound. It won't be interested in anyone else. It didn't hurt you. Not seriously, anyway."

Since the thing had already been on the loose for a while, I decided I'd feel better if I believed him. The computer blue-screened, perhaps trying to tell me something. "For somebody being stalked by a zombie, you're taking this pretty well."

Ekundayo shrugged. "Comes with the territory. Hah!" He grinned. "Okay, I can do this."

I spread my hands. "It's your show. Just tell me what to do."

He sat down in the center of the floor, pulled a box of flour out of his bag and sprinkled a handful on the floor. I didn't recognize the pattern he drew, but it was clearly not random. "Don't go blabbing about this tomorrow."

Ekundayo does not typically understand the meaning of the word "secret." "I don't like the sound of that."

"I'm just calling in a favor," he said.

"I *really* don't like the sound of that. There are favors, and then there are *favors*..."

"I just want to undo the magic someone else worked. That's not such a big deal, and it's right-handed." He shrugged and pulled a rattle out of the bag. "Not black magic. Nothing like the favors *he* called in." Then he closed his eyes and started shaking the rattle and chanting. His lips moved, but I couldn't make out the words. I had a feeling they weren't English anyway.

Ekundayo's eyes snapped open, but it wasn't Ekundayo looking out. I'd never seen anyone ridden by a loa, and I'd always assumed that it was bullshit, either an outright hoax or hysterical enthusiasm. But this wasn't a hoax. Someone—something—else was in control of my brother's body, swaying on the floor.

In another room, glass broke. I remembered the fire escape outside the bathroom window and reached for my gun. But whoever was in my brother's body smiled and shook his head. I heard no further sounds, save the humming coming from Ekundayo's throat, and even that began to trail off. His limbs moved spasmodically, though with a certain grace. The motions slowed as the humming grew fainter.

Sticking the dismount, I thought irreverently, and wondered if I should have taken the fedora off Ogun before Ekundayo invited a loa into my office.

Steps sounded on the stairs, then in the hall. I had a chance to wonder who else was in the building at this time of night, and hope that they didn't hear our little freakshow. I realized that was an exceedingly optimistic line of thinking about half a second before Balan-Gaubert burst in.

It couldn't have been anyone else. I'd never consciously imagined what a psychotic bokor might look like, but if I had he'd have fit the bill: shocking contrasts, white hair and eyes and teeth against dark skin, bright metal knife in one hand, dark metal gun in the other. A too-expressive face split into a grin at the sight of Ekundayo sprawled on the floor. I, like the absent zombie, seemed to be a non-entity.

There are moments when time seems to slow down, and this was one of them. Balan-Gaubert regarded Ekundayo, twitching and muttering on the floor. "I didn't think you had it in you," he said, still grinning. He seemed to have forgotten the gun, but not the knife. Ekundayo—or possibly the loa—said something. I couldn't tell whether it was directed to Balan-Gaubert or someone on a different plane of existence.

I had time to think about favors, time to reach for my gun. Balan-Gaubert had time to realize that there was someone else in the room. And then I fired, aiming for center mass, and kept firing.

The echo of the last shot faded and Balan-Gaubert fell to the floor. It went quiet after that. Quiet enough that I could hear Ekundayo's sub-vocal mutterings, and Balan-Gaubert's final labored breaths. I'd heard phrases like "sucking chest wound" before, but I'd never really thought about the sounds.

Eventually I realized I didn't need to keep holding my gun and dropped it on the desk. Ekundayo's mutterings turned to loud inhalations, maybe hyperventilation. No, I realized, that was me.

"Shit," Ekundayo said, and sat up.

I lurched for the bathroom. I remembered the smashed window before I opened the door, so I wasn't surprised to see the erstwhile zombie lying on the floor like a broken doll. I waited for a couple minutes, until the urge to vomit or burst into tears passed. When I came out of the bathroom, the man I'd killed was still lying on the floor. Ekundayo, propped up against my desk, looked exhausted.

"You didn't need—" he began. "I could have—"

I slid to the floor. "Called in another favor?"

He shrugged.

"That's a lot worse than undoing somebody's magic," I said. "That's got to be a pretty big favor." Not to mention left-handed. Balan-Gaubert had killed at least one man, and I had no doubt that he would have killed two more tonight. But murder had to be a left-handed thing, regardless of circumstances.

"Yeah," Ekundayo said softly. "A pretty big favor."

"Better this way. More straightforward," I shivered. "Nothing owed that you maybe won't be able to repay."

We couldn't sit in my office all night, staring at one dead man with another in the bathroom. Well, maybe we could, but we really shouldn't. I needed to pick up the phone, but my desk seemed awfully far away.

"The zombie's dead again," I added.

It was time to think of practicalities. We just needed to avoid mentioning the zombie part, and let the police draw their own conclusions about that killing. The rest really was straightforward. Balan-Gaubert was a poster boy for justifiable homicide: waving a knife and a gun, hands and clothes presumably coated in the gunshot residue from earlier in the day...I fought the urge to run back into the bathroom and wash my hands.

"Jean-Jacques," Ekundayo said listlessly. "His name was Jean-Jacques."

Jean-Jacques had died of a bullet wound sometime earlier today. He'd never been in the bathroom; that thing was just meat. I shivered again.

"What you did was..." I began, and then gave up. "I didn't think you could do that."

"Wasn't me," Ekundayo shrugged. "None of it was me."

I almost told him that seemed like a pretty good deal, but I bit my tongue.

Megan Powell

Megan Powell lives in suburban Philadelphia with one husband, two cats and four-point-five computers. Her short fiction has appeared in various magazines and anthologies, including *The Eternal Night*, *Orchard Press Mysteries*, *Ideomancer*, *SDO Detective*, *Here & Now*, *Underworlds*, *Historical Hardboiled*, *Femmes de la Brume* and *Bullet Points*. Her fantasy novel *Vocation* is available from Double Dragon eBooks and her paranormal romance *Waxing* is forthcoming from Zumaya Publications. Megan's work as an editor includes the webzines *Fables* and *Shred of Evidence*, as well as anthologies forthcoming from Cyber-Pulp and Double Dragon. She maintains a homepage at www.meganpowell.net.

Phantom Verdict

by

Steve Redwood

Ah! Que du moins, loin des baisers et des combats,
Quelque chose demeure un peu sur la montagne,
…Car qu'est-ce qui nous accompagne,
Et vraiment, quand la mort viendra, que reste-t-il?
—Verlaine

The knife in my hand clearly announces my intention, and what he has become stares up at me, fearful and uncomprehending, thin white fingers feebly clutching the sheets like asparagus sliding over the rim of a tin. Death has refused to issue a prospectus, to enable him to make adequate provision for his own eternity, so he hangs on, and leaves me no choice.

That other girl so long ago, the one who got away, the one I should have learned from. I spotted her in the college bar once. Hair that swirled dervish-like across her face in a chaotic dance of life, and eyes that flashed with the glint of a magpie's wing. Too much life: he flinched away—even then—scuttled away to safety like a cockroach when the light is suddenly turned on. When she lost patience, and soared away on the thermals of her own vitality, I foolishly picked up what I thought were the pieces, and patiently set myself to weld them together again.

His breathing is ragged, jerky, like the last drop of greasy water being sucked down the plughole. The fear that has always been there, hiding under the guise of erudition, civility, respectability, is now engulfing him. An old Financial Times is still on the bedside table; I want to wave it in front of him, let the forecasts and figures that he worshipped shower down on him and suffocate him with their merciless banality, but I realise he has to die a different way, so that the other may live again.

I was never very pretty. Sensitive boys would tell me what wonderful blue eyes I had, relieved to find an honest compliment. Others simply lunged straight for my over-

developed breasts. Oh yes, I see now why he chose me: safety—who would bother to attack a gold prospector who came back only with silt and mud? And yet...and yet, he was different. Under his touch, my breasts felt as delicate as bluebells, as fragile as a hint of honeysuckle. But those early embraces were the clutches of a promise doomed to wither, and the decades have since shuffled out of their tombs to scatter dry bones over the memories.

I often dreamed that the young man of those days simply stumbled into another dimension, that he was there waiting for me.

No more waiting.

The rain is thrashing against the window, anxious to burst in and flush away the final droppings and husks of our lives. The rasping of his breathing is the sound of someone cracking open walnuts. Is that what his heart will look like, inside? Only smaller, more wrinkled? Will his ceasing to breathe really change anything for him? Is lack of all movement really so much different from every movement planned, analysed, nervously given permission?

I now know that J. Alfred Prufrock never did finally dare to eat his peach.

But I, I will dare for him. For us.

We were walking through a park one afternoon and saw a couple of boys, no more than thirteen or fourteen years old, pushing and tormenting an old black woman on a bench. They looked round when they noticed us, and tensed as if to flee. But something told them the truth that I had yet to learn, and they casually turned their backs on us, and spat at the old woman. He walked on, dragging me protesting with him, explaining how it was wise not to interfere in these cases. Would only have made things worse for the woman, in the long run. I was in love with his learning, his knowledge, his reasonableness, so I persuaded myself to believe him. But that night I dreamed the old woman's body was hanging from the ceiling like a halalled sheep, her blood dripping between us and creating a torrent that snatched him away from me.

I foolishly ignored the Cassandra within me.

It is surprisingly easy. I look into his terrified eyes, and then I stab the knife down into his sunken chest—not too far, if he dies too quickly all is lost—and then twist to make a space for the other to escape. All I am doing is snapping a lock, and his cries of agony are to me only the welcome screech of dungeon bolts being drawn back.

He became a university lecturer, specialising—what else?—in ancient history, where the clash of armies was distant enough to be unreal, the echoes of pain deadened by time, the smell of blood long gone. I watched him shadowshuffle through the lives of the dead, while in between what was left meticulously filled in insurance and tax forms—with absolute honesty, because dishonesty might bring retribution—and fretted over pension funds, and low-risk stocks and shares, and minute scratches on the bonnet of his safety-featured Volvo, and the right amount of red wine to reduce the risk of a heart attack, and the shocking manners of his students as they slurped noisily at life.

A life without a single misdemeanour, a single crime. Except that of denying life itself.

'A man needs a little madness', said Zorba the Greek, 'or else he never dares cut the rope and be free.' In the film, at this point the music of Mikis Theodorakis cuts in with a beautiful violin melody like the rising sun.

In the film.

But I have cut the rope for him and he will be free and the music will cut in again and I—and he—will dance again.

There! There he is! Like the ectoplasm you see in horror films. Squeezing through the hole I have made, raising himself, rearing up like a male orgasm filmed in slow motion. A tiny face, an unformed pinched face, almost that of a foetus. The features are glowing, evanescent, inchoate. The head is twisting from side to side, stretching, trying to drag its body after it, but it seems trapped in the old man's chest, as if invisible hands are grasping it, holding it back.

Of course! He will not let go, even now! He is too afraid of the fury of what he might have been.

We didn't have children, though we did occasionally have sex, since that's what respectable couples are supposed to do. His well-behaved penis would politely doff its cap and slide in and out of me like a metronome, and he always seemed slightly ashamed after orgasm and quickly withdrew, though on good nights he would stay there beside me for all of a minute, before, with a kind of crabwise furtive moment, slipping out of bed and going to wash himself. All those nasty germs we keep inside our vaginas were something beyond his control, chaotic, something to be avoided.

The tiny eyes turn towards me. What is the colour of non-being? What is the colour of that which never was?

"Where have you been all this time?" I whisper.

And the answer comes back like the wind strumming a broken lute on lonely Andean peaks, as the condor silently circles. *Aborted, aborted, aborted...*

The head is still swaying from side to side, straining, and finally a wispy, insubstantial body begins to emerge, but not completely, as if it is still stuck in slime. In his final weakness, it has found the strength to try to resurrect itself, to clamber out of him into existence, but what he has become will not let go so easily.

The eyes look at me, and in their emptiness I am able to see clearly the plea for help, and perhaps for vengeance, too—vengeance for never having been allowed to live.

In a frenzy of blighted love and longing, I stab and twist, frantically clearing away the debris of bone and flesh. The glow of the tiny face is now stained by spurting blood. But no matter, he is free, and he sways towards me, gazing at last into my own soul, searching for his companion of so long ago. I rip open my dress, baring my now withered neglected breasts to him, I feel him beginning to enter me, I am preparing to go with him, wherever the journey—and then he gives a moan of despair and recoils from me and starts to dissipate...

And I know at once that he cannot forgive me for having accepted his own incarceration, the treacherous veneer of all those years, the gaudy replacements and trappings of respectability I had been offered. *"I had no choice, I did it for you, I had no choice!"* But I know that this is the eternal lie, must always be a lie, as I scream in utter despair, throw myself forward, my hands reaching out, to catch and hold the meaning of this death, but he is withdrawing back, back, into his jailer's body, with nowhere to escape to. At the end, there is just the naked face again, twisted with grief, and then that too begins to disappear, and all that remains is a mutilated old man's body.

And my own tears looming larger and larger until I drown in them.

Steve Redwood

Steve Redwood has had around 50 short stories published, including an Honourable Mention in *Year's Best Fantasy and Horror*. A humorous fantasy novel, *Fisher of Devils*, has recently been published by Prime Books, and a second science-fiction novel is under consideration. His email address is stevejredwood@hotmail.com.

Twilight Gone
by
Len Rely

Eight men in three cars are traveling a country road, the details of their lives drowned in alcohol. Their identities smeared in the ink of an obituary now taking shape, the clues of how this all came about lost to memory. Look at this doomed motorcade and try to see how it all becomes clear. Like a still from an old movie reel the first car is a microcosm of life. Distant streetlamps are reflected in a procession down its black surface, its occupants laughing over wishful thoughts of women who don't exist. One man is hoping for a fight, another started babbling philosophy the moment a bottle touched his lips, but they are all basically the same except for the small one with the open collar crouched in the back seat. He knows something no one else does, but he may be too drunk to recall. Look into his gleaming eye and see what he has in store for them. His world is a realm that leaves twilight to the half-believers and goes directly into the abyss.

The first vehicle was a black Volvo hardtop with a shiny new coat of wax. The second was a station wagon that almost dragged its belly along the ground and the third was a pickup. None of the motorists could remember exactly when and where they had started from on this fine October 31st. There seemed to be a general notion about barhopping on this particular night being a tradition from someone's lost fraternity days, but none of them had actually done it before nor could they point out the originator of the idea. The first car had the most passengers, including the small man, the one who didn't speak, who looked like he had slept in his clothes more than once.

They pulled into a tavern with an Italian name in red lights. The group was too large to sit at the bar so with a grumble from the meanest one they took a couple of tables in burgundy leather booths. The lights were low and liquor was poured without measure.

The more the philosopher drank the more he talked, but no one heard him. The bully of the group was a fat man with a beet-red face and hair cut so short it's a wonder his scalp wasn't damaged. He glared from face to face with one eye, looking for his next victim, his motive for drinking almost solely to start an argument. He had consumed an enormous amount of alcohol already. When the philosopher's ranting caught the attention of this man he grew immediately quiet and moved to the corner of the bar to sit by himself.

All remnants of conversation had died. Eyes were fixed only upon their glasses except for the small man who had not yet spoken. He cringed in the shadows at the back of the booth and the serving girl had not even noticed him. He sat on the edge of the leather cushion like a child in a child's suit worn from neglect. His chin was nestled into his open collar as he watched the others.

The fat man simply held his bottle and stared into space as if he had forgotten how to lift it to his mouth. He faced the small man's direction for several minutes until he looked as if he had just regained consciousness from a nightmare and remembered where he was.

"Who are you!" his untempered voice broke the silence.

The others looked up from their drinks. The nameless stranger said nothing.

"I want to know who you are!" the drunkard declared loudly across the table.

They all waited for the small man to respond. He opened his mouth timidly as if to speak, and something so quiet came out that only the one closest to him could make it out.

"What?" the fat man demanded. "What did you say?"

The stranger just blinked and looked at the floor. The bully could have knocked him down with just the wind from his lungs.

"What did he say?" another one asked the man sitting next to him. This man raised his eyebrows and took a swig.

"He said 'I've done it before and I'll do it again, you can't stop me, I'm the Halloween man.'"

There were looks of stupefaction for about five seconds until the fat man burst into a fit of laughter so raucous it looked like his head would explode. He stared into the little man's pale face, unable to stop himself, reddened eyes bulging. He laughed so hard he began to choke. The tavern had nearly emptied from the noise.

"Seriously, what is his name?" the philosopher commented from the bar. "I'd like to know since it was his idea to go out in the first place."

"Was it?" someone asked as they looked at each other, trying to remember. "Yes it was you!"

"The first time I saw you..." one of them recollected, "was at Ratman's beer party back in June. I remember because you had on the same clothes you're wearing now!"

"I only knew him because I picked him up hitchhiking sometime in March," Ratman stated. "He never told me about himself."

"Well, I've never seen him until tonight," another replied, several heads nodding in agreement.

"So we're all here because of some weirdo and no one knows him?" the philosopher attempted to reason.

The fat man scooted closer to their quiet host and put a massive hand around his shoulder, squeezing him.

"He already told you who he is!" he boasted. "Didn't you hear? He's the Halloween man!"

He slapped the little man on the back, almost breaking his nose on the table. The fat man's objective had changed. This creature was no source of sport in a fight but had become a plaything. A curiosity to be toyed with.

"Go on, tell us again!" the bully insisted, giving him a friendly shake.

"I've done it before...and I'll do it again," the strange man said weakly.

The fat man thumped his knee and grinned.

"Why don't you have a drink?" he asked abruptly, snapping his fingers for the serving girl.

The Halloween man shook his head vigorously. He needed to be in control tonight and had never been able to stand even a drop of alcohol. A glass was passed in his direction as his cohorts encouraged him. He squirmed and attempted to protest but was drowned in their voices. Finally there was no choice left to him as the fat man placed a hand behind his head and his mouth was pushed into the gurgling liquid to the sound of their chanting.

He choked it down, spitting violently and then held the glass to his lips by himself to appease his tormentors. They were revolting in the pleasure they derived from this. He leaned back with a sickening feeling and waited for the world to melt. Now that the drunkards were appeased he was no longer the center of attention. The tavern would be closing soon but no one was sober enough to think of looking at the time.

A curious change in the small man's expression was taking place. His eyes narrowed from timid moons to sly crevices. He sat upright with a glassy look as if he knew some terrible secret. Hot air from the liquor was coming out of his nostrils and the cauldron of worms in his stomach was suddenly quiet as if all feeling had been turned off like a switch in his brain. His small mouth widened into a grin.

His right hand went immediately to his pocket under the table and pulled out the pistol slowly by the handle. No one noticed as he held it trembling in the shadows next to his thigh. If he could not regain control he would commit the act prematurely. He tried to think of something, anything that would steady him until the time was right, and this being All Hallow's Eve, a morbid memory from his childhood came to mind. His eyes widened in recollection and he slowly returned the gun to its place.

He laughed softly through his teeth and the others looked at him.

"What's wrong with you?" one of them asked directly into his glass with a muffled hiss.

"I think he's going to say something."

This revived a new bout of semi-coherent interest voiced across the table with the gesturing of beers. At this level of drunkenness anything could set off a unanimous agreement or fight on any subject.

"There was a haunted house..." the drink loosened the strange man's tongue but he still had little chance of being heard.

"Let him speak," the philosopher said, but as usual no one paid attention to him.

Other conversations had already started, mostly spurned from whatever vile thoughts the drinker had just been living even if no one was really listening. The fat man's eyes rolled back into his head.

"Let him talk!!" he bellowed with unregulated volume that silenced the group as if someone had threatened his best friend. He stood up, almost knocking the table over, and grabbed the nearest speaker by the collar. All was quiet as the bartender watched them warily. The bully released his fellow drunkard and returned to his seat, looking down as if he had forgotten what he just said. The Halloween man finally opened his mouth.

"There was a haunted house near here when I was a kid," he said.

"There's your answer!" the fat man regaled loudly, slapping the table with his palm. "A ghost story!"

The apparent reason for their assembly on this night having been revealed, the cohorts grinned and leaned back in their seats to listen.

"And to get there you had to drive through a haunted forest," the small man continued. "The last quarter-mile of highway beginning at the last overpass was shrouded in mist. The sky was purple and the branches of trees would reach out to grab you. You could see owls and vultures with red eyes staring at you."

"Get to the part where you pull the sheet off and it's a hooker," Ratman interrupted, eager for the punch line.

"I think he means it was a *professional* haunted house, for kids," the philosopher explained. "And the last stretch of road was covered with some kind of material like a tunnel, with electrical frights and artificial light and fog."

The Halloween man nodded.

"The house itself had a different ghoul or witch in every room," he went on. "The yard was filled with carnival activities. Now all of this was thrilling to a child but as I grew older I learned the real story behind the place. You see, it had to be maintained by real people who lived there year-round, and anyone who can live and labor in a Halloween-looking mansion as a matter of business, isolated from the world for years has got to be strange. The house was owned by an eccentric old woman. After she died I heard she was a gypsy who had run from the law years ago. In the time I went there she hired a half-dumb man with a knot on his back as groundskeeper, I guess because she couldn't get anyone else."

He now had the group's undivided attention.

"When I was twelve I ran away from home because I had killed a dog. I ran through the woods until I reached the haunted property. It was strange to see the place at noon in the middle of summer when all the props were gone. In a way it was more frightening than it had ever been before. To a rapidly changing youth who had just learned to kill it was another forbidden curiosity about the real world. The hunchback was working in the field and I hid behind the shed so he wouldn't see me. But I knocked over some rusty equipment trying to get a better look, and the noise brought him running. When he went around one side I would go around the other. I was fast enough to keep him busy this way but he knew someone was there and I knew there was no way to avoid him forever. I could see him leering at me through the cracks as he ambled like a gorilla and bared his gums. Finally I took off running and a loud noise ripping through the air told me he had fired his rifle at me."

The small man looked afraid of something. The others were silent.

"I never went back there," he concluded.

"Does the place still exist?" the philosopher asked him.

He nodded, looking like he wanted to change the subject to something less reminiscent of childhood terrors.

"Well that was certainly worth coming out here and getting smashed," Ratman voiced his low standard, emptying the rest of a bottle down his gullet.

The tavern closed at eleven and the shoddy group was politely urged to move on. The night was far from over but they would have to take their business elsewhere. The men rose slowly and exited in single file, the fatigue of a stomach filled with swill making them quiet and their faces heavy. It was putting them to sleep like zombie soldiers on their way to some disjointed retreat.

Although he had consumed the least amount the small man seemed unable to control himself. From the moment he stood up it was as if all awareness had just drained out of his body and he had forgotten what he was talking about or why he had spent a year planning for this night. The more experienced guzzlers helped him to the door. If it wasn't for the story they probably wouldn't have remembered he was even there and left him behind, so it did serve his purpose. He was placed in the back seat of the black Volvo. As it pulled out he wasn't crouched with his narrow legs together like before, but wide-eyed with his mouth hanging open. He stared at the man sitting next to him and fell into him on a sharp turn only to be pushed back.

The cars stopped at a gas station where they picked up two six-packs to wash away the last of their troubles. Then they were back on the road, still having the sense to look for a place to stop before finishing off the booze. In a few minutes they were surrounded by deep woods, the country load leading them past the last sign into winding hollows with hairpin turns that threatened to cast the first car headlong into a ditch they were moving so fast.

This was a route normally taken by people on their way to hunt or camp, and even so there was so much acreage like this in the area only a tenth of it was used by men at any time of year. Of course there were locals, but their population tended to decrease, not increase, with time and many had died leaving empty shacks. The trees looked lifeless and skeletal in the insufficient light of the headlamps. The lurching was keeping the small man semi-alert, and the hair raised on the back of his neck, knowing that this was the closest he had been to the haunted mansion in a long time.

They came to a grassy lot surrounded by woods with a split rail fence on one side separating it from the pastureland beyond. This seemed as good a place as any to kill their livers, and when the Halloween man saw it he knew this would serve his intentions perfectly. The three vehicles parked and most of the men exited to relieve their bladders.

The sky was bright with a wide band of stars that cast a peculiar twilight you don't see in civilization. No one felt like lifting a finger to start a fire, or do anything else for that matter. The fat man stood reclining against the open door on the driver's side of the station wagon, bottle in hand. The man in the passenger seat was already asleep. A six-pack was sitting on the hood of the Volvo. Ratman was shirtless in the back leaning against the side of the pickup with his hat covering his face. The philosopher had walked over to the fence and pulled out a centerfold which he now held up in the moonlight. The strange man had wandered off by himself.

He stood facing the woods, his brain filled with unspoken discord and the pain of trying to stay focused long enough to remain steady. He could feel his senses failing one by one like bubbles bursting from that horrible liquid they had made him drink. His head felt swollen and it writhed like a den of serpents. He had to do it now or never.

The pistol was already in his hands where it had been the last few minutes without the others knowing. He held it out like something precious rather than a lethal weapon. He turned around to face the others. The philosopher was closest but the fat man had been watching him the whole time.

"What the hell is that?" he demanded abruptly.

This one would be the most trouble, fearless to the point of stupidity and recklessly dangerous. The Halloween man had entered his mode and said nothing in retribution to his tormentors, nor did revenge even enter his mind as he set his sights on the first of seven simple lambs awaiting the reaper.

"I've done it before and I'll do it again," he recited his immortal line.

Less than half of the men were alert enough to have any idea what was going on. For the first time the philosopher seemed to be at a loss for words. He turned toward the gunman, his mouth open.

"I don't understand," he said stupidly.

The fat man suddenly made a face that looked like his head was in a vice, throwing his bottle down which broke into fragments in the grass. He had had enough, of what no one could say, but he had had enough.

The Halloween man fired. The first shot hit the man in the stomach, immediately followed by another for good measure. The fat man was thrown backward into the open door, almost breaking its hinges, and in the same second rebounded forward landing facedown in the driver's seat with the door closing on his legs. The man sleeping on the passenger side sprang to life from the noise and the next shot went right through the windshield, killing him instantly with a lurch and a brief splash of red.

Ratman took off running for the woods. The shooter turned swiftly but there was no chance of getting a clear sight from this distance. He fired twice, enraged by this insult to his task, and missed his target by more than ten feet as the man disappeared into the shadow of the trees. The man reclining on the hood of the Volvo slipped off and the six-pack went crashing to the ground. A bullet skimmed off the black metal, leaving a long streak.

The Halloween man paused to reload. This wasn't going the way he intended. The remaining men, now fully coherent, watched in horror as their executioner slowly placed four rounds from his pocket into the chamber, the shaking of his hands making it almost impossible. The philosopher stood well in front of the others, his legs frozen. He was so close he could make out the shape of the bullets. The night was absolutely silent and the station wagon with the painted starburst on the windshield looked like it had been sitting like that for hours.

The killer didn't know how much longer he could hold it together. The pounding in his head made it impossible to count how many targets were left. Where one man crouched in the shadows he now thought he saw two, his vision turning to liquid. The philosopher looked like he was about to say something. The Halloween man wasn't finished when a body in the rear tried to make a break for it.

He fired two shots in the philosopher's direction who cried out like a child and turned rapidly to the side, clutching his face. One shot whizzed past him on the left and hit the fleeing man in the leg. The other passed on his right and missed completely. He cowered, his legs half-bent, taking frightened breaths.

For the first time tonight the Halloween man was visibly infuriated. He could not believe these mindless insignificant beings were spoiling his time-honored rite. He pointed his weapon in the air and fired as he spoke.

"No…" — BANG! — "…more…"— BANG! — "… mischief!" he shouted in a voice that was surprisingly powerful for a small man. He was wasting his shots. The philosopher could feel the heated flashes from the barrel. He tried to think of anything he could say that would delay or distract their bloodthirsty host.

"You said you've done it before and you'll do it again," he repeated in a trembling voice the words the strange man seemed to hold sacred.

The Halloween man lowered the pistol slightly and looked at him.

"You're a serial killer?" His closest victim finally put it together. "You kill only one night a year? You spend the whole year making friends so you can assemble them?"

The man nodded, holding his weapon in both hands to keep it steady.

"You don't have enough shots left to finish the job," the philosopher stated.

"I am aware of that!" the Halloween man barked, unable to control the pitch of his voice. "But one thing you must understand…"—his teeth dripped as he took a step closer—"…is that you are now in a *very* dangerous situation. I have nothing to spare on mercy. I have two of these left to ensure the four of you will never leave this field. You'll have to share, and that means someone is going to be in some serious pain."

He slowly made his way toward the middle of the group, the men staring at him with confused and fearful eyes. The man with the wounded leg was on his knees, bloodying the ground.

"I want you three to line up in front of me," the killer said. "Any man who doesn't obey in the next five seconds will be the first to die."

Figuring their chances were about even, two men bolted in separate directions. The gunman turned and fired, hitting one of them in the back; the other got away. The philosopher just stood there, his feet planted in the turf. He and the Halloween man looked at each other, both heaving.

The philosopher's face showed fear prolonged beyond the mercy of death. The thinking man had begun this night with too many thoughts to spare, purging them with drink, and now he found himself the victim saved for dead last, watching other men fall all around him. The predator was stretching out his execution like the alcohol had stretched his tongue, the ultimate torture for someone like him. Meanwhile the face of the killer was one of contempt and disbelief like a man whose buddies had drugged him into defacing his own religion. The simple act he had dreamt in perfection a thousand times had failed, and now he was nothing. He had always found it impossible to express anger, but there was no time for these thoughts now. He had fought the liquor as long as he could and now his brain was blackening.

His last victim was about to say something when he raised his weapon and put his final bullet in the philosopher's mouth. The man's head went back and then forward and his body crumpled into a heap. The gun fell from the killer's hand, which remained extended with the fingers curled upward as he stared at it, his only real moment of contemplation tonight. He was a child really who until now had never known blame.

The wounded man on his knees was beginning to wail. The woods were making sound again from the wind. The Halloween man looked around him. Some of the men had escaped, which meant he had to flee quickly, find a place to hide until his senses returned.

The police would comb the woods, the roads, everywhere. He had escaped the law enough times to know a place had to be special or none at all, and there was only one location nearby that he was familiar with. He was in no mind to relive the frights of his childhood, not tonight, but he took off running in the direction of the haunted mansion.

He followed the road for two miles, his blood pumping rotten fluid into his brain. He ambled like a gorilla, sometimes laughing, sometimes crying. He no longer had the ability to speak or think. He wasn't sure if he had just killed five men or just a dog. He only knew where he was headed. He gasped and whined like a child not caring if anyone heard him.

He reached the overpass where the haunted road began. Tumbling fog was tinted purple from the blacklights, the canvas horizon glowing crimson. He lumbered past red-eyed mechanical creatures and crooked tree limbs exactly as he remembered, cringing from their outstretched claws. His mind was completely destroyed. He stopped at the base of the hill on which the house stood.

It had been painted since he last saw it and the porch light shone on acres of green turf in place of the dusty fields from the drought days of his youth. The ground was no longer tilled but manicured like a park. The old barn was gone and there were children's' activity stations with glittered poster board. Sitting on the porch in a rocking chair at this unholy hour was the old caretaker, now senile and probably deaf, with a lantern at his feet and a shotgun in his hands.

The murderer stared warily at this man. Normally he wouldn't have expected him to still be alive, but since he was a child again it seemed fitting that the hunchback would be here. The Halloween man meandered with his fingers touching the grass around the slope of the hill toward the side of the house. In a way the sight of this place was the last straw, and he no longer knew who he was or what he had done.

He approached the carnival area where there were sufficient bales of hay stacked for a hiding place. They formed a semicircle around the front of a booth painted with images indicating a magic show. The Halloween man laughed out loud, then suddenly hushed and looked around. There were coins strewn about the ground at his feet. He dropped to his knees and began picking them up, grinning with insanity. More slipped from his fingers than made it into his pockets, making too much noise for someone trying to go unnoticed.

The caretaker picked up his lantern and stepped down from the porch, shotgun in hand. He walked in the direction of the trespasser, who stopped abruptly and stared at the approaching light source. The Halloween man shrunk against the ground. There was no way to know if the old man heard something or if he was just making the nightly rounds before going to bed. Time seemed to stand still as the flickering from behind the straw passed a weedy shadow and ignited its pointed tips. As soon as the man cleared the bales he would be seen.

The small, frightened killer had no time left. He retreated into the back yard, keeping as low as possible. He crossed the lawn and found himself in an area with no cover from the floodlights except for a single tree whose trunk cast a long black finger on the ground. Every blade of grass was two-tone and seemed to stand at attention as he backed further into empty space, and the old man appeared.

There was no longer any doubt that he could be seen. The Halloween man didn't know what to do. Chilled breath was pouring from his mouth. He wouldn't look directly at the blurred figure now approaching. He fell to his knees and put his hands together, as if in prayer to whatever merciless being he served. But like himself there was no answer.

Len Rely

Len Rely is an author of speculative fiction including the paperback novel *Mono* now available at Barnes & Noble. In addition, he has done poetry, editorial work and local news articles on the side. 75 publications to date include *Writers Choice, Gothic Press, Smoking Pen, Dark Truths, Peer Amid, Underworld Magazine* and *Redsine*.

Harbinger
by
Steven L. Shrewsbury

"A man can die but once. We owe God a death."
—William Shakespeare
Henry IV, Part Two

"I can do nothing for you, Mr. Silverstein, or should I say, Magus Martin?" the youthful doctor asked his husky patient. "Time's up."

Black eyes drilled holes in the doctor from a face without pity. The patient looked away from the young man and gripped the sides of his head. Glancing at the diplomas on the wall, Magus Martin massaged his gray temples and grumbled, "How many years out of residency are you?"

The young doctor said impassively, "Please don't pull on your hair so hard. You'll tear your scalp. Honestly, Mr. Martin..."

"Magus, Dr. Rosen," the stocky man corrected, soothing down frazzled hair. The patient in his mid-fifties glared at the smooth face opposite him and thought a China doll's skin would be jealous of this yuppie's features.

"All right, Magus." Dr. Rosen hesitated, his thin lips pursed. "Look, your religion or hobbies are no concern of mine. The health of your body is. I care not a jot if you think yourself a Wizard or a Carnival huckster to these New Age fools. In these past months you have aged beyond your 55 years."

"I live in this vile bag of flesh, doctor!" He bit his lip and gripped his goatee, restraining rage, but it spilled forth anyway. "You think this is unknown to me?" Magus snapped, his hands running down over a withering neck. His fingers fondled a chain which weighed heavy on his chest. With trepidation the Wizard glanced down to see an old silver pentagram, fading.

"I have treated you as a favor for your dear mother. Surely, a shame she passed on yesterday."

"I know your mother was one of her bridge partners," Magus mumbled, buttoning his black suit coat. He adjusted a blood red tie over the pentagram and took a breath. Never in his life for all of the drugs and spells did Magus Martin ever feel his ribs rattle before that day.

Dr. Rosen frowned. "Not many doctors would touch a man of such a dark reputation, not to mention the consuming factor of a lack of medical insurance."

When the young doctor waved a reedy hand at the line of X-rays and CAT scan proofs, Magus Martin squeezed his eyes shut. Even a man with no medical education saw the tumor behind Martin's eyes in the negatives. When Magus Martin blinked, he perceived an old friend, a tiny dark dot that floated around in his field of vision. On his left eye, he saw the tiny shape dancing in the glow of the proofs. "But you tell me I'm doomed, that this tumor in my brain cannot be reduced."

"That's correct. No amount of surgery or radiation can affect it in the advanced stage it now has achieved. I cannot believe you never suffered discomfort until now."

Magus rubbed his left eye, causing a fount of bright lights to zigzag. Still, the tiny black dot floated in his field of vision, bobbing like a buoy in the water. "You've never explained the little friend in my eye. I always wondered if that is when the tumor started to grow, when I could see this tiny spot in my eye."

Dr. Rosen sighed in resignation. "Magus! The eye surgeons saw nothing. You know what they told you it was."

"Light reflecting off scar tissue, bah!" Magus swore and soothed down the sleeves of his black shirt, removing specs of lint.

"Do you believe in miracles?" Dr. Rosen posed quietly.

Pulling his lapels tighter, the dark eyes of Magus leered at Dr. Rosen. "For most of my life I've made my own miracles, doctor! I have always been able to make bad things happen to good people. Be it potions, powders or incantations, I can bring a Jew to the cross or make a nun act like a whore. Do you know how many times I've won the lottery?"

Dr. Rosen smirked. "You always pay in cash, Mr. Wizard."

Magus nodded and his voice lowered, "And yet…"

"None of it can stop the tumor?" Dr. Rosen sighed and buttoned his white smock. "I don't pretend to believe in all of that magick nonsense of yours or the other cults in San Jose. If you had such power to affect others or cause strife amongst these dark groups, then cure thyself!" He laughed, desperately trying to make the situation lighter and shrugged. "Sorry, I couldn't resist!"

Magus closed his eyes and heard the voices in his head, the one that demanded life for life in various spells. The same leading tone that caused him to sign his soul away in Egypt and crucify his guides, that made him forget the tone of his father. Magus blinked and saw the pyramids in his mind's eye...those majestic mountains of bricks where he first beheld the tiny dark dot so many years ago. Oh, it never hung there as a constant, but when the pain of life increased, when his health turned bad, his tiny friend returned. He once named it his Harbinger, for it seemed to herald bad tidings or ill omens. This day Harbinger sported a purple corona.

"You cannot stop yourself, eh? Restraint has never been one of my virtues." Cracking his knuckles, the older man reached for the door to the doctors office, shoved it closed and stated, "Neither can I resist."

The small doctor never moved as Magus Martin crossed the room, grabbed Dr. Rosen's stethoscope and used it as a tourniquet. The entire action took only a few minutes as the Wizard's superior strength coursed through his arms as he throttled the doctor. Veins pulsing in his neck, Magus lowered the doctor to the floor, trying to ignore the shifting colors of the halo around his Harbinger. Smashing his fist into the doctor's Adam's apple, crushing it completely, the dying man stared into the gaping eyes of Dr. Rosen. In Magus' left eye the tiny dot floated and glowed purple for a moment...then returned to a black hue.

Standing up straight, adjusting his clothes, he ran both hands down either side of his long black goatee, and then locked the door behind him. He knew there would be no escape from this crime, but his life would be gone by the next day. As he exited the office Magus approached his Mercedes, every step resounding in his skull like a distant tympani drum. He whispered, "So much to do."

Rubbing his eye again, Magus Martin noticed his Harbinger was a tad larger.

When Magus Martin climbed out of the car outside his three-story home, his attention focused on a shabby homeless man. This individual dug in the sacks of garbage near the curb. Ignoring this person, Martin closed the door of the car and spotted a sleek lime green Plymouth Prowler sitting near the garbage bags. "Mr. Deron Castellan. How convenient," he muttered, fully aware of who owned the car.

As he jogged up the sidewalk made of ornamental olive-colored stepping stones, Magus heard the voice of the homeless man cackle and say, "I'm eating your soul! Hah! I'm eating your soul!" Exhaling while he unlocked the glass door, Magus Martin never looked back.

Once inside his home, the aroma of incense and cigarettes hit his nose. The smoke irrigated his left eye moderately and the Harbinger jumped. Never shedding his jacket, Magus strolled through the stylish living room, refurbished in Edwardian splendor. As always, he reached out and touched the swirls on a table top, adoring the woodwork when he passed by and considered himself blessed. He paused and reached into an ancient cabinet full of his father's possessions.

The darker realm of the hallway that connected to the master bedroom made the Harbinger in his eye appear to suddenly take on a pink halo. The odor of candles and the regular rhythm of grunts came to Magus Martin just before he opened the bedroom door.

The master bedchamber, all scarlet shag carpet and mirrored walls, was an enormous locale more akin to the dimension of a recreation room. It was just that, in fact, he mused. Listlessly, he watched the muscle-bound man in a black leather hood pound away at his wife, suspended from the ceiling in a swing made of leather straps and silver chain links. They never paused in their actions as Magus closed the door and stepped closer to them. His wife of four years wore a leather mask and all of her blonde hair was pulled through a hole in the top of the helmet she wore.

"Martin!" She grinned through ruby lips visible from a zipper opening in the hood. Her plume of hair whipped back and forth as Mr. Castellan gripped her fishnet covered calves. "Come join in! Deron dropped by!"

Magus Martin nodded, thinking nothing of this for she was married to Deron Castellan as well. "No, Bonita, not today," Martin said as the hulking man paused, then continued to enter her.

Through the zipper mouth hole in the mask Deron chuckled and said, "Don't tell me you are getting jealous, old man!"

Magus Martin laughed and wiped his left eye. "No, of course not. You see, I never had a problem with you screwing her or me while I was here." Magus Martin then removed a small pistol from his jacket. "You see? Bonita is no more important to me than the German Luger that my father removed from a soldier in France. A possession in this world of happy things, I can take it or leave it."

Mr. Castellan stopped thrusting, but never let go of Bonita's slick legs. "What are you talking about? How did it go at the doctor's?"

Magus shrugged. "As bad as possible, really. Doomsday. That's irrelevant now. You see, I wouldn't want you using my father's gun, either, when I am gone."

Bonita's eyes widened in the mask until the Wizard could no longer see her eyelids.

Mr. Castellan slipped out of her, yet never moved his feet an inch.

"Hell, Castellan, you wiping your ass on my toilet paper after I'm gone is intolerable," Magus remarked as he shot the tall man in the face, causing Deron to recoil away from the chain-swing and slam into a freshly cracked mirror on the wall…made imperfect from the bullet and slippery with his brains. Not a moment passed when Magus Martin aimed and pulled the trigger three more times. Every time the report of the gun rang in his ears and the Harbinger glowed a different shade— green, blue, and red glows for bullets to her vagina, abdomen, and open mouth. Bonita convulsed and struggled before succumbing to the inevitable. Her motions were enough to put the swing in motion. While the shadow of the swing interrupted the glow of candles gracing Deron's face, the hooded face received another shot, though he was certain the man was dead.

Standing at the door, he felt no remorse as the Harbinger grew in his left eye. It stopped developing; remaining only a tad larger than it was in the doctor's office. Every time the swing moved across his field of vision, the corona of Harbinger was orange. Every time that pendulum swung, he recalled that time was short.

Grabbing for a Diet Coke in the refrigerator, he hesitated and then pulled out a regular Coke. Magus took a sip as he scooped up Mr. Castellan's keys off the kitchen table. Knowing the police would look for his Mercedes soon, he went out to get into the garnish lime-colored Plymouth Prowler.

The homeless man, clad in grungy sweat pants and a green army jacket riddled with holes shouted, "I'm eating your soul, Magus!"

As he opened the shiny car door, Magus Martin made eye contact with the homeless man. The filthy face, covered in whiskers and sores, was biting into a rancid apple. As the churning lips of the homeless man parted and tiny worms tumbled free, Magus said, "By God, you are!"

Driving away from the curb, he checked his watch and blinked. Harbinger was steady and dark, yet never leaving. He seemed to hear the wheels grind on the paved road as he drove.

Removing his cell-phone from his jacket, Magus concentrated on the road and pressed out the number.

A deep voice said over the line, "If you have this number you may be damned already."

"I'd have never guessed," Magus replied.

Slightly taken aback, the deep, threatening voice said, "Who? Martin? Is that you?"

"Yes, Reverend Nighthawk. Can I speak with you?"

A short silence ended when Reverend Nighthawk replied, "I have little to say to you, old man. Your magick is old and weak. Your refusal to get with the times has led to your practical banishment with the new generation. They crave new ways, they pine for new thrills…they hunger after a new song, sung by me."

"Lovely," Martin retorted. "I received some terrible news today and was wondering if I could come by to see my old student."

"You're joking."

Martin smiled. "No, I'd love to come and see my favorite Indian."

"Native American, you jackass," Reverend Nighthawk grumbled. "You are still an exclusionary bastard, Martin. The way you treat individuals you better hope that there is no karma to repay in the next life."

"Spare me."

"The way you are petty and vindictive, Martin, I'd say you will be lucky if you come back as a rat!"

"Perhaps I'm going for a *roach*, Reverend. Besides, I care little for squabbles over the afterlife. You believing an assembly line for reinstating souls exists is no more preposterous than accepting eternal damnation."

"Yes, yes…"

Magus giggled, "Only I have really spoken to one demon before. I doubt you have talked to a reincarnation tech, eh?"

With a deep sigh, the Reverend Nighthawk asked, "What else do we have to say to each other?"

"My health is bad, Reverend," Martin explained, putting a gentle tone to his words. His eyes, somewhat weary, glanced to the passenger seat of the Plymouth Prowler at the other object he liberated from his father's collection case. "I thought we could bury the hatchet, once and for all."

"Papa, not that it isn't good to see you," the eight-year-old girl with dark hair stated as she glanced out the window of the pickup truck, "but when did Mama say you could pick me up from school? She never would let you come and get me before."

Magus held his left eye and pressed on it with the palm of his hand. Harbinger was larger and pulsing with a violet hue. He tried to maintain his breathing and turned on the radio. "Your mother had a change of heart this afternoon, Chloe," Magus said.

Chloe crossed her legs, adjusted the plaid skirt of the Catholic school uniform, and asked, "Papa, when did you get a truck?"

"It belongs to a friend, an old student of mine," he muttered as he drove away from the school.

On the radio, the voice seemed faint to Magus Martin, but he understood the words. His daughter, estranged from him for years via a previous marriage, never paid attention to the words. "Police are reporting a possible link between a strangled cardiac surgeon, a double shooting homicide of an interior designer and an area lawyer now that two more bodies have been discovered. One, a leader of a religious order of the Ebony Dawn, was found murdered in the exact same fashion as a San Jose suburban homemaker. The murder weapon, rumored to be a Native American Indian stone battle implement, was —"

Magus switched the radio and exited the main road.

"Why are we going to a graveyard? Are you going to show me where they will bury Gramma tomorrow?"

Martin barely made eye contact with her wide, brown eyes. "Yes, Chloe, that's it. It will be good for the soul to preview the site."

The child laughed. "Papa, you on hallowed ground?" Chloe smiled and made the sign of the cross. "Uh, sorry Papa."

Magus Martin laughed heartily as the thud of his heartbeat slammed into his ears. The sun seemed brighter than usual so he donned a pair of wire-rimmed sunglasses that were sliding around on the dashboard. His head ached badly; his left eye was full of tears and the Harbinger. It was so large, he hoped he retained enough time to complete his mission.

He parked the black Chevy Silverado and climbed out of the truck. After helping his daughter down, he took her hand and they walked amongst the stones. A few times, he stepped wrong and stumbled. Chloe tried to right his progress and said, "Papa, you're sick. The color of your face is terrible!"

Pausing, Magus Martin took a few breaths and noticed his Harbinger was almost covering his eye. Being half blind, he focused ahead with his right eye and said, "Your Papa has seen better days, dear."

"You should think on light, not all of this dark and creepy stuff, Papa," Chloe told him, helping him step along.

"Lecturing the old man all the way to the grave, hmm?" he mumbled and gave out a weak laugh. "If you didn't have a confrontational mind, I wouldn't believe you were mine!"

He saw Chloe glance up at him only to give him a horrified look. "Papa, you're bleeding!"

Quickly, he wiped his right hand across his lips and felt the blood flowing from his nose. Blinking his eye hard, he felt the tears start from his left eye again, yet when he touched his cheek, the only liquid on his fingers was scarlet. "We are here."

"You need to see a doctor," Chloe implored her father as he stopped in front of a gaping hole in the ground…a fresh grave.

"The one I visited today gave me no comfort, only fatalism," he rasped, removing the sunglasses. Blood painted the inner lens on the left side from his eyelash. Instinctively, Magus snapped the glasses to free them of the liquid. Inadvertently, he spattered the crimson fluid all over the stone next to the fresh grave. He read the words slowly, "Irving E. Silverstein. Your grandfather was a good man, Chloe. Too bad you never met him."

"Gramma Selma is with him now," she said confidently.

Magus went to one knee, holding the left side of his head and trying to rub the Harbinger out. "You believe that?"

"Papa, you are ill. We better go."

Magus shook his head and slipped the German gun out of his coat. The weapon rested on his knee as he said, "Don't you see, girl? It has to end here, Chloe. It has to end today. I did nothing but wrong with the gifts given to me and I must rid the world of my influence."

Chloe swallowed and stared at the gun. "Papa…"

"It isn't your fault," Magus Martin said as he rose up. Suddenly, he could see out of his left eye. It was like a revelation of the sunlight pouring in clean and no obstruction hindered him. Confused, he shook his head from side to side, trying to comprehend what had happened. His clear eyes focused on his daughter and he said, "I made a deal, long ago, for power and influence in this world. The gift I received from beyond couldn't stop this rock in my skull from growing."

"But Papa…" Chloe implored, her eyes going from his bloody face to the barrel of the trembling gun.

"If I learned anything, it was that all of this is about blood. Don't you even see it in that silly Roman Catholic school of yours? Jesus was a blood sacrifice just like the goats or children or horses to the pagans. In the blood is where the code exists, and there is real evil in the world. I must get rid of the evil I left behind."

"Am I evil?" Chloe asked, spreading her arms out.

Magus Martin set his feet firm in front of the grave, aiming at her chest. He blinked and saw the irony of her pose...mimicking that of a statue of the Virgin Mary not ten feet behind her. "You can be. Now, I must stop that chance."

Abruptly, his eyes looked up and saw the return of his Harbinger. This time it wasn't a jagged piece of matter, but a churning, oblong mass of ebony. Magus tried to take a deep breath but couldn't. The giant black form straightened out on the sides and edges, forming into a definite shape. Trying to scream, attempting to breathe, Magus raised his gun but found that he couldn't move. His left eye burst, ruining half of his field of vision as the black Harbinger took on the shape of a rectangle.

At last Magus could move, but the shuffling of his feet only provided him a way to fall backwards. The stocky man plummeted into the fresh grave intended for his mother and mashed into the soft earth below. Looking up with his one good eye, he saw the shape of his daughter, glowing white, again posing like the Madonna on a dashboard—the glow accentuated by the blackness behind her. Overwhelming his daughter from behind was the giant rectangle of darkness. It passed through her and sealed over the edges of the grave...and then Harbinger opened, showing him at last what was inside.

His own grave.

As the light of the world flickered out, Magus Martin fell again.

In time, he opened his eyes only to see his Harbinger at full magnitude. Complete darkness surrounded him and he was alone.

This sensation of withoutness burned. Bad.

Steven L. Shrewsbury

Steven L. Shrewsbury, 35, creator of Dack Shannon, Thor Alexander, and the Majestic Universe, is the author of close to 300 published tales online or in print. His tales have appeared in print magazines like *Eldritch Tales, Fighting Chance, Dark Wisdom, Black Petals* and *Mystery Buff.* Over a hundred of his poems are out there in magazines like *Penny Dreadful, Bible of Hell* and *Deathrealm.* His first book, *Nocturnal Vacations,* was released in 2002 by Publish America. His second book, *Depths of Savagery* was released in May, 2003 from Double Dragon Publishing. His third Book, *Bulletproof Soul,* will soon be released from Black Death Books.

He has appeared in many anthologies, most recently the hardback *Cemetery Poets, Atrocitas Aqua* and *Labor Pool,* and soon will appear in *Scriptures of the Damned* and *Scary* from DDP. His more recent acceptances have been to the anthologies *Deathgrip-2, Historical Hardboiled, Ghostbreakers, R'yleh Beastiary* and *Kings of the Night.* His website is http://www.stevenshrewsbury.com

Now I'm Waiting
by
William P. Simmons

I never loved Momma, and Momma didn't love me, but in our way, we needed each other—someone to fill the lonely, dust-choked hallways and somberly lighted rooms of our needlessly large Victorian home with at least a *suggestion* of life. A touch, a word, a smile, even if false, was our protection against the threat of complete silence, a brief reprieve from loneliness.

Me and Momma shared a room together until my Junior year of high-school. That autumn, between stomp-and-rush mornings of burnt toast breakfasts, lonely schoolyard paper sack lunches, and late-night dinners spent in shadows and strained silence, I began to notice changes across the once familiar landscape of my scrawny, pale adolescent body. Changes that both disgusted and excited me as I explored myself with uncertain hands.

Finally, on a dark, dank, leaf-curtain October morning, disgusted at the black patches of crinkly hair springing in patches beneath my penis, I worked up the courage to tell Momma I wanted my own room. My own bed. Some privacy in a world where it was a precious commodity.

"Why?" she asked after an uncomfortable pause, peering down at me as if she'd caught me doing something filthy.

Silence.

Wind rushed a dying ghost-spray of leaves, leftovers from crippled spring, past the kitchen window. In the fluid wave of shadows cast, drowned, and re-lit by streams of weak sunlight sneaking through partially open curtains, she studied me. Her expression, a cold slash of grim surprise, tightened the wizened features of a face already stretched taunt over sharp bones.

"You certainly don't have anything I haven't seen before," she finally said. She smiled—a maggot's curl revealing chipped, yellowed teeth. "Why do you suddenly need privacy so badly?" That look, then, that quietly suggested all the filthy things I could have been doing; the horary old sneer that thought I was a dirty, dirty boy.

Momma had a hard, grating voice—rusty nails rubbed down a pane of glass—and I fumbled for the right words, squirming beneath her unblinking stare. She stood close enough for me to smell the raw tuna she ate everyday for lunch. I froze when her squishy, flannel-covered breasts lingered against my arm.

She stared at me as if daring me to move, and something in her eyes mirrored the predatory hunger I'd noticed in the girls at school as they watched the boys fighting or playing football in the freshly mowed soccer fields.

I jerked away from the clamminess of her touch, wanting to cry or scream—wanting to hurt her like her closeness hurt me. Instead, I ran upstairs where I sulked in the moist, choking darkness until she came up later that evening and stretched across the damp, creaking mattress to sleep.

She didn't say a word.

She didn't have to.

Her touch said enough.

We didn't talk for days.

The third afternoon, after school, she was waiting in the hall. She waved me upstairs, and, opening the door to the mushroom-smelling room where she kept her yarn, nick-knacks, and other debris accumulated during a life spent collecting, said, "You can sleep here," before walking silently away. That evening, after an unbearably long dinner spent staring into the greasy corpse-lumps of mashed potatoes so I wouldn't have to see the red cracks of anger cris-crossing her leathery cheeks, I moved what few personal items I possessed into the room. Nothing much, just a few rarely used school books, some outdated toys, and the clothes that Momma picked out for me.

Lying there naked was an adventure. Closing the door was like declaring that small space of polished wood and lingering mothballs my kingdom, and I felt a wonderful surge of happiness when I slid under the thin covers. My skin tingled with a hundred new sensations as I memorized the lick of cool sheets against my belly, the liberating freedom of shedding underwear like bad memories.

But I couldn't sleep.

The wind whispered against the eaves. The downstairs television bled strange voices. Above them, I heard the first creak of bare feet approaching my door. Shivering, I strained to make out the sly, creeping shuffle. A soft, meaty flip-flop. Closer...

Head propped up against the lumpy pillows, entranced by the low whisper of a cracked voice mumbling, I cowered from the shadows cast by whips of stray moonlight bleeding through the window and stared through the dancing particles of dust and age dancing across the hardwood floor.

Outside the door there came the sound of heavy, strained breathing.

A monster, I thought, trembling, hating myself for believing such foolishness, but quite convinced that if I fell asleep something huge and dark and terrible would slam open the door and be on me before I could shout. Something behind the door was listening to the thudding panic of my heart.

When the shadow sighed, I couldn't pretend any longer.

No, not the bogeyman.

Just Momma.

Just my mother, against the door, listening to my movements.

And somehow, that was so much worse.

Momma wore her age like old clothes smeared with dust and pain.

Even as a child, her hair had been streaked with sluices of grey, strangled in a tight bun across her slightly curved forehead. Her almond, dark green eyes were headlights glaring beneath thin eyebrows. Those eyes didn't just look at you; they looked *through you.*

When my classmates grew and moved to careers and wives and the military, I hired out as a stock-boy for Miller's Hardware, just five minutes down our street while my classmates grew into the wide-open spaces of their lives, breaking free from Harper's Mill to walk and run and conquer a world larger than anything I'd ever imagined. A world I wouldn't *let* myself imagine.

Joseph Miller, an old, bent man with a dripping eye and nervous tick that scrunched his sandpaper skin into hard-edged wrinkles, was friends with Momma from way back. She seemed friendly with every old bird on our block. I ran the hardware's floor on thankless errands from eight in the morning till five at night. All the while, day after thankless day, Momma was there, looking on, whispering disappointment from the perch she occupied in my mind.

Sometimes I tucked myself into a deep envelope of silence during my lunch-break or late at night when I'd sneak among the elm trees to enjoy the strangely soothing lullaby of the evening wind. Those were the times, the few precious moments of freedom, that I thought about my father, who'd been killed when a rope holding a pile of heavy pine on the back of a truck had snapped and crushed his spine.

I wasn't allowed to his funeral, but Momma liked to describe how handsome he'd looked in the coffin. Momma was always telling me things like that, reminding me about death like other parents tell their children about the Tooth fairy or Santa Claus, pointing out how lonely life was, and how very, very much I depended on her.

After awhile, I believed her.

"Take them down, dear," Momma said after dinner, seated in her faded brown sofa with a warm bottle of cola. She meant the photos, of course. Mom was a great collector of photographs. There was one of me in a baseball cap in the park, another where I was crying in the backyard. The tired geography of my life was lined up over the fireplace—my youth trapped in faded colors. The last photograph Momma took of me was when I was fifteen. I was standing in our yard, smiling awkwardly.

"Look how dear you were in your outfits," Momma cooed. "What happened to that boy?"

"I don't know, Mother."

"*There* was a boy who loved his mother."

After she died, I stuffed the pictures in the attic.

I contemplated burning then, but that would have been too easy. So instead, I tucked them in a box where they could fade and warp in the moist darkness.

But I'm getting ahead of myself.

Marian…I have to tell you about Marian while there is time.

I met her Friday night, two months ago at Pete's, a dusty, warm watering-hole where Momma dragged me every weekend for a ritual of embarrassment she delighted in, reminiscing about my father with her rotten toothed cronies as I sat at the bar, hearing her emphasize all his fine qualities, reminding me of the many ways I'd failed to measure up.

I would never have approached the frail shadow of a girl sitting a few stools down, casually looking me over beneath the weak-lit clouds of cigar smoke and dully burning ceiling lights. I had no experience with the opposite sex. There had always been bills to pay, Momma's feet to soak, baths to run, photographs to look at—old pains to be scraped open like ugly, bleeding pimples by a woman I was afraid to even admit I hated.

"I hope you don't mind." Her voice was soft, relaxed when she walked over. I immediately wanted her to keep talking. "I hate drinking alone." She smiled warmly, a bit uncertain. "Do you mind?"

"…What?" *(See? I'm a real smooth talker!)*

"If I take a seat," she laughed.

Her voice was soft, and I must have nodded, for she eased delightfully curved thighs over the barstool beside me. Soft brown hair hugging slim shoulders, quick to laugh, Marian was attractive in a simple, unprepossessing way. I've never been much for the spiked heels and red panties type, and there was something provocative yet distinctively fragile about Marian. Something I wanted to know better. I was just starting to share cautious little slips of information about myself when, like a wedge of ice shattering the serenity of a quiet evening, Momma's announced, "I'm ready to leave."

Marian touched my arm. "Would you like to get together tomorrow night?"

"I don't feel well," Momma said, edging her intimidating bulk between us.

"Hello." Marian nodded to her before looking back to me, undaunted. "Should I come by around seven?"

Momma was silent on the walk home. Her back acted up later that night, and the next morning, her arthritis was so bad she could barely move. It was Sunday, so I didn't have to work at the store. I spent the morning waiting on her. The afternoon was for dishes and preparing the nightly meal. She came out in the kitchen when I was peppering a thick wedge of bloody meat.

"Is that enough for us both?" she asked.

Careful to stare at the frying pan, I said, "It's enough for one. You know I'm seeing Marian tonight."

"If you have to." She shrugged. "Though I can't pretend to know what you see in a common slut."

"She isn't a slut, Momma."

"You've known her for what, one night? How do you know *what* she is?"

Then she hobbled away.

Should I tell you that Marian showed up at seven? Should I describe the nervous, pleasurable thrill that licked my spine when she shifted close to me in the movie-house, or how I hardened in her cool-hot hands? There's nothing I'd rather do, believe me...nothing in this world that I'd rather remember than the butterflies in my stomach, the hope that I'd finally found someone. Nothing I'd rather do than relate how good it was, the first time we made love—on our second date, at her house—and give this story the obligatory happy ending.

But there isn't time. She'll be back any minute now.

After our second date, I returned home to find Momma sprawled at the bottom of the stairs. Her arms felt clammy, and when I tried to pick her up, her watery eyes peeled me where I stood.

"I lost my footing," she whimpered. Her hair was matted, the wrinkled slopes of her withered cheeks glazed with pain.

My fault! It was my fault it had happened. Mine, because I hadn't been there with her, for her! We spent the remainder of the night on the sofa, looking at my old school pictures and drinking warm colas.

The next morning, I called Marian and canceled our date. What I didn't tell her—what I couldn't find the courage to admit, was that, in my mind, I'd already decided I couldn't see her again. It would be better this way. For Momma. For me. For Marian…

I was still hanging on the phone, staring into it, when Marian broke the connection. It felt like a scalpel had severed my only connection to the outside world.

That Friday, we were on the sofa watching television when Momma told me to fetch her coat. We hadn't gone to the bar for two weeks because of her back, and I had hoped it would become a permanent deal, an unspoken trade-off. I'd give up Marian and she'd surrender her weekly humiliation of me.

But there was just no keeping her away that night.

When we arrived, a huddled group of old men dressed in ratty jackets and memories of youth greeted Momma with drunken cries and helped her up on a stool. I ordered a watery beer for me, a cola for Momma. Smoke hung like funeral blankets over the crowded room. A country-western song bled from a pair of cracked, dusty speakers wired up in the corners. Each one sounded the same as the one before it. Thankfully, I couldn't hear much of the nasal whining over the drunken stupor falling like bricks around me. In a dark corner behind a warped pool table, two students fought and ignored the weeping, red-faced girl who tried to stand between them. Occasionally, Momma peered over at me, eyes aflare with animal cunning.

Do you know that, as a child, I wasn't allowed to have pets?

"We'll keep each other company," Momma had told me. "Who needs a filthy animal to look after?" So I placated myself watching the neighbor's grey tabby whenever it crept into our yard. Memorized by the glaring insanity of its eyes; one morning I followed it's pace to a cracked sundial standing in the middle of a tangled pile of weeds in our yard. Beside it, a crippled blue jay twitched with a broken wing. There was no way the poor thing could have escaped. The cat, bared fangs and red, lolling tongue, must have sensed this, because it took its time. Head low, tail flickering, it slowly toyed with the dying creature, eyes mad with the promise of pain and blood.

The way Momma looked when Marian opened the door.

Marian had cut her hair high and flat against her ears. She wore a simple dark blouse over tight jeans. Nerves knotted my stomach. The room became unbearably hot. I wanted nothing more than to sneak outside for a taste of fresh night sky. I certainly didn't expect Marian to take the stool beside me.

Half a dozen emotions filled my head, and I couldn't find words for one of them as strained silence strangled my nerve.

"It's her, isn't it?" she suddenly said, staring past me.

My heart rolled in my ears, exquisite bursts of internal thunder that laughed *coward, coward, coward...*

Marian shook her head. "She doesn't control you," she said in a half plea, half scolding tone. "You're a man for Christ's sakes—Jesus, why don't you act like one?"

After that, the night comes back in fragments.

The doctors say to expect this, not to push for complete recall. The medicine eases the pain, so giving up some of my memories is a fair exchange.

I was talking to Marian one minute, preparing to stand, when, as though the world had tilted and knocked me back, Momma was beside me.

She was the cat, Marian the bird.

"My boy doesn't need to be mixed up with a gutter wench," she said clearly. "Find someone else to leech off of." The old men at the bar laughed and banged their beer mugs. Strangers watched from tables, amused and surprised and...hungry? Yes, I think that's it. They were thankful, eager for amusement.

Marian looked to me for support, but I hurried for Momma's coat. Defeated, ashamed, I took her flabby arm and walked her to the door, driven to a strange, unrecognizable fury when I noticed the smoldering triumph in her eyes. Disorientated, sick with embarrassment, I must have lost my footing on the sidewalk. By the time Momma screamed, it was too late.

I didn't, *couldn't* have done it on purpose. And I certainly can't be blamed for the truck driver, who, it was later determined, had been drinking.

One minute, Momma had been with me, the next, she was on the street. Right before the truck cracked her open, I saw her staring up at me. She moaned once, struggling to keep her life from slipping out in dark, red flowers around her twitching legs.

"An accident," the police determined unconcernedly.

I tried very hard to believe it.

Marian called two days after the funeral.

At first I didn't know what to say, a condition her lingering silence didn't help. Finally, her voice bled from the phone in a mixture of pity and sadness. The anger was gone, replaced by a tone that promised something that I had never really had—something that I couldn't even find words for to name.

"I'm so sorry," she said. "I never dreamed...I never wanted this to happen."

"I know."

"Can I, well, would you like some company?"

Shaken by Momma's death

—rage in those eyes, knowing—

unwilling to stay in this great, empty house alone, I did one of the few impulsive actions of my life.

"I...well, I'd like you to...what I mean to say is, would you come over and keep me company? Just for a few days?"

That afternoon, she dropped by with a few changes of clothes and held me. I abandoned myself to the excitement of having a woman in the house, in my bed, humming contentedly in the kitchen, stretched out invitingly across the sofa. I'm sure Marian was as happy as me, and that's what made our first fight so surprising. There was no reason for it—I can't recall how it started. But for one moment, just two nights after she'd moved in, I looked across the dinner table and found myself recognizing something in her eyes that froze my blood.

Something I refused to accept.

Of course it was a joke of the ceiling light, a repressed shadow that made me imagine a greenish hue drowning Marian's brown pupils. Guilt that made me see rage and hunger spilling from the face I'd covered with gentle kisses just that morning.

"What on earth's wrong with you?" Marian asked, looking up from her plate. Beneath the drooling kitchen light, she licked a piece of chicken off her lips and *smiled*.

I turned away, trembling slightly, and wouldn't face her until she moved from the table and I felt her leaning above me. It was Marian looking worriedly down at me. Marian who took me to bed, her lithe body wiggling over mine, coating me in the warm whisper of heavy breathing. *Marian*, not Momma who whispered, "That's okay, honey. Let me make it better." Marian who kneaded me erect. Marian who wrapped warm dampness over me, twirling my hair afterwards.

Marian…

Later that night, I woke to what I thought at the time had been a cold hand in the darkness. And for a horrible moment—a heartbeat of primal, undeniable terror, I thought I heard—no, thought I *felt*—the presence of someone leaning against the door.

Someone listening, waiting, giggling softly.

Creeping across the cold floor, stretching my hand to the brass knob, time froze until I finally, slowly, carefully opened the sturdy square of oak that separated me from…

Nothing.

Only the hallway, dark and silent and forever.

Marian snoring peacefully behind me.

I crept along the hall, leaned over the banister, and squinted through early morning shadows to the room below. There it was again, bare feet whispering across the floor.

The fist shot from the darkness to punch my back.

I struggled frantically to keep my footing…wobbled…tried to shout when I slipped on the first step. The floor and walls circled madly as the bottom of the floor rushed up to meet me.

The doctors released me this morning.

Marian made a show of crying when there were people crowding the room, but she didn't fool me, not even when she wrapped her arms around me and pressed her face against my neck and told me how very much she loved me.

—*Oh, God, I was so worried. I'll help you get over this!*—

But the dry, ancient lips curving against my neck had nothing to do with love.

I could have asked to stay in the hospital, but why? Who knows where Marian went? And without her, why live at all?

Momma was always the smart one, and when I saw her in the doctor leaning over me, and staring from the concerned faces of nurses, I realized there was no use running.

On the way home, she chatted about widening the garden and holding our wedding in the summer. She wheeled me up the ramp built during my hospital stay and helped me into the bathtub before she stopped and shook her head. She had forgotten something in town.

"Will you be alright? I'll just be gone a few minutes." She hummed as she walked down stairs and shut the door.

And now I'm waiting.

Waiting, sitting uselessly in the dirty, cool tub water. Unable to use my legs, unable to do anything but listen.

The downstairs door just opened…

She's in the hall now.

Marian is in the hall.

Marian, not Momma…

Don't you see?

It *has* to be Marian!

William P. Simmons

Holding a Cum Laude Honors Degree in Literature from the State University Of New York, William P. Simmons is an award recommended author, poet, reviewer, freelance journalist, and editor. His story "Telling Stories in the Dark" was recommended for a Bram Stoker award, as was his original anthology *Vivisections*. "The Wind", "When It Comes" and "They Never Come Back" have received Honorable Mentions in volumes of *The Year's Best Fantasy and Horror*. His first collection, a chapbook entitled *Becoming October*, was critically successful, receiving raves from T.M. Wright, Tom Piccirrili, Tim Lebbon, Gary A. Braunbeck, etc. His short fiction and poetry has appeared in 8 of the 9 acclaimed *Darkness Rising* anthologies (2-9), *Octoberland*, *Decadence* (2), *Gothic.Net*, *ChiZine*, *Flesh&Blood*, *The Edge: Tales Of Suspense*, and others. Further pieces are slated to appear in *ChiZine*, *The Blackest Death*, and *Dark Lurkers*.

Besides fiction and poetry, William has also contributed numerous book reviews, columns, and essays to such publications as *All Hallows*, *Cemetery Dance*, *Hellnotes*, *Gauntlet*, *Mystery Scene*, *Rue Morgue*, *Infinity Plus*, *Wormwood*, etc. As an interviewer he has spoken with some of the top names in the field, including William F. Nolan, Hugh B. Cave, Graham Masterton, Ramsey Campbell, F. Paul Wilson, Poppy Z. Brite, Caitlin R. Kiernan and many, many others. His feature interview series include Our Ladies of Darkness and Fear Focus, and his columns include Digging Up Bones, Literary Lesions, and Folk Fears.

Undaunted Press will publish *Dark Harvest*, a collection by William and fellow author Paul Melniczek. In 2003/2004, Prime Books will publish in hardcover and paperback his new collection *By Reason of Darkness*, which has received advanced critical praise by Al Sarrantonio, Graham Masterton, Gerard Houraner, and Hugh B. Cave. He has just completed a mammoth collection of exclusive, revealing interviews with some of the field's top names entitled *Dark Dialogues: Conversations With Architects of Fear and Wonder*, and he is currently working on a new collection for a respected specialty hardcover publisher, *The Autumn People*.

William currently lives in Potsdam, NY with his wife, Valarie, and his daughter, Bonnie Lee Simmons.

Gene the Sailorman
by
Dan Thomas

Spring of 2002.

That was when my Uncle Gene came home from the war.

Not Afghanistan but the Pacific Theatre, by way of Pearl Harbor and Bethesda Naval Hospital in Maryland.

You see, without a doubt, Gene was the last U.S. serviceman to return from WWII—57 years late.

Unless you've been residing in a cave in Borneo, you no doubt read Gene's incredible story in the tabloids and saw him on *60 Minutes* and the like. A story, as you probably know, with a tragic ending.

Of how Gene Hammontree, a 23-year-old Torpedoman First Class, was rescued from the *U.S.S. Blowfish* by a deep diving salvage crew. Hoping to make as big a media splash as the *Titanic* find caused, the salvagers were looking for the aircraft carrier *Yorktown* in eight thousand feet of water when their remote robots glommed onto this submarine resting on the shelf of an undersea volcano.

The submarine (one of those old diesel-electric jobs, not a modern nuclear type), was resting in about five hundred feet of water, making it reachable by divers with special helium scuba gear. On a lark, two divers made the plunge to the old boat, and by tapping on the hull with hammers they determined some forward compartments weren't flooded with water (the sub looked like it had taken a depth charge hit near its engine room, the divers later reported to the media).

Even more amazing, something from inside the rust bucket tapped back.

It was like a real cool *Twilight Zone* I'd seen on the SciFi Channel. Anyway, these divers knew it had to be loose machinery. They knew no one could still be alive in that iron coffin.

The divers got ballsy. Maybe they were high on the gas they were sucking. They went to a forward hatch and, with a lot of strain, managed to pry it open using special crowbars. Inside was what they called an "escape trunk." They entered the claustrophobic chamber, closed the hatch on top of them and, using their searchlights, located a big red valve and turned it.

The escape trunk drained and wham, they were inside a place that had been in total darkness for 59 years. In what has to be one of the coolest meetings in history, these two divers removed their flippers and clambered down a ladder and ran smack dab into Gene, wearing greasy dungarees and a T-shirt that was more "hole" than cloth. Gene was blinking like crazy from the divers' searchlights.

Those two Mike Nelson types nearly chewed through their mouthpieces. And Gene, I guess he was just happy for the company.

When the diver dudes concluded the air was okay to breath, they removed their helmets and started chattering like the Chipmunks, because of the helium still in their lungs.

And Gene, all he could manage to say was, "One of you Joes got a smoke I can bum?"

Unlucky for Gene, neither of his guests smoked. What they were able to do for Gene was get him the hell out of there. One of the divers stayed with Gene while the other left the sub, returned topside to the salvage ship and dove back down with a diving suit and helium tank for Gene.

Then the three left together, and Gene, a tear in his eye, bid adieu to the *Blowfish*, his home for more than half a century.

"By god she was a rusty old bitch, but she'd been home and a feeder," Gene was quoted as saying.

What happened next was a whirlwind of media activity that thrust Gene Hammontree (he was my father's uncle, which actually made Gene my great-uncle) into the international spotlight. For a number of weeks he even out-inked Osama bin Laden and the Enron assholes and was a hotter topic of discussion than menopause.

Just how Gene managed to survive all those years inside that pitch-black derelict sub without aging to any degree was widely discussed in the scientific community. Two Utah State professors (later discredited) theorized chlorine gas leaking from the sub's batteries had combined with propellant seeping from the torpedoes to make a weird aerosol that kept Gene alive in suspended animation.

Anyway, if the Navy brass had gotten their hands on my Uncle Gene first, I'm sure they would have hushed the whole thing up, and Gene to this day would be imprisoned on one of those super-secret islands off the coast of Vietnam where the U.S. servicemen who caught the Black Rose and other horrible STDs are kept.

The Navy thought Gene was a fake. But there was no denying he was wearing Gene Hammontree's dog tags, that he looked just like Gene Hammontree did in old family photos, that Gene Hammontree was a crew member of the *Blowfish* (he had this cool *"USS Blowfish"* flying dolphin tattoo on his left bicep to prove it), that the *Blowfish* was reported overdue and declared lost with all hands at the Battle of Midway, June, 1942.

Between you and me, I think what really frosted the Navy was Gene's insistence on collecting 59 years of back pay. But hell, at Gene's old enlisted man's pay grade of $21 per month, it only amounted to about $14,800, not exactly a figure that would bust the national treasury.

Public sentiment, all aglow with the resounding success of the War on Terrorism, forced the issue, and Gene was paid off, honorably discharged, given a three-block long parade in Silver Spring, Maryland (co-sponsored by the Cracker Jack people) and flown home on a Dow Angel Flight for terminally ill kids.

"Home" being his only surviving relations: nephew Jim Hammontree and Jim's wife Betty, and their son Michael (that's me) in Aurora, Colorado.

Uncle Gene arrived with about ten reporters dogging his heels. For a few days, it was a real zoo. Then things settled down. I could tell my mom and dad were a little upset about Gene living with us. I guess because I was younger than they were (almost 18 at the time; I'm 19 now), I was able to adjust and take it much better. Actually, I think my mom and dad were scared shitless of Gene.

The fact is, I had more in common with Gene than my folks did, which is why Gene took to me right off, called me his "buddy" and "pal." Heck, we even looked a lot alike. In many ways, he was just a big kid learning about and reacting to all kinds of new things; just like me. We had to share the same bedroom (we lived in a tract, two-bedroom home near the dying Buckingham Shopping Center—still do). My dad bought a small twin bed for Gene at the Denver Mattress Company, which suited my new roommate just fine.

"I'm kinda used to being tucked in tight at night," Gene told me. "Wide open spaces give me the jitters." Heck, a lot of times Gene would sleep in the closet with the door slid shut. It wasn't just the confined space he craved, but the darkness, too. Gene hated it when I read at night with the lamp on.

On hot, mid-summer nights, I'd hear Gene nightmaring in the closet, gibbering in his sleep and calling out to his old shipmates, "swabies" with names like "Skee," "Curly" and "Bad Ass Budowski." As loud and crazy as it got, it was better than when Gene beat off after watching some piece of T&A shit on cable TV (ask Gene what he thought was the greatest thing that had happened to the world since he went into the service, and he'd tell you it was the advent of television). I'd lie there in bed, praying for my uncle to get his grunting over with and get his rocks off.

One thing Gene didn't seem to take to was modern day food. He wouldn't touch anything that came out of a microwave. Salads and vegetables were out. Just clowning around, Gene would playfully bite my arm and whine that he was "hongry," which really drove my mom up the wall. Truth be known, it bothered me, too. Gene's teeth were pretty fangy after all those years in that sub. A Houston dentist had promised to donate his time to fix Gene's teeth, as part of a promotion with the Colgate people, but so far nothing had come through. Eventually my mom found something Gene would eat—Spam. On Sundays it was baked Spam with pineapple rings on it for Gene.

I can tell you that Gene did like his cigs and beer, though. He would go on and on about a brand of beer they didn't market anymore called Green Beer, but settled for Coors or anything else he could get his hands on. When he got a buzz, he'd slur on and on about all kinds of shit—his shipmates, some prostitutes he knew in Honolulu, the horrible shudder a sub made when it was depth charged, standing watch under the Southern Cross, shit like that. Sometimes he'd get to bawling about the buddies he'd lost in the war, and my dad would roll his eyes and get a disgusted look on his face.

My mom and dad, they didn't smoke or drink at all. Still don't.

Like I said, Gene and I got along just fine. I wish I could say the same about my friends. My (then) girlfriend Jennifer was cool towards him. Gene liked her though, said she was a "juicy broad." There was the time I left Gene alone with her in the living room while I went into the kitchen for Cokes. When I came back, Gene's right middle finger was stiff and Jennifer had this funny look on her face. Jennifer and I broke up soon after that, which is too bad, because she was a real hottie.

Eventually it came down to the fact I was the only person who could stand to be around Gene.

Weekday afternoons I'd come home from my shit job flipping burgers at the Original Hamburger Stand (in the fall I was going to attend Denver Community College and study business administration) and give a pill to my dog Taffy, an arthritic cocker spaniel who must have been 120 years old in dog years. I'd coax Taffy out of her dog house (*drag* her was more like it), jam a plug of peanut butter (the pill inside) into her black gummed mouth, then wait until she choked it down before Gene and I took off in my 1993 Ford Escort.

Gene loved to go riding with me. But for some reason he hated riding in my father's 2000 Mitsubishi, though it had air conditioning. We'd go out to Cherry Creek Dam and swim (Gene loved the water and was a strong swimmer). Or we'd go shopping, mostly at hardware stores—Gene sporting these cool shades because the light hurt his eyes. Begrudgingly my dad turned over some of his basement workshop space to Gene and even let Gene use some of his precious tools. Gene was a mechanical whiz and seemed the happiest when he was farting around with one of his projects.

Not that it was all sweetness and light. There were some rough spots, too. The roughest being one Sunday afternoon when we were barbecuing hamburgers in the backyard. It was on the eve of all the horribleness. Gene, as usual, was telling my dad he preferred his meat very rare. But my old man ignored Gene's request and cautioned him against salmonella.

Our next-door neighbors, the Sasakis, happened to be playing badminton in their own backyard. Soon after dad took the burgers off the grill, Gene happened to look across the chain link fence and noticed—for the first time, I guess—that the Sasakis were of Japanese heritage.

Well, Gene went postal. He ran to the fence and called them (Ed Sasaki and his wife Evelyn, their daughter Susan) a bunch of "dirty Japs" and "yellow bastards." My father reacted with more balls than I thought he had in him, dragging Gene away from the fence.

Gene got pissed at my dad and took a swing at him, clipping my old man's left cheek with his knuckles. My father immediately went into the garage and came back with an old Louisville Slugger of mine and threatened Gene with it.

Finally, Gene backed off. Meanwhile, my mom was apologizing all over the place to the Sasakis. It was real embarrassing. I mean, hell, the Sasakis were almost more American than we were. Ed worked out of his home as a desktop publisher, making newsletters for all kinds of companies. I felt bad for the Sasakis, but I felt bad for Gene, too, tried to understand his point of view. He had, after all, seen a lot of his buddies blown up in the war.

We didn't eat outdoors that afternoon but took our burgers inside and ate at the kitchen table. Gene pouted. My father fumed. My mom cried. It was a mess. I knew trouble, real trouble, was brewing.

The next afternoon when I got home (my folks had gone downtown to the Colorado Department of Social Services to see if they could get Gene institutionalized), Gene was nowhere to be found, which put me on edge.

I went out to Taffy's doghouse to give her a pill. Her butterscotch-colored forelegs and paws were sticking out of the house. I called to her and she didn't budge. So I lost patience, took hold of her paws and yanked.

What I saw made me hurl. The rest of Taffy looked like a picked over Thanksgiving turkey. I waved the flies away. Christ, even her eyes were gone.

"Gene, you fuck!" I yelled, knowing he had something to do with this.

I spun and spied Gene on the Sasakis' back porch. It looked like he was playing with their girl, Susan. Christ! Gene was buck naked, a heavy boner slapping against his thighs.

I rushed closer and was relieved to see Gene wasn't having sex with the girl—he was gorging on her left thigh. My body vibrated with revulsion. I ran into the garage, retrieved the baseball bat and was over that fence in a flash.

I swung the bat square on the back of Gene's head, cracking his skull. He yowled and glared menacingly at me, his cheeks puffed with meat, blood dripping down his chin.

"Jap lover," he mumbled. "Fucking Jap lover!" Chunkers missiled from between his hellish teeth and he started choking.

Susan was beyond help, so I gave Gene another whack along the side of his face for what he'd done to Taffy. Gene went down hard.

I left him there, next to Susan's gnawed on body, and went inside.

Mrs. Sasaki was lying on her back on the kitchen table, her trunk dissected like a frog in biology class, the poor woman's purple marbled breasts akimbo. Instead of straight pins to hold the flayed flesh apart, Gene had used butcher knives and shish kebab skewers. Some of her internal organs had been removed and set aside, nibbled on.

I retched up the last of the bile in my stomach. Hot snot hosed out of my nose.

Downstairs I located Ed Sasaki in his office. He'd been decapitated, his gore-tailed head resting on its side on top of a Macintosh computer monitor. The rest of Ed was still hard at work, fingers poised at the keyboard. The computer beeped an error message. On the wall, painted in blood, were the words: "DEATH TO TOJO!"

I went back upstairs and had to use the bat on Gene again to get him away from the girl's corpse. Then I turned a garden hose on him, spraying the blood and gristle off him.

That cooled him off quick. He mewed like a kitten, started bawling, said he was sorry, came up with all kinds of lame-oh excuses. "It was the bright sun" or "post traumatic stress syndrome," or some other bullshit.

I hefted the baseball bat and thought seriously about finishing him off then and there. His face was a pulpy mess with mashed banana for a nose.

"Please, Mike," he whined at me, "I want to go home."

"You are home," I snapped.

"No, *home.*"

I'm ashamed to admit that I felt a twinge of pity for him, even though he had done monstrous things. I knew what he meant. He didn't belong here. I'd felt that way many times in school, being somewhat of a nerd myself.

I put the bat down.

"Okay," I said, exhausted. "I'll get you home."

The best I could do was put him on a bus for LA. From there, he was on his own. If he wanted to swim all the way to the South Pacific, that was fine by me. I figured I could do no more.

I gave him another shot with the hose to get as much blood off his face as possible. We went inside and Gene, still crying, put on pants and a shirt. I took the money I'd saved to buy a DVD player—$89—and hoped it would be enough to get my uncle to the coast.

Before we left, Gene went downstairs and retrieved his latest "project," which he packed in a brown paper grocery sack.

On the way downtown to the bus depot, I said to him, "Uncle Gene, I've been meaning to ask you. All those years in that sub, what did you eat?"

Gene gave me a sheepish grin—flashing those gnarly teeth at me—and said, "Curly, Skee, Bad Ass Budowski."

I nodded. That explained it. I didn't ask whether Gene's shipmates had willingly succumbed to his cannibalism; I didn't want to know.

At the bus depot I bought Gene a one-way ticket to Los Angeles and stayed with him for nearly half an hour until the bus departed. I didn't say much to him. He could tell I was pissed. Every time I heard a police siren I flinched.

Finally I broke down and bought him a donut and a cup of coffee. They announced the bus was leaving and I walked him to the gate, shook his hand.

"Good luck to you, Uncle Gene."

"Luck to you, Mike."

The bus pulled out and I was relieved, though I knew I'd catch hell when I got home.

Well, I'm sure you know the rest of the story. Gene's bus stopped in Las Vegas for a rest stop. Gene, stretching his legs, was approached by a bunch of Japanese tourists to snap their pictures outside the Gold Nugget casino.

Gene lost it, pulled the fuse on his "project" and blew himself up as well as twelve innocent people and half a block of downtown Vegas. Twenty-three more bystanders were seriously wounded. The FBI was sure it was a 9-11 type attack, until they found bits and pieces of Gene (including his dog tags) and his bomb.

Me, I wasn't prosecuted as an accessory because of my then status as a juvenile. A lot of people thought I'd gone through enough hell anyway. The court has ordered me to undergo psychological testing and counseling. And though I'm no kid anymore, they're flying in an expert on children and war to talk to me. The whole thing left me crazy numb.

My parents were devastated by the whole thing. The media returned to re-camp at their door. I know my dad would have a nervous breakdown, if he'd just let himself. I don't know whether the Hammontrees will ever be a whole family again. The scars left by my Uncle Gene cut deep to the bone.

I wish now they'd never found the son of a bitch!

Dan Thomas

Dan Thomas' background includes journalism, advertising, low budget filmmaking—and writing dozens of short stories for men's magazines. His horror novel *The Reckoning* was recently published by Black Death Books. Dan's lurid novella *Dark Highway* is forthcoming from the Demonic Clown imprint, also from Black Death Books.

The Poetry of Necromancy
By
C. S. Thompson

I had just delivered a lecture. It was one of those cowardly little lectures about myth and archetype. The value of storytelling to cultures everywhere. Watered down profundities. After I gave up my other studies, this was all I had left of them.

I was walking with my hands in my pockets, feeling typically melancholy. Musing about the ways in which we trade magic for lesser things. The ways in which we dissect our nightmares until they can no longer terrify us, until the only thing we're scared of us is this fatal boredom.

That, and the messages that still creep in from the other places. When I saw the bum begging for change, I was mildly nervous. He was clothed in filth and rags, and his eyes were rather shark-like. He didn't look contrite enough for a beggar. That was cause for suspicion.

The sign with which he begged for spare change was decorated with an ominous chaos of random symbols—peace signs and smiley faces, the A of anarchy, and one shape as complicated and exotic as the stylized signatures of graffiti taggers. I wouldn't have spoken with him, but I knew that sign. I would never have expected to see it here. I stopped at the mouth of the alley and peered in at him, crouching there.

"Does it really help?" I asked him, pointing.

He grinned at me slyly. "It doesn't work *all* the time. They'd catch on if it did. All it does, really, is improve the odds. I drink better most nights as a result."

"I was only a dilettante, myself," I said. "Not a true adept. Oh, I studied the grimoires. I memorized the poetry of necromancy. But I was always too terrified to try it for myself."

"Or maybe you didn't believe."

"Yes, perhaps." I nodded. "But where would belief have gotten me?"

I didn't intend this as an insult. But the implication was obvious. If goetia led anywhere worth going, you couldn't prove it by him. His magician's tower was a heap of piled cardboard and an alleyway cluttered with beer cans and discarded condoms.

"You're confused." He grinned. "But I am willing to enlighten you. The grimoires have no poetry in them. If you found it there, you brought it there. Those books are all-too-human."

He paused for a moment, fished in his pile of rags and came out with a bottle. It was a sickly green variety of Mad Dog 20/20. He offered me a taste, but I refused. Then he drank deep, and grimaced. He wiped a spilled drop of wine from his chin.

"They're all-too-human," he repeated, "Just look at the titles of their alleged workings—how to find treasure, how to get revenge, how to find out if your wife is lying. Petty, horrid little things. But they can lead to worldly success."

I just stared back at him. No contradiction was needed. But he didn't take offense; instead he laughed at me. "The poetry of necromancy is found somewhere else. It's not high poetry, really—no, it's more like a limerick. Light verse to pass the decades. But it's a lonely kind of fun."

"What are you talking about?"

I stepped into the alley. He looked up at me curiously. Perhaps he had waited for a long time to give this lecture, in a world without apprentices.

"Let's say that what we call life is a type of dreaming. A dream of the living, and the dead have their own dreams too. Slow dreams. Dead dreams."

Something about the way he said that made me shudder.

"Yes, the dreams of the living are fast," he said, "And the dead dreams are slow. There's no other difference."

"And so you, as a necromancer…"

"I read the slow dreams like a sheet of music. And then I play them."

I suppose he must have thought that I was looking at him skeptically.

"I assure you, it's true. And there is nothing more horrible on this side of the grave."

He chuckled and coughed up phlegm. Tubercular phlegm, disease ridden. He was swarming with life.

"No, nothing more horrible on this side of the grave. But on the other side…"

He pointed to a small wet lump of brown hair with white eyes. I could smell it rotting.

"Just look at that rat there," he said. "The perfect vessel."

He patted it like a pet. I swallowed deeply. His madness was compelling. I wanted to leave at that moment. There was nothing I wanted more. But I had to watch.

"I'll play its dreams for you," he said. And then he closed his eyes and stopped breathing. At first I wondered if he was dead, and I wasn't sure if I should try to do something or just make an anonymous call from the nearest pay phone. But then he took one deep breath that shook his body. It was as if he was drawing water from a very deep well. And when his eyes opened again they seemed to shimmer with starlight.

I peered a little closer. The light was not his own. His eyes reflected the sky of early evening like two pools of clear water. But underneath that, they were all but empty. They had turned into rat's eyes—and the rat was now moving.

It got two legs underneath it like a drunk standing up. The bottom half of its body was trying to help. Maggots poured out of a wound in its belly. The body fell apart. Both halves collapsed to the pavement again, now all but separated. Gravity had defeated its strange ambition. The creature's legs churned at the air. It knew nothing about hopelessness. As long as it was under this compulsion it would go on trying to stand.

The necromancer was laughing.

"Do you see what I mean?" he said. "It is strictly for amusement. But it's a gallows humor, I'm aware of that. The kind very few could stomach."

"I didn't think it was funny."

"So very sensitive. Such scruples." He laughed again.

I turned away as if to leave. But the sight of it held me. Once the command was set in motion, it seemed that contact was not required. The necromancer was no longer in the trance, but the rat still moved. And the poor creature's tormentor had not finished with his lecture.

"You understand now why the Haitians do not fear the zombi. They fear becoming a zombi. And that's the real horror, isn't it? To be a dead thing, and yet *compelled*. To have earned your rotten little rest, and still be forced to toil. And after all, what would the dead even do if they awoke from their sleep? Decayed hands wouldn't have the strength to dig through six feet of earth. They'd be trapped down there. *Trapped like rats.*"

He giggled at that.

"So they wouldn't eat our brains?" I laughed. Weak humor to hide my fear.

"No. What would they want with them? They would do nothing at all. That's the one bit of wisdom I gleaned from your precious grimoires. Death is the only condition more powerless than life."

He stood up suddenly, and things fell from him. Dust, fragments of brittle old leaves. Other things that squirmed as they fell.

"Come with me. I'll show you."

"I'm not going anywhere with you."

He came in at me suddenly. I had no time to protect myself. Before I could even put my hands up, he was as close as a lover, grinning his idiotic, knowing grin; his breath smelling of turpentine.

He gripped my tweed jacket and hissed at me, as if he had been to my lecture. "This is not an archetype," he whispered, "This is not a reality, either. It is not a mere construct, it is not a concept, but it is not just the truth. These things are mysteries."

He let me go, and I followed him. I had found no mysteries in academia.

We crept surreptitiously through the growing darkness of the city, as if this was how he always traveled, so as never to be seen. From one pool of shadow to another, from one corner to the next. If our city had been at war we would have been safe from any sniper.

It was a slow way to get from one place to another, but it revealed subtleties I had never had the time or inclination to notice in the past. Light splashed across dark pavement like oceans or galaxies. Alleys that faded out into who-knows-what, and strange shapes just past visible, crouching in the dimness. Children with pale, smudge-streaked skin and huge, staring eyes, peeking out from the corners of buildings and then disappearing. All the weird beauties of a place that was dying; Baudelaire's flowers of evil blooming secretly in the unseen corners.

And then the cemetery. It was like another city. If ghouls existed outside the realm of nightmares, they would have felt at home there, haunting that broken necropolis. Our city had been prosperous once, or so everyone assured me. Once upon a time, a long time ago, before the mills went away. Those early prosperous families left their mark upon the cemetery. Grotesque and romantic carvings sprouted like tumors from old shattered mausoleums. Here there was a knight with a sword, there an angel with a book. And everywhere graffiti. One tag said *Asian Disciples.* Another, strangely, said *John the Baptist.*

Something moved. Or did I imagine that?

"You're a romanticist," said the necromancer. He spat on the ground. "Ghouls eat corpse flesh."

I followed after him, silent in my thoughts. I already felt like a fool. We came through into another part of the cemetery. A place where the poor were buried, and I thought *the poor shall always be with you.* Because even in those more prosperous times, few people rated such gothic extravagance. In this section there were only crumbling old stones. Some of them had crude carvings. Some had none. Many of them had toppled. These graves went as far back as the 1700s. And here the necromancer stopped. He had come to his punch line, or rather the last line of his grim limerick. His demonstration of what I had called the poetry of necromancy.

He crouched down low over one of the graves. I noticed suddenly that he was much like a spider. Very much like a spider indeed, his limbs repulsively long and thin and his hair like wires. He put his ear to the ground.

"Yes, it's still happening." He nodded. He turned his head around to look at me, and again his eyes reflected starlight. He was smiling at me. I could hear the rustling of leaves and branches, the movement of tiny creatures through the fallen leaves. I could hear everything for a few moments, as if he'd turned up the world's volume.

"You do it," he laughed.

I came over to join him. Suddenly I remembered what he'd said to me earlier. What would the dead even do if they awoke from their sleep? They'd do nothing at all.

"Don't worry," he said, as if he was a little boy showing pornography to his friends. "There's six feet of dirt between them and us, never mind their coffins. They'll never make it through."

He grabbed my arm and forced me down. I put my ear to the earth.

Was that the sound of something frantically trying to dig?

C. S. Thompson

C. S. Thompson is the president of the Cateran Society, an organization devoted to researching and practicing the historic Gaelic martial arts. He is a poet and translator, and an author of crime fiction, horror, dark fantasy, and a manual on the use of the Highland broadsword. He is the author of *A Season of Strange Dreams* (BeWrite Books), a novel set in the same fictional city as "The Poetry of Necromancy." He is a board member of the Fellowship for Celtic Tradition LLC, and a member of the Celtic Martial Arts Research Society. He is 31 years old, and lives in Portland, Maine.

Happy Days with Dick and Jane
by
Lavie Tidhar

See Dick. See Jane. See how they run.

Behind them, the house is ablaze; the fire a false dawn illuminating the suburban skyline.

See Dick. See him run.

Dick's breath comes ragged, the air cutting through his innards like broken glass. Every breath is agony and yet he must get away, must escape before night truly falls. His short legs, never athletic, feel as though they are being stretched on a torture-machine until they are about to break.

'Keep moving!' Jane is ahead of him, her long, smooth legs moving gracefully on the asphalt road. There is the sound of a loud explosion behind them—and even through the pain Dick grimaces at the choice of words, as if an explosion is ever quiet—and he picks up pace, trying to get away from the nightmare.

See Dick. See Jane. See how they run.

They run through a neighbourhood in ruins; houses half-consumed by fire, cars overturned and covered in ash. There is broken glass everywhere, fallen lampposts. Red dust covers everything, the product of the roofs' broken slates, ground to a choking powder.

Ahead of Dick, Jane is slowing down. 'Quick, in here,' she calls, and then she is pulling Dick strongly by the arm and he is guided into a pool of darkness, a hole in the ground, where he collapses in an untidy, painful heap.

It is dank below ground. As Dick's breath calms down he notices the smell, first of all. He looks aside, and sees that Jane had noticed it also, but is trying to pretend it isn't there: the smell of rotting, decaying flesh. Human flesh.

See Jane. See Dick. See them hide.

Jane is watching through the hole. The place where they are hiding was once, it becomes apparent, somebody's basement. Dick bumps against a rake leaning against the wall. He curses quietly.

There is a silence all about them, a silence and an absence of light. True night is falling. 'Are they gone?'

Jane turns at the sound of his voice. 'No.' There is a tightness in her voice.

Dick joins her at the hole, peering outside in a near-sighted grimace. He searches for his glasses, realises they are lying, no doubt long ground into dust, at the basement of the house they had just left ablaze.

'What can you see?' He can't hide the tremor of fear in his voice.

'Two of them.' Jane's voice, like his own, shakes with a fear she can no longer control 'They've been following us.' Dick's eyes widen. 'Two Spot-spawned.'

See the dogs.

They move on the asphalt at a leisurely pace, feeling the broken suburban space with their presence.

See them snarl.

The dogs' fur is dirty and crusted with blood. Their teeth glint as the light gradually grows, as the full moon rises.

Smell the blood on their muzzles.

They come closer, sniffing the air as they approach. In their hidey-hole Dick bites on tightened fists, praying that the stench of death in the cellar would protect them. Unconsciously, he reaches down to feel his penis and the touch comforts him.

Jane pretends not to notice, but her eyes betray her disgust.

They draw deeper into the cellar, and wait, huddled together as if they were children again.

It begins with the book Dick had found.

Janey is nine and, at a whole year older than Dick, she doesn't take any crap from her little brother. Crap is a good word, and Janey mumbles it to herself at night. She knows not to use it in front of the adults, but in front of Dick she wields it like an expert.

'This book is crap, *Dick!*' she cries, and tries to grab it off him. It is a disgusting little book, mouldy and brittle, with dirty pages yellowed from age. Dick shouts in rage and runs away from her, still holding on to the book. Janey follows.

See Dick. See Jane.

See how they run.

But Dick is too quick for Janey, and by the time she captures him, red-faced and out of breath, the book is gone.

'Where is it?' she demands. Dick gulps air and doesn't answer. 'Where is it!'

No answer.

'If I catch you with that *crap* book I will *burn* it!' she stomps her foot and walks out. Dick grins uneasily behind her.

Dick has hidden the book. The book is safe. The book is Dick's.

The book teaches Dick wonderful things. It has illustrations in it, very *detailed* illustrations; it teaches Dick about animals, and about religion, and about science.

When Dick is fifteen he finally starts his experiments. Dick has grown, but the book is exactly the same. At first the experiments are small: mice from the pet shop, a wounded bird found in the yard, ants and beetles and snails by the handful.

Dick is a quick, bright student.

At sixteen, Janey is permanently Jane. She no longer chases her weird little brother around. She has better things to do.

Jane has discovered boys.

Dick listens, sometimes, when Jane brings her boyfriends home with her. Mom and dad are out, and usually they come back late, if at all, and come back separately. Dick doesn't like listening to them when they *are* together. He doesn't like it, the shouting and the threats and, even worse, the silences. He much prefers listening to Jane and her friends and the stuff they get up to in Jane's bedroom, with only a thin wall to separate them from him.

When he is alone Dick spends all his time down in the cellar, down in his *laboratory*. He has the book, and a healthy interest in what he likes to call *zoology*, and *anatomy*.

The rituals in the book require blood, more and more blood, but they work, and Dick gains powers: small at first, such as to cause a group of bullies at school to suddenly clutch at their heads in pain when they'd attacked him, or to cause Susan Pond, who is fat and stupid and sits in the front row, to suddenly wet herself in front of everyone.

The powers grow with the size of the sacrifice. Or rather, as Dick would have elaborated had there been anyone for him to lecture to, the volume of blood was what counted. And though Dick was initially surprised to learn how much blood can come from even the smallest creatures, his new requirements demanded larger prey.

One night Jane comes home with Peter and Ellen, the twins from next door. Dick is in his room, and he can hear them as they come in, laughing and bringing with them the smell of cigarettes and cheap perfume. Dick hears bumps in Jane's room, as of three people trying to get together into a small space. And then the noises begin, and Dick masturbates as he listens to them, masturbates and makes plans.

'Are Peter and Ellen coming back?' he asks Jane the next morning. They sit by the kitchen table alone. Mom and dad have not yet returned; likely wouldn't return before the evening, if at all.

Jane shoots him a quick, dirty glance. 'What's it to you, shithead?'

'I like them,' Dick says through a mouthful of cold egg. 'I want you to ask them back. For a...repeat performance of last night.'

'Were you listening to me?' Jane's face is slowly turning red in anger. 'You little *pervert*!'

Before she can go any further Dick swallows the remains of the egg, then, in a calm, studied movement lays down a large tape recorder on the table and presses play.

'Did they wear their little sailor outfits, Janey?' he asks through the quiet hissing of the tape and the much louder grunts and screams that emanate from it.

'What do you want?' Jane finally says. Her face looses its colour; its paleness makes the set of her jaws more pronounced.

Dick doesn't gloat at his older sister. Despite their fights, the brother and sister are close. Indeed, sometimes too close. Dick suspects his sister quite enjoys the performance.

'I want you to bring them over again. The same as before. Get them in the room, get them going, then slip out. And take their clothes with you when you go.'

For a moment, Jane looks almost disappointed. Then an ugly smile spreads over her face. 'Just a practical joke, is it? OK, little brother, you got yourself a deal.' She reaches her hand across the table. 'Now give me the tape.'

With another seemingly casual movement that was yet ever so studied, Dick presses the button to eject the tape. Jane catches it.

'I hope nothing happens to the tape,' Dick says, 'but if anything does, don't worry, I made copies just to be safe.'

Jane flips him the finger and, turning her back on him in one smooth motion, walks out of the room.

The next few weeks are quiet. Dick uses his powers only once, sacrificing a frog he'd found by the garden pond in exchange for a brief, unsatisfying form of invisibility that gets him into the girls' locker room at the end of a basketball game, but which fails just as he is about to come, his pants around his legs, over two of the cheerleaders. He is forced to turn them unconscious, ensuring their memories of the past five minutes would be lost forever, then marches home, seething. His experiments could not go on like that. He needs something bigger, something more *complex*, something that had gallons and gallons of blood.

That weekend, mom and dad disappeared again, and by tacit agreement Friday is chosen for Dick and Jane to play each his or her own part.

Dick waits in his room. At midnight drunken laughter sounds outside, and soon the door to the house is loudly opened.

He waits as Jane leads the twins into her bedroom. He hears Jane speak, hears a squeak of excitement from Ellen and a strange sort of grunt from Peter.

He hears clothes being taken off, and then the door to Jane's room opening and closing, and the turn of a key in the lock.

He opens the door to his room before his sister has time to knock. She is naked herself, and her white, athletic body glows in the light of the full moon streaming in from Dick's window.

'Here,' she says, thrusting the pile of clothes in her hands towards him. There is a satisfied grin on her face. 'And what do you propose to do *now*?'

'Now,' Dick says, 'is my business. I suggest you stay in mom and dad's room tonight.'

Jane looks like she is about to protest, but Dick pulls out two tapes from underneath his mattress and hands them to her.

'Now go.'

He waits until she disappears down the corridor, then returns to the mattress and pulls out a large hunting knife and two syringes. He hides the knife in his belt, and takes the two syringes on a little tray and goes over to Jane's room.

He knocks on the door. 'Guys? It's me, Dick. Jane wanted me to give you something. Something *special*.' He turns the key and opens the door.

The twins are squeezed together into Jane's small bed; Peter's tanned skin stands in marked contrast to his pale, delicate sister.

'What have you got for us, little man?' Peter says in a jovial tone. 'And where has our graceful hostess gone to?'

'Oh, Pete, be nice!' Ellen says, and smiles at Dick. 'Hi, Dick.' Two small, round nipples, the colour of blackberries, provide the only colour to her skin.

'Hi Ellen.' He lifts a syringe off the tray. 'Who wants to go first?'

'What is it, little man?' Peter gets out of bed and towers over Dick, his semi-erect penis almost touching Dick's trousers.

'Why don't you take your pants off and join us?' Ellen asks, winking at him.

'It's some new drug Jane'd got somewhere,' Dick says, ignoring her. 'You want to try it or not?'

Peter doesn't think for long. 'Yeah, sure,' he says, presenting his arm. 'Shoot.'

Dick administers the drug, first to Peter and then to Ellen, and waits as they drop off onto the floor a full minute later.

Ellen's light figure presents little problem, and he half-drags her, half-carries her down to the basement.

Peter, however, is a different matter, and Dick realises he has a problem.

He goes and knocks on his parents' door.

Jane opens the door in a huff. 'What do you want?' Her kimono is untied and she is naked underneath it.

'Found dad's porno stash, have you?' he says. Then, 'look, I need a favour.'

'Forget it.'

Dick feels his self-control slipping for the first time. 'Please, Jane. I need your help.'

She looks at him with one eyebrow raised. 'So?'

Dick tells her about the book.

'You *kept* it? You little shit!' Jane is quite impressed at her brother's ingenuity.

'...so you could have anything you want,' he says excitedly. 'anything!'

Jane tightens the kimono around her and grins at him. 'Let's go.'

She follows him to her room and helps him drag the unconscious Peter to the basement.

Dick unlocks the door to the basement. The thick wood of the door is peeling yellow, dirty paint, but that is nothing compared to the stench of decay that hits Jane from within the cellar.

She gags, but then picks up once more one of Peter's lifeless hands and helps Dick drag him the rest of the way into the dark room below the house. A sense of immediate, imminent danger captures Jane. Her eyes try to get used to the darkness in the basement, which is illuminated only by the light of the moon through two high, narrow windows— really nothing more than holes in the ceiling. The moonlight turns the shadows in the room agitated and, for lack of a better word, lively; as much as she tries she is unable to pin them down. The shadows seemed to move around her like living things, lurking in the corner of her eye, appearing and disappearing with a quiet sense of menace.

'Don't worry, sis.' Dick's voice, despite his apparent calmness, shakes a little. Whether in fear, excitement or both Jane can't tell. 'They need the blood to materialise. And in exchange for the blood, they'll give us power.'

Underneath his calm exterior Dick is bursting with smug excitement. The plan worked! No one knew the twins came to their house that night. And he had his sister sharing it with him.

'Tie them up against the altar,' he says. 'They'll come around soon. Oh, and stick something in their mouths so they can't fucking talk.'

Jane does that, ignoring the moving shades that dance around her. They seem attracted to the twins, seem to recognise in them the source of their approaching nourishment.

Suddenly, there is a howl from outside the house.

'What was *that*?' It was a sound Jane had never heard before, the cry of a tormented creature consumed with violence and lust, as of a maddened wolf.

Dick looks almost embarrassed. 'Oh,' he says. 'You remember when Spot disappeared?'

Jane's eyes go round.

'I did an experiment with him. It went wrong, and when it was over he was different, more different than I expected. I kept him, *it*, in a cage down here but he tore his way out of the cage and broke the door down.' Dick shudders. 'I hope he never mates.'

Dick prepares the ceremony. When the twins return to consciousness he begins the ritual, and Jane watches in fascination as Dick slowly begins to mutilate Peter and Ellen, cutting first their ears, then their toes, then just letting the knife flow over their skin, leaving long deep gashes that begin to ooze blood.

As the twins' blood falls on the altar the shades become at once deeper and more pronounced. Dick is reciting as he cuts, words in a strange language, words that seem to have a physical force in the small room.

See Dick. See Jane. See the blood.

Later, Jane will remember the exact moment the twins died; there is a loud, unearthly hissing sound, as of air passing through a very small hole, and then the twins collapse together, and the shades come truly alive.

The shades maraud inside the room, dark and alien beings whose movement is like that of melted wax; they crow in strange voices, screaming words in that same ancient language Dick had so haltingly spoken during the ritual.

And then they are gone, and the darkness lessens.

The next week, and the week after, and the week after that, are a swirl of emotions, of new sensations, of the taste of power.

Jane can do no wrong. She can make the bus stop for her at will; she can control boys' minds; she can get straight A's at school. She has power.

And Dick, Dick rules. Invisible, he wanders the girls' toilets, the girls' showers. And not invisible, too: he can control minds, he can make people do whatever he wishes.

See Dick. See Jane. Feel their power.

When the power wanes, brother and sister seek new prey.

Jane comes home one night with Pam and Penny, the sisters from across the road. Their black skin glistens in the moonlight as the knife leaves sinuous trails of blood across it.

From time to time they notice the changes.

The burned cars, the torn houses, the ravaged corpses left carelessly in the street in broad daylight. The men and women whose eyes cannot be seen, who walk in the shadows, who bring with them hate.

They watch one night from a safe distance as the creature that was once Spot forces itself on a female dog, and Jane shudders as she hears the screams of pain, almost-human, coming from that encounter.

And, later, the spawns of that encounter.

'Dick?'

'Yes?' Dick nervously licks his lips, not turning away from the sight of Spot.

'I'm scared.'

Shades seem to multiply around them; a thicker, inky darkness congealing like blood.

'Don't be,' Dick says. 'We're OK as long as we...as long as we...' the words stick in his throat.

'Have fresh sacrifices?' Jane turns to him and grabs his arm. 'Have you looked around lately? Have you seen many *people*?'

Dick shrugs her hand off. 'Don't worry,' he says again. 'There are plenty of people about.' He glances at Spot again and then turns away, something like panic in his eyes.

The shades follow them all the time now, hiding in whatever genuine darkness there is, lurking in shadows when there isn't one.

'It's a prison,' Jane says to Dick one day. 'And we're releasing them from it. Have you asked yourself what will happen when they all come out?'

But Dick hadn't. And when the day comes that there are no more fresh bodies, when there are no more people, Dick and Jane burn the house and try to escape; until they find themselves hiding in a hole in the ground, with two dogs moving towards them.

The dogs' red eyes stare directly into the hole. Then, they seem to twinkle suddenly, like a flame passing through a diamond, and the dogs move casually away until they are out of sight.

'They knew we were here,' Jane says. 'They knew!'

Besides her, Dick begins to cry, snot dripping from his nose into his lap. 'They're never going to let us get away,' he says. 'Never. We might as well give up now.'

But Jane wouldn't let him. She grabs hold of him and lifts him up, and slaps him until he stops crying.

Then they crawl out of the hole and begin to run down the road, past more overturned cars, past more demolished houses, as shades congeal around them in a cloud of darkness.

See Dick. See Jane. See how they run.

Lavie Tidhar

Lavie Tidhar is the winner of the 2002 James Ragan Poetry Prize and the 2003 Clarke-Bradbury International Science Fiction Competition. He grew up in Israel and South Africa and travelled widely in Africa, Asia and Europe. His short stories are due to appear in several anthologies, including *Vivisections II, DeathGrip: Legacy of Horror* and *Dark Streets After Hours,* and magazines in America and the UK, as well as in translation in France, Spain, Israel and China. He writes a regular review column for DuskSite.com and his non-fiction has appeared in *The Fix, Nova Express* and *Foundation.* He currently lives in London.

The Tongueless
by
Paul A. Toth

Before the crash, I was a reporter. I have a good memory. I remember almost everything about that night.

I can see my car weaving through the curves around Lake Fenton, the roads wet from an earlier rain. The tar looked like black onyx. Clouds blotted out the moon.

Look up, I thought: I am seen. I have been located. The game's up.

No, think again; just the ordinary regrets and sorrows. I often have dreams about airplanes crashing. Hoping for bad news is an occupational weakness. It's natural.

The trees were bushy and dark. They swelled and shivered in the headlights, distracting me. The windows steamed up. I could smell my skin. The wind tugged and tore and pulled. I couldn't hold the car still between the yellow lines. Ghosts from my mind moved about. The headlights revealed their fluorescent stick figures running in the fields. Some of them shot through the air like tracers. I rubbed my eyes.

Bad things happened on this road. There isn't such a thing as an evil road, I told myself, but there are good roads and bad roads, better made and worse made roads, lucky and unlucky roads, statistically safe and dangerous roads. It's based on numbers and if you're good with numbers, everything adds up. Otherwise, it's a mystery and you can believe anything you want, like the Bermuda Triangle.

Not long to go now, ten minutes and I was home. The big curve was coming up. If I handled it right, I'd get a momentary sensation of floating.

I pushed the accelerator down. The tires gave a little, spitting mud and rocks, then took hold again, and then lifted. For a moment we floated, the car and I, sailing the space of a raindrop over the tar, through the slim expanse of a second. The colors traced past, spraying fiery light like sparklers (the ghosts of everyone who had been killed on this road—impossible).

We moved toward another field of light, decelerating, the interior of the car illuminated, the dust of cigarette ashes covering the steering wheel and instrument panel. The spectrum of colors rushed towards a central point, then exploded with the sound of snapping, twisting, popping, smashing glass, metal and plastic.

I think I smelled gasoline.

Then it was dark and there was an interlude, silent and empty, motionless.

I suppose, though I cannot remember, that the strings were tuning, the reeds trilling the scales. Disorder permeated the air, but forms stirred. Consciousness, though muted for now, would soon intrude, drunken, seized with some unfathomable motive.

My nerves burn.

Push back, with your hands on the wheel. It's crumpled.

The air is aflame. If the sun was up the road would seem to bend in the heat, but the sun is—

It's dark. I'm blind.

Turn your foot toward the door. It's already almost open. Kick it. Your shoulder is burned, slide the seatbelt strap off. Good, now your body is free. Excellent. You've got guts.

See those lights, what are they? I remember them—missiles, I think. This must be a war. My head is bandaged. This is a supply road. I'm trying to make my way along it to the Red Cross tent. Those "ghosts" are explainable. Anyway, I'm hallucinating. I can't trust myself. It could be any year, any time and I could make up any sort of story involving lights. It doesn't mean a thing. The Bermuda Triangle.

Sure, that's what you think. Watch out for oncoming traffic. The helicopters are coming. The wind from their blades may sweep away the lights, but they'll come back. This is one hell of a news story, the dead along the roadside, coming to visit their biographer, flaunting their bright colors, saying, "Thought I was black ink on newsprint, then maybe a paycheck, and then a drink, a videotape, a pack of cigarettes. You asked for our deaths and now we're asking for yours. Come along, over here, in the grass."

I'm going off the road now but because there is something not far from here, a lake, and I'm thirsty. My throat is dry. Dry with blood from a wound. I wonder where the wound is—above my mouth, I know that much.

That blood was squeezed out of your articles.

Now that's just plain stupid. I've got to watch my footing. Those blades of grass are over 300 feet tall.

The blood's running down your face. If you'd stop a moment and look at yourself, you'd see that.

Blood from of my articles, huh? I didn't cause those accidents, I only recorded them. I want a boat. I think if I got into a boat and sailed away, I'd be safe. I've got to get to a boat.

There is a whole population of people in the same state of mind, right now. You're in an earthly purgatory. But don't believe me. Go find your boat! But I'm telling you, those ghosts can swim. They're land, sea and air ghosts.

That cave, between those trees, must be a tunnel out of here. It probably goes underneath the trees all the way to the nearest water. In it fish swim at your feet. In that water I will forget everything and start all over again.

Presumptuous, as usual. An easy way out of everything.

Who is talking to me? Do lights have the ability to force sound out? I didn't think so. And now, there's the tunnel. This didn't even happen, once I'm there. So whoever's talking can forget about me.

"There he is."

"You stay with the pickup and call for backup. I'll go get this guy."

New voices—the game's up. They'll find my tunnel like in The Great Escape. It doesn't look too good. I gotta move. Follow the owl.

"Hey, wait there."

Wait? Okay. I'll wait. I'm stupid. I'll let you trap me. Throw a net over my head. Take me to the Kommandant.

"Hold up. I'm with the township. Let me take a look at you."

So look. There's the entrance. I'm going with the cold, quiet fish.

"I've got you. Take it easy. Let's get you back to the road."

"Sixty-two, over?"

"Sixty-two. Located second victim."

I'm in your arms, now. You're leading me away. You're going to save my life and send me home early. I thought I'd escaped. I almost made it.

When I came to the next day, someone prodded me with a rolled up newspaper.

"Open your eyes slowly."

I looked and saw Dave Kukla, the assistant editor. "Front page." He held up the newspaper. "I wrote it."

The headline read: "Accident Kills One—'Miracle' Spares Weekly's Tom Hamilton'."

"I'll read it later."

"Let me read it to you."

"Not now."

"Okay, later. But I have a present for you. Sergeant Alistair gave me this."

I held out my hand. He placed a dictation tape in my palm.

"From the other car?" I asked.

"For your collection."

"I don't know that I want to know."

"Do you remember anything?"

"Everything."

"Sorry. I thought you'd want it."

I placed the tape on the nightstand. "I'll probably want it later. Thanks."

"Sure. I can't stay. But," he said, dropping the paper at my side, "thank God you're all right, Tom. That's how we all feel."

I've reported lot of accidents. Along the way I developed a hobby: Local paramedics and cops gave me the cassette tapes from the car stereos of crash victims. Or sometimes I went to the junkyard and removed the tapes myself. The stereo had to be old so the cassette wouldn't flip over automatically. That way I could be sure which song was playing as the car collided.

I kept a box of these tapes at home. I catalogued the name of the song with the article I wrote for the newspaper. "Two Men Die in Collision" (September 2, 1986 issue) went with "Rocket Man," for example.

These songs became intimately connected with the victims. A trip to any local store, restaurant or elevator, where many of the songs were likely to be playing, was like having a specific, geographical location of my brain probed by a surgeon. It began to seem as though I was walking in the land of the dead, their cars perpetually spinning out of collisions, faces repeatedly slamming into car windshields as I watched. I can't explain how this preoccupation first took hold, except that during the Christmas rush a cashier's dreams are invaded by coins, bills, the clicking of numbers.

I have come to think of that time just before the accident as pre-shock. It was going to happen and I was lingering, waiting. Like a war correspondent, I had wanted to be wounded so that I wasn't merely a voyeur. Now that I held the tape in my hand, which I had been told was taken from the Dictaphone that lay at the victim's feet, I wondered if I wanted to know any particularities at all about the man I had killed.

Because I caused that accident to occur. I was a murderer and everything about the crime except my motive had already been solved.

I took the tape and a portable stereo to my back porch. It was raining again, but harder than it had in quite a while. I set the stereo on the yellow wire lawn table and sat in the chair beside it.

The week of the accident had been slow for news. I dreamed of burning airliners every night. I took that curve too fast. As the car went airborne I turned my brights on, lighting everything, blinding the oncoming driver. That was my retirement plan. One last story, then I was gone, joining the procession that for all I know marched down that long road every night, an invisible marching band blaring silent horns while cars ran over their shadows. I suppose they came in red, yellow and green, unrestricted by speed limits.

That's how I knew something was about to happen. No mystery there.

Now I had to hear the end of the story. I made it happen, Kukla wrote the words, all except the last passage. I pushed the play button and rested my hands behind my head, staring into the trees behind the fence. This time the victim would have the last word.

"Are you listening to yourself talk? Yeah, I'm listening. [Laughter] No, really, I'm making this tape so that I can listen to it at the end of the night and know that this is what I feel and think. This is evidence that I must then destroy. It's only purpose is to strengthen my will.

"For some time I—you—I have been unable to conceive a single declarative sentence. Every action is in doubt. If I pick up a fork, it might be a murder weapon. I've done a lot of reading. It gets me nowhere. Maybe I'm sick, a brain tumor. I've lost my own opinions. I do not have opinions nowadays. I do not lift off, descend, arrive, crash. No, I circle the airport, waiting for directions home.

"I do not love or hate my wife; I love, hate and feel nothing about her.

"As they say, I'm on the fence, a mugwump, worse than evil, nothing, blank, zero, stagnate, unredeemable. I am, in short, a ghost. I'm not an angel or a devil. I am undefined. I am a word that does not signify. My name is Goo-ga. Goo-ga the Lost.

"I want to be tyrannized. I wish I were a dissident. I'd have these choices forced upon me. I would become a martyr. I would die happy. I want to be deprived of food, water and oxygen. I want to be dragged across the pavement. I want my hands raked across glass. I want to be interrogated. I want to be kicked, robbed, bludgeoned. I want prostitutes to laugh at me and spit in my face. I want my wife to cut my arms and legs off.

"I'm not deserving of hell. As my last friend, as yourself, I am begging you to listen to these words, to appraise the situation, to calculate the only solution, and to execute orders. Any time will do. The sinless are waiting for me. They're getting impatient. I can hear their voices. They are moaning in the trees. Wait, only some of them are calling me. There, where it's bright. There—[Horn blaring]"

The voices were confusing, yes. They came from the trees behind my house. They said many things; each had a unique perspective. They never left the roadside. They hesitated, hanging on, hoisting their opinions like flags in the mud.

It was incoherent in that place, out of key, dissonant. They'd abandoned one form and not yet assumed another. The best they could hope was that a few stories would be told of their lives at their funerals, plus, perhaps, a respectable obituary. But nothing new about them would be reported again.

How the rain fell that night. I wished them all a peaceful night. I knew they would soon disappear, one by one, only to be replaced by others. I wondered how long it took them to finally fall asleep and be taken into the larger dream.

The rain came down harder. Maybe it would flood. Flood away! I trusted the storyteller now that I knew he wasn't me.

Paul A. Toth

Paul A. Toth lives in Michigan. His short fiction has appeared in *The Iowa Review Web*, *The Barcelona Review*, *The Mississippi Review Online*, *Exquisite Corpse* and many others, with nominations for the Pushcart prize and Best American Mystery Stories. His novel *Fizz* will be published in late 2003 by Bleak House Books. He recently completed his second novel. His official website at http://www.netpt.tv includes complete credits, news and audio stories.

The Nameless
by
Ray Wallace

He didn't want this. He didn't want any of this. But there it was, lying on the bed, the evidence that it was real, that it was happening whether he wanted it or not. Just looking at the bed made him want to throw up, all the blood and the sight of the naked, dead hooker there, ripped open from pubis to sternum, ribs cracked wide revealing the destruction wreaked upon her internally.

Wreaked by him.

He could still taste her, taste her heart, the last part of her he had eaten, could vividly remember the other things he had chewed up and swallowed—her liver, spleen, kidneys, her large intestine.

Yes, he wanted to throw up.

But he knew he wouldn't, hadn't any of the other times. What he had done was necessary, was now required by his body, by what it was that he had become.

By what that fucking bitch had turned him into.

That's what kept him going, the thought of finding her, doing to her what he had done here tonight. Not to mention a few other even more unpleasant things he had planned, especially for her...

Ariella.

The woman who had taken him to higher highs and lower lows than anyone he had ever known.

The woman he had loved like no other.

"Oh, God, why?" he moaned, then tore his eyes away from the bed and what lay there, made his way into the small, ill-lit bathroom so that he could clean up, rinse out his mouth. It was time to move on, find another sleazy motel to stay in where he could await the inevitable return of the hunger, where he could then appease that hunger. And move on again and again, always looking, always asking about her, for he knew that she was still somewhere in the city—he could *feel* it—and he knew that at some point he would find her.

And when he did…

She lay in the dark, naked, legs spread wide, masturbating with a human thighbone, so full of the ecstasy of the kill. All the while she thought of Jake, out there, alone, trying to figure it out, fighting it, fighting it, but always giving in, learning little by little what it meant to be a predator, a murderer, a cannibalistic serial killer.

What it meant to be immortal.

She began to moan as she moved toward climax, brought the bone in and out more rapidly, pictured him tearing open some poor, unsuspecting little whore, burying his face in her organs much as he used to bury it between her legs. God, she used to love that, the way he would use his tongue…

And afterward, he would always tell her how incredible she tasted, how beautiful she was, how she almost made him believe in God because she *had* to be an angel, that no mere mortal could be as perfect as she was. Then she would go out and screw someone else, and tell him about it, prove to him that she was no angel. She could see at those moments that he hated her, that he could have killed her, but he never did because that hatred was born of a love so fierce that it hurt them both. And that's why she did it, why she would fuck other men—and the occasional woman—because even as that love made her feel like the most special person in the world, it also scared her. No one had ever truly cared for her like that before and she just didn't know how to handle it.

She was crying now, thinking of him, of what she had done to him. But even as she wept she came, gripped the bone firmly with both hands, flailed her body about in the darkness and wailed out loud as a tumult of emotions swept through her.

A short while later, she lay there panting, feeling the room's cool air play over her sweat-dampened skin. Then a door opened and a figure stood in the rectangle of light, looked in at her, asked, "Is everything alright?" in a thick, Russian accent.

She made no move to cover herself, simply lay there on the bed, staring up at the man-shaped silhouette, imagining how she must look to him. Removing the bone from between her legs, she casually tossed it to the floor where it landed next to the ruined corpse there, the thing that had once been a laughing, dreaming, breathing young man, was now nothing more than a broken carcass from which she had torn loose the femur that she had just finished with.

Forcing a smile she said, "Yes, everything's fine. Why don't you close the door, come over here. I think I can use some *live* meat."

Slowly, silently, the figure pulled the door shut and Ariella's bedchambers were once more claimed by darkness.

Jake remembered the change, how it had happened, how Ariella had returned one night after a month-long absence saying she was sorry, that she didn't ever want to fight with him again, that she had missed him terribly. He didn't even ask her where she had been, didn't really want to know, had just been so happy to see her. And in the bedroom she had told him how she wanted to be joined with him forever and had pulled out a razor blade, cut her hand and his, pressed the bleeding wounds together. And all the while she had kissed him so fiercely that he hadn't cared, would have done anything for her, let her do anything she wanted to him. Then they had sex, rough, violent sex, and when they were finished she said she had to go, to take care of some things, that she would be back later. And she had left him there, sweating, lying on the floor.

Left him to die.

Or to be reborn.

He had fallen asleep where he lay, not bothering to turn off the light, and awoke some time later consumed with sickness, his body racked with pain, his brain burning with fever. All he could do was lay there in a ball, puking and moaning and crying, praying for death.

At some point there were hands on him, caressing him, and he opened his eyes and saw an angel. His angel.

Ariella.

"Please..." he whimpered, or tried to. "Make it stop..."

"Shhhhh..." she said. "You're going to be alright. Everything's going to be alright."

She had a cool, damp cloth pressed to his forehead, all the while telling him how good things were going to be, how he wasn't going to die, that he was going to make it, how they would live forever...

He mercifully slipped from consciousness.

On and on it went, from sleep to waking agony, for an eternity it seemed. But when it was finally over he discovered that it had only been one night, a single night spent in Hell, and here he was, once again, in the land of the living, in his bedroom, the curtains drawn against the morning light, his head in Ariella's lap, her fingers running through his hair.

In the shower she told him things, crazy things, about how he would never grow old or get sick ever again, about how strong he would be when he fully recovered, how quickly any wounds would heal, and how bad the sunlight would hurt him.

Jake had laughed, mind still tinged with delirium, had asked, "What are we then? Fucking vampires?"

But Ariella hadn't laughed, had said, "No. Not vampires. Close, but not quite. We are something else, need more than mere blood to survive. We are something humans had never deemed fit to name. And I can't say that I blame them."

Jake couldn't help it, laughed again at the absurdity of what she was saying.

Later on, though, he discovered that her words were anything but humorous.

Nicolae claimed to be able to divine the future by eating the brains of his victims. He believed the fresher the brain the better. Ariella thought that he was more than a bit delusional, but who was she to argue? He was the man in charge. And besides, it did seem as though his predictions were right some of the time. But she chalked them up to mere coincidence and lucky guesses. The one time she had attempted such a foretelling she simply felt as though she had taken some bad acid and her appetite had disappeared for three days. Not an experience she wished to repeat.

A sudden rapping at the door to her bedchambers tore her away from the memories of that strange, hallucinatory event. For more than an hour now she had been sitting in a nightgown at an open window, thinking, a cool autumn breeze playing with her long, dark hair as she stared at the city laid out below and before her, at the myriad lights of the sprawling metropolis among which Jake would be wandering at this moment.

Searching for her.

The rapping came again and so she stood, crossed the room, the thick carpeting soft beneath her bare feet, opened the door.

Eric was there, a tall, thin, skin-headed young man—at least he *appeared* to be young—with a dyed red goatee. He said, "Nic's going to perform a divination," in his surprisingly high-pitched voice. "He wants everyone present."

"Of course. I'll be right down."

A short while later, after changing into a pair of shorts and a red blouse, she was downstairs in the living room—or the "dying room," as it was jokingly referred to among the other twelve members of the coven. A young woman lay hog-tied on a large wooden table—the room's lone piece of furniture—a gag in her mouth, her eyes wide with fear.

"Now that we are all here," said Nicolae from where he stood at the head of the table, where Ariella went and stood beside him, "I wish to inform you of recent news of the rogue."

Ariella looked around the table, at Eric and the ten other strange and beautiful faces staring back at her, handpicked by Nicolae over the one hundred and eighteen years of his existence. Some of them were nearly as old as he was. Some were much younger. Ariella was the youngest. And the most beautiful. And she knew that the five other females of the coven hated her, were insanely jealous of her position within the group. They would have destroyed her if it wasn't for Nicolae. She was his queen and therefore untouchable. That is, as long as she pleased him. And what if, at some point, he grew tired of her, as he had of those before her? Then she would have no protection, would be at the mercy of the others, mercy she knew they had in very limited supply. At the same time she was afraid to leave, could only wonder what Nicolae would do if she tried, knew that her own sadism paled in comparison to his.

Immediately upon joining the coven she had become aware of this situation, had almost as quickly devised a plan. And so one evening when her and Nicolae were searching for prey down at Sector 7—the nightclub where she had first met the strikingly handsome man with the captivating accent—she had disappeared into the crowd, had left the club and made her way back to Jake's apartment, had given him the dark gift, had stayed with him through the worst part of the change, made sure he was going to make it. Then she had left him again, to grow strong on his own, to search for her and at some point find her, to hopefully bring her plan to the sought-after conclusion.

"He has become rather famous of late," continued Nicolae after a brief pause, gently stroking the head of the terrified woman on the table. "The news is full of the bodies, mostly of prostitutes, which have been found all over the city. The media has even released a rather crude description of the man who may be responsible. Fortunately for us, the mortals believe it to be the work of a particularly heinous serial killer, or group of serial killers, for how could one person be responsible for such a trail of carnage? It is obvious that this rogue is a fledgling, lacks guidance, has never been taught the supreme importance of properly disposing of the remains, of not attracting attention to himself, to our kind!" The last words were accented by grabbing the bound woman's hair, by repeatedly lifting her head and banging it down on the table. A moan escaped from behind the gag.

"There are a few questions that need answered here." Once again, Nicolae was his former, calm self, softly petting the woman's hair. "First: who is this rogue? Secondly: what is it that he wants? And lastly: where can we find him? Anyone have any ideas?"

He scanned the faces before him, expected no response, got none. Then his eyes were on Ariella and as she met his look she was filled with a cold certainty that he knew, that he must have followed her that night, had seen where she had gone, knew exactly who this rogue was, why he had been created.

But he said nothing to her, simply smiled at her, then turned his attention to what lay on the table.

"I thought not, which brings us to what it is that I am about to attempt here."

With that he reached down and grabbed the head of the woman lying in front of him with both hands, said to her, "I'm sorry, but I'm afraid this is going to hurt a great deal." Then he began to squeeze.

The woman's bright, blue eyes began to bulge from their sockets as Nicolae used his superhuman strength to apply pressure at her temples. Ariella started breathing deeply as a now-familiar rush of pleasure came over her at the sight of the woman's thrashings, at the sound of her muffled screeching. Harder and harder Nicolae squeezed until there was an audible *pop!* as the skull between his hands caved in, and just like that the woman's struggles ceased. Next came the tearing away of the scalp and the opening of the cranium. A short while later Nicolae was holding the woman's brain in his hands.

"With this I will see what is to be," said the leader to his assembled minions. "And with any luck I will be shown what part, if any, the rogue will play in the future of our family."

So saying, Nicolae ate the mysterious organ that had so recently been the seat of consciousness of an innocent, beautiful young woman. When he was finished, a chair was brought into the room to which Nicolae allowed himself to be tied. Then the table was pushed against a wall and the "family" made themselves comfortable on the floor before their patriarch, waited for the divination to begin.

They did not have to wait long.

Suddenly, Nicolae's body tensed, was straining against its bonds, his hands opened, fingers formed into claws, mouth stretched wide in a scream. Two of the males present jumped to their feet, held the chair so that their leader would not topple to the floor. Then the scream faded and Nicolae relaxed and began to speak.

The divination started the way it normally did, with a lot of talk of fire and darkness and the end of all things. The other members of the family sat enraptured as they always did, but Ariella was not impressed. It was an easy thing to prophesize of such things. Then he went on to tell of the leaders and the countries that would fall before the end of the world, and he even spoke of the end of their kind. After an hour of this, the divination finally got interesting.

"And there will be blood," said Nicolae in a harsh whisper. "So much blood. Within the walls of this house. For he will come. The rogue. Jake is his name! *His* blood! And *mine*!" His gaze suddenly found Ariella, locked with hers. "All for you…"

He paused for a moment, looking into a place that only he could see.

"And there will be death. A final death. For one of our kind. For either him or me!" His eyes bored into Ariella's, would not let her go, threatened to pull her into that place he was gazing into. "But it is dark…so dark…hard to see…I must get closer, stare into the face of the fallen one…Yes! It is he! The rogue! In this house he will meet his doom…"

And suddenly Nicolae fell silent, said nothing for some time, and it seemed that no one else could find anything to say either.

Ariella sat holding herself in the silence, shaking, wondering if it could be true, hoping that he *had* followed her that evening, that he had not truly seen the future. But for the first time she had her doubts. What if he really did possess such ability?

Then as the wind and the rain began to lash the house, as lightning illuminated the room's curtained windows, Nicolae said in a calm, sane voice, "Untie me."

Later on, after they had made love—or the closest thing two of their kind were capable of—Ariella lay next to Nicolae in the darkness, crying as she thought about the person she used to be, what it was that she had become. And what she had done to Jake, the only person who had ever truly cared for her.

It was mid-October when Jake found the house.

Nearly two months had passed since the change, since he had become some nameless, unspeakable thing. The city was in a panic over the trail of cannibalized corpses he had left behind and the authorities had banded together in a manhunt of previously unseen proportions.

A week earlier, they had nearly caught him.

He had been dozing on the floor of another motel room, satiated by his earlier meal, the remains of which were still in the bathtub, when there came a pounding on the front door.

"Sir?" came a voice from beyond the door. "Sir, are you in there?"

Instantly alert, he had rushed to the window, peeked around the curtains, saw the motel's balding manager and two uniformed police officers outside.

One of the cops turned to the manager and said, "Alright, open it up."

Jake didn't wait to see the man pull out his key ring, place the key in the lock. He was running to the bathroom, smashing out the small window there with his bare hands, climbing through, mindless of the myriad cuts he suffered in his escape. Then he was in the small alley that ran behind the motel, the sound of footsteps coming after him, someone yelling, "Stop! Police!!" Shots were fired. A bullet whizzed past his head and bright pain blossomed as one hit him in the back of the thigh.

He cursed and grabbed at the wound but barely even slowed, turned down a few more dark alleys, made his way into an abandoned apartment building where he sat quietly, listened to the sounds of pursuit pass him by.

Already the pain in his leg was ebbing, the wound closing as were those caused by the glass of the broken window, another demonstration of just how inhuman he now was. He was concerned though, not by the physical harm he had endured, but by the close call he had just experienced. It seemed that he was getting careless, had made someone suspicious, enough so that they had reported him to the police. From now on, he would have to be twice as cautious as ever before.

It was the following night that he heard about the house.

He was in another, even sleazier motel with another hooker. And this one was a talker.

"Oh, yeah, there's all kinds of freak shows out there," she had said in her cheap, Brooklyn accent. "If you can think of it, honey, someone out there's into it." As she undressed, the skinny streetwalker had gone on to recount all manner of requests she had fulfilled for various customers: S&M, domination, golden showers, bizarre role-playing incidents, bestiality (dogs were as far as she would go, thank you very much. Except for that one time with the orangutan...).

Then there was that really weirdo place on the outskirts of the city, the big mansion where a group of people lived who were rumored among her fellow prostitutes to be some sort of cult. She had even attended a party there once, had tried to talk to some really good-looking guy with this amazing accent—"You know, like from Russia or somewhere."—into some high-priced kinky stuff. But he had merely looked at her like she was a piece of fecal matter and had wandered off, leaving her to find someone else interested in her offer.

It had been a great party although it was said that there were others who had attended who had never been seen again...

This story had hit Jake like the bullet he had taken the night before. Recently he had been dreaming of a house, a big house on a hill overlooking the heart of the city, all those lights laid out below. And in his dreams he would stand in front of the house, convinced that Ariella was inside, but for some reason he was too afraid to go in and find her.

After he had gotten directions to the mansion, he had killed the hooker—quickly and painlessly out of gratitude for the information—had eaten his fill of her, then had left to find the place he was now certain he had been searching for all along.

And here it was, just as it had appeared in his sleep-visions, an old mansion built on a hill on the edge of the city.

He was afraid, here, in real life too.

But Ariella is in there, he told himself. *She had to be.* And the thought of what she had done to him, of what he had had to endure, filled his mind, and he was overcome with a rage that made his fear seem a feeble thing. Fueled by that rage, he ascended the steps that led up to the front porch and the double doors there which he smashed open with a mighty kick.

Then he was standing in an unlit foyer, the room darker than the night outside, and all of his pain and fear and hatred poured forth from him in a single word: *"Ariella!"*

Again he screamed and this time when he fell silent a voice said from directly behind him, "Well, well, well. Look what we have here." A voice with a thick, Russian accent.

He turned around but no one was there.

Then he heard laughter coming from inside the house, and when he looked in that direction again someone or something slammed into him from behind, dragged him into the mansion's darker interior. He was kept off balance, pushed through one room after the next until he was finally let go, allowed to fall to the floor of a large room which had but one piece of furniture, a table pushed against one of its walls. A few candles stood in the corners atop elaborate holders, providing the room's feeble illumination.

Jake quickly got to his feet, looked about him, saw that he was not alone.

Figures stood in the room's three entranceways, close to a dozen of them, half of them male, half female, all of them young looking and beautiful in their own, unique ways. And a part of him knew that all of them were the same thing he was.

"Welcome to the family," said that accented voice from behind him again.

This time when he spun around someone was there, a man of stunning good looks, his perfectly etched features dancing in the candlelight.

"So you are the famous serial killer we've heard so much about," said the man in a mocking tone. "It is an honor to have you here, sir."

Once again there was laughter, coming from the others.

"Where is she?" asked Jake in a tight voice.

"She? Oh, you must mean my beautiful Ariella. Of course that is why you are here. Unfortunately, she did not wish to attend tonight's entertainment, did not think she could bear to witness the events that I have foretold. She is elsewhere, awaiting my return, there to pleasure me once I have disposed of you."

And so another emotion was added to the dangerous mix already fueling Jake's thoughts and actions: jealousy. He finally had someone before him whom Ariella had been with, someone he could direct the pain of all the past betrayals toward.

With a roar, Jake launched himself at the man before him, grabbed him by the throat, drove him backward into the wall there with all of his superhuman strength, pulled him out of the hole created by the impact, slammed him into another wall, another…Then the man broke Jake's hold and drove him through a wall, into another room which soon resembled the one they had just left, brought to ruin by their conflict. At some point they ended up back in the foyer. On and on they fought, each raining blows upon the other, biting and tearing at each other's flesh. Jake felt as though he were being hit with a sledgehammer, that a hawk with razor claws had been turned loose on him, felt the blood running freely over his skin. *Whack!* He felt ribs break. *Whack!* There went a knee. He knew that some of his shots were landing also, felt bone give way beneath a couple of them, felt flesh rending beneath his grasp. But he also knew that his opponent was older than he and apparently stronger. It did not take him long to come to the realization that if the battle continued like this he would be defeated.

Suddenly the man was on top of him, had him pinned down, was laughing as he placed a hand on each of Jake's temples.

"Now that wasn't very nice," came the voice out of the darkness above him. "Showing up and wrecking the house that took me all these years to save up for. All that stealing and cheating for this? Do you know how much it will cost to have it all fixed? And not to mention the way you have treated me!...Oh, well, I must admit that it was fun. I haven't had a good fight like that in, oh...sixty, seventy years. But I'm afraid that the fun must now end for, you see, it would do me no good at all to have a rival such as you around."

And with that the hands on either side of Jake's head began to squeeze...

It felt as though his head were in a vice, that at any moment his skull must surely crack. He opened his mouth to scream...

That's when the massive chandelier directly above the two combatants came on, and the pressure to his head suddenly abated.

Both men turned and looked towards the grand staircase that descended into the room, saw Ariella standing there. And Jake knew immediately that all his thoughts of hurting her were simply those. Thoughts. That he would never hurt her. That he just wanted to be with her. The sight of her caused a far deeper pain than all his wounds combined, a pain born of loneliness and longing. And he heard those feelings reflected in her voice as she said, "I'm so sorry Jake."

It was all he needed to hear.

With the last of his strength he thrust upward, driving his assailant into the chandelier, which exploded in a shower of light and crystal, imprinted on his brain the sight of the blood—his and his foe's—which smeared the walls, puddled the floor. Then he threw himself aside as the great fixture fell from the ceiling and landed on the floor below with a deafening crash, the other man pinned beneath it.

Darkness again, then hands on him, familiar hands, pulling him from the room, saying, "We must go. Now. Come on, before the others try to stop us."

Then they were outside, beneath the stars, and Jake moaned as the physical pain of his ordeal assaulted him. He nearly collapsed but Ariella held him up with tender strength and told him that he would be alright, that everything was going to be alright...

His wounds healed, of course, and he eventually came to accept what it was that he had become. Having Ariella with him helped.

At some point they heard that Nicolae had survived the battle, that he still had his family, had found a new queen.

"Good for him," Jake said as he drove a new sports car through the night-shrouded streets of a city far from the one where he had been reborn. "Good for him."

"Someone's happy," said Ariella from the passenger seat.

He turned and smiled at her. "We're together. How could I not be happy?"

She leaned over and kissed him.

"You hungry?" he asked.

"Starving."

"Me too. I found a place the other night, just around the next corner."

A few moments later they were there. He pulled up to the curb, rolled down the window. A scantily clad young woman approached.

"How much?" Jake asked the prostitute.

"For the both of you? A hundred."

He looked at Ariella. "What do you think?"

"Mmmm, tasty."

"Alright, get in." He opened his door, pulled his seat forward, motioned for her to get in back. She did. He closed the door.

Ariella reached over and took his hand, lifted it to her mouth, gave it a little bite.

Oh, it's going to be a wild one tonight, thought Jake then he put the car in gear and drove off into the darkness.

Ray Wallace

Ray Wallace hails from Brandon, FL, a suburb of Tampa he affectionately refers to as "Satan's Spawning Ground." There he runs a record label with his brother, composes electronic music, and writes his fiction. He has published stories in such publications as *Cthulhu Cultus, Erotic Fantasy: Tales of the Paranormal, Monster's Ink, Shadowland, Thirteen Stories, Welcome to Nod, Whispers from the Shattered Forum,* and at *Bloodfetish, Bloody Muse, Camp Horror, Dark Muse, Delirium,* and *Errata* (a story written with Geoff Cooper and Brett Savory). A few of his other stories have appeared at *The Chiaroscuro* website where he took first place in a fiction contest. He also wrote a long running book review column for *The Twilight Showcase* webzine and now writes reviews for *Chizine* and *SFReader.com.* He is currently slaving away at his first novel.

Lisa's Shortcut
By
Nicholas James White

Interstate

Interstate somewhere which connects to something—you get off at the end. Thanks. Having no clue the man at the wheel drives, he looks at his useless navigator (who snores a lot), and quietly repeats the directions in an attempt to see which one sounds more correct. Was it east or west? Do you hit the exit or drive past it? Should I stay or should I go now?

Lisa, the sleeping navigator occasionally moves around in the passenger seat and talks to herself in her sleep. Not an intelligible, interesting kind of speech, not something to get the blood flowing; she mumbles. The driver hates this and occasionally tries to converse with her while she sleeps. The closest thing he gets to language is a "hunh?" Paul the driver stares blankly at the road; he does this so when she does spring to life, she looks awkward. On the basis that he has just met this woman, and has no real allegiance to her, Paul instead of taking the exit cruises down a back road a few kilometres after the exit. He can see the overall flatness of the landscape begin to majestically change as huge forests pop over the horizon. A forest like God is old. The forest was getting even taller upon Paul's approach.

The forest herself was mostly evergreen and its canopy was thick. The kind of forest where by early evening its floor was pitch black and its nocturnal animals were out by 6:00 pm. There was nothing but bats, possum, raccoons and the occasional deer. And with the death of the day Paul found rebirth cruising into an off-beaten path at the forests edge. Oddly enough at just about sunset—right at the start of the forest—Lisa woke. Paul had decided Lisa was the best liar at the diner only a few hours before. As opposed to what he expected to be a story about visiting a sick mother or aunt, Lisa did in fact admit she had no real home, and she did in fact sleep with truckers in exchange for a consentient change of scenery. Lisa was a hopeless drifter. But at least she admitted it. Paul connected with her with stories of his failed band and how they almost got into the music business in a big way. Lisa almost went to collage. Despite the stereotypes, Paul immediately concluded upon their meeting that Lisa was indeed very eloquent and versed in current events. She was not Daisy Duke as Paul had hoped. She was something better. Paul had felt guilty about approaching her like a stripper or prostitute avoiding big words and serious conversation—Lisa coped with this well and never threw it back at Paul. This was why Paul was driving Lisa out of state and in no way expected sex from the arrangement. Paul just wanted conversation on an endless, mind-numbing trip. Anything else would be a bonus but still a fantasy.

Moondance

"Where are we?" Lisa asked softly.

"My guess—middle of nowhere." Paul grinned as he replied.

"You're not one of them rapists, are you?" Lisa said mockingly in her best southern twang.

"No, I be watcha call a serial killa, baby," Paul said very straight-faced in his best twang.

"Honestly, I thought this would be a shorter route; if it really bugs you I can turn it around."

"No, no," she replied, placing her hand on his shoulder. "If we're both clueless as to where we're going, then who's to decide the best route?"

"Touché," he replied as he fumbled with the radio dial.

There were tire marks on the road they were now cruising down, which meant that at least someone in the past day had used the road. This made Paul sigh relief, but only in his mind. In the worse case scenario they had only driven straight into this place and had taken no turns; thusly, although a huge pain in the ass, Paul could just turn around.

The static of the radio gave way to "Moondance".

"Do you mind? I love this song," he asked politely.

"Go ahead. I like it too."

Bonus: smart and she understood the overwhelming goodness of Van Morison. She's a keeper, he thought. She'll do just fine. The song dripped out of the speakers to mix with the gorgeous starry backdrop that was Paul's wrong turn. He placed his hand out the window to feel the breeze. The air smelt fresh too.

"It's fucking *beautiful*," she said slowly

"Lets just stay in here." She placed her hand around his neck and began to scratch.

Oh shit, she knows to do that. Where's a jeweller? he joking thought. Oh man—just propose right now.

He turned his head so to rub against her arm like cat would. He needed to show affection at this point, lest the all-too-important neck scratching and rubbing stop. He felt like he was 16 again. He smiled at Lisa.

"It does not get better than this," Paul explained.

"Well, I guess there might be one way it could," she said, looking him straight in the face.

Wow. Paul one, the rest of single men in the world, zero. He pulled over just before a hill. Paul though about oncoming cars but then decided against being such a wussy. As soon as he pulled the hand brake she was atop Paul and reclining his seat back. Paul realized he was entering what could only be a porn or urban legend type of scenario. And he loved it. She kissed him deeply and undressed him quickly; he followed suit. They made love—yes, Paul thought, not sex—right there. Under that starry blanket they both appreciated.

Afterwards Paul stepped out to suck up some of that sweet air he had been enjoying earlier. Then they both hit the tree line to relieve themselves. As they headed back towards the car, neither of them felt awkward, nor did either show any regret. Paul opened the trunk and rummaged past his black gym bag to find his essential supply of booze for boring hotel nights. He popped open his cooler and handed Lisa a beer.

"Sorry, it's not a cigarette but I felt I had to commemorate this with something, you know?" he said jokingly.

She smiled and began to drink. He smiled back, looked at the sky again and drank as well. They held hands as they sat on the hood.

Their moment was shattered by the distinctive blast of a shotgun.

Paul heard the wail of buckshot ricocheting off a hubcap as his left rear tire vomited out its last fleeting spouts of air. Paul recoiled almost into a ball, spilling beer on his shirt. He grabbed Lisa's trembling hand and pulled her off of the hood and scurried with her behind the other side of the car—hoping that there was no shooter on this side as well. He was glad he wore black—it covered his form well—but he had Lisa to contend with; she was wearing a white shirt and khaki pants—in the moonlight that sort of thing lights up. Paul knew they were both fat targets at the moment and he desperately tried to snake his hand into his trunk to get his gym bag. Lisa, teary-eyed, slapped his shoulder and frantically pointed to people coming down the road. There were four to be exact.

"Fuck," Paul said softly.

The men said nothing but motioned with their guns for Paul and Lisa to stand, which they did. The men were all taller then Paul but some not quite as built. Paul softly sized them up and hoped they were as stupid as they looked. Some of the men were clad in some sort of redneck militia uniforms, the others in what looked like farmers overalls, all very, very filthy.

"What do you want?" Paul said flatly, puffing out his chest. He was a built guy and hope these white trash highwaymen would recognize and respect that.

One of the men smashed the but of his gun into Lisa's head, who immediately fell. Paul promptly smashed his fist into the mouth of the man who stuck Lisa, only to be quickly dispatched in the same fashion by one of the other men. He could only see up to their muddy boots as they kicked in his chest and head. The dark forest went totally black.

As he slept he remembered how it was just a few months ago. There was an amazing clarity to his dreams but perhaps because of the cruel nature of this sleep they were cruel unpleasant dreams. Not nightmares, no. Simply unpleasant realizations of the drifting path he had chosen. Its beginnings and what he understood to be its eventual ending. He remembered the strip club—the rude bouncer—what he did and how he fled. And the next week, the bar—the rude patron and what he did. From then on the scenario was the same and his newfound illegality kept him from a fixed residence. But what did he care? His musical aspirations had failed, and not that it justified anything, but he knew that was it. Past hating collage and not being good with his hands, Paul knew that if he didn't get a band going it was over. Paul had nothing to loose. Hence the drifter/outlaw lifestyle he had chosen. This cowboy bullshit is played out, he thought—but still strangely appealing. Paul's formula was flawless: do something stupid in one county where no one knows your name, then drive to the next. Repeat. Paul's spinning dreams bled into spinning reality as the black slowly drifted away.

Rude Awakenings

When Paul did wake the headache was not as bad as he thought it would be. However his sides, shoulders and waist hurt; and when he looked down he knew why. From just below his collar bone to his waist Paul was wrapped in barbwire, like a three-year-old's attempt at Christmas wrapping. Here ya go, Daddy, a Chwistmus Pawl. Paul wanted to scream, but would that make the situation worse? He could see one of the highwaymen rummaging through various silver-looking tools all laid on a slab directly in front of him. The man had long greasy hair and a lean build; his clothes looked like a dressed-down kind of military uniform, camel pants, something you'd wear paintballing. The man looked up at him, smiling.

"Its as bad as you think! And worse than you could have imagined!" the man said manically.

"Gonna fix you up really real nice!"

"Fuck you," Paul replied.

The room was a dirty beige colour; it led Paul to believe they were in a basement of sorts, or maybe a cellar. Something with a lot of concrete to soak up sound, at any rate. The chair he was strapped to seemed like a very old dinning room chair, circa late 40's early 50's. Paul, it would seem, was tied down with what appeared to be chicken or maybe barbwire. He tried to subtly move but that only made him subtly bleed. But the chair itself was frail. Paul noted that. To the immediate left was what looked like an old coal chute. The chute was holding very dry crackling wood. To the right a thick wooden door

"You just give me one second. I want that bitch you came with to see something. I have this really interesting hobby," he said, moving towards the door.

He paused just before the door and spoke, not turning around.

"It's called torturing the shit out of people," he said authoritatively.

After he left Paul began to thrash up and down. Using his legs and calf muscles to lift the chair and then smash it down again on the floor. The wood began to give way. It cut and it hurt, but he didn't care. He kept smashing till he heard the door begin to creak open. Lisa, in a filthy white shirt and khakis, and what looked like a pillowcase around her head, stumbled in, followed closely by the greasy sadist. A thousand thoughts of the nature of his abductors flew through Paul's addled brain. Where they trying to scare him? Where they this insane? What had they done to Lisa or what where they going to do? That thought, as horrible as it sounded to Paul, gave him strength—because now what were they going to do to *them*.

The wiry creep moved confidently to the coal furnace, opened it and with a rag from his back pocket, pulled out a long poker. Lisa remained still and standing, her hands bound behind her with what looked like the same barbwire. The creep held up the poker and waved it towards Paul, the end of the instrument glowing a dull cherry red.

"Now this will only hurt a lot," the thing joked.

He placed the poker on Paul's chest. The searing sound hit before the pain, which was a sick sort of white-hot sensation. When the poker was pulled away it felt as if the pain went down deeper into his chest like a diving bird, and like that swooping bird, crested up again a few moments later.

"Fuck...you! Inbreed!" Paul screamed.

His shoulders began to shake and he rocked back and forth in pain.

Again the sizzle, the pain and the rocking.

"Fuck!"

The sizzle, and now twisting of the instrument.

"Cocksucker!"

Paul slammed the chair up and down in discomfort while his captor giggled and marvelled at his own craftsmanship. The wire was still cutting, now over the fresh burns.

"You're dead for that," Paul said calmly as his chair snapped.

His captor moved back as Paul regained his footing and bulled the sadist into the table ahead of them, his head butting the redneck's scruffy jaw. As his captor fell to the floor Paul had precious seconds to pull of his wire constraints. Paul, despite the ripping and stinging, did not hesitate. The whole time thinking, *What I am gonna do to you...*

With the wire on the floor and new adrenaline in his blood, he quickly stomped his heel down between the legs of his would be captor. Again and again. The man cried beneath Paul's shoes. With his interrogator whimpering on the ground, Paul began to swing his foot into the ribs of his hated captor. The highwayman grabbed at Paul's legs and Paul felt a special satisfaction. Paul picked the highwayman up by his greasy hair. The man kicked and screamed as Paul dragged him towards the furnace.

"No please!!"

"No shit! This upsets you, hillbilly?"

"Gosh, I am ever so sorry!"

Paul pushed the hillbilly's head into burning ambers. He looked back to see Lisa still frantically spinning her cloth covered head around.

Best she didn't see it anyways. The hillbilly kicked and cried as Paul pushed his face deeper into the coals. Eventually the kicking stopped. It smelled like hell. When he threw the body aside, it looked as if the face was made of tree bark. Smoke rising from the nose.

Paul headed towards Lisa and gently removed her mask. Her eyes were teary but they lit up regardless. He hugged her and gently began to untie her wrist restraints. She seemed shaky, but who wouldn't be.

"Are you hurt?" Paul asked cautiously.

"I'm OK; they didn't really do anything else other than toss me around a bit," Lisa explained

"Who are they?"

"I have no idea, but I'm sure they heard us, so let's get out now."

Paul looked to the slab in the middle of the room. The devices all looked like they were either for surgical purposes or for a slaughterhouse. Some of the blades were rusty, some shiny and new looking. Not wanting to think about it anymore than absolutely necessary, Paul grabbed what looked like a hunting knife off the table, the only knife he could properly identify, as well as a few scalpel-like tools, which he gave to Lisa. Lisa herself promptly walked over and picked the poker up from the floor. Simultaneously they both headed towards the door.

The stairs that led above were solid but made of a very old wood. It led Lisa to believe they were probably in an old farmhouse, or possibly a large cabin. The both moved sideways up the steps. Lisa led with her poker held in a batting position, as to dispatch any assailants. The steps were dimly lit with what looked like a sliver of moonlight at the top coming from underneath another heavy old door. Lisa placed her hand on the door.

"Just swing—don't think about it," Paul whispered into her ear.

Lisa gently pushed the door open and recoiled back to swing. There was nothing but a dimly lit room. A kitchen. Darkness and nothing more. Lisa moved in slowly. The cupboards were scratched and the wood itself rotted. There was a small table in the centre of the room, which did contain some freshly eaten chicken bones. Or something's bones. For whatever reason, the other captors were nowhere to be seen. This in no way relaxed the two of them. To their left was a den of some kind and straight ahead an exit. They wasted no time and bolted towards the rickety wooden door which they both quietly prayed led to a main road.

Crashing behind them, one of the taller highwaymen burst into the kitchen from the den, flipping the old table in his wake.

"Where's Jimmy?" he demanded in a very deep voice.

Paul assumed Jimmy was a friend, or more likely a brother as this particular captor had a similar but taller appearance. Uber-Jimmy.

"I killed him. Where the fuck is my car?" Paul said coldly.

Lisa couldn't believe someone in a situation this scary could be this confident.

"*Son of a bitch,*" Uber-Jimmy replied softly.

"Fetch my fucking VE–HICKLE you dumb backward-ass bumpkin," Paul shouted.

"And I may just not kill you too."

"Fuck 'em both up!" Uber-Jimmy shouted, directing his voice to the den.

Uber-Jummy ran at Paul and the two locked arms and tussled into the fridge at the back of the kitchen. The door behind Lisa burst open to reveal another Cletus, this one looking almost identical to Uber-Jimmy. She turned and swung the poker wildly at him. It caught him on the shoulder and he fell into the wall. She continued her assault knowing full well that if she failed in disabling him she would suffer a fate much worse than anything she could dream up.

Jimmy's first brother and Paul were slamming each other into the walls and cupboards of the kitchen, both locked by grabbing each other's shirts and by the angry contempt-filled stares held by both men. Jimmy twisted the knife out of Paul's hand and began to punch him just under the rib cage. The sting was as bad as the poker. Paul wanted to scream but before he could, Jimmy first began to use those same bony knuckles across his mouth and temple. Paul collapsed.

Worst Case Scenario

What a change he had felt in this Lisa girl. In the brief time he met her he was brining his whole life around and neither of them knew it. He could give up his addictions for her. His needs were no longer his needs but that of a disease, a virus. He had found his antidote. A girl he would be proud to show off to his friends. God, how long had it been since he had seen them? A year? Year and quarter? Paul missed every Friday going to Hogan's pub early and staying till about 11, then staggering across the street with the boys to Club Noir. God, how did security ever let us guys in? Paul never got angry there. Place was packed with friends and strangers who just wanted to have fun. Funny how one bad experience in an unfamiliar place can set off everything.

Lisa screamed. Paul woke on the floor. His hands bound with rope this time. Mercifully. He was in the den. Jimmy's brothers are peeling away Lisa's filthy shirt with Paul's stolen hunting knife. Lisa herself had a massive black eye.

"Were gonna do you so she can watch. Then do her so you can watch," one of the twins explained.

"Then gouge out yer fuckin eyes!" the other twin snapped back.

One of the pair left the den for a moment only to return with Paul's black gym bag. Paul knew he was fucked. His captor laid the bag out in front of Lisa, grabbed her by the back of her head, and pointed to the bag.

"Your boy over here ain't what you think!"

Paul reached into his pocket where he had stashed one of the scalpels.

"He's one of those highway perverts you read about in the news," his captor explained, using grandiose gestures.

Paul found the blade and began to quietly rub the blade against his rope restraints.

"He's the kinda guy to pretty a pretty thing up such as yourself, rape em, them leave dead in a ditch or woods somewhere!"

The rope slowly began to give way.

"Fuck, I'd like him had he not killed my boy Jimmy. Now he's gotta get fucked and die!"

Paul remained still on the floor looking at his captors—making eye contact—so they would not notice his restraints falling off. The second captor dumped Paul's bag on the floor and the night at that moment became infinitely worse then Lisa could have imagined. It was all there. His machete, his rope, his handcuffs, his ski mask. His life—his thing that he did. Would she believe them? They were the textbook definition of what we in the modern era would call a *psychopath*. Lisa wept. He would not have done her. Paul only did the people who hurt him or made him angry. Only that stupid bouncer at that stupid club; why didn't he go to Hogan's with the boys?

"Now I am gonna freshen you up and she's gotta watch!" the second brother said.

With his hands down his pants, rubbing in a furious motion, he put his free hand on Paul's shoulder. He pushed Paul flat on the floor. Paul did not resist—too focused on concealing the blade and holding his ropes where they should be. Paul watched as the pig moved directly behind him and began to tug at his belt. In one quick motion Paul

slammed the blade into the pig. As disgusting as it felt, he was happy to know the blade struck the genitals.

"Fuck!" The pig squealed.

Paul spun around onto his back quickly to kick the wounded animal aside. The brother was already on top of him. Paul on his back blindly slashed up at the molester's face, catching him on the check. Jimmy's brother moved back and Paul sprang to his feet, rushing into and stabbing the blade in where he could. Lisa moved quickly away from the confrontation in an attempt to loosen her restraints. Paul turned to see the brother lying on the floor, clutching his groin with a look of disbelief.

"Please don't. I only have my daddy left," he whimpered.

Paul tossed the scalpel aside.

"Thank you."

Bending over to picked up the machete, the other brother tried to get up right again but it was too late. Paul lobbed the blade right into his molester's forehead. Walking over he simply placed his foot on the pig's head and jerked the blade out. He turned to Lisa who was now free and picking up the bloody scalpel for herself.

"We have to find my car right now."

"No shit." She giggled, tears in her eyes. Paul wondered if she believed them.

The two ran out the house together. Down a rickety set of stairs leading from the kitchen. Lisa and Paul realized it had been an old cabin. A dingy, cold and grey cabin. Could it have been anything else? Lisa wondered. It looked like it was built at least fifty years ago. Woods surrounded the cabin itself. Only one path or driveway led to what appeared to be the road they were driving along. And not sixty steps ahead of them was Paul's car, with, it appeared, no flat tires. Next to the vehicle were a jack and a tire iron.

"Great! They were gonna steal your car too!" Lisa smiled.

Sundance

Paul looked to her and smiled—but paused. From the tree line behind her he could see a hulking man running in their direction. Paul pushed Lisa towards the car and clutched his machete. The man slowed his pursuit and began to walk calmly towards Paul. The man himself was huge; his arms looked to be the same width as Lisa's waist, his chest and gut expanded to grotesque proportions. The beast's complexion was a

ghostly kind of white. And his hair short but greasy, like his progeny. From his belt he pulled out two large hooks—the kind one would use for gutting fish. He clutched them one in each hand and let them softly swing back and forth. The sun quietly rose over the horizon.

"Well, fuck you then," Paul said.

"You people have just pissed me off now."

The man lunged at Paul, bringing the hooks down, narrowly missing Paul's head. As he ducked, Paul swiped his weapon against the father's massive side, cutting deep. He swung again at the beast's face, but the hulk countered with the hook. With each swing the monster's reflexes proved to be much faster then he appeared: blocking every lunge and every swipe. Paul swung down low and faking a follow through only to try and bring the machete up to the monster's face. The monster swung one of his hooks down hard enough to snap Paul's weapon. Too close to swing the behemoth, he punched Paul across the cheek, tossing him aside. When he hit the ground he thought he had heard the car start. As he looked up he could see the hooks above him; one after the other they slammed into his chest. Paul screamed and shrieked as the man slowly pulled him up. Desperately clutching his attacker's wrists to minimize the tearing. He tried punching but each hit made the man move back— tearing Paul. Paul heard the engine roar as Lisa drove onto the grass towards them. Tires squealing, Paul punched his assailant between the legs as hard as possible. He released the hooks. Paul leapt aside as Lisa barrelled down on the monster. His massive framed slammed down onto the hood and was seemingly sucked beneath the vehicle by some unseen undertow. Lisa could hear a cracking sound as she rolled over him.

Paul clutched his badly pierced chest, trying to not look at the holes. On his knees, holding his chest together, a painful reappraisal of the situation was necessary for Paul. Even if Lisa didn't believe the brothers Jim, she would have certainly seen the instability in Paul. Paul the cowboy, Paul the drifter, Paul the serial killer. Where did he go from here?

Out of Sate

In the early morning light he could see Lisa driving back and forth over the slain monster. She has heart. Oh man, even all bruised and scared she's beautiful. The guys would love her—he could start over. No one

was looking for him yet. What a story they had to tell—a book deal—and a new beginning.

Lisa backed off of the creature and reversed slowly on the driveway leading to the road. She looked at Paul, who had very little of his shirt left and was covered in blood and dirt. He looked like he was about to cry. Lisa reached over and opened the passenger door for him.

"I think you need a tetanus shot."

"Yeah, maybe I do," Paul said, crying.

Paul climbed inside and held her hand. Funny had one bad experience in an unfamiliar place can set off everything.

Nicholas James White

Nicholas James White lives in the Greater Toronto Area in Ontario Canada. He has a long time love affair with the horror genre and writes horror short stories. He is currently working on a full-length novel.